Northern Guardians
Sea of Tears
Raglam
of the World
Ironpass
Northwarden
Dencamp-on-the-Teeth
Kenting Rush
Cutter's Gap
Highcastle
WOLD
Wolfram
Cavell Keep
Prank's Stone
The Blackwood
High Fastness
EASTERN KINGDOMS
THE KINGDOM
Dolth
Rodez
Ran
Euper
Romney
Tiburn
Sloop
The Straits of Ilthros
THE KINGDOM OF ROLDEM
Roldem
Bas-Tyra
Sadara
Lyton
Silden
Malac's Cross
Cheam
Rillanon
Salador
Timons
The Sea of Kingdoms
The Grey Range
Deep Taunton
Mallow Haven
The Green Reaches
The Peaks of Tranquility
Pointer's Head
Peaks of the Quor
Jonril
GREAT KESH
Kampari
Spires of Light
Ishlana
Mother of Waters
Zacara
Caralién
Khattara
Kesh
DARK HAVEN
Ishap's Deep
Hattaresh
Sunnom
Wasra
Overn Deep
Kimri
Grimstone Mountains
Tupa
Jalôme
Queral
The Great Sea
The Guardians
Ahar
Hansulê
Ashunta
The Girdle of Kesh
Brijanê
Telêman
The Clasp
Dong Tai
The Belt
LESSER KESH
(KESHIAN CONFEDERACY)
R.M. Askren 2002

EXILE'S
RETURN

Also by Raymond E. Feist

KING OF FOXES
TALON OF THE SILVER HAWK

MAGICIAN
SILVERTHORN
A DARKNESS AT SETHANON

FAERIE TALE

PRINCE OF THE BLOOD
THE KING'S BUCCANEER

SHADOW OF A DARK QUEEN
RISE OF A MERCHANT PRINCE
RAGE OF A DEMON KING
SHARDS OF A BROKEN CROWN

KRONDOR: TEAR OF THE GODS
KRONDOR: THE BETRAYAL
KRONDOR: THE ASSASSINS

With Janny Wurts

DAUGHTER OF EMPIRE
SERVANT OF EMPIRE
MISTRESS OF EMPIRE

EXILE'S

Conclave of Shadows: Book Three

RETURN

Raymond E. Feist

An Imprint of HarperCollins*Publishers*

HarperCollins books may be purchased for educational, business, or sales promotional use. For information please write: Special Markets Department, HarperCollins Publishers Inc., 10 East 53rd Street, New York, NY 10022.

FIRST EDITION

Eos is a federally registered trademark of HarperCollins Publishers Inc.

Designed by Renato Stanisic

Helmet illustration by Paul Robinson

"Midkemia" endpaper map by Ralph Askren, D.V.M.
"Novindus" frontispiece map by Ralph Askren, D.V.M., with grateful acknowledgment to Claire Naylon Vaccaro

Printed on acid-free paper

Library of Congress Cataloging-in-Publication Data

Feist, Raymond E.
Exile's return / Raymond E. Feist.—1st ed.
p. cm.—(Conclave of shadows ; bk. 3)
ISBN 0-380-97710-9
1. Exiles—Fiction. 2. Imperialism—Fiction. I. Title.

PS3556.E446E95 2005
813'.54—dc22 2004056324

05 06 07 08 09 JTC/RRD 10 9 8 7 6 5 4 3 2 1

This one's for James,

with all the love a father can give

Contents

Acknowledgments

As always, I am indebted to those who created Midkemia and allowed me to use it. Without their generosity I might be flipping burgers. So, Steve A., Jon, Anita, Conan, Steve B., Bob, Rich, April, Ethan, and everyone else who contributed, my thanks.

Thanks to Ralph Askren for the fine map work.

Special thanks this time around to a group of people who have provided me with seemingly endless support and friendship through personal craziness: Andy Abramson, Richard Spahl, and Kim and Ray McKewon.

My deepest affections and appreciations to The Ladies: Annah Brealey, Jennifer Evins, Heather Haney, Candace Serbian, Jennifer Sheetz, Tami Sullivan, Rebecca Thornhill, Amaliya Weisler, Elyssa Xavier, and a special thank you to Roseanna Necochia. In many different ways you have all made life resonant and interesting. Your friendships have made me a far richer man than I deserve.

I also, once again, thank Jonathan Matson.

Thanks to my mother, for being there.

Lastly, and most deeply, to my children for their love and beauty; they drive me crazy while keeping me alive.

Exile's
Return

NOVINDUS

R. M. A. 2004

May see thee now, though late, redeem thy name,
And glorify what else is damn'd to fame.
—Richard Savage, *Character of Foster*

ONE

CAPTIVE

The riders came at him.

Kaspar, who had until the day before held the title of Duke of Olasko, waited, holding his chains ready. Moments before he had been deposited on this dusty plain by a tall white-haired magician who, with only a few words of farewell, had vanished, leaving the exiled nobleman to face an approaching band of nomads.

Kaspar had never felt this alive and vitalized. He grinned, took a deep breath and flexed his knees. The riders were fanning out, and Kaspar knew they judged him a risk even though he stood alone, barefoot and without any weapon save for heavy chains with manacles and leggings attached to each end.

The riders slowed. Kaspar counted six of them. They wore alien garments, loose-fitting outer robes of indigo over white blouses belted at the waist with whipcord;

ballooning trousers were tucked into black leather boots. Their heads were covered by wrapped turbans, with a length of cloth left hanging on the right. Kaspar judged that this could be quickly raised to cover mouth and nose against a sudden dust storm or to hide identity. The clothing looked less like a uniform than tribal garb, he decided. And they carried a variety of lethal-looking weapons.

The leader spoke in a language Kaspar didn't understand, though there was something oddly familiar about it. Kaspar replied, "I don't suppose there's the remotest chance you speak Olaskon?"

The man Kaspar had identified as the leader said something to his companions, made a gesture, then sat back to watch. Two men dismounted and approached Kaspar, drawing weapons. A third behind them unwound a leather cord, with which he obviously intended to bind their new captive.

Kaspar let his chains drop slightly, and slumped his shoulders, as if acknowledging the inevitability of his circumstances. From the manner in which they approached, Kaspar knew two things: these were experienced fighting men—tough, sunburned plainsmen who probably lived in tents—and they were not trained soldiers. One glance gave Kaspar the one fact he needed to make his decision on how to act. None of the three men still on horseback had drawn a bow.

Kaspar allowed the man with the leather bindings to approach, and then at the last instant he kicked out, taking the man in the chest. That man was the least dangerous of the three at hand. Kaspar then swung his chains, releasing an end at the same instant, and the swordsman on his right who had judged himself out of Kaspar's reach was slammed across the face with the makeshift weapon. Kaspar heard bone crack. The man went down silently.

The other swordsman was quick to react, raising his sword and shouting something—an insult, battle cry, or prayer to a god, Kaspar didn't know which. All the former duke knew was that he had perhaps three or four seconds to live. Instead of moving away from the attacker, Kaspar threw himself at the man, coming up hard against him as the sword fell through empty air.

He got his shoulder under the man's armpit and the momentum of the missed blow carried the nomad over Kaspar's shoulder. Kaspar's powerful arms pushed up hard and the man spun through the air, landing hard upon the ground. The breath seemed to explode out of his body and Kaspar suspected he might have cracked his spine.

Kaspar sensed more than saw that two archers were unlimbering their bows, so he sprang forward, and with a diving shoulder roll, came to his feet holding the closest man's sword. The nomad who had held the binding leather was trying to come to his feet and draw his own sword at the same time as Kaspar stepped by him, smashing the man's head with the flat of the blade. The man fell over without a sound.

Kaspar might not be the swordsman Tal Hawkins had been, but he had trained as a soldier most of his life, and now he was in his element, in-close brawling. He ran at the three riders, two with bows and one with a slender lance, that man leveling his weapon as he put his heels to his horse's barrel. The animal might not be a seasoned warhorse but it was well trained. It leapt forward as if sprinting from the starting line in a race and Kaspar barely avoided being trampled. He almost took the point of the man's lance in the chest, but with a quick move to the left evaded it. Had the horse started only a yard or two farther back, he would have been moving too fast for Kaspar's next move, which was to continue twisting and reaching up with his left hand, grab the rider by the back of his robe and yank him from the saddle.

Kaspar didn't wait to see the man hit the ground, but used his momentum to keep turning until he was facing the closest rider, who was trying to draw his bow. Kaspar reached out with his left hand and grabbed the man's ankle. He yanked it back and then up and the bowman fell from the saddle.

Kaspar spun, looking for the last opponent, or to see if one of those he had unhorsed had regained his footing. He turned twice before accepting his situation. Slowly he stood up and let the sword fall from his fingers.

The last bowman had calmly moved his horse away a few yards, and now sat quietly in the saddle, drawing a bead on Kaspar. It was hopeless. Unless he was a terrible shot, Kaspar would never avoid the arrow pointing at his chest.

The man smiled and nodded, and said something that Kaspar took as "good," then flicked his gaze to someone behind Kaspar.

Suddenly one of the riders he had embarrassed smashed his forearm into the back of Kaspar's neck, driving him to his knees. Kaspar tried to turn as he heard metal clanking, and he realized someone was approaching with his discarded manacles. Before he could get his head around, cold iron slammed into the point of his jaw. Bright lights exploded behind his eyes for an instant before he lapsed into unconsciousness.

Kaspar's jaw throbbed. His neck hurt and he felt sore all over his body. He was disoriented for a moment, then remembered the confrontation with the nomads. He blinked, trying to clear his vision, then realized it was night. From the variety of aches he experienced when he tried to move, he assumed the riders had spent a fair amount of time kicking him after he had been knocked unconscious, displaying their displeasure at the manner in which he had received their request for him to surrender.

He judged it a good thing he hadn't killed any of them, for that would have probably earned him a cut throat. He realized his chance of escaping that encounter had been slim. He struggled upright, no mean feat with his hands bound behind him with leather cords. But he also knew that a trained fighting man might stand a better chance of survival among people like these compared to a common field hand or house servant.

Looking around, he discovered he was secured behind a tent. His bindings were tight around his wrists, and those in turn were tied by a tough rope to a tent stake. He could move around a few feet, but there wasn't enough slack in the rope to enable him to stand. A quick inspection of the stake revealed he could probably pull it out, but if he did, he would bring down the tent, clearly informing his hosts of his attempted departure.

He was dressed as he had been when taken. He did a quick physical inventory and judged that nothing was broken or sprained too badly.

He sat quietly and considered things. His instincts about these people seemed correct so far. From what little he could see beyond the tent, this was a small camp, perhaps just the six riders and their families, maybe a few more. But he could see a picket line for horses, and by rough estimation there were at least two or three mounts for every person here.

On the other side of the tent he heard voices, speaking

softly. He strained to listen to the alien language. He sat back. A word here or there was tantalizing to him.

Kaspar had a quick grasp of languages. As heir to his father's throne, it had been judged necessary for him to learn the educated speech of the surrounding nations, so he spoke fluent, unaccented King's Tongue—the language of the Kingdom of the Isles—as well as those languages related to his native Olaskon, all descended from Roldemish. He also spoke flawless court Keshian and had taken the time to learn a little Quegan, a variant on Keshian that had evolved on its own after the Quegan Kingdom had successfully revolted from the Empire of Great Kesh nearly two centuries earlier.

In his travels he had picked up patois and cants from half a dozen regions of those foreign nations, and something about what he was now hearing sounded very familiar. He closed his eyes and let his thoughts wander as he eavesdropped on the conversation.

Then he heard a word: *ak-káwa. Acqua!* The accent was thick, the emphasis different, but it was Quegan for "water"! They were talking about stopping somewhere for water. He listened and let the words flow over him without trying to understand, just allowing his ear to become used to the rhythms and tones, the patterns and sounds.

For an hour he sat there, listening. At first he could recognize one word in a hundred. Then perhaps one word in fifty. He was recognizing one word in a dozen when he heard footsteps approaching. He slumped down and feigned unconsciousness.

Kaspar heard two sets of footfalls draw near. In a low voice one man spoke. Kaspar heard the words "good" and "strong" from one man. There followed a quick conversation. From what Kaspar could judge, one man was arguing to kill him where he lay because he might be more trouble than was he was worth, but the other argued he had value because he was strong and good at something, probably with a sword, since it was the only skill Kaspar had demonstrated before being overwhelmed.

It took total control on Kaspar's part not to move when an ungentle boot prodded him to see if he was truly unconscious. Then the two men departed.

Kaspar waited and when he was certain they were gone, he chanced a peek and caught a glimpse of the men's backs as they walked around the tent.

He sat up.

He fought to keep his mind focused on what he was hearing, and started to wrestle with his bindings. The danger would be to become so intent upon escaping he wouldn't hear anyone approach. He knew his best chance for escape was this first night, while they thought him still unconscious. He had very few advantages. They probably knew the surrounding countryside and were experienced trackers.

His only edge was surprise. Kaspar was a skilled enough hunter to know what cunning prey could do. He needed at least an hour's start on his captors, but first he had to free himself of the leather bindings around his wrist.

He gave in to the unreasonable desire to test the bindings, and found them tight enough to cause pain when he tried to pull his hands apart. He couldn't see, but they felt like rawhide. If he could get them wet they would stretch and he might be able to slip them off.

After a futile period of struggle, he turned his attention to the rope he could see. He knew he would have little chance of getting the rope off the peg without bringing down the entire tent, but he could think of no other option. He had to turn first one way, then the other, to come to the conclusion that this was impossible with his hands tied behind him.

Kaspar sat and waited. As the hours dragged by, the camp quietened. He heard footsteps and once more feigned unconsciousness as someone came to check on him before turning in for the night. He let minutes drag by until he was certain that those inside the tent were asleep. Then he sat up. He glanced at the sky and was greeted with a display of alien stars. Like most men of his ocean-going nation, he could navigate by the stars, either on land or sea, but above him lay constellations unknown. He would have to rely upon basic navigation skills until he became used to the display above. He knew where the sun had set, marked in his mind by a spiral of rock in the distance he had glimpsed just before sunset. Which meant he knew where north was.

North and east was his most likely route home. Kaspar had read sufficiently to know where the continent of Novindus lay, relative to Olasko. Depending on where on this continent he found himself, his best chance to get to Olasko was to work his way to a place called the City of the Serpent River. There was almost no trade between this land and those on the other side of the world, but whatever trade there was started in that city. From there he could find his way to the Sunset Isles, and from there to Krondor. Once in the Kingdom of the Isles, he could walk home if he had to.

He knew he was almost certain to fail in the attempt, but whatever was to happen to him, let it happen as he struggled to return home.

Home, he thought bitterly. A day earlier he had been home, ruling his nation, before being taken captive in his own citadel, defeated by a former servant he had thought as good as dead. He had spent the night in chains considering the dramatic reversal of fortune that had overwhelmed him, and had fully expected to be hanged by now.

Instead, Talwin Hawkins, his former servant, had forgiven him, and he had been banished to this distant land. Kaspar was uncertain as to what exactly had transpired over the previous few days. In fact, he was beginning to wonder if he had truly been himself for the last few years.

He had heard guards talking outside his quarters while he had been awaiting what he anticipated would be his execution. Leso Varen, his magician advisor, had been killed in the battle for the citadel. The magician had first come to him years earlier, promising great power in exchange for Kaspar's protection. His presence had been only a minor distraction at first and he had from time to time provided useful service.

Kaspar took a deep breath and returned his attention to gaining his freedom. There would be time for more reflection on his past, assuming he lived long enough to have a future.

Kaspar was a broad-shouldered man of unusual strength, but his looks were deceptive. Unlike many men of his build, he kept himself limber. Expelling all the air from his lungs and hunching his shoulders forward, he pulled his knees hard up against his shoulders, sticking his head between his thighs, forcing his feet between his bound wrists. He could feel ligaments protest as he stretched his arms as far as possible, but he managed to get his hands in front of him.

And almost pulled the tent down in the process. He found himself able to lie down, easing the tension on the rope and peg. He studied it. The bindings were indeed of rawhide, and he set to them with his teeth. Using saliva, he got the simple knot wet, gnawing at it until it loosened. For long minutes he worried at the loops of the knot, then suddenly it came loose and his hands were free.

He flexed his fingers and rubbed his wrists as he slowly stood up. Forcing his breathing to a slow, deep rate, he crept around to the front of the tent. He peered around the edge of the tent and saw a single guard sitting with his back to the fire at the other end of the camp.

Kaspar's mind raced. He knew one thing from years of experience: more harm came from indecision than from bad choices. He could attempt to silence the guard, thereby possibly gaining several hours on the pursuit that would certainly follow, or he could simply leave, and hope the guard didn't come to check on him before dawn. But whichever choice he made, he had to act now!

Without conscious effort, he took a step in the guard's direction. He trusted in his instincts: the risk was worth the potential reward. The guard hummed a simple tune, perhaps as a device to keep himself alert. Kaspar trod lightly on the balls of his feet and came up behind the man.

Some change in the light as Kaspar stepped between the guard and the camp fire, a slight sound, or just intuition, made the man turn. Kaspar lashed out as hard as he could and struck him behind the ear. The guard's knees wobbled and his eyes lost focus and Kaspar struck him across the jaw. The man started to fall, and Kaspar caught him.

He knew his freedom was measured in seconds as he stripped the guard of his headcover, and sword. But the man had smaller feet than him and his boots were useless to Kaspar.

He cursed the soldier who had taken his boots on the night of his capture. He couldn't attempt an escape barefoot. He lacked the calluses of those who traveled without boots and while he knew little of the terrain around him, what he had seen told him it was rocky and unforgiving. He remembered a small copse of trees on a distant hillside to the northeast, but doubted he could effectively hide there. What other cover might be nearby was unknown to him; he had had no time to study his surroundings between his arrival and the confrontation with his captors. His only escape option would be to find a pair of boots and put as much distance between himself and his captors before they awoke, climbing into the rocky ridge above them where the horses couldn't follow.

He stood silently for a moment, then hurried quietly to the largest tent. Holding the sword at the ready, he gently moved aside the tent flap. Inside he could hear snoring. It sounded as if there were two sleepers, a man and a woman. In the gloom he could see little, so he waited and let his eyes adjust. After a moment he saw a third body near the left side of the tent, a child from the size of it.

Kaspar saw a pair of boots standing next to a small chest, where he imagined he'd find the chieftain's personal treasure. Kaspar moved with the catlike stealth uncharacteristic of a man so large. He quietly picked up the boots and saw they were of a size he could wear, then moved back toward the tent flap. He paused. Conflicting urges tugged at him. He was almost certain to be overtaken and recaptured, perhaps killed this time, unless he could find an advantage. But what? While he pondered, valuable moments passed, time never to be regained that would count against him as he sought to distance himself from this place.

Indecision was not part of Kaspar's nature. He glanced about in the gloom and saw the chieftain's weapons where he would expect them, close at hand in case of trouble. He inched past the sleeping couple and took out the nomadic leader's dagger. It was a long, broad-bladed thing designed with a single purpose, to gut a man at close quarters. There was nothing dainty about it, and it put Kaspar in mind of the daggers worn by the nomads of the Jal-Pur desert of Kesh. He wondered idly if these people were somehow related. The language of the Jal-Pur was unrelated to Keshian, but Quegan had been a dialect of Keshian, and these people's language bore a faint resemblance.

Kaspar took the blade and crept closer to the tent flap. He peered in the gloom at the child. In the dim light he couldn't see if it was a boy or girl, for the hair was shoulder length and the child's face was turned away. With a quick, downward thrust, Kaspar drove the dagger through the floor cover into the earth below. The slight sound caused the child to stir, but not wake.

Kaspar left the tent. He glanced quickly around and saw what he needed, a filled waterskin. He then looked longingly at the line of horses, but ignored them. A mount would give him a better chance of survival, but trying to saddle one was likely to wake someone, and whatever chance his warning in the tent might earn him, stealing a horse from these people would certainly outweigh it.

Kaspar moved out of the village and toward the trees and the hills beyond. What he had seen before his capture indicated that it was rocky terrain and perhaps these horsemen might be disinclined to follow if the way was too harsh. Perhaps they had a rendezvous to make, or perhaps Kaspar's message might give them pause.

For unless the chieftain was a fool he would understand what Kaspar had done. The dagger next to his child would say, "I could have killed you and your family while you slept, but I spared you. Now, leave me alone."

At least that's what Kaspar hoped the man would understand.

Dawn found Kaspar climbing over broken rocks, high into the hills. There was almost no cover above the small copse of trees he had seen the day before, and he struggled to find a place to hide.

He could still see the camp below, though by now it was a distant dotting of tents on the floor of the wide valley. From his vantage he could see that this valley was a choke point of a broad plain, flanked on his side by broken hills with a plateau opposite. On the other side of the valley, a vast mountain range rose in the distance. Snow-capped peaks suggested that these mountains would be difficult to cross. The military man in him admired the defensibility of the location, should someone choose to place a fortress where the nomad's camp was. But scanning the horizon, he realized there was nothing to protect here.

The valley lacked apparent water. The trees he had passed through were a variety unknown to him. They were scrawny, had tough black bark, thorns, and obviously needed very little water to survive. Everywhere he looked he saw rocks and dust. The valley below and the cut through the rocks told him that once a river had flowed through here. Shifting land or a change in climate had caused it to dry up and now its only function was to mark a quick passage for horsemen between one place and another, both unknown to Kaspar.

Distant sounds informed him his escape had been discovered, and he returned his efforts to climbing, feeling lightheaded and slightly weak. He had not eaten for at least two days, depending how he calculated the time. He had been dragged before Talwin Hawkins and his allies in chains at night and transported here instantly at dawn. He must truly be on the other side of the world.

He needed rest and food. He had found some sort of dried meat and hard cracker in a pouch on the side of the waterskin, and planned on devouring these when time permitted, but for the moment he was content to put as much distance between himself and the nomads as possible.

He reached a ridge, on top of which a narrow path ran. He pulled himself up off the rocks and turned to look at the distant camp. Tents were being folded and the tiny dots he took to be men and horses appeared to be moving at a sedate pace. There was no sign of pursuit below him. Kaspar took a moment to catch his breath and regarded the path.

It was wider than a game trail. He knelt and examined it. Someone had taken the trouble to compact the earth beneath his feet. He followed it as it climbed, leading him away from the area above the camp, and soon he found a rock face on his right that showed marks made by tools. The sun was partially blocked by the rock face, so he sat and ate the cracker and some of the dried meat. He drank about a third of the water in the skin and rested.

He seemed to have escaped and it appeared that his message to the tribe's chieftain had been understood. No riders fanned out in search, no trackers climbed the hills below him. He was free of pursuit.

The air was dry. He reckoned his orientation from the rising sun. The trail he was on had once been a military road, which appeared to have been abandoned for some reason or another. The surrounding countryside was harsh and ungenerous, so there seemed little reason to claim it. Perhaps it had once served as a highway for a nation no longer claiming this region.

He knew the heat of the day would be punishing, so he sought out shelter. None was evident. He decided to spend a while along this old military road, for if nothing else it offered him a vantage point. He allowed himself one long sip of water, then replaced the stopper in the waterskin. He had no idea how long it would be before he found another supply.

The snatches of conversation he had overheard the night before led him to believe water was a source of concern to his former captors. He assumed they would be heading for a new source, so he decided to walk the trail in parallel to their course.

A hour went by and he noticed that the distance between himself and his captors was growing. They walked their horses, but they were traversing flat terrain and he was picking his way along broken stones. The roadbed was flat for a dozen yards or more at a time, then would be interrupted by breaks, overturned stones and gaps due to slides in the hillside below. Once he had to climb down half a dozen yards in order to circumnavigate a collapsed section.

By midday he was exhausted. He removed his shirt and tied it around his head as a rudimentary covering. He didn't know how he knew, but he vaguely remembered as a boy being told that the body could withstand sunburn as long as the head was shaded. He drank another swallow of water and then chewed the jerked meat. It was tough and with little fat, and very salty. He resisted the urge to drink more, determined to permit himself just one more mouthful when he had finished the food.

It took a while to chew the meat, but at last he finished and he took that one long drink. He sat regarding his surroundings.

Kaspar was a hunter. Perhaps not the hunter Talwin

Hawkins had been, but he had enough wilderness lore to know he was in dire circumstances. Whatever rain visited this harsh countryside did so infrequently, for there were no signs of vegetation save the tough trees that scattered the landscape. The rocks he sat upon had no grass pushing its way up between cracks, and when he turned a stone over, there was no moss or lichen growing on the shaded side. This country was dry most of the time.

He let his eyes follow the ridge upon which he walked and he saw that it ran toward the south. To the east he saw nothing but broken plains, and to the west the arid valley. He decided he would take this trail for a while longer, and look for anything that would keep him alive. The nomads were heading south, and if he didn't know anything else, he knew that eventually they would be heading for water. And to survive, he needed water.

For that was the task at hand: survival. Kaspar had many ambitions at the moment, to return to Opardum and reclaim the throne of Olasko, and to visit vengeance on his traitorous Captain Quentin Havrevulen and Talwin Hawkins, formerly of his household. As he walked, a thought arose. The two men weren't actually traitors, he guessed, as he had condemned both to imprisonment on the isle known as the Fortress of Despair, but whatever the legal niceties were, he'd have them both dead.

He'd probably have to rally forces loyal to him and seize the citadel from them. Most likely Talwin had forced his sister Talia to marry him, to claim his throne, and Havrevulen was almost certainly in command of the army. But he'd find men who remembered who was the rightful ruler of Olasko, and he'd reward them handsomely once he was back in power.

His mind churned and he advanced plan after plan as he trod the roadway, but whatever plan presented itself he first had to overcome several significant obstacles, starting with the fact that he was on the wrong side of the world. That meant he would need a ship and crew, and that meant gold. And to get gold he would have to contrive of a way to earn it or take it. And that meant finding civilization, or what passed for it on this continent. And finding people meant he had to survive.

He glanced around as the sun reached its zenith, and decided that right now, survival looked improbable. Nothing stirred in any direction he looked, save a small cloud of dust marking the passage of the nomads who had captured him.

However, he considered, standing still only guaranteed his death, so he would keep moving as long as he had the strength.

He marched on.

Survival

Kaspar lay dying.

He knew his time was short as he sheltered under an overhang from the afternoon sun. He had been three days on the trail and his water had been used up at dawn. He was lightheaded and disoriented and had stumbled down the side of the ridge to a shaded area to wait out the heat.

He knew that if he didn't find water by nightfall, he most likely would not awake tomorrow morning. His lips were cracked and his nose and cheeks peeled from sunburn. Lying on his back, he ignored the pain from his blistered shoulders as they rested against the rocks. He was too tired to allow the pain to bother him; besides, the pain let him know he still lived. He would wait until the sun was low in the west, then work his way down to the flat land below. The landscape was bleak and unforgiving: broken rocks and hardpan lay in every direction. He realized that the magician who had transported him here had given him little chance for survival; this was a desert by any measure, even if it lacked the flowing sands he associated with that name.

The few trees he had encountered were lifeless and dry, and even the underside of rocks were without a hint of moisture. One of his teachers had told him years ago that water could sometimes be found below the surface in the desert, but Kaspar was certain it wouldn't be at this elevation. Whatever streams had graced this landscape ages before, any water was now long vanished; if any remained, it would be in those gullies that were his goal, down below the cracked surface toward which he staggered. For a brief moment he paused to catch his breath, which was now labored; no matter how deeply he inhaled, he couldn't seem to get enough air. He knew it was another symptom of his plight.

Kaspar had never seen so bleak a place. The great sand ergs of the Jal-Pur of northern Kesh had seemed exotic, a place of shifting forms, a veritable sea of sand. He had been a boy with his father, and a lavish entourage of royal servants from the Imperial Keshian court at his beck and call, amid a mobile village of colorful tents and opulent pavilions. When his father hunted the legendary sand lizards of the Jal-Pur, servants were always nearby with refreshing drinks—water scented with herbs or fruit extracts, cleverly kept cool in boxes packed with snow from the mountains. Each night was a royal feast, with chilled ales and spiced wine.

Just thinking of those drinks caused Kaspar near-physical pain. He turned his fevered thoughts to his current surroundings.

Here there were colors, but nothing remotely attractive to the eye, just harsh ocher, dingy yellow, the red of rusted iron, and a tan muted with gray. Everything was covered by dust, and nowhere was there a hint of green or blue indicating water, though he had noticed a shimmer to the northwest, which might be a reflection of water on the hot air.

He had only hunted once in the hot lands of Kesh, but he remembered everything he had been told. The Keshians were descendants of the lion hunters who roamed the grasslands around the great lake called the Overn Deep, and their traditions had endured through the centuries. The old guide, Kulmaki, had counseled Kaspar, "Watch for birds at sundown, young lord, for they will fly to water." For the last two days he had scanned the horizon in vain; but not a bird had he seen.

As he lay exhausted and dehydrated he lapsed in and out of consciousness, his mind alive with a mix of fever dreams, memories and illusions.

He recalled a day as a boy when his father had taken him hunting, the first time he had been permitted to accompany the men. It had been a boar hunt, and Kaspar had barely the strength to handle the heavy-tipped boar spear. He had ridden close to his father as he took the first two boars, but then he had faced his own, he had hesitated, and the pig had dodged the broad head of Kaspar's weapon. He had glanced over and seen the disapproval in his father's eyes, and he had charged after the boar into the underbrush, without heeding the warning of the Master of the Hunt.

Before the men could catch up, Kaspar's horse had chased the boar into a thicket where it had turned at bay. Kaspar had done everything possible that was wrong, yet when his father and the others had arrived, he stood ignoring the gash in his leg, standing triumphant over the still-thrashing animal. The Master of the Hunt put the animal down with a quick arrow, and Kaspar's father had hurried to bind his son's leg.

The pride Kaspar had seen in his father's eyes, despite the admonishing words about foolish acts, had branded the boy for life. *Never be afraid.* He knew that no matter what, any choice must be made fearlessly, or else all would be lost.

Kaspar remembered the day when the mantle of rulership had fallen on his shoulders, and he had stood mutely by, holding his baby sister's hands while the priests applied torches to the funeral pyre. As smoke and ash rose to the heavens, the young Duke of Olasko again pledged to be fearless in all things, and to protect his people as if he was facing that boar.

Somewhere it had all gone sour. Seeking a proper place in the sun for Olasko had somehow turned into naked ambition, and Kaspar had decided that he needed to be King of Roldem. He was eighth in line for succession, so a few accidents and untimely deaths would be all he required in order to unite all the disparate nations of the east under Roldem's banner.

As he lay there thinking this, Kaspar's father appeared suddenly, and for a moment Kaspar wondered if he had died and his father had come to guide him to the Hall of Death, where Lims-Kragma would weigh the value of his life and select his place on the wheel for its next turning.

"Didn't I tell you to be cautious?"

Kaspar tried to speak, but his voice was barely a croaking whisper. "What?"

"Of all the weaknesses that beset a man, vanity is the most deadly. For through vanity can a wise man turn to folly."

Kaspar sat up and his father was gone.

In his fevered state, he had no idea what the vision of his father meant, though something told him it was important. He didn't have time to ponder this. He knew he couldn't wait until sundown, his life was now being counted out in minutes. He stumbled down the rocks to the flatlands, heat shimmer rising off the gray and ocher rocks, stumbling over the broken shards of stone once made smooth by ancient waters.

Water.

He was seeing things that weren't real. He knew that his father was dead, yet now the spirit of the man seemed to be marching before him.

"You placed too much faith in those who told you what you wished was true, and ignored those who tried to tell you what was true."

In his mind, Kaspar shouted, "But I was a force to be feared!" The words came out an inarticulate grunt.

"Fear is not the only tool of diplomacy and governance, my son. Loyalty is born from trust."

"Trust!" shouted Kaspar, his voice a ragged gasp as the word seemed to scrape along the inside of a parchment-dry throat. "Trust no one!" He stopped, nearly falling over, as he pointed an accusing finger at his father. "You taught me that!"

"I was wrong," said the apparition sadly and it vanished.

Kaspar looked around and saw he was heading in the general direction of where he had seen the reflected shimmer. He staggered along, lifting one foot and putting it down before the other. Slowly he halved the distance, then halved it again.

His mind continued to wander as he relived events from his childhood, then the downfall of his reign. A young woman whose name he could not recall appeared before him, walking slowly for a minute, then vanished. Who was she? Then he remembered. The daughter of a merchant, a girl he had found fair but whom his father had forbidden him to see. "You will wed for reasons of state," he had been told. "Take her to your bed if you must, but leave aside foolish thoughts of love."

The girl had wed someone else.

He wished he could remember her name.

He stumbled along, several times falling to his knees, only to rise once more on will alone. Minutes, hours, days passed, he had no way of knowing which. His mind was turning in on itself as he felt his life begin to wane.

He blinked, aware that the day was fading and he was now in a small gully, heading downward.

Then he heard it.

A bird call. Slightly more than the peep of a sparrow, but a bird call.

Kaspar forced himself out of his lethargy and blinked. He tried to clear his swimming vision, and then he heard the call again. Cocking his head, he listened, and then a third call came.

He staggered toward the sound, mindless of the treacherous footing. He fell, but caught himself on the walls of the deepening gully.

Tough grass appeared beneath his feet and his mind seized on this one fact: if there was grass, there must be water below. He looked around and could see no sign of it, but he could see a stand of trees ahead. He pushed himself forward until he had no strength left, and fell to his knees and then onto his face.

He lay panting, face down on the grass; and he could feel the moisture of the blades against his face. Weakly, he dug at the grass and his fingers clawed up the loose earth. Below it he felt dampness. With his last shred of will he pulled himself to his knees and drew his sword. The odd thought came to him that should his old swordmaster see him use a blade this way he would be up for a beating, but he ignored the whimsical thought and plunged the blade into the soil. He dug. He used the blade as a gardener would a spade and he dug.

He ripped and pulled with the last of his strength and forced a hole into the ground with near-hysterical purpose, tearing the dirt aside as rapidly as a badger digging a burrow. Then he smelled it. The damp smell was followed by a hint of gleaming moisture on the blade.

He plunged his hand into the hole and felt mud. He tossed aside the sword and dug with bare hands, and then plunged his fingers into water. It was muddy and tasted of clay, but he could lie on his stomach and pull up a meager handful at a time. He filled his cupped hand, raised it to parched lips and drank. At some point he rubbed some water on his neck and face, but over and over he raised his cupped hand to drink. He had no idea how many times he did this but eventually he collapsed, his head striking the ground as his eyes rolled up into his head and consciousness fled.

The bird scratched at the seeds, as if sensing danger nearby. Silently, Kaspar watched from on his stomach behind a depression a few feet away, masked by a line of thorny brush, as the bird—some sort of sage fowl he didn't recognize—pecked at the seed, then picked it up in its beak and gobbled it down.

Kaspar had recovered from his ordeal enough to pull himself into the shade that morning, leaving it only to drink what he could dredge up from his impromptu well. The water came harder each time, and he knew this little reservoir would soon be exhausted. He had decided near mid-afternoon to venture deeper into the gully, to see where it led, and to find another place to dig for water.

Near sundown he had found the tree. He had no name for it, but it bore a tough-skinned fruit. He had cut several down and discovered that once the skin was cut with a blade, the meat was edible. It was also pulpy and tough, and the flavor was nothing to delight a hedonist, but he was desperate. He ate a few bites, despite being consumed by hunger, and waited.

It seemed they weren't poisonous. He ate several before cramps gripped him. They might not be poisonous, but they were tough on the stomach. Or perhaps three days without food had caused his stomach to act more tenderly.

Kaspar had always possessed a healthy appetite and had never known hunger more pressing than skipping a midday meal because of a hunt or sailing off the coast. Others in his father's household had complained bitterly when he pressed on, and he laughed silently to imagine how they would react in his current circumstances. The laugh died as he realized they would all likely be dead by now.

The bird came nearer.

Kaspar had placed seeds in a line leading to a snare he had fashioned from the materials at hand. Painfully he had woven tough fibers pulled from the bulb of a strange-looking cactus; it was a trick shown him by his Keshian guide. He had ripped off the end of the bud and yanked hard, producing a sharp tip attached to a long fiber. "Nature's needle and thread," the guide had said. He had struggled, but in the end he had produced a line twice the length of his arm. His hands and arms were covered in cuts and puncture wounds, testament to his determination to fashion a snare from the thorn-covered branches of the local plants.

It took every ounce of will for Kaspar to remain silent and motionless as the bird approached his snare. He had already started a small fire, which was now banked and waiting to be fanned back into flame, and his mouth positively watered in anticipation of roast fowl.

The bird ignored him as it worried at the seed, attempting to break though the tough outer husk and get to the softer inner kernel. As Kaspar watched the bird finished the tiny morsel and moved to the next seed. For an instant, Kaspar hesitated as a pang of doubt seized him. He felt an almost overwhelming fear that somehow the bird would escape and he would slowly starve to death in this isolated place.

Genuine doubt almost paralyzed him to the point of losing the bird. The fowl tossed the seed in the air and it landed just far enough from where Kaspar had placed his snare that he felt sure it would escape. However, when he yanked his line the trap fell exactly where he had judged it would land.

The bird fluttered and squawked as it tried to escape the thorny cage. Kaspar endured punctures from the iron-like points as he lifted the small cage to reach under and seize the bird.

He quickly wrung its neck and even before he had returned to the fire he was plucking its feathers. Using the tip of his sword to gut the bird proved a messy prospect. He wished now he had kept the dagger instead of using it to warn off the nomad chieftain.

Finally the bird was dressed and spitted and he was turning it over a fire. Kaspar could hardly contain himself waiting for the bird to cook. As the minutes dragged on, the cramps in his stomach were from anticipation more than anything else.

Throughout his life Kaspar had developed a strong self-discipline, but not eating undercooked bird was the toughest test he could remember. But he knew the dangers of eating undercooked fowl. One bout of food poisoning as a young man left an indelible memory.

Finally he judged the bird finished, and with disregard for burned lips and tongue he set to with a frenzy. All too quickly he was finished, having eaten every shred of meat and the tiny bit of fat the scrawny thing had possessed. It was the best meal he could recall, but it merely whetted his appetite. He stood up and looked around, as if he might spy another bird waiting to be snatched up and eaten.

Then he saw the boy.

He looked to be no more than seven or eight years of age. He wore homespun and sandals, both caked with dust. He had as handsome a face as Kaspar had ever seen on a child and a serious expression. He was dark blond and he studied Kaspar with wide, pale blue eyes.

Kaspar remained motionless for what seemed minutes, and then the boy turned and fled.

Kaspar took out after him a half-moment later, but he was weak from hunger and deprivation. His only goad was fear that the boy would alert his father or the men of his village and while Kaspar feared no man living, he knew he was too weak to give much account of himself if faced by more than one man.

Kaspar labored to keep the boy in sight, but soon the child had vanished down a gully and between some rocks. Kaspar followed as well as he could, but after only a few minutes of climbing where he had seen the boy disappear, he stopped as dizziness gripped him. His stomach grumbled and he belched as he sat down. He patted his middle and in a moment of giddiness laughed at how he must look. It had only been, what? Six or seven days since he had been captured in his citadel in Olasko, but he could feel his ribs already. Near starvation had taken its toll.

He forced himself to be calm and then stood up and looked around for signs. He was perhaps as gifted a tracker as any man born to nobility in the eastern kingdoms. Kaspar had few vanities, but his skill at tracking and hunting were not among them; he was as good as he thought he was. He saw scuff marks on the rocks and when he climbed up them he saw the pathway.

Like the ancient abandoned road, this was an old path, made ages ago for carts or wagons, but now used by animals and a few humans. He saw the boy's tracks heading straight away from him and followed.

Kaspar was amused by the thought that the only other nobleman he knew who had skills to match his own as a hunter was Talwin Hawkins, the man who had overthrown him and taken away all Kaspar held dear. Kaspar stopped and caught his breath. Something was wrong: he was light-headed, his thoughts unfocused. Those scant bits of fruit and one tiny bird were not enough to keep him more than barely alive. His thoughts were wandering and he found that as disturbing as the constant hunger and dirt.

He shook his head to clear it, then resumed walking. He forced his mind to something approaching alertness and considered Talwin Hawkins. Of course he had been justified in his actions, for Kaspar had betrayed him. Kaspar had sensed his sister's growing attraction to the young noble from the Kingdom of the Isles. Personally, he had found Hawkins likeable, and he admired his skill with a blade and as a hunter. Kaspar paused for a moment. He found himself confused as to why he had chosen to make Hawkins the dupe in his plan to assassinate Duke Rodoski of Roldem. It had seemed a good idea at the time, but now he wondered how he had arrived at that conclusion. Hawkins had been an able servant and as a bonus had employed that wily old assassin, Amafi. They were a redoubtable pair and had proven their worth early and often. Yet he had chosen to put all blame for the attempt on Rodoski's life on Hawkins.

Kaspar shook his head. Since leaving Olasko, he had several times felt that something had changed within him, something more than just dealing with his dire circumstances. After a while it occurred to him that it had been his friend Leso Varen who had suggested that Tal Hawkins could pose a threat.

Kaspar blinked and realized his mind was drifting. He turned his mind to finding the boy before an alarm could be raised. There were no signs of any habitation nearby, so Kaspar decided the boy might yet be some distance from his home. He focused on the boy's tracks and followed them, picking up the pace as his sense of urgency rose.

Time passed and the sun moved across the sky, and after what Kaspar judged nearly half an hour, he smelled the smoke. The path had led him down into a defile, but now as it rose up and he followed it around a tall rock formation, he saw a farm. Two goats were confined in a pen and in the distance were a few cattle, an odd breed with long sweeping horns and brown-speckled white hides. They cropped grass in a green meadow. Behind a low mud-and-thatch building a full two or more acres of crops swayed in the breeze: corn, Kaspar thought, though he couldn't be certain. And in front of the building stood a well!

He hurried to it and pulled up a bucket on a long rope. The water was clear and cool and he drank his fill.

When he finally dropped the bucket down into the water, he saw a woman standing in the doorway of the building, the boy peering out from behind her. She leveled a crossbow at him. Her face was set in a determined expression, brow knit and eyes narrow, her jaw clenched. She said something in the same language used by the nomads and it was obviously a warning.

Kaspar spoke Quegan, hoping she might recognize a few words, or at least infer from his tone his intent. "I will not harm you," he said slowly as he sheathed his sword. "But I have to see what you have to eat." He pantomimed eating and then indicated the house.

She barked a reply and motioned with the crossbow for him to be off. Kaspar was enough of a hunter to know that a female protecting her young was worthy of the greatest caution.

He slowly approached and again spoke slowly. "I mean you no harm. I just need to eat." He held his hands palms outward.

Then the aroma hit him. Something was cooking inside and it almost made Kaspar ache to smell it; hot bread! And a stew or soup!

Calmly he said, "If I don't eat soon, I'm as good as dead, woman. So if you mean to kill me, do it now and be done with it!"

His reflexes saved him, for she hesitated an instant before tightening her fingers on the release of the crossbow. Kaspar threw himself to the left and the bolt split the air where he had stood a moment earlier. Kaspar rolled, came to his feet and charged.

As soon as the woman saw that her bolt had missed, she raised her crossbow to use it as a club. She brought it crashing down on Kaspar's shoulder as he forced his way through the doorway. "Damn!" he shouted as he wrapped his arms around her waist, bearing her to the floor.

The boy shouted angrily and started striking Kaspar. He was small but strong and Kaspar could feel the blows. He lay on top of the struggling woman and held tightly to the hand that still held the crossbow. He squeezed until she cried out and released it, then stood up just in time to avoid being brained by the metal skillet the boy swung at his head.

He grabbed the boy's wrist and twisted, causing the youngster to shout as he let go of the skillet. "Now stop it!" Kaspar yelled.

He drew his sword and pointed it at the woman. The boy froze, his face a mask of terror.

"All right, then," he said, still speaking Quegan. "One more time: I am not going to hurt you." He then made a show of putting away his sword. He moved past the woman and picked up the crossbow. He handed it to the boy. "Here, lad, go find the bolt outside and see if you can manage to crank it up. If you must kill me, feel free to try again."

He pulled the woman to her feet and studied her. She was rawboned, but he could see she had been pretty once, before a hard life had aged her. He couldn't tell if she was thirty or forty years of age, her face being burned to brown leather by the sun. But her eyes were vivid blue and she held her fear in check. Softly he said, "Fetch me food, woman." Then he let her go.

The boy stood motionless, holding the crossbow as Kaspar looked around. There was only one room in this hovel, but a curtain had been hung so the woman had a bit of privacy when she slept. Her sleeping pallet and a small chest could be glimpsed from where he sat. Another pallet was rolled up under a single table. There were two stools. A makeshift cupboard sat next to an open hearth upon which there sat a kettle of simmering stew. An oven below it had just produced bread, and Kaspar reached down and grabbed one of the still-warm loaves. He tore off some of the bread and stuffed it into his mouth. Then he sat down on one of the stools. He looked at his unwilling hostess and said, "Sorry to be such a boor, but I prefer ill manners to starvation."

As the flavor of the bread registered, he smiled. "This is very good." He motioned to the stew pot and said, "I'll have some of that."

The woman hesitated, then moved to the hearth. She ladled some of the stew into a bowl and placed it before Kaspar, then handed him a wooden spoon. He nodded and said, "Thank you."

She stepped away, gathering the boy to her side. Kaspar ate the stew and before asking for another bowl, he looked at the motionless pair. Quegan didn't seem to be working, but it was the closest language to what he had heard the nomads speak. He pointed to himself and said, "Kaspar."

The woman didn't react. Then he pointed to them and said, "Names?"

The woman might be frightened, he thought, but she wasn't stupid. She said, "Jojanna."

"Joyanna," Kaspar repeated.

She corrected him. "Jojanna," and he heard the soft sound of an "h" after the "y" sound.

"Joy-hanna," he said, and she nodded as if that were close enough.

He pointed to the boy.

"Jorgen," came the reply.

Kaspar nodded and repeated the boy's name. He started to help himself to more stew and judged he had consumed most of their evening meal. He looked at them and then poured the content of the bowl back into the pot. He contented himself with another hunk of bread, then pointed to them. "Eat." He motioned for them to come to the table.

"Eat," she repeated, and Kaspar realized it was the same word, but with a very different accent. He nodded.

She carefully ushered the boy to the table and Kaspar got up and moved over to the door. He saw an empty bucket so he picked it up and turned it over to use as a makeshift stool. The boy watched him with serious blue eyes and the woman kept glancing at him as she put food on the table for the boy.

When they were both seated, Kaspar said, “Well, Jojanna and Jorgen, my name is Kaspar, and until a few days ago I was one of the most powerful men on the other side of this world. I have fallen to this low estate, but despite my scruffy appearance, I am as I have said.”

They looked at him uncomprehendingly. He chuckled. “Very well. You don’t need to learn Quegan. I need to learn your language.” He hit the bucket he sat on and said, “Bucket.”

The woman and her son were silent. He stood up, pointed to the bucket and said the word again. Then he pointed at them and gestured at the bucket again. “What do you call this?”

Jorgen understood and spoke a word. It was unlike anything Kaspar had heard. He repeated it and Jorgen nodded. “Well, it’s a start,” said the former Duke of Olasko. “Maybe by bedtime we can speak enough for me to convince you not to cut my throat while I sleep.”

Three

Farm

Kaspar awoke on the floor of the small hut.

He had slept in front of the door to prevent Jorgen or his mother from fleeing. Levering himself up on one elbow, he peered around in the early morning gloom. There was only a small window near the chimney to his right, so it was still quite dark in the room.

The boy and woman were both awake, but neither had moved from their respective sleeping pallets. "Good morning," Kaspar said as he sat up. He had confiscated their crossbow and any sharp utensil he judged capable of inflicting serious injury and had piled them up out of their reach. He trusted his instincts, as a hunter and a warrior, to awaken him should either of his reluctant companions attempt to harm him, so he had slept well.

After rising slowly, Kasper started returning the implements to their proper locations; the woman would have work to do. He had spent the balance of the previous afternoon and evening pointing at objects and asking their names: slowly unraveling this new language. He had learned enough to surmise that their dialect was related to ancient Keshian, spoken in the Bitter Sea region a few centuries before. Kaspar had studied Empire history as much as any noble boy was forced to and vaguely remembered references to a religious war which had sent Keshian refugees fleeing west. Apparently some of them must have landed nearby.

Kaspar always had possessed a flair for languages, though he now wished he had spent a little more time speaking Quegan—an offshoot of the same Keshian dialect these people's ancestors had spoken. Still, he was getting along well enough if he ever decided to stay and farm around here.

Kaspar looked at the boy and said, "You can get up."

The boy rose. "I can get out?"

Kaspar realized his inaccuracy and corrected it. "I mean get up, but if you need to go outside, do so."

Despite his early behavior toward them, Jorgen had expected to be beaten or killed, and Jojanna had expected to be raped. Not that she wasn't attractive enough in a weather-beaten fashion, Kaspar conceded, but he had never acquired a taste for unwilling women—not even for those who feigned willingness because of his wealth and power.

The woman rose and pulled aside the small privacy-curtain while the boy rolled up his bedding and stowed it under the table. Kaspar sat on one of the two stools. She went to the banked fire in the hearth and stirred the embers, adding wood. "You need wood?" Kaspar asked.

She nodded. "I will cut some more this morning, after milking one of my cows. She lost her calf to a mountain cat last week."

"Is the cat troubling you?"

She didn't understand his question so he rephrased it, "Is the cat returning to take more calves?"

"No," she said.

"I'll cut the wood," said Kaspar. "Where is the axe?"

"In the . . ." He didn't recognize the word, and asked her to repeat it. Then he realized it was an oddly pronounced variant of the Keshian word for "shed." He repeated it, then said, "I will work for my food."

She paused, then nodded and started to prepare the daily meal. "There is no bread," she said. "I make it the night before."

He inclined his head, but said nothing. They both knew why she had not baked last night. She had sat fearfully, waiting for him to assault her, while he repeatedly asked odd or pointless questions about the names of things.

Slowly, he said, "I will not harm you or the boy. I am a stranger and need to learn if I am to live. I will work for my food."

She paused, then looked into his eyes for a moment. As if finally convinced, she nodded. "There are some clothes that belonged to my . . ." She spoke a word he didn't understand.

He interrupted. "Your what?"

She repeated the word, and said, "My man. Jorgen's father."

The local word for husband, he gathered. "Where is he?"

"I don't know," she replied. "Three . . ." Again a new word, but he didn't bother to interrupt; he'd find out later if she meant days, weeks, or months. ". . . ago he went to market. He never came back." Her voice remained calm and her face emotionless, but Kaspar could see a sheen in her eyes. "I looked for three . . ." Again a word he didn't understand. "Then I came back to care for Jorgen."

"What is his name?"

"Bandamin."

"A good man?"

She nodded.

Kaspar said nothing more; he knew she must be wondering what would have happened if Bandamin had been home when he had shown up. Kaspar said, "I'll chop wood."

He went outside and found the axe in the shed next to a small pile of logs. He saw Jorgen feeding some chickens and waved the boy over to him. He motioned to the dwindling pile and said, "Need more soon."

The boy nodded and started speaking quickly, pointing to a stand of woods on the other side of the meadow. Kaspar shook his head and said, "I don't understand. Speak slower."

It was clear Jorgen didn't understand him either, so Kaspar mimicked the boy talking rapidly, then spoke slower.

The boy's face brightened in understanding and he said, "We will cut down a tree over there."

Kaspar nodded and said, "Later."

He was still weakened by his ordeal of the last few days, but he managed to carry enough wood into the hut to keep the fire going for almost a week.

When he put the last armload into the bin next to the hearth, Jojanna said, "Why are you here?"

"Because I need water and food to live."

"No, not here on the farm," she said slowly. "I mean here . . ." she waved a circle around her, as if indicating a larger region. "You are—" a few words he didn't understand "—from far away, yes?"

"A foreigner." He nodded. "Yes, from very far away." He sat down on the stool. "It is hard to tell without . . ." He paused. "I don't have the words—" he said at last. "—yet; when I do, I will tell you."

"Truth?"

He studied her face for a moment, then said, "I will tell you the truth."

She said nothing as she looked him in the eyes. Then with a single nod, she returned to her work in the kitchen.

He stood up. "I will go and help the boy."

Kaspar went outside and saw Jorgen heading into the meadow. He stopped briefly, realizing he had no idea what needed to be done. He had owned tenant-farms in Olasko, but the closest he had ever been to one was riding past on horseback. He had a vague idea of what they produced, but little concept of how they did it. He chuckled to himself as he set out after the boy. He couldn't start learning quickly enough, he decided.

Felling a tree was far more difficult than Kaspar had anticipated, given that he had only seen it done once before, when he was a boy. It had almost landed on top of him to the evil delight of Jorgen, once the initial fear of injury had passed.

He had stripped off all the branches and then cut the bole into manageable sections, which he had lashed up with large leather straps that should have been fastened to a horse's harness. He had discovered that the family's only horse had vanished along with Jorgen's father, so now Kaspar played the part of the horse, dragging the timber to the house across the damp meadow. He strained and heaved forward and the recalcitrant log followed him in jumps and starts.

Pausing to catch his breath, he said to Jorgen, "It seemed like a good idea back there."

The boy laughed. "I told you we should have cut it up and carried the wood back to the house."

Kaspar shook his head in disbelief. Being told off by a child; it was a concept so alien to him he found it amusing and irritating at the same time. He was used to people deferring to him automatically, to saying nothing critical in his presence. He leaned into the harness again and said, "If Tal Hawkins and his bunch could see me now, they'd be on the floor laughing."

He glanced at Jorgen who was obviously amused, and found the boy's mirth infectious. Kaspar began to chuckle as well. "Very well, you were right. Go back and fetch the axe and we'll chop this thing up right here."

Jorgen scampered off. Kaspar didn't relish the idea of a dozen or more trips across the meadow, but without a horse his idea was just plain folly. He stretched as he turned to watch the boy run to where they had left the axe and the water bucket.

Kaspar had been at the farm for eight days now. What had started off as a fearful experience for the boy and his mother had begun to settle into a relatively calm situation. He still slept by the door, but he no longer gathered up potential weapons. He had chosen that spot to give Jojanna as much privacy as was possible in a one-room hut, and also for security reasons. Anyone attempting to come through the door would have to physically move Kaspar first.

Kaspar was still vague about the geography surrounding the farm, but he had no doubt that they were constantly plagued by dangers. Bandits and marauding bands of mercenaries were not uncommon in the area, but the farm was far enough removed from the old high road—the one Kaspar had stumbled along—that few travelers ever chanced across it.

Kaspar stretched again and relished the strength in his

muscles. He knew he had lost weight during the three days without food and water, and now the constant exercise of farm-work was further reducing his bulk. A broad-shouldered man, the former Duke of Olasko had always carried his weight effortlessly, and he had indulged in food and wine of the highest quality. Now Kaspar had to wear the missing Bandamin's clothing because his own trousers were starting to fit too loosely around the waist. He had let his neatly-trimmed beard grow, lacking a razor, mirror, or scissors. Every morning, before washing his face in the water bucket, he caught a glimpse of his reflection and barely recognized himself—sunburned, his dark beard now filling in, and his face thinner. He had been here less than two weeks—what would he look like after a month? Kaspar didn't want to think about it; he intended to learn as much as he could from these people and then leave, for his future was not farming, no matter what else fate might hold in store for him. Still, he wondered how Jojanna would fare once he left them.

Jorgen had tried to help Kaspar, but as he was only eight years old, he was often drawn away by boyish interests. His regular chores involved milking the cow who had lost her calf, feeding the chickens, inspecting fences, and other small tasks a small boy was competent enough to perform.

Jojanna had taken up as much of her husband's work as she was capable of, but a lot of it was just not possible. While she was as hard a worker as Kaspar had ever met, even she couldn't manage to be in two places at the same time. Still, he marveled at how industrious she was; rising before dawn and retiring hours after the sun set, to ensure that the farm would be maintained just as her husband had left it.

Kaspar had hundreds of tenant-farmers on his estates,

and had never once given thought to their toils, always taking their efforts for granted. Now he appreciated their lives to a significant degree. Jojanna and Jorgen lived very well in comparison to most Olaskon farmers, for they owned their land, a small herd, and produced saleable crops; but when Kaspar compared their situation to his old way of life, he realized they lived in near-poverty. How much poorer were the farmers of his own nation?

His nation, he thought bitterly. His birthright had been taken from him and he would have it back or die in the attempt.

Jorgen returned with the axe and Kaspar set to chopping the tree into smaller sections.

After a while the boy said, "Why don't you split it?"

"What?"

Jorgen grinned. "I'll show you." He ran back to the shed and returned with a wedge of metal. He stuck the narrow end of the wedge into a notch and held it. "Hit it with the back of the axe," he told Kaspar.

Kaspar glanced at the axe and saw that the heel was heavy and flat, almost a hammer. He reversed his hold on the handle and swung down, driving the wedge into the wood. Jorgen pulled his hand away with a laugh and shook his hand. "It always makes my fingers sting!"

Kaspar gave the wedge three powerful blows and then, with a satisfying cracking sound, the bole split down the middle. Muttering, he observed, "You learn something new every day, if you just stop to pay attention."

The boy looked at him with a confused expression and said, "What?"

Kaspar realized he had spoken his native Olaskon, so he repeated it, as best he could, in the local language and the boy nodded.

Next, Kaspar set to breaking up the rest of the bole and

then chopping the remaining split rails into firewood. He found the repetitive effort strangely relaxing.

Lately, he had been troubled by dreams, odd vignettes and strange feelings. Small glimpses of things barely remembered, but disturbing. The oddest aspect of these dreams were the details which had escaped his notice in real life. It was as if he was watching himself, seeing himself for the first time in various settings. The images would jump from a court dinner, with his sister sitting at his side, to a conversation with a prisoner in one of the dungeons under his citadel, and then to a memory of something that happened when he was alone. What was most disturbing was how he felt when he awoke, it felt as if he had just relived those moments, but this time the emotions were not consistent with how he remembered them before the dream.

The third night he had one particularly vivid dream-memory; a conversation with Leso Varen in the magician's private chambers. The room reeked of blood and human excrement, and of alien odors from things the magician insisted on mixing and burning in his work area. Kaspar remembered the conversation well, for it had been the first time Varen had suggested to him that he should consider removing those who stood between himself and the crown of Roldem. Kaspar also remembered how appealing he had found the idea.

But he had awoken from the dream retching from the memory of the stench in the room; at the time he had visited Varen, he had hardly been aware of it, the smell had not bothered him in the slightest. Yet this morning he had sat bolt-upright before the door of the hut, gasping for breath, and had almost disturbed Jorgen.

Kaspar encouraged Jorgen to speak about whatever was on his mind, as his constant prattle sensitized Kaspar to the local language. He was becoming quite conversant, but was also frustrated. For all their good qualities, Jorgen and Jojanna were simple farm people who knew almost nothing of the world in which they lived beyond their farm and the village a few days' walk to the northwest. It was there they sold their cattle and grain, and from what Kaspar could discern, Bandamin had been considered well-to-do by local standards.

He had been told about the great desert to the northeast, commanded by a race called the Jeshandi, who were not like the nomads who tried to capture him. They were the Bentu, a people who had migrated from the south in Jojanna's father's time. Kaspar calculated that it must have been during the war which had ended with the defeat of the Emerald Queen's army at Nightmare Ridge in the Western Realm of the Kingdom of the Isles. Olaskon intelligence had gathered as much information as they could when Kaspar's father had been Duke, and some tidbits had been gleaned from agents working in both the Kingdom and Kesh, but what Kaspar had read left him certain that a large part of the story was never reported.

What he did know was that a woman known as the Emerald Queen had emerged somewhere to the far west of this continent of Novindus and had waged a war of conquest among the various city states, forging a vast army—which included, according to some reports, giant-sized serpent men—and had gathered a fleet for the sole purpose of invading the Kingdom of the Isles.

While no reason was forthcoming as to why this had happened, and while it defied all conventional military logic, it had still happened. Krondor had been reduced to mostly rubble and the rebuilding of the Western Realm was still underway nearly thirty years later.

Perhaps, thought Kaspar as he finished chopping wood, I'll learn something more about it while I make my way across this land. He looked at the boy and said, "Don't just stand there. Pick up some wood. I'm not going to carry it all."

The boy grumbled good-naturedly as he carried as much as he could: a decent amount of kindling, and Kaspar carried as much as he was able. "I'd give a lot for a horse and wagon," he said.

"Father took the horse when he . . . went away," said Jorgen, huffing with exertion.

Kaspar had grasped the various terms for time and now realized that the boy's father had left three weeks prior to his appearance at their farm. Bandamin had been taking a steer to the village, called Heslagnam, to sell to an innkeeper there. He was then going to purchase some supplies needed for the farm.

Jojanna and Jorgen had walked to the village when he was three days overdue, only to be told that no one had seen Bandamin. Somewhere between the farm and Heslagnam, the man, his wagon, and the steer had simply vanished.

Jojanna was reticent to speak on the subject, still hoping after almost two months that her husband might return. Kaspar judged it unlikely. This area had little that passed for law. In theory, there was a covenant among those who lived in the region, enforced at times by the nomads to the north, the Jeshandi, that no one troubled travelers or those who cared for them. The origin of this covenant was lost to history, but like so many other things even that had vanished like smoke in a wind when the Emerald Queen's army had ravaged this land.

Kaspar deduced that this farm's relative wealth, in cattle as well as crops, was the result of Bandamin's father being one of the few able-bodied men who had evaded being enlisted into the Emerald Queen's army at swordpoint. Kaspar felt frustrated by the gaps in his knowledge, but he pieced together a picture of what had probably happened from things Jojanna had said.

Her father-in-law had managed to hide while many others were pressed into service for a battle on the other side of the mountains to the southwest—the Sumanu, she called them. He had benefited by finding strays from abandoned farms, as well as seed grain and vegetables. He had found a wagon and horses, and over a few months had come to this little dell and established his farm, which Bandamin had inherited.

Kaspar put the wood in the wood box behind the hut and started back across the meadow to fetch more. Looking at the tired boy, he said, "Why don't you see if your mother needs your help?"

Jorgen nodded and ran off.

Kaspar stopped for a moment and watched the child vanish around the corner of the hut. He realized that he had given no thought to being a father. He had assumed the day would come when he would have to wed and breed an heir, but had never considered what actually being a father would mean. Until this moment. The boy missed his father terribly; Kaspar could see that. He wondered if Bandamin's disappearance would ever be explained.

He set off to fetch more wood, admitting to himself that farm life was a great deal more arduous than he had ever imagined. Still, that was where the gods had placed them on the Wheel of Life, he considered; and even if he was back on the throne of Olasko, he couldn't very well beggar the treasury buying horses and wagons for every farmer, could he? He chuckled at the absurdity of it all, and flexed his aching shoulders.

Kaspar looked up from his meal. "I must leave," he said.

Jojanna nodded. "I expected that would happen soon."

He was silent for a long moment, while Jorgen's eyes went back and forth between them. Kaspar had been a fixture in their house for more than three months, and while at times the boy mocked him for his ignorance over the basics of farming, Kaspar had come to fill the void left by his father.

But Kaspar had more concerns than one boy from a distant land, despite having grown used to his company. He had learned all he could from them. He spoke the local language passingly well now, and he had come to understand as much about the customs and beliefs as Jojanna knew. There was no reason for him to stay and many reasons for him to leave. He had spent months moving only a few miles from where he had been deposited by the white-haired magician, and he still had half a world to travel across.

Jorgen said at last, "Where are you going?"

"Home."

Jorgen seemed about to say something, then he fell quiet. Finally he asked, "What will we do?"

Jojanna replied, "What we always do."

"You need a horse," Kaspar said. "The summer wheat will be ready to harvest soon, and the corn is ready now. You need a horse to pull your wagon to market."

She nodded.

"You will need to sell some cattle. How many?"

"Two should bring me a serviceable horse."

Kaspar smiled. "One thing I do know is horses." He neglected to mention that his expertise lay in the area of warhorses, hunters, and his sister's sleek palfreys, not draft animals. Still, he could spot lameness, smell thrush in hooves, and gauge the temper of the animal, he supposed.

"We shall have to go to Mastaba."

"Where is that?"

"Two, three days' walk beyond Heslagnam. We can sell the cattle to a broker there; he may have a horse to trade," she said flatly.

Kaspar was silent through the rest of the meal. He knew that Jojanna was fearful of being alone again. She had made no overtures toward Kaspar, and he was content to leave things as they were. He hadn't been with a woman in months, and she was attractive enough in her rawboned fashion, but the confined quarters coupled with his concern for Jorgen had kept them apart.

Jojanna alternately hoped against hope to see her husband again, then mourned him as if he were dead. Kaspar knew that in a few more months she would accept him in Bandamin's place permanently. That was another reason why he felt it was time to leave.

"Perhaps you can find a workman who might come here to help you?"

"Perhaps," she said in a noncommittal tone.

Kaspar picked up his wooden plate and carried it to the wash bucket. From then until they went to their respective sleeping mats, there was silence.

FOUR

VILLAGE

Kaspar, Jojanna, and Jorgen trudged along the old highway.

They walked at a steady pace, as they had for the previous two days. Kaspar had never realized how tedious it was to walk everywhere. He had lived his entire life using the horses, carriages, and fast ships at his disposal; in fact, the only time he had ever traveled by foot was during a hunt or when taking a stroll through a palace garden. Going more than a few miles by shank's mare was not only fatiguing, it was boring.

He glanced back to see how Jorgen was doing. The boy walked behind the two plodding steers. He held a long stick and flicked the animals with it when they attempted to veer off to the side of the road to crop the plants—not that there was an abundance of fodder, but the contrary animals seemed intent on investigating every possible source unless they were constantly prodded.

Kaspar felt anxious to move along, yet resigned to the reality of his situation. He was on foot and alone, save for the company of Jojanna and her son, and without protection, sustenance, or experience of this hostile land. What little Jojanna had told him revealed that the area was still reeling from the ravages of the Emerald Queen's army, even though it had been almost a generation since those terrible events.

The farms and villages had returned quickly, despite the absence of most of the men. Old men and women had eked out their livings until the young had matured enough to work, wed, and have more children.

The lack of civil order had lingered; an entire generation of sons had grown up without fathers, and many were orphans. Where once a string of city-states had controlled the outlying lands, now chaos ruled. Traditional conventions had been supplanted by the law of warlords and robber barons. Whoever ran the biggest gang became the local sheriff.

Jojanna's family had survived because of their relative isolation. The local villagers knew the whereabouts of their farm, but few travelers had ever chanced upon it. It had only been through the lucky happenstance of Jorgen's search for the lost birds that Kaspar's life had been saved. He could easily have starved to death within a few hours' walk of a bounty of food otherwise.

As they walked, Kaspar could see a mountain range rising to the west, while the land to the east fell away and turned brown in the distance, where it bordered a desert. Had he stayed a captive with the Bentu he would have become a slave; or if he had planned his escape badly, he'd most likely have died in the arid lands between those distant mountains and the range of hills along whose spine this old road ran.

He caught sight of a shimmering in the distance. "Is that a river?"

"Yes, it's the Serpent River," Jojanna said. "Beyond it lies the Hotlands."

Kaspar asked, "Do you know where the City of the Serpent River lies?"

"Far to the south, on the Blue Sea."

"So I need to go downriver," Kaspar concluded.

"If that is where you wish to be, yes."

"Where I wish to be is home," said Kaspar with an edge of bitterness in his voice.

"Tell me about your home," asked Jorgen.

Kaspar glanced over his shoulder and saw the boy grinning, but his irritation died quickly. To his surprise, he found himself fond of the boy. As ruler of Olasko, Kaspar knew he would eventually have to marry to produce a legitimate heir, but it had never occurred to him that he might actually like his children. For an idle moment he wondered if his father had liked him.

"Olasko is a seafaring nation," said Kaspar. "Our capital city, Opardum, rests against great cliffs, with a defensible, yet busy harbor." As he plodded along, he continued, "It's on the eastern coast of a large—" he realized he didn't know the word for continent in the local language, "—a large *place* called Triagia. So, from the citadel—" he glanced at them and saw that neither Jojanna or Jorgen looked puzzled by the Keshian word "—from the citadel, you can see spectacular sunrises over the sea.

"To the east are table lands and along the river are many farms, quite a few like your own . . ."

He passed the time telling them of his homeland, and at one point Jorgen asked, "What did you do? I mean, you're not a farmer."

Kaspar said, "I was a hunter," a fact he had already shared with the boy, when he dressed out a slaughtered steer to hang in the summer house—as he thought of the underground cave with a door they used to store perishables. "And I was a soldier. I traveled."

Jorgen asked, "What's it like?"

"What's what like?"

"Traveling."

"Like this," he said. "A lot of walking, or sailing on a ship, or riding a horse."

"No," said Jorgen, laughing. "I mean what were the places like?"

"Some like these Hotlands," answered Kaspar, "but other places are cool and rainy all the time . . ." He told them of the nations around the Sea of Kingdoms, and talked of the more entertaining and colorful things he had seen. He kept them amused and distracted until they crested a rise and saw the village of Heslagnam.

Kaspar realized that he had expected something a bit more prosperous, and felt disappointed. The largest building in sight was obviously the inn, a two-story, somewhat ramshackle wooden building with an improbable lime-colored roof. A single chimney belched smoke and the establishment boasted a stable in the rear and a large stabling yard. There were two other buildings that appeared to be shops, but without signs to herald their merchandise. Kaspar was at a loss to know what one could or could not buy in the village of Heslagnam.

Jojanna instructed Jorgen to herd the two steers into the stable yard while she and Kaspar went inside.

Once through the door, Kaspar was even less impressed. The chimney and hearth had been fashioned from badly mortared stones and the ventilation was poor; as a result, the establishment was reeking with the odors of cooking, sweaty men, spilled ale and other liquids, moldy straw, and other less identifiable smells.

The inn was presently unoccupied, save for a large man carrying in a keg from somewhere at the rear of the building. He put it down and said, "Jojanna! I didn't expect to see you for another week."

"I'm selling two steers."

"Two?" said the man, wiping his hands on a greasy apron. He was a thick-necked, broad-shouldered man with an enormous belly, and he walked with a rolling gait. He bore a handful of scars on his forearms, exposed by rolled-up sleeves, and Kaspar recognized him as a former soldier or mercenary. He could see that under the fat lay enough muscle to cause trouble.

He looked at Kaspar as he spoke to the woman. "I don't even need one. I've got a quarter still hanging in the cold room and it's aged pretty nice. I could maybe take one off your hands, stake it out in the back, then slaughter it next week, but not two."

Jojanna said, "Sagrin, this is Kaspar. He's been working at the farm for his keep, filling in for Bandamin."

With an evil grin, the man said, "I expect he has."

Kaspar let the insult slide. The innkeeper looked like a brawler and while Kaspar had no fear of any man, he also didn't go out of his way to court trouble. He'd seen too many of his friends die needlessly in duels as a youngster to believe that there was any profit in borrowing trouble. Kaspar said, "If you can't use the beef, we'll try the next village . . ." He looked at Jojanna.

"That would be Mastaba."

"Wait a minute," said Sagrin. He rubbed his hand over his bearded chin. "I don't have much by way of coin or trade goods. What do you have in mind?"

"Horses," answered Kaspar. "Two."

"Horses!" echoed Sagrin with a barking laugh. "Might as well be their weight in gold. Some Bentu slavers came through here a couple of months back and bought two of mine, then came back the next night and stole the other three."

"Who else has horses to sell around here?" asked Kaspar.

Sagrin rubbed his chin as if thinking, then said, "Well, I'm certain you won't find any up in Mastaba. Maybe downriver?"

Jojanna said, "You know that traveling downriver is dangerous even for armed men, Sagrin! You're trying to scare us into making a better bargain for you!" She turned to Kaspar. "He's probably lying about there being no horses in Mastaba."

As she turned to leave, Sagrin's hand shot out and he grabbed her arm. "Wait a minute, Jojanna! No one calls me a liar, not even you!"

Kaspar didn't hesitate. He reached out, grabbed Sagrin's hand, and pressed his thumb hard into a nerve below the other man's thumb. A moment later he pushed the heavy man, and as Sagrin resisted the push, Kaspar grabbed his dirty tunic and pulled. Sagrin stumbled for a moment and then his old fighter's reflexes came into play. Rather than landing hard, he rolled to the side and came up, ready to brawl.

Instead of attacking, Kaspar stepped away and said calmly, "I'll have my sword in your throat before you can take a step."

Sagrin saw a man standing confidently, his sword still at his side. He hesitated for a moment, then whatever fight he had left in him vanished. With a grin he said, "Sorry for my temper. It's just that those were hard words."

Jojanna rubbed at her arm where he had grabbed it.

"Hard, maybe, Sagrin, but you've tried to get the better of Bandamin and me before."

"That's just trading," said the stout innkeeper stepping forward, his hands held with palms outward. "But this time it's the truth. Old Balyoo had the one extra mare, but the old girl's spavined, and not even fit to foal, so he might have put her down already. Other than that, horses are harder to find around here than free ale."

Kaspar said, "What about a mule?"

"You mean to ride a mule?" asked Sagrin.

"No, I want it to pull a wagon and a plow," said Kaspar, looking at Jojanna.

"Kelpita has a mule he'd probably trade for the price of a steer," said Sagrin. He motioned to the bar. "Why don't you fix yourselves up with something to drink while I go ask him?"

Jojanna nodded as Jorgen entered the inn, and Sagrin left, tousling the boy's hair as he passed. Jojanna went behind the bar and poured ales for herself and Kaspar, filling another cup with water for Jorgen.

Kaspar watched as they sat at a table, then joined them. "Can you trust him?"

"Most of the time," she answered. "He's tried to take advantage of us before, but as he said, it's just bargaining."

"Who's Kelpita?"

"The merchant who owns that large building across the road. He trades down the river. He has wagons and mules."

"Well, I don't know much about mules, but in the army—" he paused "—the army I was with for a while, they used them instead of horses for the heavy hauling. I do know that they can be difficult."

"I'll make him work!" said Jorgen with youthful eagerness.

"How much will the steer bring?"

"What do you mean?" Jojanna looked at Kaspar as if she didn't comprehend.

"I've never sold a steer before." Kaspar realized that he had little idea about the cost of many items. As Duke he never paid for anything out of his own purse. The gold he carried was for wagering, brothels, or to reward good service. He had signed documents allocating the household budget for the entire citadel, but he had no idea what his housecarl paid to the local merchants for salt, or beef, or fruit. He didn't know what food came as taxes from his own farms. He didn't even know what a horse cost, unless it was one especially bred as a gift for one of his ladies or his own warhorse. Kaspar started to laugh.

"What?" asked Jojanna.

"There are many things I don't know," he said, leaving his meaning ambiguous. She looked at him pointedly and he elaborated. "In the army other people—quartermasters, commissaries, provisioners—made all our arrangements. I just showed up and the food was there. If I needed to ride, a horse was provided."

"That must be nice," she said, her manner showing that she didn't believe him.

He considered what he did know about the prices of luxury items, and asked, "How much does a steer bring in silver or copper around here?"

Jorgen laughed. "He thinks we have coins!"

"Hush!" snapped his mother. "Go outside and find something useful to do, or at least play, but go outside."

Grumbling, the boy left. Jojanna said, "We don't see coins here often. There's no one making them. And after the war—" he didn't have to be told what war; all references to "the war" meant the Emerald Queen's rampage "—there were many false coins, copper with silver painted on them, or lead covered in gold. Sagrin sees a few from time to time from travelers, so he has a touchstone and scales to tell the true from the false, but mostly we barter, or sometimes work for one another. Kelpita will list what he's willing to exchange for the steer, then consider if it is worth a mule. He might want both steers in return."

"No doubt he will," said Kaspar. "But that's negotiating, isn't it?"

"He has what I want, and doesn't have that much use for a steer. He can only eat one so fast."

Kaspar laughed, and Jojanna smiled. "He'll then trade it to Sagrin who will slaughter and dress it out, and Kelpita will be able to eat and drink here for a while at no cost, which will please him and vex his wife. She doesn't like it when he drinks too much ale."

Kaspar waited without making further comment. Again he was visited by the thought that Olaskon peasants must lead similar lives. In Olasko there would be merchants whose wives grew bitter when they drank too much ale, ex-soldiers who owned run-down inns, and little farm boys out looking for someone with whom to play. He sat back and reflected that it was impossible to know each and every one of them. He barely recognized half the household staff at the citadel, let alone knew their names. But even so, he should have been mindful of what kind of people looked to him for protection.

He was visited by an unexpected rush of sadness. How little care he had given. A torrent of images swept through his thoughts, much like the dreams he had experienced.

"What's wrong?" asked Jojanna.

Kaspar looked at her sideways. "What?"

"You've gone all pale and your eyes are brimming with moisture. What's wrong?"

"Nothing," he said, his voice surprisingly hoarse. He swallowed hard, then said, "Just an unexpected old memory."

"From a war?"

He shrugged and nodded once, saying nothing.

"Bandamin was a soldier once."

"Really?"

"Not like you," she added quickly. "He served with a local militia when he was a boy, with his father, trying to make this a fit place to live in."

"Seems they did a good job."

She shrugged. "I don't know. We still have bandits and raiders to worry about. The Bentu slavers will take a free man and head south; they'll sell him to a rich farmer or a miller, or if he's a warrior, take him to the City of the Serpent River for the games."

"This City of the Serpent River. How far is it?"

"Weeks by boat. Longer by foot. I don't really know. Is that where you will go?"

"Yes," answered Kaspar. "I need to get home, and to do that I need a ship, and the only ships that travel to my homeland are there."

"It's a long journey."

"So I gather," he said flatly.

After an hour, Sagrin returned and said, "Here's what Kelpita will do . . ." He outlined a trade of some goods, seed at a future date, and some trade with another merchant in the next village. At the end, Jojanna seemed satisfied.

Kaspar said, "Throw in a room for the night, including supper, and you have a deal."

"Done!" said Sagrin, slapping his hands together. "We have roasted duck and some stew for tonight's meal, and the bread was freshly baked this morning."

As he walked to the kitchen, Jojanna whispered to Kaspar, "Don't expect too much. Sagrin can't cook."

Kaspar said, "Food is food and I'm hungry."

Then Jojanna said, "You still have no horse."

Kaspar shrugged. "I'll find a way. Perhaps I'll find a boat heading downriver."

"That would be difficult."

"Why?" asked Kaspar as he moved to pour himself another ale while Sagrin worked in the kitchen.

"I'll tell you over supper. I had better go find Jorgen."

Kaspar nodded, drank the ale. *A man could have a worse life than being married to a woman like Jojanna, with a son like Jorgen*, he thought to himself. Then he looked around the pitiful inn and thought, *But he could have a much better one, too.*

Kaspar came awake first. Jojanna and Jorgen slept on two cots that served for beds in the inn and Kaspar lay on a pallet on the floor.

Something had disturbed his rest. He listened intently. Horses!

Drawing his sword, he hurried along the hall and down the stairs. He found Sagrin already waiting in the common room, holding an old blade. Kaspar motioned for the stout old soldier to move to one side of the door as Kaspar hurried to the window.

He counted five riders. They milled around and chattered. One pointed toward the inn and another shook his head and pointed up the road. They wore heavy cloaks, but Kaspar could see enough of their garb to recognize them for what they were: soldiers.

After a moment, they turned as a group and rode north.

Kaspar said, "They're gone."

"Who were they?" asked Sagrin.

"Soldiers. They wore cavalry boots. I could see a single stripe on their tunics, though I couldn't make out its color—white or perhaps yellow. They bore identical swords, but no bows or shields. They wore turbans with feathers on their heads."

"Damn," said Sagrin. "They must have decided to go to Mastaba, but they'll be back."

"Who are they?"

"There is a bandit to the south, in the city of Delga—if you can call it a city—who calls himself the Raj of Muboya. Those are his men. He's claiming all the land between Delga and the banks of the Serpent Lake, and he's garrisoning the towns and villages. The bastard is also taxing people."

Kaspar said, "Is he offering protection?"

"Of a sort," answered Sagrin. "He protects us from the other renegades and bandits around here, so he can pluck us like chickens himself."

"It costs money to govern," said Kaspar.

"I do just fine without a government," said Sagrin.

"Find enough people with swords to agree with you, and you might convince him. Those five I saw could probably run this entire town without additional help."

"You're right," said Sagrin as he sat heavily in a chair. "I'm what passes for a warrior in these parts. A couple of the farmers are strong, but none are trained to fight.

"I only know what I know because my father formed a militia when I was a boy and we fought a lot of thugs in our day." He pointed to the scars on his arms. "Make no mistake, these were honestly earned, Kaspar. But now I'm an old man. I would fight, but I know I wouldn't win."

"Well, this Raj might not be the first bandit to found a dynasty. Where I come from—" He dropped the thought, then said instead, "If he can bring order and safety to people like Jojanna and Jorgen—women and children—that would be a good thing, no?"

"I guess. Whatever is going to happen will happen. But I reserve the right to complain."

Kaspar chuckled. "Feel free."

"Are you staying with Jojanna?" he asked, and Kaspar took his meaning.

"No. She's a good woman who hopes that her husband is still alive."

"Slim chance. If he is, he's toiling in a mine, working on some rich merchant's farm to the south, or fighting in the arena down in the City of the Serpent River."

"I have my own plans, in any event," said Kaspar. "They don't include being a farmer."

"Didn't take you for one. Soldier?"

"For a time."

"Something else, too, I wager," said Sagrin. Heaving himself out of the chair he added, "Well, I might as well get started; the sun will be up in an hour and I rarely fall back to sleep easily, especially if I must sleep with a sword in my hand."

Kaspar nodded. "I understand."

He now knew what his next step must be. He needed to head south. There was a man gathering an army there, no matter what he called himself, and he had horses.

Kaspar needed a horse.

FIVE

SOLDIER

Kaspar waited silently.

He crouched behind some low brush while a patrol of cavalry rode by. He had encountered two other patrols over the last week since leaving Jojanna's farm. Given what little he knew of these people, he had decided to avoid contact with them. Common soldiers had a decided tendency to use weapons before asking questions, and Kaspar had no desire to end up dead, a prisoner, or enlisted into any army at the point of a sword.

Leaving the farm had proved more troubling than he had expected. Jorgen seemed especially disturbed by the prospect of being alone with his mother again. On the other hand, the mule would help with all the heavy work, and Kelpita had a son who would come and work with them during harvest so Jojanna wouldn't lose her grain.

Kaspar considered how they would have fared had he

never arrived. They'd still be scrabbling to run the farm and wouldn't have had enough wood or the mule.

Still, it had been harder to say goodbye than he had anticipated.

A couple of days before, he had skirted a village that appeared to be a staging post for the local patrols, and then had bartered a day's work at a farm just off the road for a meal. The food had been meager and they had only offered him water to drink, but he had been glad for it. Kaspar remembered the lavish meals that had been the hallmark of his court, but quickly pushed the memory aside. He'd happily kill someone for a cut of hot rare beef, a bowl of his cook's spiced vegetables, and a flagon of good Ravensberg wine.

Certain the riders were now gone, Kaspar returned to trudging along the road. What had been a broken old highway appeared to be in better condition the farther south he moved. There were signs of relatively recent repair-work at various places he had passed over the last two days.

As he rounded a bend in the road, he saw a large town in the distance. The land around him was getting progressively more verdant and abundant. Whatever else this Raj of Muboya had done, he had pacified the territory around his capital to the point at which farmers were prospering again; farms lined the road and orchards were visible up on the hillsides. Perhaps in time this more peaceful aspect would be visited upon the area where Jorgen and his mother lived. He would like to think the boy had a chance for a better life.

As he approached the gate of the town he saw signs of harsh justice. A dozen corpses in various stages of decay were on display, as well as half a dozen heads impaled on stakes. The men had been hung by ropes on crosses of wood, "crucified" in the Quegan language. He had been told it was a nasty way to die; after a while the body could not prevent fluid from gathering in the lungs and a man would drown in his own spit.

At the gate a squad of soldiers waited, each dressed like those he had seen on horseback, save that they lacked the cloaks and fancy hats. These ones also wore metal helms with chain guards over their necks.

One sauntered over to intercept Kaspar. "Your business in Delga?"

"Just passing through on my way south."

"You have an odd accent."

"I'm not from around here."

"Your trade?"

"I'm a hunter now. I was a soldier."

"Or maybe you're a bandit?"

Kaspar studied the man. He was thin and nervous and had a habit of looking down his nose when he spoke. He had a weak chin and his teeth were gray. Whatever his rank here, he would be a corporal at the most in Kaspar's army. He knew the type: self-important, not bright enough to realize he had risen as high as he ever would. Without taking obvious offense, Kaspar smiled. "If I were a bandit, I'd be a damn poor one. All I'd have to show for my labors is this sword, the clothing on my back, these boots, and my wits." The soldier started to speak, but Kaspar cut him off and continued, "I'm an honest man, and am willing to work for my keep."

"Well, I don't think the Raj has need of any mercenaries today."

Kaspar smiled. "I said I was a soldier, not a mercenary."

"Where did you serve?"

"Somewhere I'm sure you've never heard of."

"Well, get along and see you don't cause any trouble. I've got my eye on you." He waved him on.

Kaspar nodded and walked though the gate. Delga was the first real town he had visited in this land and it had more hallmarks of civilization than Kaspar had encountered in any settlement so far. The inns near the gate were run-down and as seedy as Sagrin's, which was to be expected. The better inns would probably be located near the merchants' quarter, so he walked until he reached a market square, which at this hour of the afternoon was thronged with people. Delga had all the signs of being a prosperous community and the people seemed content in their daily tasks.

Kaspar had studied governance all his life, for he had been born to rule. He had seen enough fools, madmen, and incompetents to last a lifetime and had read about many others. He knew that the populace were the foundation of a strong nation and they could only be taxed to a certain point. Kaspar's plottings and intrigues had been designed, in part, to minimize the need for overt military confrontation, which was always an expensive undertaking that put a great burden on the people.

Not that Kaspar had cared much for his people's happiness, one way or the other—he hadn't even considered the plight of commoners until he had met Jojanna and Jorgen—but he was concerned for welfare of his nation in general, and that meant maintaining a contented populace.

Whatever else, the people of Delga didn't look overburdened or worried. They showed none of the signs of being concerned about government informants or tax officials seeing too many luxury goods on display.

The market was a riot of colors and sounds, busy with afternoon trading. Occasionally he heard the sound of coins being counted out or a jingling purse, so he judged that hard money was returning under the Raj's care.

At first glance, it seemed this ruler had the support of his people. Uniformed men, wearing a different livery, were strolling through the market, their eyes constantly searching for trouble. Kaspar guessed they were constables or the town watch.

He made eye contact with one; a broad-shouldered man with a scarred face and neck. The man stopped, but Kaspar didn't avert his gaze and walked over to him. The man wore a blue tunic, but instead of displaying the high boots of a cavalryman with his trousers tucked in the tops, he wore balloon-legged pants that almost hid the boots entirely. His sword was a shorter weapon, and he wore no helm, but rather a felt hat with a broad brim.

"Good afternoon," said Kaspar in greeting.

"Stranger," said the man curtly.

"I take it you are a constable?"

"You take it correctly."

"I was wondering, where might I go to find work around here?"

"Your trade?"

"I'm a skilled hunter and a soldier," Kaspar continued politely.

"If you bring in game, you can sell it at the inns, but the Raj has no need for mercenaries."

Feeling as if he had already had this conversation, Kaspar didn't debate this point. "What about laboring?"

"There's always need for those able to heft a bale or lift a crate at the caravanserai." He pointed south. "Through the town and outside the gate. But you're too late today. All the hiring is done at first light."

Kaspar nodded his thanks and moved through the town. All at once, he was struck by a sense of the alien and the familiar. These people dressed differently and their accents and voices sounded strange to his ear. He had thought himself comfortable with the language, but now he realized he was only used to hearing Jojanna's and

Jorgen's two voices. This was a town, a good-sized one, on its way to becoming a city. He passed new construction work and saw men eager to be about their business, and found the pace and rhythms of the settlement familiar.

Reaching the outer gate, Kaspar found that the caravanserai was indeed quiet. As the constable had warned him, most of the business of the day was done. Still, it was still an opportunity to ask questions. He went from caravan to caravan and after a few conversations he had the feel of the place. He discovered that a caravan making for the south would be departing in a week's time, and the caravan owner said he should return then to seek a position as a guard, but in the meantime he had nothing to offer Kaspar.

By the time the sun began to set, Kaspar was tired and hungry. There was nothing he could do about the latter, but he could at least find a place to sleep if he was quiet about it. This land was hot, despite it being early spring—if he could judge the seasons on the other side of the world. The nights could get chilly, but they were far from cold.

He found some workers sitting around a fire and speaking softly, and asked permission to join them. They seemed content to let him, so he settled in and lay behind two men who spoke of things he could only imagine: villages whose names he had never heard before, rivers that coursed through alien landscapes, and other things familiar to them, but foreign to Kaspar. For the first time since coming to this continent, Kaspar wished not only to wreak destruction on Talwin Hawkins and those who had betrayed him, but simply to go home.

The wagons bumped along the old highway. It was a rugged ride, but it was a ride. Kaspar was glad not to be walking. He had finished an arduous week of work, loading and unloading wagons for scant wages—scarcely enough to pay for food. He had lost even more weight; he had to buy a whipcord belt to keep his trousers from falling down. He had supplemented his income by playing knucklebones with some of the other workers, but on the last day his luck had faltered and now he was barely more than a few copper coins ahead. But at least he *was* ahead, and every little improvement was an advantage. He had endured. Though it had been one difficult week for him, the other men had suffered a lifetime of difficulty. For Kaspar, the most telling characteristic was their complete lack of hope. For these workers, each day was an exercise in survival; tomorrow would take care of itself.

Kaspar felt a mixture of impatience and resignation. He was anxious to make as much progress as possible every day and to return home as rapidly as he could to settle accounts, but he knew the journey would take time, and that time was also dependent on many factors outside of his control.

His struggle across the harsh wilderness before he found Jorgen and his mother had been simple physical hardship, but the week he had spent laboring at the caravanserai had been as miserable a week as he had ever spent. It had exposed him to a level of human wretchedness which he'd never experienced before in his privileged life.

He had learned that the War, as it was known locally, had taken place when Kaspar was just a boy. The Kingdom of the Isles had defeated the armies of the Emerald Queen at the battle of Nightmare Ridge, when Kaspar had been barely out of nappies. Yet the effects were still being felt decades later.

Many of the laborers were the children of people driven from their homes by the advancing horde. The enemy had enlisted every able-bodied man they found, giving them the choice at sword-point: to fight for them, or die. Women were taken as whores, cooks, and menial laborers, and even some young boys were forced to serve with the luggage carts.

Thousands of children had been orphaned, and there had been no one to care for them. The weak had died, and those who did survive grew up wild, without any sense of family outside their gang of thugs, or loyalty beyond a petty bandit chieftain.

Bringing order to such a place would tax the wits of the most talented of rulers, Kaspar thought. He knew that if he was given the task, he would begin much the same way this Raj of Muboya had: by consolidating a core area, making sure it was stable and prosperous, and then expanding the sphere of influence, turning the influence into control. The young Raj might do this for most of his life before facing any organized opposition to the north.

As Kaspar had lived with the porters and teamsters for a week, they answered his questions and he had learned a great deal about the local area. To the east lay the Serpent River and beyond that the wasteland controlled by the nomadic Jeshandi; it seemed they had no interest in what occurred on this side of the river. But across the Serpent they ruled supreme; even the Emerald Queen's army had been sorely pressed on that flank by the Jeshandi. Kaspar had read reports of the war from his father's archives when he was a boy and given the immense size of the Queen's army, Kaspar assumed the Jeshandi had to be a formidable cavalry to have avoided obliteration.

To the west rose the Sumanu Mountains and beyond them vast grasslands that rolled down to the River Vedra and a string of petty city-states. That natural barrier protected the Raj from conflict to the west. To the south, other minor nobles and self-styled rulers held territory, but from the rumors, the Raj was already halfway to winning a happy little war with one of his neighbors in that direction.

But far to the south, on the coast of the Blue Sea, lay the City of the Serpent River, about which these locals knew little. Once, it had held sway from the sea all the way up to the Serpent Lake, and had been ruled by a council of clans indigenous to the area. More than that, Kaspar didn't know. Still, that was where ships docked, some from as far away as the Sunset Isles, the southern Keshian cities, and sometimes even Queg and the Kingdom. Which meant a way home for Kaspar. So, that was where he was bound, war or no war.

The wagons continued to bump along and Kaspar kept his eyes scanning the horizon in case trouble appeared unexpectedly. He thought it was unlikely, as the farther south they traveled from Muboya, the more peaceful the countryside seemed. At least, until they ran into the rumored war.

Kaspar sat at the rear of the wagon. The only thing he had to watch, besides the horizon, was the team of horses pulling the wagon behind his, and the dour expression of Kafa: a taciturn old driver with little good to say when he said anything at all.

The driver of his wagon was a voluble man named Ledanu, whom Kaspar tended to ignore, since his words tumbled out aimlessly as his mind wandered. Still, Kaspar had grown tired of the relative silence and judged he could endure a little of Ledanu's rambling if he could glean a bit of useful information from among the flood of words.

"Tell me, Ledanu, of this next city."

"Ah! Kaspar, my friend," said the little man, eager to impress his new wagon mate with his expertise. "Simarah is a most wonderful place. There are inns and brothels, baths and gambling houses. It is *very* civilized." Kaspar sat back and endured a torrent of details about the establishments that Ledanu found most convivial in each aforementioned category. Kaspar realized that any useful intelligence, such as the disposition of soldiers, the politics of the region, its relationship with neighboring cities and such would be lacking. Still, it was useful to hear something about the place, as it would be Kaspar's next home until he could conspire to find a way south again.

Kaspar leaned against the doorway, waiting to see if anyone would appear this morning requiring laborers. It was traditional for those seeking day-labor to meet before sunrise in a small market near Simarah's north gate. Kaspar had found work every morning for the first week after arriving in Simarah, and the pay was better than it had been in Muboya.

There wasn't a full-scale war underway as yet, but some sort of border skirmish was developing down south, between Muboya and the realm of someone calling himself the King of Sasbataba. Soldiers were being recruited, and because the pay was relatively good, most workers were taking up arms. So Kaspar had been constantly employed. He had also rediscovered his gambling luck, and so had enough coin in his purse to feed himself for another week should work stop. He could also afford a room—little more than a cot under the stairs—at a local boarding house. He ate simple food and didn't drink, so he actually ended each day with a little more wealth than he had at the start.

He had hoped for another caravan to pass through the town, heading south and that he could again find a position as a guard, but during the conflict with King Sasbataba, all supplies and goods heading south were under strict military escort. A sense of urgency was overtaking him as he waited to continue his journey home.

Three men approached the market and all the workers came to their feet expectantly. Kaspar had seen these three before over the last few days. The first two always hired about two dozen men between them, but the third had lingered for a while, looking closely at the men in the area, as if searching for some unseen quality, and had then departed alone.

The first man shouted, "I need three pickers! Experienced orchard men only!"

The second said, "I need strong backs! I've got cargo to load. Ten men!"

But the third man simply walked past those racing to present themselves to the first two men hiring, and approached Kaspar. "You there," he said, his words colored by a strange accent. "I've seen you here for a few days." He pointed to the sword at Kaspar's side. "Know how to use that thing?"

Kaspar smiled, and it wasn't friendly. "If I didn't, would I be standing here?"

"I need a man who can use a sword as well as having other talents."

"What talents?"

"Can you ride?"

Kaspar studied his would-be employer and realized this man was dangerous. Whatever he was about to suggest was probably illegal, and if so, Kaspar stood to make good money from doing it. He studied the man's face for a moment and found little in it to recommend itself. He had a thin nose that made his dark eyes look too close together. His hair was oiled and combed flat against his head, and his teeth were yellow and uneven. His clothing was of a fine weave, if simply cut, and Kaspar noticed that his dagger had an ivory handle. But the most noticeable thing about the man was his expression, one of fatigue and worry. Whatever he needed done would undoubtedly be dangerous, and that might mean a healthy wage. After considering the question, Kaspar said, "As good as some, better than most."

"I can't place your accent. Where are you from?"

"A lot of places, most of them very far from here, but most recently up north, around Heslagnam and Mastaba."

"You're not from the south?"

"No."

"Any problem with having to fight?"

Kaspar was silent for a moment, as if considering his answer. He knew that if a horse was involved in the bargain, he was taking the job, no matter what the task; he didn't plan on returning to Simarah in this lifetime. If he didn't like the job, he'd steal the horse and ride south. "If the job is to fight, I'm no mercenary. But if you mean can I fight if I need to, yes, I can."

"If things go as planned, you only need to be able to ride, my friend." He motioned for Kaspar to follow him. As he walked away, he said, "My name is Flynn."

Kaspar stopped in his tracks. "Kinnoch?"

Flynn spun around and spoke in the language of the Kingdom of the Isles. "Deep Taunton. You?"

"I'm from Olasko."

Flynn glanced about and in the King's Tongue said, "Then we're both far from home, Olaskon. But this may be the gods' way of providing us both with what we need, because unless I'm sadly mistaken you didn't just decide to come down here to this godforsaken side of the world out of choice. Follow me."

The man named Flynn hurried along a series of streets in the seedier part of the merchants' quarter, then turned down a long alley. Kaspar kept his face immobile and tried to maintain a calm demeanor, but his heart raced. Flynn had been the surname of one of his boyhood instructors; a man from a region known as Kinnoch, part of a nation long ago overrun by the Kingdom of the Isles. But the inhabitants had retained their strong cultural identity and still spoke a language used only among their community. Kaspar's instructor had taught him a few phrases, to indulge a curious boy, but even that much would have been considered a betrayal by other clan members. The men of Kinnoch were redoubtable fighters, poets, liars, and thieves; prone to drunkenness, sudden bursts of rage, and deep sorrow, but if this man had found a way to this godforsaken side of the world, he might well have the means to return to civilization.

Flynn entered a warehouse which looked drafty, dusty, and dark. Inside, Kaspar saw two other men waiting. Flynn stepped to one side and nodded, and without warning the other two men drew their swords and attacked.

OPPORTUNITY

Kaspar leapt to his right.

Before his attacker could react, Kaspar had drawn his sword and spun round to deliver a crushing strike to the man's back.

Flynn's blade scarcely blocked the blow as he shouted, "Enough! I've seen enough." He still spoke the King's Tongue.

Kaspar took a step back as the other two men did likewise. Flynn quickly resheathed his blade and said, "Sorry, my friend, but I had to see if you really could use that thing." He pointed to Kaspar's blade.

"I said I could."

"And I've known women who said they loved me, but that didn't make it true," countered Flynn.

Kaspar kept his blade out, but lowered it. "You have a problem with trust, it seems."

Flynn nodded, a wry smile on his lips as he said, "You're observant. Now, forgive me, but we had to be sure you'd wits enough for trouble at any time. These lads wouldn't have killed you, just cut you up a little if you hadn't been able to defend yourself."

"Your test almost got your friend here crippled for life," said Kaspar, as he pointed to a wiry man with shoulder-length blond hair who was not amused by Kaspar's observation. He said nothing, but his blue eyes narrowed. He nodded once at Flynn.

The third man was broad-shouldered, thick-necked, and covered with hair everywhere, except for his balding pate. He laughed; a short bark like a dog's. "It was a good move, I'll grant."

Kaspar raised an eyebrow and said, "You're a Kinnockman, or my ears have never heard that accent."

The blond man said, "We're all from the Kingdom."

"I'm not," said Kaspar. "But I've been there."

The two men looked inquiringly at Flynn, who said, "He's from Olasko."

"You're even farther from home than we are!" observed the blond man.

"I'm McGoin, and he's Kenner," said the burly man.

"I'm Kaspar."

"So, we're four kindred spirits; men of the north." Kenner nodded sagely.

"How did you get here?" asked Kaspar.

"You first," urged Flynn.

Kaspar thought it best to hide his identity. These men might think him a liar, or they might seek to use such knowledge to their benefit and his disadvantage in the future. Mostly, he decided that his former rank hardly mattered now; he was on the wrong side of the world and had been stripped of his title and lands. He might tell them more, later, after he had heard their tale.

"Nothing very fancy, really. I got on the wrong side of a magician who has enough power to relocate the people who annoy him. One minute I'm in Opardum, the next I'm up near Heslagnam with half a dozen Bentu riding toward me."

"You got away from Bentu slavers?" asked McGoin.

"No," said Kaspar. "First they caught me; then I escaped."

Flynn laughed. "Either you've a touch of magic yourself, or you're enough of a liar to be a Kinnockman."

"I haven't that honor," said Kaspar.

"Magicians," observed Kenner. "They're a curse, no doubt."

"Well, that one certainly was," said Kaspar. "Still, he could have landed me halfway across the ocean and let me drown."

"True," said Flynn.

"Now, your story."

"We're traders out of Port Vykor," began Flynn.

Instantly Kaspar knew Flynn was lying. It was far more likely that they were pirates out of the Sunset Isles.

"We were a consortium put together by a trader out of Krondor, name of Milton Prevence. When we reached the City of the Serpent River we found a clan war underway. We couldn't even come into port, because two clans were battling over who controlled the harbor.

"So, we turned around and looked for a landing." He pointed to his companions. "There were thirty of us when we started."

Kaspar nodded. "A few merchants and how many guards?"

Flynn shook his head. "None. We are traders, but all of

us have learned to take care of ourselves. McGoin started off as a felter's apprentice, and got into the wool trade. From there it was fine clothing, and the silks you can buy down here are the best he's seen, even better than from Kesh.

"Kenner's specialty is spices, the rarer the better. Me, I specialize in gems."

Kaspar nodded. "All highly transportable and not too bulky, save for the silk."

"But it's light," said McGoin. "You can pack the hold of a ship and she'll barely lower a yard on the waterline."

"So what happened?"

Kenner took over the narrative from Flynn. "We had two choices. We could have turned west and sailed on to the City of Maharta to trade up the Vedra River; lots of commerce, lots of exotic goods, but also, lots of crafty traders and less advantageous deals."

"What was the other choice?" Kaspar asked.

"There's a place where the Serpent River loops to the east, almost reaching the coast. It's less than a week's walk from the beach to the river, so we didn't bring horses—we'd just buy them here if we needed to ride. At the river there's a town called Shingazi's Landing. Used to be a small trading post, but now it's a good place to catch a ride upriver."

McGoin added, "So, that's what we did; we hired a boat and set upriver, figuring there'd be goods up there no Islesman had ever seen before."

Flynn laughed. "Talk about gods cursed arrogance. We're not faint-hearted men, Kaspar, but there were thirty of us when we started and all of us knew how to take care of ourselves.

"But the farther north we traveled, the madder things became."

"How long have you been here, Kaspar?" asked McGoin, interrupting the story.

"Six, seven months. I've lost track."

"How far north did you go?" asked Flynn.

"Mastaba."

"Then you didn't get close to the Serpent Lake," said Flynn. "That area's a no man's land. There are these nomads—"

"The Jeshandi. Yes, I've heard of them."

"They prevent anyone settling around the lake, but there are other people up there, too. To the south of the lake rise the Sumanu mountains, and that's where we—"

"Start at the beginning, Flynn," said McGoin.

Flynn took a deep breath, as if preparing to tell a long tale. "We found a riverboat at Shingazi's Landing, a well-built craft with a wide-keel and shallow-draft; the kind you could walk the deck with poles and haul with ropes when need be.

"The captain explained that there were no significant ports until a town called Malabra, which was as far north as he would sail, but he'd sell us the boat. Several of us had some riverboat experience so we felt confident that by the time we reached Malabra we'd have everything sorted out. We agreed that Prevence would be the commander of the entire expedition and that a man named Carter would act as boat-captain upon leaving Malabra.

"The trip up to Malabra took three months. Everything seemed fine for a while. Then, we hit some weather and had to shelter on the shore. A couple of days later, we encountered bandits, who stalked us for five days on horseback while we struggled to stay midstream. They took three men with arrows before giving up."

Kenner said, "We should have known. We hadn't

found one decent trading opportunity and we'd already lost three lives; we should have known . . ."

"But we carried on," continued Flynn. "By the time we got to Malabra, two more men had died from fever." He paused, as if trying to remember. "We did all right, at first. We set up a trading post, in a warehouse not unlike this one. The language wasn't that difficult, because we had a dozen men who could speak Quegan, and the two dialects are similar. It was around that time things started to—" He looked at his companions, as if asking for help.

McGoin said, "Some of the local people started bringing items to the warehouse to sell to us. We were carrying plenty of gold—a fair amount by Kingdom standards, but a royal treasury here. I expect you've noticed their lack of coinage; it looks like they're still paying the price of that war my father fought in.

"But, the things they brought in . . . well, at first we thought they were just—what's the word?" He looked at Kenner.

"Artifacts."

"Ya, that's it," said McGoin. "From some long-dead civilization—these things were really old."

"What kind of things?" asked Kaspar, now caught up in their story.

"Some of them were masks, like those temple priests wear in festivals, but like nothing we've ever seen. Animal faces, and other creatures—well, I don't know what they were. And jewelry; lots of it. Some of it was pretty ordinary, but other pieces . . ." He shrugged.

Flynn continued. "I've traded in gems all my life, Kaspar. I've seen common baubles and gifts fit for the Queen of Isles, but some of these pieces!"

"Why were they willing to trade such valuable trinkets for gold?"

"Imagine a farmer owns a necklace which is worth a lifetime's toil—but he can't sell it, trade with it, or eat it—it might as well be a bucket of dirt," said McGoin. "But he can spend a bag of coins a little at a time and buy what he needs for years."

"So we bought all the jewelry," said Flynn.

"Tell him about the ring," said Kenner.

Kaspar looked around the warehouse and saw a stack of empty bags, waist high, so he went over and made himself comfortable. Flynn said, "We had some rings brought in. Some were gold, but most weren't. Some were set with gems, and a few were of really good quality. But a lot of them were plain metal bands with odd markings on them."

Kaspar tried to not sound scornful, but he said, "Let me guess. Magic rings?"

Flynn glanced at the other two who nodded, then he reached into his belt-pouch and brought out one. It glowed in the gloom of the warehouse.

Kaspar stood up, walked over to Flynn and took the ring. He examined it: it was made from a dull metal, not unlike pewter, save it glowed. "Anyone try to wear it?" asked Kaspar.

Flynn said, "A man named Greer did. He put it on and it seemed to do nothing, for a while. Then, suddenly, one night he attacked and murdered Castitas. McGoin had to kill Greer to keep him from slaughtering more of us. Then, I put it on to try and work out what had happened to Greer, but after a while I started seeing things. No one's worn it since then."

"Why didn't you throw it away?"

"You ever heard of Stardock?"

Kaspar had, but he shook his head. He decided it would be better to feign ignorance—if he was going to pass himself off as a common man, he couldn't appear too worldly. "Can't say I have."

"It's an island in the Great Star Lake, on the border of Kesh and the Kingdom. A community of magicians live there, very powerful—"

"And rich," interjected McGoin.

"—and rich," agreed Flynn. "We'll sell the ring to them."

Kaspar looked around the room. "Something tells me there's more to this than the ring. Look, if I have this right, you were thirty prosperous merchants who brought along enough gold that if you three had just decided to do away with the other twenty-six, you'd be set for life, right?"

"It was a small fortune," said Kenner.

"So I assume you're not murderers, but astute traders and now have goods that are worth more?"

They nodded.

"So, there's a reason you're not just hiring a bunch of mercenaries for protection as you head south and find a ship for home?"

The three men glanced at one another. At last Flynn said, "We were coming to that. The ring is just a trinket. I mean it must do something special, as two men are dead because of it, but the ring's not worth all this bother. There is something else."

Flynn motioned to the far side of the warehouse and the four men moved to where he indicated. A wagon was standing there, a simple freight-hauler almost indistinguishable from those Kaspar had seen wending their way though the streets of his own city. In the bed rested something covered by an oiled canvas, and from the size of it, Kaspar already had an idea of what it could be. Flynn jumped into the wagon and pulled back the edge of the canvas.

It was a body, at least Kaspar thought it was one, or perhaps it was just an empty suit of armor. But whatever it was, it was unlike anything he had ever seen before.

Kaspar climbed up next to Flynn and removed more of the canvas. If it was armor it looked seamless. It was black, with a dull golden trim along ridges at the neck, shoulder, wrist, thigh, and ankles. Kaspar knelt and touched it. It was made of metal, but a smoother one than any he had seen before. Whoever owned it would be tall, taller than Kaspar's two inches over six feet.

Back in Opardum, Kaspar had purchased the finest armor known in the Eastern Kingdom, from the Master Armorers from Roldem, but this was far beyond their ability to fashion.

"Hit it with your sword," said Flynn, leaping out of the wagon to give Kaspar room. Kasper stood, drew his sword, and swung lightly against the shoulder plate, and the blade rebounded, as if he had struck hard rubber. Kasper again knelt next to the figure.

"Is there someone inside it?" he asked.

"No one knows," answered Kenner. "We can't find any way to remove the helm or any other part of it."

"It has an ill aspect," observed Kaspar, speaking slowly.

The helm was simple, as if a cylinder had been cut at an angle and then had the sharp edges rounded off, leaving a continuously smooth line from shoulder to crown, without any edge or point. Then it was pinched slightly in front, so that from above it looked slightly teardrop in shape rather than truly round. Both sides of the helm were flanked by what could have been wings, but unlike the wings of any creature Kaspar had hunted; they were shaped like a raven's, yet curved back slightly, following the sides of the helm, and they were webbed like those of a giant bat—but this was no normal bat. A single eye slit allowed for vision. Kaspar attempted to peer inside.

"Can't see a thing," observed McGoin. "Jerrold even

tried to hold a torch up close and almost set his hair on fire trying to look in."

"There's something there: a glass or quartz, or something hard enough to stop a dagger's point," said Kenner.

Kaspar sat back. "It's unique, I'll admit. But why haul it all the way across the ocean to Stardock? There must be someone around here who'll give you a fair price for it."

"It's magic, no doubt," said Flynn. "And around here magicians are scarce and poor." He looked at his two friends, and added, "We did try to find buyers at first, but quickly realized this land is too destitute. We could have taken what we could find and then returned home, and along with the gold we still had and what we'd purchased, we could have lived very comfortable lives."

"But we're not thieves," said Kenner. "We had partners and some of them had families. We could have given a small share of the profits to each of them, but would that have compensated for losing a husband or father?"

Kaspar slowly said, "They knew there'd be a risk traveling here."

"Yes, but I have a wife and three sons," said McGoin, "and I'd like to think that if I was buried up north, one of my companions would return home and give my widow enough to care for our sons and their futures."

"Noble sentiments," said Kaspar jumping down from the wagon. "What else?"

Flynn handed Kaspar a sword. It was as black as the armor, and when he put his hand on the hilt, a slight vibration seemed to shoot up his arm. "Feel it?" asked Flynn.

"Yes," said Kaspar and he handed the blade back. It was lighter than he had expected, but the vibrating made him feel uneasy.

Flynn walked over to the armor and said, "Now watch." He took the ring out of his pouch again and held it close to the metal. It immediately switched from a dull glow to a brilliant shine. "There's no doubt about the armor's magic, I think this proves it."

"Persuasive," agreed Kaspar. "Now, what does all this have to do with me?"

"We need an extra man," said Flynn. "The fact you're from the north and also wish to return to the Kingdom is a bonus. We were just looking to hire a clever swordsman to travel with us to the City of the Serpent River—we're hoping that the clan war is now over." Flynn put his hand on Kaspar's shoulder. "But, as I said, perhaps the gods have placed you in our path for a reason, for a man who will go the entire distance through his own desire is better than any hired sword could be. We're prepared to make you an equal partner."

Kenner seemed on the verge of objecting, but then said nothing while McGoin nodded.

"That's generous," said Kaspar.

"No," replied Flynn. "Before you agree you must know everything. Not all our lads died before we found this thing." He pointed to the wagon. "The peasant who showed us where the armor lay would have nothing to do with retrieving it, wouldn't go near it once he had uncovered it. We had discovered enough riches to live like kings, so after we loaded up four wagons worth, we headed south.

"By the time we reached your town of Heslagnam, there were only six of us left, and we were down to one wagon. We'd abandoned a nation's wealth on the road behind us."

Kaspar didn't like what he was hearing. "So, someone wasn't happy about you taking the body, armor, or whatever it was."

"Apparently so. We were never attacked during the day, or while resting in a town or village, but at night, alone on the road, things started to happen."

"One night Fowler McLintoc just died. Not a mark on him," said Kenner.

"And Roy McNarry went off to relieve himself one evening and never came back. We looked for a day and found not a hint of him," added McGoin.

Kaspar laughed, a short bark that sounded halfway between dry amusement and sympathy. "Why didn't you just leave the bloody thing and take the rest?"

"By the time we'd figured out that it was the body they wanted, it was too late. We had already abandoned the other three wagons. We measured out the best of the gems—they're in a bag over there—and concealed most of the jewelry and other valuable artifacts; we found a cave, marked it, and just left it all there. We sold the horses for food along the way, and eventually got here. But every week or so, someone always died."

"This tale is not persuading me to go with you."

"I know, but think of the prize!" said Flynn. "The magicians will pay a king's ransom for this thing, and you know why?"

"I'm eager to learn," said Kaspar dryly.

Flynn said, "I believe you are a man of some education, for you speak the King's Tongue like a noble, yet you're from Olasko."

"I've had some schooling," Kaspar admitted.

"Do you know the tale of the Riftwar?"

"I know that one hundred years past an army invaded from another world through a magic rift and almost conquered the Kingdom of the Isles."

"More," said Flynn. "There's a lot that was never written in the histories. I heard something from my Grand-da—who served as a luggage boy at the battle of Sethanon—and it concerned dragons and ancient magic."

"Spare me your grandfather's fireside tales, Flynn, and get to the point."

"Have you ever heard of the Dragon Lords?"

Kaspar said, "I can't honestly say I have."

"They were an ancient warrior-race, who lived upon this world before men; they were even here before the elves. They were a race of dragon riders who could perform powerful magic. They were crushed by the gods during the Chaos Wars."

"That's theology, not history," said Kaspar.

"Maybe, maybe not," answered Flynn, "but the temples teach it as doctrine, and while no mention is made of the Dragon Lords in the texts, the legends still remain. But look at that thing, Kaspar! If that's not a Dragon Lord, straight out of its ancient tomb, I don't know what it could be, but I'll wager the magicians at Stardock will want to know, and will pay to find out."

Kaspar said, "So you need a fourth man to carry this thing north, help ferry it from Port Vykor to this Stardock, and then ask a reward from the magicians?"

"Yes," said Flynn.

"You're mad," said Kaspar. "You should have stowed it in the cave and brought the treasure out with you instead."

Kenner, McGoin, and Flynn looked at one another. Finally Kenner said quietly, "We tried. We just can't."

"What do you mean you can't?"

"We tried to do what you said; but after we sealed the cave, we were no more than half a mile down the road before we had to turn around and go back. Then we stored all the gold and other goods, and fetched this thing out."

"You are madmen," said Kaspar. "I could go with you for a horse and the price of passage to the Kingdom, but I couldn't promise to stay with you after that. You've given me too many good reasons to say no." He paused for a moment. "In fact, I think I'll say no right now and avoid the trouble."

Flynn shrugged. "Very well. Try to leave."

Kaspar jumped down from the wagon, his sword still in his hand. "What do you mean?"

"We won't stop you," said Flynn. "That's not what I meant."

Kaspar started to circle the three men. When he reached the door of the warehouse he said, "I bid you good fortune gentlemen, and hope we may hoist a drink together in a Kingdom tavern some day, but I doubt we will; this commission has all the hallmarks of a doomed undertaking and I'll have none of it, thank you."

He turned, pushed the door open, and tried to step through.

He couldn't.

DECISION

Suddenly, Kaspar hesitated.

He wanted to step through the door, but something made him wait. He turned and said, "All right, I'll think about it."

Flynn nodded. "You can find us here, but we have to be on the road by the day after tomorrow."

"Why?" asked Kaspar.

"I don't know," said Flynn. "We just can't stay in one place too long."

Kenner added, "You'll understand."

Kaspar shrugged off the compulsion to stay and left the warehouse.

He wended his way through the early morning throng and found a cheap inn where the ale wasn't too dreadful. He rarely drank before his midday meal, but today he made an exception. He spent more of his meager purse than he should have, but deep inside he already knew he would join Flynn and the others. Not because of some nonsensical magical coercion, but because he wanted to; these men could get him closer to home in the next six months than he could manage on his own over the next two years: he was no sailor, and would have to work for months to save the cost of his passage, and ships plying the waters between Novindus and Triagia were scarce in any case. Even taking a vessel to the Sunset Islands would cost him the local equivalent of two hundred gold coins—that was half a year's work for a skilled craftsman in Olasko.

No, this way he would at least gain a horse and his passage to the Kingdom. From there he could walk home if he must.

He finished his ale and returned to the warehouse, finding the three men waiting. "You're with us?" asked Flynn.

"To Port Vykor," said Kaspar. "After that, we'll have to see. I want a horse, enough gold for decent lodgings and food along the way, and my passage from Salador to Opardum. You can keep the rest of your wealth. Agreed?"

"Agreed," said Flynn. "Now, we should prepare to leave at first light tomorrow. There's a caravan heading south loaded with supplies for the military and while we can't join it officially, we can shadow it for a while; it would keep bandits away from us."

"Very well," said Kaspar. "But first we have to find a coffin."

"Why?" asked Kenner.

"Because down here people bury their dead, they don't burn them, so a coffin under the tarpaulin will attract a lot less curiosity than that . . . thing will." He pointed to the wagon. "You could drive it all the way to the City of the Serpent River without one, but I doubt you'll get it past customs at Port Vykor. A late companion being brought home to rest, though—where do they bury the dead in the Kingdom?"

"Up around Quester's View, I think."

"That will have to do," said Kaspar. He regarded his three new companions. "And if we do manage to get to the City of the Serpent River we will have to spend some of your booty on clothes. You gentlemen need to look more like cultured men of commerce than brigands and ruffians."

McGoin ran his hand over his five days' growth of beard and said, "You've the right of it, Kaspar."

"Do you sleep here?"

Flynn and the others nodded. Flynn said, "We tried sleeping at inns along the way, but it's impossible. You find yourself waking up, anxious to make sure that thing is safe."

"Sometimes, two or three times a night," nodded Kenner.

"So, now we sleep under the wagon," said McGoin.

"Well, you three can sleep here if you must, but I'm for a hot bath, clean clothing, and a night in a good inn. Give me some coin, Flynn."

Flynn dug out some silver pieces and handed them to Kaspar. "I'll see you at first light."

Kaspar left the inn and indulged himself for the first time since losing the citadel. He found a tailor and purchased a new tunic, trousers, and small clothes, as well as an outer jacket and a new felted beret with a metal pin clasping a false ruby. Then he found the best bathhouse in the town—which wasn't close to the standard of the great bathhouses in Opardum.

Afterward, Kaspar felt refreshed and reinvigorated. He took a room at an inn off the main town square, and discovered an agreeable barmaid who, after only a little coaxing, arrived at his door after the other guests had retired and her chores were finished.

An hour after drifting off into a deep, satisfied slumber, Kaspar came awake with a start. He glanced around the room and felt disoriented. Slowly, he realized where he was and rolled over to inspect his bedmate.

She was a pretty thing, no more than nineteen years old and typical of her calling; a poor girl hoping to catch a rich husband, or at least, garner a generous gift for her favors. Only time would tell if she ended up married, or in a brothel.

Kaspar put his head down again but sleep refused to return. He turned over and tried to clear his mind of images, but each time he started to drift off he would catch a disturbing glimpse of the wagon in his mind's eye, and of what rested upon it.

Finally, he rose and dressed, leaving the girl a small gift of silver. If Flynn proved correct, there would be ample wealth to replace it soon enough.

He was opening the door quietly as the girl awoke. "Leaving?" she asked sleepily.

"I have an early day," Kaspar said, closing the door behind him.

He made his way carefully through the dark streets, mindful that few lawful folk were about this late. Finally he reached the warehouse and opened the door to find Kenner awake and the others sleeping.

Kenner approached him, treading softly, and said, "Knew you'd be back before dawn."

Kaspar ignored the urge to respond with a jibe, and simply replied, "Why are you awake?"

"One of us is always awake. It'll be better now that you're here. What's the time?"

"About two hours after midnight," said Kaspar.

"Then you can take the next three hours and wake McGoin after that." Kenner climbed underneath the wagon, pulled a blanket over him, and settled in to sleep.

Kaspar found a crate to sit on, and kept watch. Kenner was quickly asleep and so he was left with his thoughts. He resisted the urge to go to the wagon and lift the tarpaulin. Kaspar refused to believe that any unnatural compulsion had forced him to be here. He was here out of choice.

He cursed all magicians and all things magical as he thought about his recent past. It was too much of a coincidence, but he rejected the idea of fate or that the gods wanted him to be here. He was no one's pawn. He had enjoyed the company of a magician, but Leso Varen had also been his advisor; and while many of suggestions he made to Kaspar had been repulsive, the benefits had largely outweighed the costs. Varen had been influential, perhaps the most influential advisor in Kaspar's entire court, but Kaspar had always made the final judgment and given the final order on what would or would not be done.

Dark memories flooded his mind as he considered the arrival of Leso Varen. The magician had appeared one day in open court as a supplicant seeking a place to rest for a while; a simple purveyor of harmless magic. But he had become a fixture in Kaspar's household very quickly, and at some point, Kaspar's view of things had changed.

Had his ambitions always come first, Kaspar wondered suddenly, or had the magician's honeyed words held greater sway?

Kaspar pushed away these unwanted thoughts; he felt deep bitterness toward anything that reminded him of his home and everything he'd lost. He turned his attention instead to what Flynn had said.

Kaspar struggled to keep events in order. Though it

was rare for traders from Triagia to venture to Novindus, it was not unheard of. And for such a group to be here, seeking riches heretofore unseen around the Sea of Kingdoms, was perfectly reasonable. That both he and these men would arrive in this small town and discover a common interest was an improbability, but it could still be just a coincidence.

Besides, fate had nothing to do with where the white-haired magician had deposited him; certainly, there had been the high probability that Kaspar would not survive his first few minutes there. How could any agency or power know that he would escape and survive the wilderness? It was not as if someone watched over him; Kaspar had struggled hard for a long time to get to that square where he met Flynn.

He stood up and paced the floor quietly. The entire situation was beginning to fray his nerves. He was loath to consider that something beyond self-interest might influence him. Like many men of his position he had paid service to the gods—making offerings in the temples and attending services on certain holidays—but that had been out of duty, not conviction. Certainly, no Midkemian would deny the existence of the gods: there were far too many stories from reliable sources attesting to the direct intervention of this or that god over the ages. However, Kaspar was almost certain that such omnipotent beings were far too busy to preoccupy themselves with his particular circumstances.

He glanced at the wagon and then quietly approached the thing under the tarpaulin. Lifting the canvas, he looked at the dark helm. It wore a baleful aspect if ever he saw one. Kaspar reached out and touched it, half expecting some sign of life—a vibration or feeling—but his fingers brushed only cold metal, though it was unlike any metal he'd ever known. He studied the figure for a while longer, then replaced the covering.

He returned to the boxes and sat for some time, wrestling with the uneasy feeling he had gained by staring at the lifeless object. Then, he realized what was troubling him. As he regarded the armor, corpse, or whatever it was, he couldn't dismiss his instinct that it wasn't dead. It was merely lying there. And it was waiting.

Kaspar had fallen into a long conversation with the *jemedar* in charge of escorting the caravan weaving just ahead of their wagon. Given the officer's age, Kaspar assumed that a jemedar was the equivalent to a lieutenant in the Olaskon military. Certainly, the *havildar* who rode at the young man's side was as crusty an old sergeant as you'd find in any army.

At the end of their conversation, the jemedar—named Rika—agreed to allow Kaspar and his friends to follow the caravan at a discreet distance, without officially being part of it. He had inspected the coffin, but had not insisted on opening it. Obviously he didn't consider four men to be a threat to his company of thirty.

So Kaspar sat astride a decent, if not memorable, gelding, who could probably make the long journey to the City of the Serpent River—so long as enough rest, food, and water were found along the way. Kenner rode a dark bay, and McGoin and Flynn drove the wagon: a solid, unremarkable freight hauler designed for mules or oxen rather than horses, but which moved along at a good rate in any event.

Flynn had shown Kaspar the contents of the other chest in the wagon, and Kaspar had been forced to admire their resolution to distribute the spoils among the families of their late companions; the gold and other items in the chest would have made the three extremely wealthy men for life.

Something about this entire enterprise was bothering Kaspar, however. No matter how hard he tried to convince himself that everything was mere coincidence, no matter how improbable it was, the more he eventually became convinced something else was wrong.

He had experienced the same odd feeling when spending time with Leso Varen—the same detached sense that he was viewing his own life from a distance. But this time, he was fully aware that it was happening.

Perhaps his three companions were correct and the armor—as he had come to think of it—did have some sort of power over those who came into contact with it. Maybe he would have to go all the way to Stardock to be free of it. But whatever happened, he knew that it was but one leg of a long and arduous journey, but one which might get him closer to his goal than he could have hoped for mere weeks ago.

At midday, he and Kenner switched places with Flynn and McGoin and rode the wagon. With the soldiers still in sight there seemed little need for guards, yet both riders were anxious and kept peering back at the road from time to time.

Finally, Kaspar asked, "Are you afraid of being followed?"

"Always," said Kenner, without offering further explanation.

Despite the army sentries one hundred meters up the road, the four men took turns standing guard around their own fire. Kaspar drew the third watch: the two hours in the deepest part of the night.

He practiced all the tricks he knew to stay awake. He had been taught these by his father the first year he had traveled with the army of Olasko on a campaign; he had been just eleven years old.

He didn't look into the fire, knowing it would mesmerize him, capture his eyes, and then render him blind should he need to look into the darkness. Instead, he kept his eyes moving, otherwise imaginary shapes would rise up and cause false panic. Occasionally, he glanced skyward at the waning moon or distant stars, so that he would not fatigue his eyes staring at nothing.

An hour into his watch he noticed a flicker of movement over by the wagon, barely visible in the gloom. He moved quickly to the wagon, and at the very edge of the firelight he saw something again. He kept his eyes on the spot as he said, "Wake up!'

The other three men woke up and Flynn asked, "What?"

"Something's out there, beyond the firelight."

Instantly, all three men came out from beneath the wagon and spread out, weapons drawn. "Where?" asked Kenner.

"Over there," said Kaspar, pointing to where he had seen the figure.

"Kaspar, come with me," said Flynn. "Keep us in sight, and watch our backs," he instructed the other two.

The two men moved forward slowly, swords at the ready. When they reached the place Kaspar had pointed to, they found nothing but an empty field. "I could have sworn I'd seen something," said Kaspar.

"That's all right," said Flynn. "We're used to it. It's better to be safe than to do nothing."

"This has happened before?"

Returning to the relative warmth of the fire, Flynn said, "It happens a lot."

"Did you see who it was?" asked Kenner.

"Only a shape."

McGoin crawled back under the wagon. "That's good."

"Why?" asked Kaspar.

"Because it's not serious," said McGoin. "When you can see what it is . . . then it's serious."

"What's serious?" asked Kaspar as the others settled back under the wagon.

Kenner said, "I wish I knew what it is."

Kaspar said, "This doesn't make any sense."

"No, it doesn't," agreed Flynn. "Keep an eye out and wake me in an hour."

The rest of the night passed uneventfully.

As they reached the village of Nabunda, the patrol escorting the caravan peeled off to report to the local commander. The jemedar waved a good-natured goodbye to Kaspar and his companions as they rode into town.

"We need to find storage for the wagon," said Flynn, "then get some information on conditions to the south of here."

It took the better part of the day to find a suitable place for the wagon, as every warehouse was full. Eventually, they settled in a corner of a public stable, and paid three times the normal price.

Nabunda was thronged with people drawn to the conflict. There were soldiers' wives and camp followers, as well as those who found soldiers eager customers or easy marks—thieves and mountebanks, pickpockets and tailors—all vying for whatever trade came within their reach.

As they gathered at a crowded inn, Kaspar observed, "This border skirmish has all the signs of becoming a full-blown war."

"How can you tell?" asked Flynn as they pulled out their chairs.

An older but still attractive barmaid approached and took their order for supper. After she had left, McGoin said, "I thought you said you weren't a mercenary."

"I wasn't, but I was a soldier," said Kaspar. "I spent most of my life in the Olaskon army, if truth be told."

"Why'd you leave?" asked Kenner.

Without wishing to provide too many details, Kaspar explained, "I was on the losing side of the last war." Looking around, he said, "But I've seen enough stand-up fights to recognize groundwork when I see it; and all of those who customarily use wars to feather their own nests." He pointed to a corner table where a card game was well underway. "I don't know the game, but I'll wager that fellow with his back to the corner is the one who initiated it, and I'll also wager that he's using his own deck."

Kaspar then pointed to another small group of men in common garb who gathered in the opposite corner. "Just as I'll wager those gentlemen are merchants, not unlike yourselves. A tailor whose clientele—like our young Jemedar Rika—wish their uniforms to fit just so, or a boot-maker whose specialty is riding boots, fine enough to catch a general's eye. Perhaps there's a tinker in their midst, for many wives will be cooking for their man on the eve of battle, and their pots will need mending." He looked back at his friends. "Yes, this has all the makings of a full-scale war, my friends."

Flynn looked troubled. "Getting south may prove difficult."

"You'd be surprised," said Kaspar. "War is chaos, and from chaos springs opportunity."

The food arrived and conversation fell to a minimum.

There were no rooms to be had in the town, so the four companions returned to the stable. The stable lad was fast asleep in the loft, and their arrival didn't wake him.

"Some watchman," observed Kenner as the first three to sleep got under the wagon.

Kaspar fell asleep swiftly, but was troubled by a restless sense of danger even though no images came to him. Then he felt a presence close to him and opened his eyes.

The armor was standing over him. Through the dark helm two evil, red eyes glared balefully down. Kaspar lay motionless for an instant, and then with a sudden, catlike quickness, the armored figure drew his black sword and raised it to strike at Kaspar.

Kaspar sat up, striking his head on the wagon with almost enough force to knock himself unconscious. His vision swam and darkened for a moment as he shouted and fumbled for his sword.

Hands grabbed him and Flynn cried, "What is it?"

Kenner said, "It's only a dream, man."

Kaspar blinked the tears out of his eyes and saw Flynn, who had taken the first watch, kneeling above him. Kenner was still lying by his side.

Kaspar crawled out from underneath the wagon and looked around. Then he looked at the tarpaulin and pulled it back. "I could have sworn—" he muttered, putting his hand on the coffin.

Flynn said, "We know."

McGoin said, "We've all had that dream; it's as if that thing comes to life."

"All of you?"

"At one time or another," said Kenner. "You just can't be around it long before it starts to haunt you."

"Get back to sleep if you can," said Flynn.

"No," said Kaspar, rubbing his sore head. "I'll take the rest of your watch and my own. I'll wake McGoin at two hours past midnight."

Flynn didn't argue and left Kaspar to stand a long watch. Kaspar wrestled with the dream, for it had been vivid and intense. He was troubled by the sensation he'd received when he touched the box. For the briefest instant it had vibrated under his fingers, just like the black sword.

Even after he awoke McGoin, Kaspar couldn't sleep.

COMMANDER

The guard signaled them to stop.

Flynn urged the horses to the side of the road while the rider approached. He was a subedar, which would roughly have made him a senior corporal or very junior sergeant in the Olaskon army. His patrol had dismounted and was dug in around a narrow cut through a low hillock, taking cover behind rocks, brush, and a few felled trees.

He rode up to them and said, "The road ahead is closed. We've come up against a squad of Sasbataba regulars who've occupied a village."

"You going to take them out?" asked Kaspar.

"My orders are to make contact, pull back, send word, and wait for reinforcements."

"A cautious approach," said Kaspar, looking over the ragged patrol under the subedar's command. "Given how tired your men look, probably a good one."

"We've been on the line for a month," said the subedar, obviously not in the mood for further conversation. "If you want to head south, you'll have to find another way around."

Kaspar rode over to Flynn and relayed this to him, adding, "There was a road leading to the southeast out of that last village we went through."

"I can't think of a better alternative," said Flynn, and he started to head the wagon around.

They had only been on the road north for a few minutes when a large contingent of cavalry came past at a steady walk. Flynn pulled the wagon off to the verge of the road and waited until they had passed before continuing their journey.

The village—Higara—they had driven through only two hours earlier now looked like a military camp. Guards ran to take their positions along the road, ignoring the wagon as it rolled into the little village, but Kaspar knew that wouldn't continue very long. A commissary wagon was being unloaded and it was clear that the village inn was being converted into an operational headquarters.

"Looks like the Raj is getting serious about whatever that subedar and his patrol has found back there," Kaspar observed.

Flynn and the others nodded agreement. Kenner said, "I don't know much about armies, but this one looks big."

Kaspar pointed north. "From the size of that dust cloud I'd say it is very big. I'm guessing there's at least a full regiment heading this way."

They tried to hurry along invisibly, but as they turned down the southeast road, a squad of soldiers barred their way. "Where do you think you're going?" asked a tough-looking subedar.

Kaspar rode over to where the man stood, dismounted and said, "We're just trying to find our way to the City of the Serpent River, and avoid that offensive you're staging."

"Staging an offensive, are we?" asked the soldier. "And what makes you say that?"

Kaspar looked around and laughed. "I think the large regiment of infantry coming down the road, following the three cavalry companies I saw ride through here earlier offered a pretty convincing clue."

"What's in the wagon?"

"A coffin," Kaspar replied. "We're outlanders, from across the Green Sea, and we're trying to get to a ship so we can bury our comrade at home."

The sergeant, as Kaspar thought of him, walked to the back of the wagon and pulled off the box's cover. "You must have been very fond of the fellow to haul him halfway around the world to plant him. Plenty of fine soil around here." Inspecting the coffin, he said, "There will be plenty of bodies in a day or so." He climbed up on the wagon and saw the chest, snug against the seat where Kenner and Flynn sat. "What's that?"

Kaspar said, "We're merchants, and that's our profit for this journey."

The subedar said, "Unlock it."

Flynn threw Kaspar a desperate look, but Kaspar said, "We have nothing to hide."

Flynn gave Kaspar the key and he opened the chest. The subedar said, "This is a fortune. How do I know you came by it through honest means?"

"You have no reason to think otherwise," Kaspar countered. "If we were brigands we would hardly try to transport this through a battle zone. We'd more likely be traveling north, drinking and whoring!'"

"There may be something in your story, but it's no

longer my problem. This is a matter for my commander to look into."

He ordered everyone to dismount and motioned for two of the guards to take the wagon to a stable. When all four men were on foot, he said, "Follow me."

He led them to an inn where a command center was being set up, and told the four men to stand in the corner, quietly. They did as he requested. Kaspar observed the subedar as he spoke to a junior officer and then to a senior official.

The higher-ranking soldier stood in a dusty but finely-cut tunic which was decorated with gold piping around the collar and cuffs. On his head he wore a white turban; a flourish of horse hair, dyed a bright crimson, protruded grandly from a silver pin in its center. He had a neatly-trimmed beard, not unlike the style that Kaspar had favored for many years. He waved for the four men to approach him.

The commander said, "My subedar has reported that you claim to be merchants."

"We are, my lord," said Kaspar with just enough deference to be respectful.

"You are a rough-looking company for reputable traders."

Kaspar looked him straight in the eye. "We've been though a great deal. There were thirty in our company when this enterprise began—" Kaspar neglected to mention his late arrival "—and now we are four."

"Hmm, and apparently you've managed to collect an impressive amount of booty."

"Not booty, my lord, but honest profits," said Kaspar remaining calm and persuasive.

The commander looked at him for a long minute, then said, "You're foreigners, which is in your favor, as I can't believe even the idiot-king of Sasbataba is muddle-headed enough to try and pass off four foreigners, complete with a wagon, coffin, and a fortune in gold, as spies.

"No, I'll trust you, simply because I don't have the time to decide if you're merchants or criminals. That's for the local constabulary to worry about. Me, I've got to figure out how to thread a rope through the eye of a needle."

Kaspar glanced over at the table where a map lay stretched out. He had read enough military maps in his day to be able to judge the situation in a glance. "That narrow in the road two miles up is a double-edged sword."

"You have a good eye for the situation, stranger. Were you a soldier?"

"I was."

The commander gave Kaspar a long look, then said, "An officer?"

"I commanded," was all that Kaspar said.

"And you got a look at that pass in the road?"

"I did, and it's a position I'd want to defend, not attack from."

"But the bloody problem is that we need to be on the other side of it."

Kaspar didn't ask permission but simply turned to the map. He studied it for a moment, then said, "You might as well bring back your cavalry. They're next to useless employed there, unless you want to see them picked off two at a time as they ride through."

The commander waved the junior officer over and said, "Send a rider and tell the cavalry to fall back to the village. Leave a messenger squad at the front, too."

"As long as I'm giving you advice," said Kaspar, "the men holding the pass look like they haven't seen a hot meal in a month."

"I'm aware of the situation."

Looking at the map, Kaspar said, "And if I may ask you for some advice, will the southeastern road take us around the conflict?"

The commander laughed. "By a wide margin. That road will eventually take you to the Serpent River; from there you could travel by boat, but it's a dangerous trek these days." He sighed and said, "In my grandfather's time, the City of the Serpent River kept things quiet upriver for hundreds of miles. Local rulers also helped to keep the area relatively calm, save for an occasional skirmish or two. Back then, a merchant could travel practically anywhere without an escort, but now, you'd be well advised to postpone your journey, unless you hire a company of mercenaries to go with you, and they are very hard to find in these parts."

"All wearing your colors?" asked Kaspar with a smile.

"Or Sasbataba's." He fixed Kaspar and his companions with a baleful look and said, "If you were a little less gray, I'd press-gang the four of you on the spot." He held up his hand and said, "But for the time being, I'll settle for one more piece of advice. I appreciate fresh eyes; look at this map and tell me how you'd deal with that bottleneck."

"Without knowing the deployment of the defenders and what resources are available, I'd simply be guessing."

"Then assume that there are sufficient forces in a village about an hour's ride south of the gap. The enemy probably has several companies of archers situated in the rocks around the gap, and in the woods on the other side."

Kaspar looked at the map for a long time, then he said, "I'd go around them."

"And leave them at your back?"

"Why not?" He pointed to a spot on the map. "Here you have a nice wide little valley, but what? Three days west of here?" He moved his finger in a line. "I'd keep enough men here to make noise and confound any scouts or spies they might have nearby, then send a couple of squads of infantry right up to the gap, trumpets blowing, flags flying, and then dig in. Make it look as if you're going to wait them out for a while.

"Then, while the infantry keeps them busy, I'd send those three companies of cavalry, including any horse archers you can scrape up, and send them west. Leave the mounted infantry behind Sasbataba's men in the woods and hills, and ride through that village. Instead of having you bottled up, their archers are now trapped and you've got the village."

"Not a bad plan. Not a bad plan at all." He looked at Kaspar and asked, "What is your name?"

"Kaspar, from Olasko." He turned, "These are my companions, Flynn, Kenner, and McGoin from the Kingdom of the Isles."

"And the unfortunate in the wagon?"

"The former leader of our expedition, Milton Prevence."

"The Kingdom of the Isles? I thought that land a myth," observed the Commander. "My name is Alenburga, and I'm a General of the Brigade."

Kaspar bowed slightly. "It's a pleasure to meet you, General Alenburga."

"Of course it is," said the commander. "Some of my fellow officers would have hung you just to be done with the bother." He signaled to his subedar. "Take these men to the corner-house and lock them up."

Flynn started to say something, but Kaspar held his hand up to silence him. "For how long?" he asked the General.

"Until I judge whether this damn-fool plan of yours has merit. I'll send the scouts out this afternoon and if all goes well, we'll both be heading south again within the week."

Kaspar nodded and said, "If it's not too much bother, we would like to see to our own provisions."

"It's no bother, but save yourself the trouble, there's no spare food in the village. My commissary has commandeered everything we can chuck into a cook pot. But don't worry. We'll see you're fed. Please, join me for supper tonight."

Kaspar bowed and he and his friends fell in behind the subedar. They were led to a small house just off the town square and shown inside. "Guards will be outside the doors and windows, gentlemen, so I suggest you settle in. We'll come fetch you at suppertime."

Kaspar led the others inside and looked around the makeshift jail. It was a small building with two rooms: a kitchen and a bedroom, and outside lay a modest garden and a well. Everything remotely edible had been picked out of the garden, and the cupboard was bare. Seeing only two beds in the other room, Kaspar said, "I'll take the floor tonight. We'll alternate."

Flynn said, "I guess we have no choice."

Kaspar grinned and said, "No, but we may have some luck out of this."

"How is this lucky?" asked Kenner.

"If General Alenburga doesn't hang us, he may well escort us halfway to the City of the Serpent River. An army is better than any band of mercenaries for protection."

McGoin went to the bed and threw himself down on it. Through the door he said, "If you say so, Kaspar."

Kenner sat down on a chair between the hearth and table in the main room and asked, "Did anyone remember to bring a deck of cards?"

After three nights, supper with the General and his staff became a standing invitation. Alenburga's staff consisted of five younger officers and a senior advisor, an over-colonel. The General proved to be a genial host. While the food was hardly banquet-hall fare, it was tastier than the rations Kaspar had been eating on the road, and even though there was no wine, there was ample ale, and the General's commissary proved able to come up with quite a variety of dishes given the scant ingredients available to him.

After the meal, the General asked Kaspar to linger, while he had Flynn and the others escorted back to their quarters. When they had gone, he sent away his batman and ordered the guards outside. Producing a pair of cups, he fetched a bottle of wine from a bag near his sleeping pallet and said, "I don't have enough for the officer's mess, but I have a couple of bottles stashed away for moments like these."

Kaspar took the proffered cup and said, "What's the occasion?"

"A tiny celebration, actually," said the General. "I'm not going to hang you."

Kaspar raised his cup and said, "I'll drink to that," and took a sip. "Very good," he said afterward. "What's the grape?"

"We call it sharez." The General took a drink. "It grows in several regions close by."

"I shall have to fetch a bottle or two home, so—" he was about to say so that his housecarl could provide samples to wine traders in Opardum, and seek out the same grape in the Kingdom or Kesh, but then the reality of his new life came tumbling over him, "—so I can recall these pleasant evenings once or twice more."

"Finding a pleasant evening in the midst of war is welcome," agreed the General. "In any event, my scouts have reported that the situation is much as you anticipated. There are desultory patrols that can easily be neutralized, and a clear line of attack on the western flank. Now I know for certain you're not spies."

"I thought you had come to that conclusion some time ago?"

"One cannot be too careful. It had occurred to me that your story was so improbable, and your demeanor so unlikely, that you could be incredibly clever spies. I doubted it, but as I said, one cannot be too careful." He smiled and drank again. "Our enemies would not hand us a major victory simply to lull us into a false sense of superiority. Besides, if we take the two villages to the south, Sasbataba will be forced to sue for peace or be utterly defeated. The King's an idiot, but his Generals are not fools. We'll have a truce in a month from now."

"Something to look forward to," said Kaspar.

"It should make your journey to the City of the Serpent River somewhat easier," observed the General. "You have no idea how nasty some of these border skirmishes can get and the terrible effect they have on commerce."

"I believe I do," said Kaspar.

The General looked at him a long moment, then said, "You are a noble, yes?"

Kaspar said nothing, but he nodded.

"Your companions, they do not know?"

Kaspar sipped the wine and after a moment said, "I do not wish them to know."

"I'm sure you have good reason. You are, I gather, a very long way from home."

"Halfway around the world," said Kaspar. "I . . . ruled a duchy. I was the fifteenth hereditary Duke of Olasko. My family had direct ties to the throne of Roldem—not the most powerful, but one of the most influential kingdoms in the region—by descent and by marriage. I . . ." His eyes lost their focus as he remembered things he hadn't thought about since meeting Flynn and the others. "I fell prey to the two worst faults of a ruler."

Alenburga said, "Vanity and self-deception."

Kaspar laughed. "Make it three then: you neglected ambition."

"The power you inherited wasn't enough?"

Kaspar shrugged. "There are two kinds of men born to power, I think. Well, three if you count the fools, but of those with a mind to rule, you are either a man content with what providence has given you or you will always seek to enlarge your demesne. I was given to the latter disposition by nature, I fear. I sought to rule as much as possible and hand down a legacy of greatness to my heirs."

"So ambition and vanity in large measure."

"You seem to understand."

"I am related to the Raj, but have no ambition save to serve and bring peace to a troubled region. My cousin is as wise a young man as I have ever met. I have no sons, but even if I had, I could not imagine a finer young man to care for what I have built. He is . . . remarkable. It's a shame you'll never meet him."

"Why never?"

"Because, you are anxious to be on your way as soon as you can, and heading north to Muboya is hardly along your planned route."

"Then I guess you're right. So, we're free to leave?"

"Not quite yet. If we lose, based on this mad plan of yours—"

"Mine?" exclaimed Kaspar with a laugh.

"Of course it is, if we lose. If we win, I am the genius responsible for the stunning victory."

"Of course," said Kaspar, lifting his cup in salute and then drinking.

"It's a shame you're so intent on returning home. I expect there's a wonderful story behind how a powerful ruler of a nation finds himself traveling with a band of merchants on the other side of the world. Should you choose to remain, I know I could find you a position of some authority here. Men of talent are at a premium."

"I have a throne to reclaim."

"Well, you can tell me about that tomorrow night. Go and tell your friends that if we prove victorious in the next few days, you'll be on your way in a week. Good night to you, Your Grace."

Kaspar smiled at the use of the honorific. "Good night to you, my Lord General."

Kaspar returned to the house and bade the soldiers who escorted him a good night. As he entered, he wondered how much of his past he would reveal to the General over the next few days and he realized that talking about it to someone who understood the nature of rulership had been a relief. Then, for the first time, he felt the need to examine some of the choices he had made. He was less than a year removed from his previous life, yet at times it seemed much farther away than that. And many of those decisions now gave him pause: why had he desired the crown of Roldem so ardently? After spending months shoveling steer-manure over Jojanna's vegetables, carrying crates for mere coppers a day, and sleeping in the open without even a blanket for warmth, ambition seemed an almost ludicrous concept.

Thinking of Jojanna made him wonder how she and Jorgen were doing. Perhaps there might be some way to send them a message, to pass along a tiny part of the wealth he carried in that wagon. What he would spend on a new set of clothing when he returned to the Kingdom would make them the richest farmers in the village.

He sighed and put that thought away. There was still a very long way to go.

NINE

MURDER

Kaspar bounced on the seat.

He was taking his turn driving the wagon, a skill he decided he had never really needed to learn, as they traveled a relatively rocky portion of the old highway. The wooden wheels groaned and creaked every time they bounced over a rut in the road, and the constant rattling was leaching out any patience Kaspar had. He would be so very glad to see the last of this wagon.

He turned his mind away from his physical discomfort and took in the scenery. The land around them was turning cooler, and a darker green as they headed south. Kaspar found the notion that the hotter lands were in the north, along with the season here being opposite of his homeland, very odd. They were heading into the hottest part of the summer in this region, readying for the Midsummer's Festival, Banapis, while in his homeland of Olasko, the Midwinter's Festival would be celebrated.

The landscape was charming though, thought Kaspar, a series of rising hills and meadows, green farms and thick forests set away from the road. A high range of mountains was visible in the distance to the southwest. Kaspar knew from discussions with those on the road that those would be the Mountains of the Sea. The Serpent River was closer now, running a course to the west before turning south again, and they would reach a ferry landing two days south of Shamsha. Here they could abandon the wagon and book passage on a river boat heading down to the City of the Serpent River. They were seventeen days south of Higara and still two days away from Shamsha, the first thing that would pass for a small city according to what travelers they had encountered had told them.

Now that they were away from the many nameless villages they had driven through, Kaspar found the dreams were returning. From the occasional outcry as one or another of his companions awoke from a troubling dream, he knew the others were suffering from the same affliction.

Kaspar rode up beside Flynn and said, "If there's a temple in Shamsha, maybe we might find a priest to take a look at our dead friend?"

"Why?" asked Flynn.

"Doesn't it disturb you just a little that the farther we get from where you dug him up—"

"We didn't dig him up," Flynn interrupted. "We traded with those who did."

"Very well," Kaspar said. "How about, since you came into possession of him, people have been dying all the time and the farther away we get from where you got him, the more vivid and troubling the dreams have become?"

Flynn flicked the reins to move the sluggish horses

along. He was silent a while, then said, "You're suggesting it's cursed?"

"Something like that." Kaspar paused then said, "Look, we all know that once someone gets involved or . . . touches the damn thing . . . well, however it works, we can't just leave it. Maybe you're right and the magicians at Stardock will want it and pay a bounty for it, but what if they can't . . . get us to give it up?"

Flynn flicked the reins again. "I didn't think about that."

"Well, think about it," suggested Kaspar. "I would really like to be able to make a choice about where I go once we reach Port Vykor."

"But your share . . . ?"

Kaspar said, "We'll talk about it when we get there. Riches are not something I dwell on; getting home is."

A moment later he saw something in the distance. "Smoke?" he said to Flynn.

"A fight?"

"No, it looks more like we're getting within a day or so of the city. Probably smoke from the city hanging in that low valley ahead." He looked around. "We should camp soon, and get an early start. If we push it, we'll be in Shamsha by sundown tomorrow."

The area through which they passed was lightly forested, with farms scattered around the countryside within an easy ride of the highway. Several streams cut through the landscape as well as two rivers of sufficient size to require that bridges be erected over them. They found a patch of pastureland not too far from the road, next to a stream, and Kaspar was thankful for that; he was planning on a hot bath in Shamsha, but a quick rinse in the cold stream before then would be welcome.

So often had they made camp together that the four

men followed a well-worn and silent routine. Kaspar watered the horses, and watched the other three fall into easy rhythms, Kenner starting the fire, getting ready to prepare the evening meal, McGoin seeing to the horses' fodder when Kaspar brought them back, while Flynn unloaded the bedding and foodstuff from the wagon.

Kaspar was developing a strange relationship with these men; he wouldn't call them friends exactly, but they were comrades, and he realized that throughout his entire life he had little experience with such. His only exposure to this kind of thing had been as a boy, when spending time with his father and watching a few of his father's close friends at an intimate supper, or out on the hunt.

As a boy Kaspar had always been painfully aware of the issues of rank that surrounded him as the sole heir to the throne of Olasko. He had numerous playmates as a child, and no true friends. The older he got, the less sure he was if someone sought him out for the pleasure of his company or to simply gain an advantage. By the time he was fifteen, Kaspar found it easier to assume everyone, save his sister, was seeking personal favor. It kept things simple.

Kaspar returned to where the others waited and turned the horses over to McGoin who helped him stake out the animals. Then the two men portioned out the grain to the four horses.

This done, Kaspar declared, "I'm going for a swim."

McGoin said, "I think I'll join you. I have dust in places I didn't know I had places."

Kaspar laughed at that; and even though McGoin had said it a hundred times, each time Kaspar chuckled.

The two men stripped off and waded into the stream. It was cold, but not bitter. They were far enough south in early summer, and it was refreshing.

As they swam and bathed, McGoin said, "What do you think?"

"About what?"

"About this curse business."

"I'm no master of dark lore, McGoin. All I know is that since the moment I met you lot I've felt cursed."

McGoin hesitated for a moment, blinked, then started to laugh. "Well, you're no Princess of the Festival, yourself, Kaspar."

Kaspar nodded. "So I have been told."

McGoin said, "If you don't mind me asking, what was it you and the general were on about after supper those nights?"

"We played chess. And talked about being soldiers."

"I figured something like that. I never served. I've had my share of fights—started out as a cook's monkey on caravans down into Kesh my father organized and worked my way up from there. Had more than one run-in with bandits along the way." He pointed to a nasty scar that ran down his left side from armpit to hipbone. "Got this when I was only seventeen. Damn near bled to death. My father had to sew me up with a bloody canvas needle and twine. Then I damn near died of the fever when it festered. Only a priest of Dala saved me that time, with some medicine and a prayer."

"They have their uses, the priests."

"Seen any of the temples down here?"

"Can't say as I have," Kaspar replied.

"Mostly in the cities, but once in a while you see one out in the middle of nowhere. Really strange bunch of gods. Some of the ones we know, though they've got different names. Guis-Wa here is called Yama, for one. But lots of gods I've never heard of. A spider god called Tikir, and a monkey god, and a god of this and that, and more demons and whatever you call it . . . just a lot of temples.

"Anyway, I was thinking, if you want a priest to look at what's in that coffin, seems to me we ought to think just what sort of priest we're talking to."

"Why?"

"Well, back home I tithed to Banath."

Kaspar laughed. "The god of thieves?"

"Of course. Who better than to keep thieves from robbing me blind? And I also made offerings to other gods, but what I figure is each is concerned with their own . . . I don't known, call it a plan."

"An agenda?"

"Yes, that's it! They've got their own agendas . . . But what I've been thinking is what if that thing in the coffin is something that a temple might find useful—maybe even useful enough to cut our throats and dump us in the river (all the while saying a prayer for our journey on the Wheel, of course)?"

"I think we should talk it over with the others."

"Good idea."

They returned to the others as Kenner portioned out the evening's rations. It was a staple diet Kaspar had grown inured to: dried oat cakes, dried fruit, dried beef, and water. Still, it was a banquet compared to the bitter fruit he had lived on for two days when first coming to this land.

Kaspar discussed McGoin's idea with Flynn and Kenner; despite their concerns, they decided it would still be best to consult a priest in the next city. They chatted after eating and then settled in for the night.

Kaspar awoke. He had banged his head so many times on the wagon above that he came wide awake and rolled over, his hand grabbing the hilt of his sword, and crawled out from under the wagon before standing up. He looked around, his heart pounding.

No one was standing guard. "McGoin!" he shouted, waking up Kenner and Flynn.

Both men were out from under the wagon, weapons in hand, in an instant. Kaspar glanced around and saw no sign of McGoin.

A shout from beyond the firelight had Kaspar and the others racing. Before they were three steps on their way, a scream cut through the night that froze them in their tracks. It was McGoin, but the sound he made was a shriek of terror so profound, so primal, that each man's first instinct was to turn and run. Kaspar said, "Wait!"

Flynn and Kenner hesitated, then came a gurgling, strangled scream that died suddenly.

Kaspar shouted, "Spread out!"

He had taken less than a dozen steps when he came upon McGoin, or what was left of him. Beyond him, a thing—roughly man-shape but of much larger proportions—stood in the darkness. It had shoulders twice the size of any man living, and its legs were reversed, like a horse's or goat's hind legs. The face was obscured in the darkness of a moonless night, but Kaspar could see there was nothing remotely human about it. At the creature's feet lay the body of McGoin. His head had been torn from his shoulders, and the creature had ripped off his arms and legs, tossing them aside. The trader's torso had been pulled apart so that no piece of his anatomy was recognizable; he had been reduced to so much bloody pulp and meat.

Kaspar held up his sword and shouted, "Circle behind it!"

He didn't wait to see if the others obeyed his command, for the creature was full upon him. He struck out and the creature raised its arm to block. When Kaspar's blade struck, sparks flew, as if metal was striking metal, although the sound it made was as if he had struck something made of very hard leather, and the shock that ran up his arm surprised him. He had never hit something this hard, even a man in armor in battle. He barely could hold on to his sword.

Flynn came at the creature from behind and struck it hard at the joint of head and neck, and all he did was achieve the same sparking display. Having no other ideas, Kaspar shouted, "Back to the campfire!"

He faced the creature as he backed away, fearing to turn around lest the thing prove faster. He sensed rather than saw Flynn and Kenner racing past, and he shouted, "Get brands! If steel won't hurt it, maybe fire will."

As Kasper backed into the circle of the campfire's light, he could see the monster's face. It looked like a demented ape, with fangs that were exposed when it curled back its lips. They were black, as were the gums. The eyes were yellow and had black irises. The ears looked like nothing as much as webbed bat wings, and the body like the torso of a man or large ape stuck upon the legs of a goat. Kaspar heard Flynn shout, "Step to your left!"

Kaspar did so and Flynn ran past him, thrusting a flaming torch at the creature. It recoiled, but it didn't turn and flee. After a moment, Kenner shouted, "The fire doesn't hurt it. It just seems annoyed by it."

Suddenly Kaspar had a thought: "Hold it at bay!"

He raced for the wagon and leapt into the back. Pulling aside the tarpaulin, he used his sword to pry up the lid of the coffin. He reached in and took the black sword that had been placed with the armor and jumped down from the wagon. With three strides, he stepped between Flynn and Kenner and lashed out with the sword.

The reaction was instantaneous. The black blade

struck the creature and instead of just producing sparks, the edge cut into the thing's arm. It howled in pain and stepped back, but Kaspar was on it, pressing his advantage.

He lashed out, first high, then low, and the monster stumbled back. Each cut brought a howl and finally the creature turned to flee. Kaspar leapt forward. He lashed out, taking it across the neck. The head went flying off in a graceful arc, and then dissolved into mist before Kaspar's eyes. The monster's body fell forward and also started to turn to vapor before it struck the ground. By the time Kaspar could kneel to examine it, it was gone. There was no sign of a struggle.

"What was that?" Kaspar breathed.

Kenner said, "I thought you might know. You're the one who thought to get the black sword from the coffin."

Kaspar realized the sword was thrumming in his hand as if he stood holding the rail of a ship which vibrated from slamming against the waves. "I don't know why I did that," said Kaspar. "It just . . . came to me to get this sword."

All three men were staring out where McGoin lay and Kenner said, "We need to bury him."

Kaspar nodded. "But we need to wait until dawn so we can find all . . ." He left the thought unfinished. All three men knew their companion was scattered over a wide area and the grisly task of gathering up all the pieces of him and putting them in a grave lay ahead. It was something better done by daylight.

They felt the presence before they heard anything. As one, all three men turned to see the black armor, standing upright behind them. Kaspar turned, the black blade at the ready, while Kenner and Flynn held up the burning torches and retreated.

The armor made no threatening gesture, but slowly

held out its hands, palms upward, and waited. After nearly a minute of no one moving, Kaspar took a single step forward and waited. The armor remained motionless.

Slowly, Kaspar put the sword into the armor's outstretched hands. Instantly it wheeled about and moved back to the wagon. With an inhuman hop, it jumped into the wagon, which bounced under its weight, then stepped into the coffin and lay down.

The three men didn't move.

After nearly a minute of total silence and stillness, Kenner ventured to move to the wagon. The others followed. The armor lay in the coffin as it had when Kaspar had pried open the lid. For almost another minute they just looked at it. Finally Kaspar put out his hand and touched it, ready to pull back if there was any response.

It felt exactly as it had before.

The three men exchanged questioning looks, but no one said anything. Finally Kaspar climbed up on the wagon bed and replaced the lid of the coffin. He said, "Hammer," and waited until Kenner handed him one from the tool box under the driver's seat. Without hurry, Kaspar carefully re-aligned the heavy iron nails that had pulled out with the lid and then diligently hammered them all back into place.

Then he said, "We will find a priest tomorrow."

The other men nodded. For the balance of the night, none of them closed an eye.

The wagon rolled through the streets of Shamsha, an hour before sundown. This was the first population center Kaspar would actually call a city. The walls could easily be breached by his Olaskon engineers in less than a week's siege, but that was a week longer than any he had seen so far. The guards were called prefects, which struck Kaspar as odd, as that was the title give to a rank of senior military officer in Queg. At one time in ages past, this must have been a military post. The senior prefect gave the wagon a cursory inspection and then threatened to delay them for an indefinite period until Kaspar bribed him.

The three men had been silent most of the day. They had gathered together what they could of McGoin and buried him deep in a hole in the meadow. No one had spoken as they stood around the makeshift grave, until at last Kenner had said, "May Lims-Kragma quickly speed him to a better life."

Flynn and Kaspar grunted agreement, and they packed up their camp and set off. It was nothing any of them could come to grips with. The monster and the armor coming to life were events so unbelievable that Kaspar knew the others were as reluctant to discuss it as he was; it was as if to speak of it was to admit the possibility that what they had witnessed was real.

Yet what troubled Kaspar most of all was the familiar feeling he had recognized. Something about all the carnage and evil had a recognizable quality to it. An echo of an earlier time in his life pressed into this mind, as if trying to remember a song once heard and barely remembered, yet associated with a memorable event, a festival or celebration perhaps. But in the field at night, it had been something unknown and unknowable, and like a man struggling to remember that nameless tune he at last grew tired of the process and push it aside. Better to concentrate on what to do next than dwell too long on what had already happened. It wasn't as if he could change the past.

They found an inn with an impressive stabling yard and before retiring, Kaspar inspected the wagon and watched as Kenner and Flynn hauled the chest up to their room.

When he had finished with the horses, he sought out the innkeeper.

The owner of this establishment was a prosperous man of advancing years, given to wearing a gaudy waistcoat over his puff-sleeved white shirt and almost pristine apron. He wore a knit cap that came to a long peak which fell over his left shoulder. He saw Kaspar regarding the odd red-and-white-striped hat and said, "Keeps me hair out of the soup. What can I do for you?"

"If a traveler needed to see a priest about something dark, which temple would be the right choice?"

"Well, that depends," observed the innkeeper, his pudgy face set in a smile as his watery blue eyes regarded Kaspar.

"On what?"

"If you seek to do something dark, or if you wish to prevent something dark from happening."

Kaspar nodded. "The latter."

With a wide smile, the innkeeper said, "Out the front door, turn left. Go down the street until you reach the square. On the other side of the fountain lies the temple of Geshen-Amat. They will help you."

"Thank you," said Kaspar. He hurried up to the room and informed his two companions of what the innkeeper had told him. Flynn said, "Why don't you and Kenner go, and I'll stay here?"

Kaspar said, "I think this is the type of inn where our gold will be safe."

Flynn laughed. "This chest is the least of my concerns." He motioned with his head to the window outside. "It's that thing we are burdened with that I fear. And I just feel better with one of us being close at hand."

Kaspar said, "Then open the chest. I don't know a lot of temples that work magic just because you ask nicely."

Flynn took the key out of his purse and opened the lock. Kaspar said, "Give me your belt-pouch," to Kenner, who did as he was asked. Kaspar picked over the odd sized and shaped coins, fetching out a few coppers, and half a dozen golden coins, then loaded it up with silver. "Any more and it's robbery," Kaspar observed.

Kaspar and Kenner bid Flynn farewell and headed down the stairs and out of the door.

As evening fell, the streets of Shamsha were crowded. Inns were alive with laughter and music, and many merchants were trying for that last sale of the day before closing up shop. The streets were festooned with banners and garlands, as the populace made ready for the Midsummer's Festival that was less than a week away. Street lamps had been wrapped in colorful paper covers, bathing the ground in a soft glow, lending a gaiety to the scene that put in stark contrast the dark mood Kaspar and Kenner felt. As the two men reached the market square, they saw carts being loaded up as merchants shut down their stalls to head for home.

Across the square they saw the temple of Geshen-Amat. It was a large building with wide steps leading up to an ornately decorated marble façade, a bas-relief of gods and angels, demons and men.

On either side of the base of the steps rested statues. One was a man with the head of an elephant, and the other was a man with the head of a lion. Kaspar paused to inspect them for a moment as a monk walked down the steps. He had short hair and wore only a simple brown robe and sandals.

"You seek entrance to the temple?" he asked politely.

Kaspar said, "We seek help."

"What may the servants of Geshen-Amat do for you?"

"We need to speak to the leader of your temple."

The monk smiled, and Kaspar was suddenly visited by the odd notion that he had seen this man before. He was short, balding, and had the odd cast of features you saw on certain Keshians—dark eyes, high cheekbones, and dark hair, with an almost golden tone to the skin.

"The Master of the Order is always pleased to speak to those in need. Please, follow me."

The two men trailed after the monk as he led them into the vast entrance of the temple. On both walls more bas-reliefs were cut into the stone, and every few feet a hanging lamp of oil burned, casting flickering shadows that made the bas-reliefs look as if they were moving.

Along the walls small shrines to various gods and demigods were situated, and before several of these people prayed. Kaspar realized he was observing rites in a faith he knew nothing about, for to the best of his knowledge the temples of his homeland had no counterpart to Geshen-Amat. For a brief moment he wondered if there truly was a god, and if so, were his powers and influence limited only to this land?

They reached a large hall containing dozens more shrines, but opposite the entrance rose up a heroic statue of a seated man. His face was stylized, his eyes, nose, and lips being rendered in a manner Kaspar could only call simplistic. In his homeland, as well as the other kingdoms of the north, the effigies of the gods and goddesses were of human proportions, save when they were small icons placed in roadside shrines, or adorning the homes of the faithful. But this statue was easily thirty feet from its base to the top of its head. The figure wore a simple robe, with one shoulder bare, and held out his hands, palms upward, as if granting a benediction. To its left and right, in roughly human proportion, sat the two figures Kaspar and Kenner had seen in front of the temple, the men with the heads of an elephant and lion.

Before the statue sat a lone monk, his hair white with age. The younger monk escorting them said, "Wait here, please." He continued forward and spoke briefly into the older monk's ear and then returned. "Master Anshu will see you momentarily."

"Thank you," said Kenner.

Kaspar said, "I must plead ignorance of your faith, brother. I am from a distant land. Can you enlighten me?"

The monk grinned and with unexpected humor said, "Would that enlightenment were that quickly achieved, my friend. Then we would have little work to do in this realm."

Kaspar smiled at the jest, and said, "Tell me about Geshen-Amat, please."

"He is the godhead, the one true divinity of which all others are but reflections. He is the one above all."

"Ishap?" Kaspar asked quietly.

"Ah, you *are* from a distant land. The Balancer is but one aspect of Geshen-Amat. Those who sit at his feet, Gerani—" he pointed to the figure with the elephant's head "—and Sutapa—" then the figure with the lion's head "—are avatars, sent forth by Geshen-Amat to teach mankind the One True Path. It is not an easy path, but it does eventually lead to enlightenment."

"Then what of all the other temples?" asked Kenner.

"Geshen-Amat provides many ways to travel the One True Path. There are avatars for every man and woman to embrace."

Then Kaspar understood. "Ama-ral!"

The monk nodded. "In the ancient language, yes."

"In my land that was considered a heresy and a terrible war was fought over the doctrine."

"You are an educated man," said the monk. "Here is Master Anshu."

The elder monk approached and bowed before Kaspar and Kenner. He was wry and his skin was as brown as sunburned leather, but he had bright brown eyes. His head was completely shaved, and he wore the same brown robe and sandals as the young monk. The men returned the greeting and then the old monk said, "My disciple says you are in need, brothers. What may I do for you?"

"We have come into possession of an artifact, perhaps a relic, and we believe it may be cursed."

The older monk turned to his disciple and said, "Bring tea to my quarters." Turning to Kaspar and Kenner, he said, "Please, follow me."

He led them out of a side door and through a long hallway, by the quiet. "You can barely hear the sounds of the city."

"Meditation is served by silence," said the old monk. He led them to a door and opened it for them. "Come, please."

He indicated that they should remove their boots and Kenner and Kaspar complied. The room was large but sparsely furnished. A reed mat filled more of the floor, upon which the old monk sat. There was a small, low table to one side, which he reached over and placed between them. A moment later the young monk entered and provided cups and a pot of tea. He served Kenner and Kaspar then Master Anshu. When he departed, the old monk said, "Now, tell me about this cursed relic."

Kenner started slowly, telling the entire tale of his group and how they had traded with local villagers for the artifacts they had looted from what appeared to be a tomb. When he detailed McGoin's gristly murder the night before, the old monk nodded. "It may very well be that this is a cursed item. We live on a world that has seen elder races, and the burial places of the dead are often protected by wards of dark magic. I should like to see this relic."

"Now?"

The old monk smiled. "If not now, when?" He stood up and without saying a word, motioned for the two men to put their boots on and return to the garden. He followed them outside where the young monk waited and said, "We shall accompany these gentlemen."

The young monk bowed and fell into step beside his master. They quickly made their way down the steps of the temple, across the square, and down the street to the inn.

Kenner said, "I'll go get Flynn," and went into the inn, while Kaspar led the monks through the gate to the courtyard. They approached the wagon and the old monk's steps faltered. He turned to his disciple and said, "Return to the temple at once! Bring Master Oda and Master Yongu. Hurry!"

The young monk ran off, and the Master Anshu said, "I can sense at this distance that you have something in that wagon that is . . . wrong."

"Wrong?" asked Kaspar. "What do you mean?"

"I cannot describe how I know, but whatever you have in that wagon is not merely a cursed relic or artifact. It is something more."

"What?" asked Kaspar.

"I won't know until I see it."

Kenner and Flynn exited the inn and Kenner introduced the old monk to Flynn. Kaspar said, "We seem to have something unexpected here. There are others coming from the temple."

"Why?" asked Flynn. "What's unexpected?"

"I won't know until I view what's in there," the monk said, slowly approaching the wagon.

Kaspar jumped into the bed of the wagon, drew the tool box out from under the seat, and pulled aside the tarpaulin. He used a pry bar to lift the lid of the coffin.

The old monk moved to the side of the wagon and could not clearly see into it. Kaspar held out his hand and the old master gripped it with surprising strength, and Kaspar helped him into the wagon.

The monk turned and looked down upon the black armor. His mouth opened, but no words were spoke. He exhaled a deep breath, as if sighing with relief, then his eyes rolled up into his head and he collapsed. Kaspar grabbed him to keep him from falling, and then he handed down the still form to Kenner and Flynn.

Kenner knelt beside Master Anshu. "He's alive."

Kaspar turned and looked inside the coffin. For an instant he though he saw a hint of movement in the eye-slit. But then nothing.

"See if you can revive him," he said, leaping down from the wagon.

A few minutes later, three monks entered the courtyard and when they were a few feet away from where Kenner, Kaspar, and Flynn gathered around the unconscious monk, they halted.

The leader of the three was a powerful-looking, middle-aged man, with a shocking streak of gray hair through an otherwise black mane he wore to his shoulders. He had a robe of the same cut as the others, but in black rather than brown. "Step away from Master Anshu, please," he instructed.

Kaspar and the others did so and the black-robed monk took one step forward and began an incantation, waving his hands in a complex pattern in the air. The other two monks lowered their heads as if in prayer.

Kaspar heard and saw nothing unusual, but suddenly the hair on his arms and neck stood on end! He turned to look at the wagon and saw a pulsing light surrounding it. The horses started to whinny in their stalls and become agitated, and Kaspar and the others took another step backward.

Then the light was gone and the two brown-robed monks hurried forward to attend to Master Anshu. The black-robed monk moved purposefully past the others and jumped into the wagon bed. He took a long look down at the figure in the coffin, then he put the lid back in place. He took the hammer out of the toolbox and with deft blows had it quickly fastened shut.

The old monk was beginning to revive. He came to stand before Kaspar and the others. Without preamble, he said, "That thing must be taken from here tomorrow."

He turned to walk away but Kaspar cried, "Wait a moment, please!"

The monk stopped.

Kaspar said, "Master Anshu said the armor was wrong. Is it cursed?"

"Our master is correct. The thing in the coffin is not cursed, but it is wrong. You must take it from here quickly."

"Can you help us?"

"No," said the black-robed monk. "I am Yongu, and the safety of the temple is my concern. That thing must be taken from here and the longer you tarry, the more harm will come."

"Where should we go?" asked Flynn.

Yongu said, "I do not know, but if you linger, innocent people will be harmed."

"Why the rush?" asked Kaspar.

"Because the thing in the coffin grows impatient. It wishes to be somewhere."

Kaspar looked at the others, then said, "But where?"

Master Anshu said weakly, "It will tell you where to go."

"How?" asked Flynn.

"If you go the wrong way, you will die. As long as you live, you're heading in the right direction. Now, forgive us, but we can help you no more." He raised himself to his feet, took two steps, then stopped and said, "But one thing I can tell you. Turn your steps westward."

The monks left, and Kaspar said, "Westward?"

Kenner shook his head. "But we need to go south, then sail northeast."

Kaspar shook his head. "Apparently not." He walked back toward the inn. "We leave at dawn, my friends."

Kaspar turned away at the door of the inn and Flynn said, "Where are you going?"

"To see if I can find a map," answered Kaspar. "I need to see what is west of here."

Without another comment, Flynn and Kenner went inside the inn, and Kaspar set out in search of a map.

Ten

Westward

Kaspar's brow furrowed.

He, Kenner, and Flynn sat at the table in the common room of the Four Blessings Inn, concentrating on the three maps Kaspar had contrived to purchase after the monks had left.

While he had been finding map merchants, Flynn and Kenner had returned to the temple to try to prize whatever additional information from the monks about what was "wrong" with the armor, but they came back with nothing. The monks would not speak to them. Flynn was convinced that they should not move on in the morning, to force the monks to return and speed them on their way.

"How reliable are these, I wonder?" Kaspar asked.

The stout innkeeper approached their table with three fresh cups of ale. "Planning your next journey?" he inquired.

"If we can depend on these," said Kaspar.

The innkeeper looked over their shoulder then reached out and removed the top map. "You can burn this one. I recognize it; it's a copy of a copy of a very old, inaccurate map."

"How do you know?" Kenner asked.

"Used to be a merchant-trader—like yourselves—before I settled down here. Reached an age where I was tired of thrashing bandits and dodging raiders. Let me go see what I've got locked away in my trunk. I can show you a couple of things."

He returned a few minutes later with an old map, drawn on rolled-up leather. "This I bought from a trader up in Ralapinti, when I first started out. I had one wagon, a mule, a sword which I'd won in a card game, and a bunch of junk to sell."

He unrolled it. Unlike the maps they had, this one displayed the entire continent of Novindus. As well as the original ink, there were additional notes and drawing, which Kaspar assumed the innkeeper had made. "See here." The innkeeper indicated their location, in Shamsha. "From here to here," he said, moving his finger in a line, "all three maps are pretty accurate, but after that . . ."

"We need to go west," said Kaspar.

"Well, there are two ways to do it. You can head back up north for a few days and you'll find a road heading west. It's not a bad way to travel if you're not in a hurry. You wind through the foothills of the Mountains of the Sea—lots of passes and some decent game if you're hunting along the way." He paused, tapping his finger on his chin. "I think it took me a month or so the last time I took that route. Of course, that was thirty years ago.

"Most people would just head south to the City of the Serpent River and then catch a ship to Maharta."

"Why Maharta?"

The innkeeper sat down, uninvited. He pointed to the map. "If you head straight west from here, you end up just about in the middle of the Great Temple Market Square." He scratched his chin. "From there, if you keep going west, there's not a lot you'd want to mess with.

"I take you for outlanders. You speak well enough, but I've never heard accents like yours. Where are you from?"

"Across the Green Sea," said Kaspar.

"Ha!" The innkeeper slapped his hand on the table. "I've heard tales of traders from across the sea showing up from time to time. Tell you what, after I finish supper and take care of my other customers, let's sit and talk. If you're going west, there are some things you need to know if you want to stay alive. And I'm curious about your homeland." He stood up. "I don't miss the dangers, but I do miss the excitement."

He departed and left the three men puzzling over the new maps.

It was late when the innkeeper returned. "Name's Bek, which is short for Bekamostana."

"I can see why they call you Bek," said Flynn. He introduced himself and his companions.

"Now, tell me what you need to know."

Kaspar said, "We were told to go west, so I guess that means Maharta."

Bek said, "'Queen City of the River' they call her. Once the most prosperous, beautiful, wonderful city . . . well, we used to say in the world, but that was before we learned about those places across the sea. Anyway, the old Raj,in my grandfather's time, well, he did right by his people. It's not the biggest city—that's the City of the Serpent River—but it's the richest. At least it was at one time."

"What happened?"

"The Emerald Queen is what happened," said Bek. "No one talks much about it, because everyone knows what happened; our parents taught us." He stroked his chin. "She came out of somewhere up in the north of the Westlands."

"Westlands?" asked Kenner, looking at the map.

Bek put his hand over two-thirds of the map of Novindus. "Here are the Westlands," then he covered both sides, "and in the middle lay the Riverlands, and to the east—"

Flynn finished, "Are the Eastlands."

"You catch on," said Bek with a grin. "Time was, you could travel either the Serpent River or the Vedra River almost all the way without much difficulty. Oh, there were a few bandits, according to my grandfather, but back then the City of the Serpent River controlled most of the land around the river all the way up to the Hotlands.

"The Vedra is lined with city-states, each with their own territories, but apart from a border skirmish now and then, it's pretty peaceful. It's when you get away from the rivers that things start to get nasty." He indicated the area west of Maharta. "That's the Plain of Djams. It's all grasslands. Don't go there."

"Why?"

"Two reasons. Nothing worth trading for, and it's inhabited by these really murderous little bastards, about four foot tall. No one can speak their language and they kill all trespassers. They usually stay away from the river so there are still farms on the west bank, but go more than a day's ride from the river and you're likely to end up with some poisoned darts in you. Can't see them coming. No one even really knows what they look like.

"After that, you reach the Pillars of Heaven."

"What are they?" asked Kenner.

Bek's finger pointed to a range of mountains. "Ratn'gary Mountains. Biggest mountains down here. About three days up from Ratn'gary Gulf. Legend has it you'll find two things there: the Necropolis—the City of the Dead Gods, where all the gods who perished in the Chaos Wars wait—and high above, the Pillars of Heaven—two mountains so tall no man has ever seen their peaks. And on top of those peaks is the Pavilion of the Gods, where the living gods reside.

"It's all legend, of course. No man living has ever tried to go there."

The three men exchanged glances and after a moment of silence Bek asked, "So, what is this expedition then?"

"We were told to go west," said Flynn. "That's all."

"Who told you?"

"The monks you sent me to see last night," said Kaspar.

Bek rubbed his chin. "Well, seems to me you don't ignore those sorts of suggestions. I mean, you needed some advice and got it. But you'd think they would be a little more specific than just 'go west,' wouldn't you?"

Kaspar wrestled with the idea of telling Bek about the cargo they had in their wagon, but decided the old innkeeper was unlikely to have any additional insights. He stood up. "Well, we're off at first light. We're going to offload our cargo and take a boat down to the City of the Serpent River—it sounds like a better choice than going over the mountains by wagon."

Bek said, "Takes about the same amount of time if you include all the loading and offloading, securing passage and the like, but in the end you'll have a better chance of getting there intact."

"Is it safe to assume the clan war is over?" asked Kenner.

"Never safe to assume anything about the clans down there, but most of the bloodshed is over for the time being, according to what I hear. Just make sure you bribe all the right people when going from one clan district to another. My advice would be: as soon as you get off the boat, go right at the first big boulevard. I can't recall its name, but you won't miss it. There are maybe half a dozen little alleys, then this one big street running north and south. You'll want to go straight on, 'cause that's where everyone else will be going. That would take you to the great northern market square, and all the good inns. But if you turn right, you'll stay in the Eagle Clan's area of control. They hold everything along the river, down to the docks. If you bribe a guard or two, you'll have no trouble. Find an inn at the docks and wait until a ship's bound for Maharta. Shouldn't have to wait more than a day or two as most of the sea trade from the City puts in at Maharta before heading down the coast to Chatisthan and Ispar."

"Thanks," said Kaspar. "You've been very helpful." He handed back the map.

"No, keep it," said Bek. "I've got no use for it now. My daughter married a miller up in Rolonda village—nice enough lad but I don't care much for my in-laws—and my son's in the Raj's army, so I don't think they'll be needing a trader's map any time soon."

"Thank you very much," said Kaspar.

As Kenner and Flynn started up the stairs to their room, Kaspar said, "One last question. You said that if we went straight west from here, we'd end up in the . . ."

"Great Temple Market Square," finished Bek. "That's a truth."

"Is that significant?"

The innkeeper was silent for a moment, as if considering the question. "Maybe. A hundred years back Maharta was the trading center for the entire continent. Everything going up or down river—from all the coastal cities, from Serpent River up to the distant Sulth—would pass through there. So the old Raj's ancestors built the great square so that merchants and travelers would have a place for their temples. Must be at least a hundred of them. If the monks said to go west, then maybe that's as good a place to start looking for what you seek. I've heard there are sects so small they've only got two temples in the world, one in their home town and another in Maharta!" He laughed. "Even if the city's not what it used to be, it's still worth a look."

"Thanks," said Kaspar, standing up. He rolled up the map. "And thanks for this."

"Don't mention it. I'll see you in the morning."

Kaspar slowly walked up the stairs. By nature he was a man to make decisions and he hated uncertainty. But now he found himself in a unique situation; he knew he was compelled to finish this business with Kenner and Flynn before he could think of returning home. But he hated not knowing what he was doing. Hell, he thought, he wasn't even sure about where he was going.

He reached the top of the stairs and entered the room.

The coffin was hoisted in a cargo net and then lowered slowly into the hold of the ship. Kenner and Flynn carried the chest aboard, while Kaspar finished selling the wagon and horses. They didn't need the extra gold—they had enough riches in the chest to keep them comfortable for the rest of their lives—but Kaspar was determined to play the role of trader and not bring suspicion on them.

Bek's advice had been sound. They had turned south at the corner where Bek had told them to, and were stopped only twice by warriors wearing the mark of the Eagle Clan on their tabards.

The bribes they made were not even masked, but simply the price of doing business. The second guard had even given them a token, a wooden coin with an eagle on it, that he instructed them to show to any other guards who might question them. Kaspar complained that the first guards hadn't offered them such, and was greeted by a laugh and the observation that the bribe obviously hadn't been generous enough.

Kaspar mounted the gangplank and followed Kenner and Flynn to the little cabin they would share. It was barely large enough for the two sets of bunks, one above the other. They put the chest on one of the lower bunks and Kaspar settled into the other.

"I've been thinking," he said.

"About what?" asked Flynn.

"About what the old monk said, that if we make the wrong choice, we die."

Kenner climbed into an upper bunk and lay down. "Seems a tough way of letting us know. Three wrong moves and that thing in the hold is left sitting somewhere with no one to move it."

"I think it would find someone to move it somehow," Flynn observed.

"Anyway," continued Kaspar, "I was also thinking about something Bek said, how there was a road to Maharta a couple of days north of the city. We must have passed it. Maybe McGoin died because we didn't take that road."

Kenner lay on his side with his head resting on one hand. "I don't know. I sometimes think that if we weren't caught up in the middle of this we'd be a lot more terrified."

Flynn pulled himself up onto his bunk. "Nothing special about it. Kaspar, you've been a soldier, right?"

"Right."

"Sooner or later you just get used to the blood, right?"

Kaspar was quiet for a moment. Then he said, "Yes. It becomes . . . commonplace."

"That's it, then," Flynn continued. "We've just got used to the madness."

Kaspar lay back in his bunk, content to wait for the call for the midday meal. He thought about what Flynn had just said and decided he was right: you did get used to the madness if you lived with it long enough.

But a troubling thought occurred to him then: he had been living with madness long before he had come here and encountered these men.

ELEVEN

MAHARTA

A call came from the deck.

Kaspar motioned for his companions to get out of their bunks. "We're tied fast. By the time we get this up on deck, the gangplank will be out and I'll see about hiring us a wagon."

"Buy one if you have to," said Flynn. He had already taken gold out of the chest and handed Kaspar a full purse which he put away under his tunic.

Flynn and Kenner left the cabin first and hauled the chest up the companionway. Kaspar took one last look around the tiny cabin in case anyone had left something behind. He closed the door and climbed the steps after them.

On deck he noticed two things almost instantly; the usual noise of the waterfront was missing. He had sailed into enough harbors in his life to know what to expect, and hushed voices punctuating an otherwise complete silence wasn't normal. The other peculiarity was that the only activity on deck was a boom-crew hoisting the coffin out of the hold.

Glancing around, it took a moment for Kaspar to take everything in. Kenner and Flynn had put the chest down and Kenner was pointing over the rail. Kaspar looked and saw at least two hundred armed guards had cleared the entire wharf. Where the gangplank was being run out stood what could only be called a delegation of clergy, from a temple Kaspar didn't recognize. Behind them sat what officers of the local Raj's garrison and behind them came a dray-wagon with two heavy horses pulling it. It was empty and as Kaspar watched it was quickly rolled to where the coffin would be lowered. Over to the right waited an ornate carriage.

Flynn said, "I don't think you need to worry about finding a wagon. It seems we are expected."

The moment the gangplank struck the wharf, armed guards hurried aboard. They wore a light blue livery with gold and white trim, and their helms of steel were polished to a silver gleam. As the coffin was hoisted out of the hold, the soldier in charge came to stand before Kaspar and his companions and said, "You are the outlanders who accompany that?" He pointed to the suspended coffin.

"Yes," said Kaspar.

"Come with us." The soldier turned without waiting to see if he was being obeyed, and two guards grabbed the chest at Flynn's feet while two others motioned for the three men to hurry along.

Kaspar felt a slight relief that he hadn't been disarmed. Not that he had any illusion about his ability to fight two hundred of the Raj of Maharta's finest by himself, but at least it meant he wasn't quite a prisoner . . . yet. He knew there was only a slight difference between an armed guard and an escort, but sometimes that difference separated the honored and the condemned.

When he reached the bottom of the gangway, a regally dressed elderly man stepped forward. His robes were crimson trimmed with ermine and gold braid, and upon his head he wore a conical red hat adorned with runes of gold. He motioned and half a dozen other clerics moved to the wagon as the coffin was lowered. "I am Father Elect Vagasha, of the Temple of Kalkin. Please accompany me and we'll talk."

Kaspar replied, "I appreciate the illusion that we have a choice in the matter."

The old cleric smiled and said, "Of course you don't, but it's nice to observe civility, don't you think?"

He led them to a carriage waiting by the edge of the crowd, and two footmen opened the door for him. When all were seated inside, the carriage moved off.

Kaspar looked out of the window. "This reception seems to have wreaked havoc with daily commerce, Father. And it's unexpected." He looked at the old prelate. "I assume Brother Anshu sent word of our impending arrival?"

"Indeed. He communicated with his order, which in turn sought out my own. The Brothers of Geshen-Amat are a contemplative one, given to very esoteric and mystical considerations. While they are held in high regard in matters of spirituality, there are some things which are best left to other orders. As I understand it, you are outlanders?"

"Yes," replied Flynn. "From a land across the sea."

"The Kingdom of the Isles," said Father Elect Vagasha. "We know of it. We've known of it before the coming of the Emerald Queen. As we know of Kesh and those who dwell in other parts of the world. Commerce is rare between our hemispheres, but not unheard of.

"Our religion is not practiced in your part of the world. You would consider us a martial order, as many of our brothers and fathers were soldiers before they came to the faith, while others have served under arms from first moment they took holy orders.

"Moreover, we are a brotherhood of scholars and historians. We seek knowledge as one of the many paths to enlightenment so we were the logical choice to examine this . . ."

"Relic?" supplied Kaspar.

"That's as good a word as any for now. In any event, why don't you tell me what you know about it, from the beginning, as we drive to the temple?"

Kaspar looked at Flynn, who looked at Kenner. Kenner indicated Flynn should tell the story. Flynn began, "Over two years ago, a group of us gathered in Krondor. There were thirty merchants in all, and we formed a consortium . . ."

Kaspar sat back. He had heard every detail of the story so he let Flynn's voice fade into the background as he looked out at the passing vista of Maharta.

This city, more than any other place he had visited, reminded Kaspar of home. This far south the climate was temperate and the summer weather more clement than he had endured so far. The buildings near the wharf were of brick and mortal, not the flimsier, if cooler, constructions he had encountered farther north. The streets were cobbled and the sea breeze blew away much of the stench of overcrowding he had endured in the City of the Serpent River and the other towns he had visited on his way here.

The market they entered seemed as prosperous as any he had seen, with well-fed, industrious people all around. The urchins who chased after the carriage and the wives out shopping could have easily been plucked from the streets of Opardum and deposited here. He felt a wave of nostalgia for his homeland he had not experienced so far since his exile.

As they rolled through another broad boulevard, Flynn said, ". . . and that's when we found Kaspar."

The Father Elect said, "So you were not part of this company from the outset?"

"No," said Kaspar. "I had only come to this land a few months before I met Flynn and the others. It was mere happenstance that put me in the market the day they sought a fourth sword to help them get the . . . relic down to the City of the Serpent River."

"So you had no prior interest in this item?"

"I merely sought to speed my way home. I did not come here by choice."

"Oh?" The old prelate leaned forward. "How does one travel around the world if not by choice? Certainly not as a prisoner?"

"Not in the traditional sense, Father. I was not chained in the hold of a ship, if that's what you are asking." Kaspar leaned back and sighed. "I was exiled by a very powerful magician I chanced to run afoul of and, in truth, he was more forgiving than not, for had our positions been reversed, I almost certainly would have killed him."

"At least you appreciate your enemy's clemency."

"My father used to say, 'a day spent breathing is a good day.'"

"How you ran foul of this magician is probably a fascinating story," observed the old priest, "however, let us leave it for a later conversation—should circumstances permit—and move on to what occurred once you joined the three survivors of this ill-omened expedition."

Kaspar took up the narrative from where he had met

Flynn, McGoin, and Kenner, and covered the high points of the journey, with the others occasionally adding a detail here and there. When he got to the description of the creature that killed McGoin, the priest asked some specific questions, then when he was satisfied with Kaspar's answers indicated that he should continue.

"There's not much more to say," Kaspar shrugged. "We were in Shamsha two days later boarding a boat to the City of the Serpent River. The only thing that happened there was our encounter with Brother Anshu, and I'm sure you've had a full report on that from his temple. We spent three days in the City of the Serpent River before boarding the ship that brought us here."

"And here you are," said the Father Elect. The carriage slowed. "And here we are," he added.

Kaspar looked out and saw they had entered a huge square, surrounded on all sides by temples. The one they stopped in front of was far from the gaudiest, but it also wasn't the plainest. They got out of the carriage and the prelate said, "We have quarters for you, gentlemen. By the Raj's orders, at our request, you will be guests here until it is decided what to do with you and your odd cargo."

"And how long will that be?" asked Kaspar.

"Why, as long as it takes," answered the old man.

Kaspar looked at Flynn and Kenner who both shrugged. Kaspar said nothing more as he mounted the steps into the temple.

The Temple of Kalkin was unlike any temple Kaspar had ever visited. Instead of silence, or the muted prayers of the devoted, or the singing of hymns, the main hall of the temple was filled with voice. Young men stood in groups, often with an older priest in attendance, sometimes without, sometimes listening to the older priest carefully, other times heatedly debating a point. Other brothers of the order hurried about, but nowhere did Kaspar see the silent devotion he was so familiar with in other temples.

"It gets a little loud in here sometimes. Let's retire to my apartment while your quarters are prepared," said the Father Elect.

He led the three men into a hallway, opened a door and indicated that they should enter. Once inside, a servant approached and took the conical hat and the heavy robe from the Father Elect. Underneath, Father Vagasha wore the same simple robe of gray homespun Kaspar had seen the other priests wearing.

The apartment was simply furnished, but possessed a wealth of books, tomes, scrolls, and parchments kept in cases along the wall. Otherwise there was only a single writing table and five chairs. The priest indicated that the three men should sit. He instructed the servant to fetch refreshments, then sat down too.

Kaspar said, "Your temple isn't like any temple I've visited, Father. It looks more like a school."

"That's because it is, in its own way," said Vagasha. "We call it a university, which means—"

"The whole," supplied Kaspar. "*Universitas Apprehendere?*"

"*Videre,*" corrected the old priest. "Perfect understanding is the province of the gods. We merely seek to understand everything that we are permitted to see."

Kenner and Flynn looked as if they were feeling out of their element, and Father Vagasha said, "Your friend speaks a very old language."

"Ancient Quegan, and only a little. My instructors taught me the classics from several nations."

"Instructors?" said Kenner. "I thought you said you were a soldier and a hunter."

"I was, among other things."

The servant arrived with a tray of refreshments, some cakes and tea. "I'm sorry I can't offer you anything stronger, but my order is abstemious. The tea, however, is very good."

The servant poured four cups and departed. "Now," said the cleric. "What to do with you?"

"Let us go," supplied Flynn. "We're convinced that if we don't do what that thing wants us to do, it'll kill us."

"From the story of your most recently departed friend, it sounds as if it actually saved your lives."

Kaspar nodded. "We're merely guessing."

The priest said, "One thing that surprises me is your relative calm about this. If I were compelled by some dark force beyond my comprehension, I think I would be beside myself."

Flynn and Kenner exchanged glances, and Kenner said, "After a while . . . you just sort of get used to it. I mean, at first when things started going wrong there was a lot of discussion over what we should do. Some of the men wanted to leave that thing in the cave and take the rest of the gold but . . . we just couldn't. It just wouldn't let us."

"So, it's not like we have a choice," added Flynn.

"That was our reason for seeking out Brother Anshu," said Kaspar. "I knew there was something wrong and that I should be angry about it. I am not the sort of man who's used to being told what to do. So I guess you could say I was bothered about not being bothered."

"Must have made it difficult when you were in the army," said Flynn, trying to lighten the mood.

Kaspar smiled. "At times."

"There is a . . . geas upon you," said the priest.

"I don't know the word," said Flynn.

"Nor I," admitted Kaspar.

"It's a magical compulsion. A charm that requires you to fulfil a task before you can be free of it," answered Father Vagasha. "It's one of the reasons these murderous things happen to your companions, yet you are relatively untroubled by them."

Kenner squirmed in his chair as he said, "I thought it was just . . . me being—"

"Callous?" Kaspar supplied.

"Yes," said Kenner. "Even when the first member of our party died, I felt . . . nothing."

"Nor could you, or you would not fulfil this geas." The old priest said, "My brothers are examining this relic of yours and when they are done, we shall do what we can to aid you in freeing yourself from it."

"It's evil then?" asked Flynn as if he was still uncertain.

"There are times when good and evil are not simple concepts," said the priest. "I'll be able to tell you more after we finish examining the relic. Why don't you go now and rest. You will dine with the brothers tonight; our fare is not sumptuous, but it is nourishing. Perhaps by tomorrow we'll have more to talk about."

He rose and they followed suit. As if anticipating the Father Elect's need, the servant appeared to conduct them to their quarters. To the three men the priest said, "We shall send for you later this evening."

Flynn followed the servant and said, "This may be a good thing, coming here."

Kaspar nodded. "Unless, of course, it gets us all killed."

No one spoke after that.

They dined with Father Vagasha that night, but it wasn't the next day that they spoke to him again, but nearly a week later. During that time they were left to their own devices. Kenner and Flynn tended to keep to their quarters, sleeping or playing cards, or eating.

Kaspar took up wandering the great hall, sitting quietly and listening to the discourse of teachers and students. Much of what he heard was sophomoric and predictable, idealized views of life and how the world should work, but even those with unsophisticated views expressed themselves well.

The second day in the hall Kaspar paused to listen to a particularly difficult debate, in which the priest overseeing the education of these young men would pose questions and not provide answers but allow the students to debate each point and arrive at their own conclusions.

Listening to their discussion, Kaspar sensed a promise of things to come, a glimpse from time to time of, if not original thought, at least rigor. Some of these young men would mature into original thinkers, Kaspar realized, and even the dullest among them would benefit in the long term from being here.

For an instant Kaspar found himself on the verge of rage. *This is worthwhile!* he thought. *This is where human enterprise should take mankind, to understand the world around us, not just conquer it!* He paused, surprised at the intensity of his feelings, and wondering from whence they sprang. This was not the sort of experience he was comfortable with. Where had this anger come from? It was as if he had lived his life in a place of darkness and had suddenly been shown that light existed, and all the beauty and wonder of life had always been but a step away if he had just known it! Who had kept him in darkness? Kaspar had never been an introspective man, and this revelation troubled him deeply.

Kaspar stopped himself from reacting and forced his mind away from such questions, turning his attention back to the matters at hand. Impatient with himself for feeling such conflict, he turned and left the hall. He returned to his room.

It was only the Temple's rule against strong spirits that kept him sober that night.

Over the course of the remaining week, Kaspar let the young men's debates amuse him, but he steered consciously away from the type of questions that had caused him such deep turmoil.

A week later they were summoned to the Father Elect's quarters.

As they entered, the old priest waved them over to some chairs. "Please, sit. I know you've been anxious for an outcome. We now have some sense of what must be done."

No one spoke. They watched as three other clerics entered the room. The old prelate introduced them. "This is Father Jaliel, Father Gashan, and Father Ramal." The three men wore identical robes to those worn by the other members of the order save for a small pin near the collar that Kaspar had noticed on the teachers in the great hall. The first man was elderly, while the other two were closer to Kaspar's age, somewhere in their forties.

Vagasha said, "Father Jaliel is our resident expert in ancient artifacts and relics. Father Gashan is our theologian, and has the responsibility for interpreting our discoveries as they relate to our doctrines and beliefs. Father Ramal is our historian." He motioned for the three men to step forward. "Father Gashan, will you begin? Please explain to our friends our concept of knowledge."

Father Gashan said, "If I become too esoteric, please ask me to clarify." He looked from one to another of the three men, then began. "We view knowledge as imperfect understanding. New information is always presenting itself which challenges us to re-examine our faith and view of the universe. We categorize knowledge into three categories: perfect knowledge, certain knowledge, and flawed or incomplete knowledge.

"Perfect knowledge is the province of the gods, and even their perception of it is limited. Only the True Godhead, he who is worshiped as Ashen-Genet by some, apprehends it perfectly. The other gods are but aspects and avatars of the godhead, and their perfect knowledge is limited to the area appointed to him or her.

"Our master, Kalkin, is a teacher yet even he has a perfect understanding of teaching only, not of what is being taught.

"Certain knowledge is that which we believe to be an accurate reflection of nature, life, and the universe. Such knowledge can be either correct or incorrect. When we discover a new fact of existence, we do not reject it as not being in keeping with existing doctrine, but rather re-examine the doctrine and see how it might be in error. Flawed knowledge is knowledge we know to be incomplete, to be lacking something that will progress it to certain knowledge.

"As you can imagine, the vast majority of what we know is flawed knowledge, and even our certain knowledge is suspect."

"So what you're saying," said Kaspar, "is that we can never be certain of what we know because we are not gods."

The priest smiled. "Essentially; that is a simplified answer, but it will serve for now." He paused, and then added, "Knowledge can also have another aspect, of good or evil."

Kaspar hid his impatience. This was beginning to put him in mind of the tutorials he had endured as a child.

"Most knowledge is neither good or evil. Knowing how to start a fire does not determine if you will cook food to feed the hungry or burn a man's house to kill him. But some knowledge, that which is clearly beyond the understanding of mankind, can be expressly good or evil." Father Gashan turned and looked at other two priests who nodded. "I will not labor the point, but just trust me when I say there is knowledge in the universe with the ability to transform you, to set you in a state of eternal grace or damn you to everlasting torment and suffering just because you have possession of it."

Now Kaspar and the other two men became attentive, for the implication was not lost them. Kaspar asked, "Are you saying that just by having knowledge of this . . . thing we have in our possession, we may already be . . . committed to certain consequences?"

"Perhaps," said Father Gashan. He turned to Father Ramal, who nodded.

"Our history teaches us that before man came to Midkemia, other races occupied this world," began Ramal. "Elves are one species known to have come before man. Some of that long-lived race still abide in the north, though they are in slow decline. They will endure for ages before they finally succumb to their mortality. Dragons also were here before our race, and their masters, too."

"The Dragon Lords," said Flynn. Looking at the others he said, "I told you."

"Yes, or so the ancient texts state," continued Ramal, "but of these beings we know very little. The elves say nothing of them, and it is believed that little has survived the Chaos Wars. Somewhere there may be those who have more knowledge than we do, but they are unknown to us."

Flynn said, "We were taking the relic to Stardock, to the Academy of Magicians. Perhaps—"

Father Vagasha held up his hand. "We have some knowledge of that . . . organization. Our temples have long regarded magicians as suspect. Many trifle with knowledge and power without any proper sense of context. Men of magic have attempted to utilize knowledge which is clearly evil in purpose—necromancy or communing with dark spirits—for their personal gain. Even a group which prides itself on being a servant of knowledge like the Academy at Stardock has shown itself to be too dangerous to trust with such a thing as you possess." He looked at Father Jaliel, who stepped forward.

"The armored artifact has no place in our world. It is from somewhere else."

Kaspar sat back. He had not expected that. "It's not a Dragon Lord relic?"

"No, it is not even from Midkemia."

"Is it Tsurani?" asked Flynn.

"No," said Jaliel. "No Tsurani reached our shore during the Riftwar. We were ignorant of that war until years later."

"Then what is it?" asked Flynn.

"We don't entirely know," said Jaliel. "We have ruled out many possibilities, which is a good step, but I fear we have exhausted the limit of our wisdom and knowledge."

Kaspar said, "Then despite your distrust, I suspect we still need to go to Stardock and consult the magicians."

"There is another choice. We feel that our good Brother Anshu has pointed the way. While we are an order recognized for our teaching and wisdom, others such as those of Geshen-Amat have occasional flashes of insight or experience intuitive leaps that we can't duplicate. There is a possible answer that lies to the west."

Kaspar sat up, remembering what Bek had told him when he showed them his map. "The Pavilion of the Gods?"

The four clerics looked at one another, and Father Elect Vagasha said, "You know of the Pavilion?"

"An innkeeper in Shamsha gave us a map. It's in our quarters. It shows a place in the mountains to the west; beyond that, we know little."

Vagasha looked at Ramal. "There are said to be many wondrous things in the Ratn'gary Mountains. Much of what is there is not for mortal eyes.

"At the base of the two highest peaks, the Pillars of Heaven, rests the City of the Dead Gods. Those who built the temples are lost to us, but their works endure. It is said that on top of the peaks the living gods, or their avatars, reside, and only the most gifted of mortals can achieve even a glimpse of them. But below the summit, above the Necropolis, lies a bastion. Within that dwell the Keepers."

"The Keepers of the Gate," said Vagasha. "Men who belong to a sect that has almost no interaction with other men, not even with our temples, but they are said to be custodians of the way to the gods.

"It is also said that if a man, driven by need, and committed in purpose, can find his way to the Keepers and, should he be deemed worthy, he will be permitted to petition the gods."

"Is this true?" asked Kenner.

Father Elect Vagasha smiled ruefully. "We lack certain knowledge of it."

Kaspar chuckled at the play on words. "Still, you think that this is where we must go?"

"It is where you *must* go, otherwise you risk consequences as deadly as your twenty-eight predecessors endured. What you will find there, we can only guess at."

He motioned to the servant. "We shall have a ship waiting, and provide you with an escort to the foothills below the Necropolis. More than that we cannot do. Once you reach the trail leading into the mountains, you must go alone. Now, you may return to your quarters until this evening's meal."

Dismissed, the three men returned to their quarters, and once inside, Kenner said, "I don't like the sound of it. I think we should go to Stardock."

Flynn said, "You're still worried about gold? I want this curse, or geas, or whatever it is removed! I want my life to be my own."

Kenner nodded, obviously disturbed, but seemingly unable to speak.

Kaspar sighed. "Your lives have not been your own since you found that damned thing, and neither has mine since I met you. We are fated to finish this . . . quest, for lack of a better term, one way or the other."

No one needed to hear what their alternatives were. They must accomplish whatever this mysterious mission was; or they would die.

TWELVE

RATN'GARY

The ship slammed into the breakers.

Kaspar, Kenner, and Flynn stood at the rail, their cloaks gathered closely around them as they watched the ship round Point Mataba and turn upwind for a reach into the relative shelter of the Ratn'gary Gulf. Despite the fact that it was summer, they were far enough south for the weather to be cold during a storm. Directly to the north of them, high up on the point, the trees of the Great South Forest loomed, dark and forbidding, dominating the cliffs.

They were three and a half weeks out of Maharta, on a ship procured by the Temple of Kalkin, and were nearing their destination: the Ratn'gary Gulf, below the southern end of the Ratn'gary Mountains.

Since leaving Maharta the three men had been somber, each of them overwhelmed by a feeling of helplessness in the face of what they had discovered about the geas controlling their lives. Kenner was introspective, and rarely spoke. Flynn searched constantly for a solution no one had thought of. Many of his conversations with the others touched on things he thought might have been overlooked, and each time he failed to discover something previously missed, he fell into a brooding silence for hours. Kaspar was simply angry.

For his entire life Kaspar, heir to the throne of Olasko and then Duke, had never had to ask leave of any man, save his father. He did what he wanted, when he wanted, and the only time he had been successfully balked, it had taken traitors and three armies to foil him; and yet he was still alive! The very idea that some agency could simply will him to obedience brought him to the edge of outrage.

Since coming to this land, Kaspar had reflected on many things. Things that would have revolted him as a young man now only amused him. He remembered how fastidious he had been at home, with every item of clothing needing to be cleaned and arranged just so before he dressed for his morning court or evening gala. The only time he had not cared was when he had been out hunting with his father.

What would his father have thought had he seen Kaspar at Jojanna's farm cutting wood, or shoveling steer manure? Not once had a single person he had spoken to save Commander Alenburga had ventured to guess that he might be noble born. It had taken several nights' conversations before Alenburga had reached that conclusion; but at least he had respected Kaspar's desire for anonymity. He knew that Flynn and Kenner suspected that he might have been an officer and a gentleman at one time, which would explain his education and manners, but neither of them had pressed him. He didn't know if that was their natural inclination or an effect of the geas.

Kaspar wrestled with one fact that was causing him more distress than he had ever known: that his life was not his own, nor had it been long before he had come to this land.

He was certain now that Leso Varen, his "advisor," had used his magical arts to manipulate him far beyond his normal inclinations toward ambition. Kaspar had remained quietly behind his desk in his private quarters and ordered the destruction of entire races, as part of a misguided and maladroit plan to mislead the Kingdom of the Isles. Thousands had died so that he could draw the attention of the Sea of Kingdoms away from his true goal, the throne of Roldem.

It had seemed so simple at the time. Seven convenient deaths and the grief-stricken populace of Roldem would turn their eyes northward and welcome Kaspar, Duke of Olasko, as their rightful ruler. What had he been thinking! Then he realized he hadn't; he had thought only what Leso Varen had allowed him to think.

He didn't know what made him more angry, that he had let the magician into his company so easily, or that he had lost his ability to see the madness the magician had created. Today, standing on the spray-wet deck of an alien ship in a distant land, Kaspar could quickly tick off a dozen reasons why every plan of Varen was insane. The only result of his attempt to seize power would be war and chaos. Kaspar realized that must have been the magician's plan all along; for reasons he might never understand, Leso Varen had wanted the Eastern Kingdoms, the Kingdom of the Isles, and perhaps even Great Kesh plunged into war.

Kaspar could not begin to imagine whom that would benefit. There were times when it was to a nation's advantage to have neighbors embroiled in conflict. He had engendered several such over the years, but they had only been border skirmishes, political intrigues, or diplomatic betrayals, not wholesale war involving the three most powerful nations in the northern hemisphere. Destabilizing that area was dangerous; it wouldn't take much for war between Kesh and Isles to spill over the borders and embroil the Eastern Kingdoms.

And he had witnessed the results of involving those three nations. But rather than destabilizing the area, his failed plots had convinced them to combine their efforts, disastrously for Kaspar: his capital city had been overrun in a single day! Even if Talwin Hawkins hadn't discovered the secret passage into the citadel—and curse the ancestor who had judged the citadel impregnable!—the combined might of Roldem and Kesh would have reduced his stronghold to rubble in a month. Moreover, had the rumored army from the Kingdom of the Isles arrived, then it would have shortened the sacking of Opardum dramatically.

No, the whole picture made no sense. No more than this cursed geas made sense. More than anything else, Kaspar prayed that should he survive this ordeal, someone could explain it all to him.

One of the soldiers escorting them said, "We heave to at sundown. My captain says we should spend the night aboard ship and get a fresh start in the morning."

The three men returned to their cabin, remaining quiet, each caught up in his own thoughts until they were summoned to take a quiet meal with the captain.

That morning it took the better part of an hour to get organized and haul the coffin onto the beach. The tide was running high and the breakers were pitiless, but at last Kaspar and his companions stood on the beach with an escort of thirty soldiers from Maharta and their officer.

The young lieutenant, Shegana, inspected the coffin and the sling that had been rigged so that four men could carry the burden. He obviously didn't care for this assignment and had taken no pains in hiding that fact from Kaspar as soon as they had boarded ship. They weren't even out of the harbor when he had turned to Kaspar and said, "My instructions are to get you to a certain point marked on a map given to me by the Father Elect of the Temple of Kalkin. I have also been instructed to treat you with courtesy and insure my men also show respect. I take it from what was said that you may be a gentleman or even a noble, though that was never stated explicitly. So, sir, I shall endeavor to conduct this mission to the best of my ability, but I wish to make one thing clear: if it comes to a choice between keeping my men or you three alive, my men will live, and you three will be on your own. Is that clear?"

Kaspar kept silent for a long moment, then said, "If we survive this quest, Lieutenant, I wager you'll become the sort of officer men will follow into the breech. But you'll also need to learn to be more discreet when given orders that don't please you."

The earnest young lieutenant signaled and his men picked up the coffin. They moved toward a trail that led from the beach into the bluffs. Kaspar looked at Kenner and Flynn, nodded once, and followed.

The first three days of the cross-country trip were arduous, but without incident. The trail from the beach had led up through seaside cliffs and over a plateau broken by gullies, which forced them into a fair amount of climbing.

Kaspar spotted ample game sign, and some large predators: bears, wolves, and mountain cats. As they wended their way higher into the mountains, the weather got cooler, with the temperature plunging to near freezing at night, despite it being late summer, and soon they passed into forested hills, with many streams to ford.

Evening found them in a relatively clear area, an almost flat outcropping of rock upon which they built a fire, around which Lieutenant Shegana placed sentries.

"Lieutenant, you might halve your guard and let your men get a bit more sleep," Kaspar offered. "I'm an experienced tracker and there hasn't been a sign of another human since we beached. The only thing we might fear are large predators, and the fire should keep them away."

The lieutenant merely nodded, but Kaspar noticed later that night that there were only two sentries instead of the usual four.

The next two days passed quietly, but on the morning of the third one of the advanced scouts returned with the news that the trail leading up into the mountains had been identified. An hour later the entire party reached a plateau where the trail forked, one track leading north to skirt the foothills, while another leading west rose steeply into the mountains.

Lieutenant Shegana said, "Well, gentlemen, if the good Father's directions are accurate, from here we climb until we arrive at the foot of the Pillars of Heaven, above which rests the Pavilion of the Gods." He nodded and the scout strode off at a brisk trot. The four men who were detailed to lug the coffin picked it up and the party set off.

For another day they traveled, and near sundown they reached a deep pass. The lieutenant said, "This is where we must wait. The Father Elect said that from this gap you must travel alone."

Kaspar nodded. "We'll leave at first light."

The mountains appeared to be almost without feature, a tableau of murk and shadow, with whatever light the setting sun provided being devoured by the heavy clouds above.

The lieutenant said, "This is an ill-omened place, sir. My instructions were clear; I am to wait here for two weeks and if you do not return within that time, we are to return to the ship without you."

"I understand," said Kaspar.

Kenner looked at Flynn. Then he said, "We're supposed to carry that coffin up those mountains?"

"Apparently," said Kaspar.

"I do not envy you," said the lieutenant. "And carrying that burden is the least of it."

The soldiers made a fire. There was little conversation while they ate.

Kaspar came awake in a rush, standing with his sword drawn before he was clear that the sound rousing him was Flynn's cry. In a moment he looked around and understood the source of Flynn's panicked wail. Around the ashes of the campfire lay Lieutenant Shegana and his men, faces contorted in horror, eyes wide, all of them dead.

Kenner also was on his feet, looking around as if he was about to flee. "What?" he shouted, as if an answer would make the terror go away. "What is it?" He kept looking from face to face. "Who did this?"

Kaspar put his sword away. "Someone or something that decided these soldiers had got too close to the Pavilion of the Gods."

"We're all going to die!" shouted Kenner, nearly hysterical.

Kaspar grabbed him by the shoulder and dug his thumb in, making the pain distract his attention. "All men die. We just aren't going to die today. If whatever it was that killed these soldiers wanted us dead, we'd be dead."

Kenner pulled away from Kaspar, but his eyes were now focused and the terror was ebbing from his features. "Why?" he whispered.

"I have no idea," said Kaspar. "A warning, perhaps?"

"As if we need more warnings?" shouted Flynn, his fear replaced by anger. "As if we need more death to speed us on our way?"

"Get a hold on yourself, man," Kaspar commanded. "I'd have thought you'd be used to death by now."

Flynn said nothing to that.

Kenner said, "How are we to lug supplies and that . . . thing?"

Kaspar looked around as the morning sky grew brighter. "We may have to travel in stages. We'll carry the relic and some food for half a day, then one of us stays with it while the others come back and fetch more supplies. It'll be slow going, but we have two weeks to get where we're going and then back here. I assume the ship will be there a few days after that."

Kenner said, "Then let's get on with it!"

There was no objection to that. The men started preparing for the climb up the Pillars of Heaven.

Kaspar carried the armor by its feet. Removing it from the coffin had lightened the load considerably, and the rope harness that had been used for the coffin now lent itself to supporting the armor. Now Kaspar labored with two ropes tied around the armor's feet, and looped over each of his shoulders. It was the worst part of the burden, for they were climbing, so the thing's feet would often swing down and strike him in the stomach or thighs, if he wasn't alert and kept the rope taut. The men rotated positions by the hour so no one of them would be free of bruises at the end of the day.

Kaspar had the thing's sword slung over his shoulder in a makeshift back-scabbard he had fashioned from a pair of belts taken off from the dead soldiers. It had taken an entire day to dig a shallow grave and cover the twenty-one men. Kaspar felt a pang of regret when he threw earth over Lieutenant Shegana. He had shown promise; he was the kind of lad Kaspar would have welcomed in his own army.

Kaspar looked skyward and called a halt. "I think if we're going to return for more supplies, we'd better start looking for a place to camp."

Flynn nodded and said, "It looks flat up ahead."

They climbed for another few minutes and found a small plateau. They were still close to the timberline, so Kaspar said, "I'll gather wood for a fire and stay with this thing. You two should head back to the last camp and stay the night. In the morning, gather up as much as you can carry and come back."

"This will make for slow going," said Flynn.

Kaspar looked at the mountains rearing above them. "Who knows how long it's going to take to find these Keepers? We may be up there for days. And if it gets as cold as it looks, we'll need food to keep our strength up."

Kenner looked nervous, his eyes wide. "What if . . . whatever is making us do this thinks that Flynn and I are running away?"

Kaspar grew impatient. "If you want to stay the night alone with this thing, I'll go with Flynn."

Kenner shook his head. "No, I'll go."

Flynn said, "Well, the sooner begun, the sooner finished. Let's go."

Kaspar walked a short way with them and then turned off into the woods and started gathering firewood. Kaspar found enough deadfall that he didn't need to cut anything. He gathered enough wood for two nights and then sat down. Exposed, the alien armor looked even more baleful in the fading light.

When the fire was going, Kaspar took out his rations and ate. He drank from a water skin, then opened up his bedroll. The goose down–filled roll would be welcome. It was going to be a cold night.

He kept the fire bright against any predators hunting and turned in, crawling into the bedroll. As he drifted off to sleep, Kaspar heard a wolf's howl in the distance. He opened his eyes and glanced around. It was close.

He lay still for a few minutes, listening for an answering howl. Kaspar had no knowledge of the wolves in these mountains. In the mountains of Olasko, there were three breeds of wolf as well as wild dogs. The lowland wolves were dog-sized and hunted in packs, and were the bane of farmers when winter thinned the herds of deer, antelope, and elk. Wolves would eat anything, even mice, and if game grew scarce, they'd raid farms for chickens, ducks, geese, farm dogs, barn cats, or anything else they could take. It was rumored that they'd even hunt humans if starving, though as long as he had been Duke, Kaspar had never heard a report of such.

The dire-wolves of the highlands tended to run in smaller packs, and were noticeably larger of head and shorter of leg, and they avoided humans when possible. They were only slightly bigger than their lowland cousins.

The swamp-wolves of the southeastern marshlands of Olasko were simply lowland wolves that had taken to living in the wetlands—the only difference Kaspar could see was that they had a darker coat which camouflaged them with the darker foliage.

The howl was not answered, and Kaspar drifted off to sleep.

Sometime during the night, another howl woke Kaspar, and he came alert with his hand on his sword's hilt. He listened but no sound except the wind in the trees below could be heard. He glanced over at the armor, a mute figure lying on the other side of the dying fire. After a long moment of studying the flicking light that reflected off the thing's surface, he put down his sword and returned to sleep.

It was midday when Kenner and Flynn hove into view, carrying large backpacks loaded with supplies. They sat down heavily and Flynn asked, "No troubles?"

"There was a wolf somewhere close by, but nothing more."

"Wolf?" asked Kenner. "Alone?"

"Apparently," said Kaspar as he threw more wood into the fire. "Let's see what you've got." He inspected the stores. "If I calculate this right, here's what I think we should do. Tomorrow morning, you two take the supplies . . ." Kaspar laid out a plan whereby they could move along the trail for a few days, leapfrogging one another until they had used up enough supplies to be able to carry the remainder. They rested that afternoon after ensuring they had enough firewood. Kaspar wasn't too worried about the wolf, but he knew that bears could be brazen when they smelled food, and this time of the year—late summer—they were beginning their mating rut; the males would be aggressive and the sows would be hungry, looking to store fat for the coming winter's hibernation.

As night approached Kaspar said, "We should probably stand watch. Just in case something smells our food and sneaks up on us." After his own encounter with a gray-muzzled bear, from which he emerged with his life only because Talwin Hawkins had known how to slay it, he thought it best to forgo mentioning any specifics.

Kaspar elected to take the middle watch, letting Kenner and Flynn have unbroken sleep; they would be the ones hiking the next day and Kaspar would have ample time to rest. He spent the time on guard reflecting more upon his own life.

Black memories flooded in as he considered the arrival of Leso Varen. The magician had appeared one day in open court, a supplicant seeking a place to rest for a while, a purveyor of harmless magic. But he had swiftly become a fixture in Kaspar's household, and at some point Kaspar's view of things had changed.

Had Kaspar's ambitions come first, or the magician's honeyed words? Kaspar realized he had done things that now repelled him, and that the longer he was removed from those events, the more abhorrent they became. He remembered his last day at the citadel in Opardum. He had been convinced that he would be executed once taken prisoner, so he had been determined to fight to the death. He had had no idea of who was behind this onslaught from Kesh and Roldem until Talwin Hawkins had broken into the last room Kaspar and those loyal to him defended; and then it had all made evil sense.

That Quentin Havrevulen was with him was ironic to the point of black comedy. When Talwin revealed himself to be the last of the Orosini, Kaspar at least understood his motives, and he almost applauded his guile. Talwin had been so well disguised as a squire of the Kingdom that he had fooled even Leso Varen's magic. The defeat had been swift and overwhelming.

But what had taken Kaspar most by surprise was the final disposition of his life—being banished to dwell upon his misdeeds. And he cursed Hawkins for it, because it was having precisely the effect intended. For the first time in his life, Kaspar was experiencing remorse.

Kaspar wondered how many women like Jojanna and boys like Jorgen had died. Before he had been banished to this land, he had seen them not as people, but as obstacles in his plan of conquest. His dreams of grandeur, to sit the throne of Roldem—not the most powerful nation in the world, but the most influential, cultured, and civilized—all that was vanity. Murderous vanity which gained him nothing. For what would come next? Conquering the world? Somehow contriving to bring Kesh and the Kingdom to heel? Turning the Eastern Kingdoms into more provinces? Sailing across the sea to bring order to this chaotic land? And then what? The fabled continent to the north—whose name he couldn't even recall? Invade the Tsurani homeworld? How much was enough?

And when all was done, what would he have to show for it? He was a solitary man, with only one person in the world—his sister—for whom he felt a shred of love, and there was no one with whom to share the dream.

Kaspar sat down and regarded his two sleeping companions. Flynn had a wife. Kenner a girl he hoped waited for him, but both had dreams that could be realized, not impossible fantasies of power and control. Control was an illusion, his father had told him. Now he began to understand. He envied these two men, men who were hardly friends, but at least men whom he trusted. There was nothing of ambition or avarice left to either of them. They were simply men struggling to free themselves of a curse and get back to a normal life.

Kaspar wondered what normal life would be for him be once he was free of this geas. Could he ever be satisfied with finding a woman, settling down, and fathering children? He had never really wanted to have children, though his time with Jorgen gave him a sense of what it would be like to have a son. Children had always been the eventual product of a state marriage, tiny guarantees of good behavior on the part of neighboring states. The idea of loving one's children had always seemed quaint, at best.

He woke Kenner, who nodded and changed places with him without speaking, so as not to disturb Flynn. Kaspar wrapped himself up in his bedroll and lay quietly, waiting for sleep to come.

But sleep did not come easily, for inside he felt a dull, swelling ache, a pain that was unfamiliar to him, and made him wonder if he was getting ill.

After a time he realized what this alien feeling must be, and when he did he wanted to weep, but he didn't know how.

The wolf came an hour before dawn. Kaspar sensed something a moment before Kenner screamed. Kaspar and Flynn were both up with their weapons drawn just in time to see the wolf rip out Kenner's throat.

"Grab a firebrand!" shouted Kaspar.

The biggest wolf Kaspar had ever seen was a dire-wolf he had hunted in the mountains of Olasko. It had easily been six feet from nose to tail and weighed in at over one hundred pounds. This animal was close to half as big again. The beast was seven or eight feet long, weighing as much as a man: Kenner never stood a chance once the animal leapt. Kaspar gripped his sword and wished for a spear. He did not want this monster getting in close, yet the sword was only effective as a thrusting weapon. It would have to be a near-perfect thrust to kill it.

The wolf let go of Kenner's limp body and growled a warning. Flynn had pulled a brand from the fire and held it in his left hand, while waving a sword with his right. "What do we do?" he asked Kaspar.

"We don't let it go. It's a man-eater, and it's smart enough to scout out the camp one night, and come back the next. We have to kill it, or injure it so that it'll crawl off somewhere to die." He glanced around. "Circle to your right, keep the torch in front of you. If he charges, thrust the flames in his face and try hard to cut him as he goes by. Otherwise, drive him around the fire to me."

To Kaspar's surprise, Flynn showed unusual resolve, for the beast would make even the most experienced hunter hesitate. The creature lowered his head in what Kaspar recognized as a crouch before a spring.

"Get ready! He's likely to leap!"

Flynn took the initiative, and with a short hop thrust the torch at the creature, causing it to shy away. With a torch in his muzzle, and a campfire to his right, the wolf jumped away to the rear and left, landing almost sideways.

If only I had a spear! Kaspar thought, cursing silently. He hurried around the fire and the creature turned. Seeing no flaming brand, the wolf was emboldened: he leapt at Kaspar without a warning crouch.

Years of experience saved Kaspar's life, for he recognized the single explosive leap as soon as it began. Rather than moving to his right, away from the beast as would be instinctive, Kasper spun to his left in a reverse pivot, swinging his sword parallel with the ground.

As he hoped, the blade took the creature across the chest, and as the shock ran up Kaspar's arms, the wolf let out a wailing yelp. Kaspar continued his turn, and came around, in case the wolf spun and attacked again.

Instead, he saw the creature thrashing on the ground, trying to get up on a severed right foreleg. In pain and confusion, the animal snapped at its own wounded leg, causing itself further pain. Kaspar had cut off the creature's leg above the carpus.

Flynn came over as the wolf righted himself on three legs. "Wait!" said Kaspar. "It'll bleed out. If you get too close it can still tear your throat out."

The animal tried to advance, and fell muzzle-first to the ground. It howled, scrambled up again, and tried to turn, again falling. "Bring the torch," said Kaspar.

"Why?"

"Because we need to make sure it dies."

They followed the wolf as it tried to make its way down the hillside and into the trees, but after fifty yards it fell over and lay there, panting. The two men approached close enough to observe it in the torch light, yet far enough away to remain safe.

At last the animal's eyes rolled up in its head and Kaspar took one quick step forward and drove the point of his sword into the its throat. It jerked once, then lay still.

When it was over, Flynn said, "I've never heard of one that big."

"Neither have I," said Kaspar. "This breed doesn't exist in Olasko, or anywhere else that I've heard about."

"What do we do now?" asked Flynn.

Kaspar put a hand on Flynn's shoulder. "We leave the wolf here for the scavengers. Then we bury Kenner."

The two men turned and silently returned to camp.

Thirteen

The Pillars of Heaven

Kaspar grunted with the effort.

He and Flynn had rigged up the armor so they could carry it hammocklike in a sling, with Kaspar at the head and Flynn at the feet. They had each loaded up a backpack, and now they struggled to negotiate the narrow gorge.

Rock faces rose up on either side of them. The sense of menace was palpable. It was as if the uninvited might be crushed between two giant stone palms at any time. Even in the bright morning sun it was gloomy inside the ravine, with only a strip of blue sky showing high above them.

"How are you holding up back there?" Kaspar asked. He was worried about Flynn. With Kenner's death, it seemed that whatever reserve of strength Flynn had was gone. He seemed to be a man resigned to inevitable death. Kaspar had seen that expression on the faces of prisoners led away to his dungeons, men who were to be tortured or killed for one reason of state or another.

"I'm all right," said Flynn, his voice lacking conviction. "I think I see something ahead."

"What?"

"The ravine is ending," said Kaspar. As they rounded a curve in the rocks, he could see that the terrain ahead opening up. They left the gap and entered a large plateau, with a path leading straight across it. "Let's rest."

Flynn didn't argue, and they put the armor down. Each man then unshouldered his pack and put it on the ground.

Kaspar said, "Do you see any shapes against the rocks over there?"

Flynn squinted against the brightness. It was one of those summer days when the sky was high, the air almost alive with the heat. The light was glaring after the hours they had spent in the ravine. "I think so."

They rested for a few minutes, then took up their packs again, and hoisted the armor. As they walked across the plateau, the odd shapes resolved themselves. Against the mountains, a small city had been fashioned, and the plateau gave way to a plaza.

Some buildings were cut into the rock, while others were free-standing in the plaza. Their shapes were mind-numbing, with lines and curves that confounded the eye and nagged at the senses. Hexagons, pyramids, a pentagon, a rhomboid; great obelisks jutting straight up between the buildings. These were also oddly fashioned, with a curved face, then a flat one, or a defiant-looking three-sided tower next to a spiral. "Let's put the armor down," said Kaspar.

They lowered the armor and again took off their packs,

and Kaspar walked to one of the obelisks. "It's covered in runes," he observed.

"Can you read them?" asked Flynn.

"No, and I doubt any living man can," answered Kaspar.

Flynn looked around, "This must be the City of the Dead Gods, then?"

"Must be." Kaspar looked around and inscribed an arc with his hand. "Look at the design. No human mind could imagine this."

Flynn looked around. "Who do you think built it?"

Kaspar shrugged. "The gods, perhaps. Those still living." He stared about. "Do you see anything other than tombs?"

Flynn slowly turned a complete circle. "They all look like tombs to me."

Kaspar walked over to one and saw a word inscribed above the door.

"Can you read that?" asked Flynn. "It's like nothing I've seen before."

"I've seen it before, but I can't read it." Kaspar had seen runes like these on parchments in Leso Varen's study. "It's some sort of magical writing."

"Where do we go now?" Flynn asked.

"The Father Elect said only that the Keepers abide in a bastion above the Necropolis but below the Pavilion of the Gods. We must find a way up, I suppose."

They moved deeper into the City of the Dead Gods.

The plaza ended in a massive façade carved into the face of the mountains. Four words were carved on it. "What is this place?" asked Flynn.

"The gods know, but I don't," said Kaspar. "The entrance looks like it goes straight back into the mountain."

Flynn looked around. "Kaspar, do you see any way up?"

"No. And I don't remember any trail splitting off, or heading upward."

"Kaspar, I'm tired."

"Let's rest." Kaspar set down his end of the armor and Flynn did likewise.

"No, I don't mean that kind of tired." Flynn looked pale, his features drawn. "I mean . . . I don't know how much longer I can keep doing this."

"We'll do it for as long as it takes," Kaspar said. "We have no choice."

"There's always a choice," said Flynn. "I can just wait to die."

Kaspar had seen that look before. It wasn't the same resignation he had seen after Kenner's death, the look he had seen in the faces of prisoners doomed to die. This was the look of a hunted animal when it had stopped struggling and lay back with a glazed expression, waiting for death to take it.

Kaspar took a step forward and with as much strength as he could muster slapped Flynn across the face. The smaller man reeled, then fell back, landing on his backside.

Eyes wide and filling with tears from the slap, Flynn looked up in astonishment as Kaspar came to stand over him. Pointing his finger at Flynn, Kaspar said, "You'll not die until I tell you it's time to die. Do you understand?"

Flynn sat stunned, then suddenly he laughed. He kept laughing until Kaspar realized he was verging on hysteria. Kaspar reached down, offering Flynn his hand, and pulled the other man to his feet. "Get a hold of yourself," he commanded, and Flynn's laughter ceased.

Flynn shook his head. "I don't know what happened to me."

"I do. It's despair. More men have died from that than all the wars in the world combined."

Flynn said, "I guess there's no getting around it. If we're to find these Keepers, we need to go in there."

They picked up their burden and moved toward the cavernous opening. They climbed low broad steps into a large doorway and entered.

They stopped in the center of the vast hall. A gray light infused the interior as if sunlight had been filtered through overcast skies. The walls, floors, and ceilings all seemed to glow with a soft amber hue. The hall was empty, save for four huge stone thrones, two on either side of the hall. Kaspar looked at the closest one and said, "There's writing on the base of the throne. It's in many languages. I can read the word *Drusala*."

"What does that mean?"

"I don't know. Perhaps the name of the being who is supposed to sit on that throne. Or perhaps it's the name of a place whose ruler is supposed to rest here."

The only other feature of the hall was that the wall opposite gave way to a vast cavern, leading off into darkness.

"I suppose that's the way we must go," said Kaspar.

"I wouldn't recommend it," came a voice from behind. "Unless you know exactly where you're going."

Both Kaspar and Flynn tried to turn, getting caught up in the rope harness they had rigged. By the time Kaspar had dropped his end of the armor and turned, the stranger was standing almost within touching distance.

It was a woman of middle years, her head covered in a

shawl, but enough of her hair showed to reveal some gray in the black. Her eyes were dark and her skin fair, but Kaspar suspected if she ever saw any sun she would be darker than she looked.

There was something unworldly about her, but Kaspar couldn't put his finger on what it was. Perhaps it was simply the atmosphere of the place, and the fact that she had managed to approach undetected.

"Stay your hand, Kaspar of Olasko. I am no threat to you."

Flynn appeared to be close to hysteria again. "Who are you?"

She seemed mildly amused by the question. "Who am I?" She paused then said, "I am . . . Call me Hildy."

Kaspar approached warily, his sword not entirely lowered. "Forgive my trepidation, lady, for you must understand that lately my friend and I have been visited by more strange occurrences and ill events than most men experience in a lifetime. Since we are hundreds of miles from what passes for civilization in these parts, and since there is apparently only one way into this hall, it's troubling to find anyone else here, no matter how unthreatening your demeanor. So please be forbearing if I am less than trusting at this time."

"I understand."

"Now, how do you know me?"

"I know a great deal, Kaspar, son of Konstantine and Merianna, hereditary duke of Olasko, brother to Talia. I could recount your life from the moment of your birth until this minute, but we don't have the time."

"You're a witch!" cried Flynn, making a sign to ward off evil.

"And you're a fool, Jerome Flynn, but after what you've been through, it's a surprise you're even sane." She ignored Kaspar's sword and walked past him to stand next to Flynn.

Touching him, she said, "Your suffering will be over soon, I promise."

Flynn appeared like a man reborn. One instant he had looked on the verge of total collapse, and in a the next he was a man refreshed, filled with joy and resolve. Unable to control the smile on his face, he said, "How did you do that?"

"A one-time acquaintance of mine refers to them as 'tricks.' I have more than a few." She turned to look at Kaspar. "As for who I am, you could not understand. Let's say that I am but an echo of the being I was in ages past, but contrary to the opinion of some, I'm not yet completely dead. I am here to help you, Kaspar; you and Jerome."

Kaspar turned to his companion. "You know, I never knew your name was Jerome. I've just called you *Flynn* all these months. You never said."

"You never asked," said Flynn. "And you never told me you were the Duke of Olasko!" He laughed. "I don't know why, but suddenly I feel wonderful."

"Magic," said Kaspar. He nodded toward Hildy.

"Only a little. I don't have much to spare, unfortunately."

"How did you know we were here?" asked Kaspar.

"Oh, I've been keeping track of you for some time, really," said Hildy, her dark eyes fixed upon Kaspar. "It started quite by accident, really. You came to my attention when you entertained an old adversary of mine. He resided in your citadel and caused a great deal of trouble."

"Leso Varen."

She nodded. "It's one of many names he's had over the years." She turned and looked at Flynn. "If you'll excuse us," she said.

Flynn quietly sat down on the floor, then slumped over and fell asleep.

"I haven't much time. Even keeping up this . . . appearance is difficult for long periods. I know you have questions, but for the most part they must go begging. Here's what you need to know, Kaspar.

"Circumstances have brought you to a crossroads in the fate of nations and worlds, and even the tiniest choice may have consequences beyond imagining. You were, by any measure, a cold-hearted, mean bastard, Kaspar—a murderous, ambitious, unforgiving monster."

Kaspar said nothing. No one in his life had ever spoken to him in this way, and yet he was forced to admit that every word was true.

"But you have a chance given to few men in their lifetime, a chance to change, to do something selfless and heroic, not because anyone will know, or even appreciate what you've done, but because it will restore some rightness to a world you've done your best to make wrong. It may mean the difference when you go before Lims-Kragma and are measured for your next life on the Wheel; you've spent mere weeks being a peasant farmer, so imagine what a lifetime of that would entail. Redeem yourself, and you may escape that fate." With a slight smile she added, "Though I doubt anything you could do would gain you another life of power and privilege.

"In a few minutes, Flynn will recover, and then you must enter the cavern. Therein is a path that runs beside a river. It is a difficult path to find, but if you search to the left hand side you will find it. You must not cross that river, for on the other bank is the land of the dead.

"Stay on the path and you will find your way to the bastion on the mountain. There you will meet the Keepers. They will not want to speak to you. When they attempt to turn you away, give them this." She held out her hand and Kaspar took a token from her. He examined it. It was a simple copper disk, with a rune on one side and the face of a woman on the other.

"This looks like you."

"Yes, it does, doesn't it?" She waved away further questions. "Time grows short. The Keepers will not give you much satisfaction, but you still must go there and learn what they have to teach you. Understand this: they will tell you the truth, *but it is only the truth as they know it.* Their perspective is limited. When you are finished there, you will understand where you must go next.

"But above all else, there is one thing you must believe. The fate of this world hangs by a thread. It has since an age before man, back in the time of the Chaos Wars. There are forces loose which are relentless: worse, they are clandestine and almost impossible to detect. You were the unwitting tool of these forces."

"Leso Varen," said Kaspar, not surprised. "He used me."

"As he has used others and will again."

"He's dead," said Kaspar. "Talwin Hawkins broke his neck."

"He's been dead before," said Hildy. "You will discover should you cross paths with him again that he's like a cockroach. You just *think* you've stamped him out."

"If I see him again, I'll happily test the theory with a sword's point."

"You may not recognize him. He has the facility to change his appearance. He's an annoyance to me, but a deadly risk to you. If you ever face him again, you'll need powerful allies."

"Where shall I find them?"

"You will find them when you get rid of that," she said, indicating the armor.

"What is that?"

"Something left over from a time before man. You'll learn some of the truth from the Keepers.

"Now, I must depart. Wake Flynn and take him to the

river, then follow the road. And remember, I have picked you, not Flynn. At the end, you will be alone."

She stepped back.

"Wait!" he said, "What do you mean 'alone'?"

But she was gone.

Kaspar stood motionless for a moment, the sensations of contentment and pleasure he had experienced in her presence slipping away. When he turned, he found Flynn reviving.

"Where is she?" Flynn asked, getting to his feet.

"Gone," said Kaspar

As he watched the color again drained from Flynn's face. Whatever good the woman had done had departed with her.

"Come on," said Kaspar. "We've got a trip to take. At least now I know where we're going." He studied his companion's face and knew Flynn was again in the grip of despair. Trying to force him to a better frame of mind, he said, "It's not far." He was lying, but he was concerned over Hildy's warning. "And we can put this bloody thing down and get some hot food!"

Flynn said nothing as he picked up the rope harness again and put it around his shoulders, then took up his backpack. Kaspar did likewise and when the armor was once more slung between the two men they set off.

It seemed only a short walk to the entrance to the cavern, but it took a few minutes to reach it. If the hall was bathed in a soft amber glow, the cavern ahead defined gloom. There was a faint hint of light in the distance, so Kaspar felt no need to find material for torches. He doubted there would be any to find close by. He paused for an instant at the threshold, then entered.

It seemed the faint light ahead kept retreating as they walked through the gloom of the cavern. At one point Flynn said, "Where are we?"

Kaspar replied, "I never asked." He judged it would be unwise to tell Flynn they were approaching the banks of the River of Death.

The light started growing brighter, and at last they arrived at an opening into a much larger cavern. The rocks rose up beyond the eye's ability to follow them, and the surface looked odd and slippery. Kaspar walked over and touched it. It felt like soapstone. A broad river barred their way ahead, and in the distance something could be seen coming toward them. Kaspar sensed that whatever it had come from the opposite bank of the river. As it grew nearer, it resolved itself into the shape of a man in heavy robes sculling a wherry.

"Kaspar," said Flynn. "Do we cross?" He put down his burden and quickly dropped the rope harness. "I think we're supposed to cross."

The hairs on the back of Kaspar's neck rose as he realized where they were. "Flynn, come back!" he shouted as his companion walked toward the ferry. "We're in the Halls of the Dead! If you cross the river you enter Lims-Kragma's domain! We need to look for the path on this side."

He hurried after Flynn and grabbed him by the arm.

Flynn turned and Kaspar saw an expression of utter relief on his face. "No, it's over for me. I know that now. I'm crossing."

Kaspar released Flynn's arm as the ferry touched the shore. The ferryman held out his hand, as if beckoning.

"He's waiting," Flynn said. "I must go." He removed the pouch at his belt and handed it to Kaspar. "The ring, and some other rare items." Kaspar took the pouch and stood holding it as Flynn moved to the bank and climbed aboard the wherry. By the time Kaspar could react, the ferry was already away. Flynn looked over his shoulder. "If you make it, find my family in Krondor, won't you? See they are all right?"

Kaspar could say nothing. He watched his companion vanish into the mist on the river.

Then he was alone.

For the first time since beginning this strange odyssey Kaspar felt helpless. He looked down at the alien armor and almost gave in to despair. He stood motionless for a full five minutes, his mind reeling with the improbability of everything that had happened to him since he had lost his throne, then he started to laugh.

He couldn't stop himself. If there had ever been a more colossal joke played upon a mortal by fate, he couldn't imagine what it was. He laughed until his sides ached, and realized he was verging on the same hysteria that had gripped Flynn.

Throwing back his head he roared a primal challenge, giving voice to his defiance. "Is this where it ends?" he screamed. With a single shout, he answered himself: "No!" At last he regained control and softly added, "It is not!"

He gathered his wits and looked down at the armor. After lugging it halfway across this continent, he felt resigned to having to haul it the other half by himself.

He gathered up the rope and fashioned a harness, which he worked around the armor, under the thing's armpits, and then he stood it on its feet. He got behind it and slipped his arms though the ropes and then leaned forward, hoisting the armor on his back.

As fit as he had ever been in his life, Kaspar knew that he would be in agony when he reached wherever he was bound. But, as his father used to say to him, sooner begun, sooner finished.

Pushing the image of Flynn vanishing into the gloom from his mind, Kaspar turned left, away from the river, and walked until he found a path.

He couldn't tell how long he walked. His back ached and so did his feet, but he kept on. At some point he felt as if he were climbing, and then a short while later, he saw light ahead.

He trudged upward, and found himself in another cave. This cave felt less eerie than the large cavern. He thought he must have crossed some sort of boundary and now was back in what he had come to think of as the ordinary world.

At the far end of the cave, he saw light and he hurried toward it. He had no sense of time passing. He might have been in the cavern by the River of Death for days for all he knew. He wondered if people in there ever grew tired or hungry.

He came out of a cave in the side of the mountain, emptying into a narrow trail that led up to the left and down to the right. He looked down, hoping that the bastion might be below, for a downhill walk seemed very appealing at the moment. From the angle of the sun he judged it to be nearly midday, so he must have been inside the mountain for at least one full day.

He started upward.

Kaspar had no measure of distance on this mountain, which irritated him. As a hunter he had prided himself on a keen sense of always knowing where he was. But he knew that time had passed. He had slept on the trail, lashed to the armor, after night fell, and it was again approaching midday when he saw the bastion in the distance. It seemed to sprout out of the face of the mountain itself, facing east toward the sun. By Kaspar's calculations, they had approached the City of the Dead Gods from the east, so he must have wended his way completely around the mountain to get here.

He trudged up the trail and found that it ended before a large oak door which was wide enough to admit a small cart. He saw no handle, lever, or knocker, so he balled his fist and pounded on the gate.

Nothing happened for several minutes, then the door swung open. A man of advancing years, gray-haired and -bearded, in a simple brown homespun robe, opened the door. "Yes?"

"I seek the Keepers."

"They see no one," the man said, about to close the door.

"Kaspar, Duke of Olasko, is hardly 'no one,'" Kaspar replied, leaning on the gate. "Here, show this to whoever you need to show it to." He handed over the copper disc.

The man looked at it and nodded. "Wait here."

A few minutes later he returned with another even older man who asked, "Who gave this to you?"

"The woman whose likeness is engraved on it. She called herself Hildy, though I suspect that's not her real name."

"Indeed," said the older man. "You may enter."

Kaspar stepped inside and saw that he was in a small courtyard, most of which was occupied by a vegetable garden. When the gate was closed behind him, Kaspar unburdened himself of the armor.

The two men looked at it, and the older one said, "What is that?"

"I was hoping you could tell me," said Kaspar. "The Father Elect of the Temple of Kalkin bid me bring this to you."

"What are we to do with it?" asked the younger of the men.

"I have no idea," said Kaspar, "but nearly fifty men have died to bring it here."

"Oh, my," said the younger man. "That was hardly necessary. I mean, it's very nice, I'm sure, but as you can see, we have little need for armor here."

Kaspar said, "I think you miss the point. I'm here to see the Keepers. Where may I find them?"

The two men looked at one another. "Why," said the elder, "we are the Keepers. You have found us. I am Jelemi, and this is Samas." He pointed to the armor. "Leave that there. No one will steal it."

Samas chuckled at the joke. "We're the only ones here."

"Come inside," said Jelemi. "That disc you brought has earned you a meal, a warm bed, and some conversation before you leave tomorrow."

"Tomorrow?"

"Yes," said Samas, motioning Kaspar toward the entrance of the bastion. "We are not permitted to entertain. It's part of our job. We must be vigilant and alert. Guests would distract us."

"Distract you from what?"

"Why, protecting the gods, of course."

Kaspar faltered for a step, then got his feet back under him. He decided it would be best to sit down and get something to eat before he attempted to unravel this strange mystery.

FOURTEEN

KEEPERS

Kaspar ate slowly.

It wasn't until food was put before him that he realized he was famished. He also knew that if he ate quickly, he might earn himself stomach cramps. The meal was simple—boiled vegetables, bread baked a few days before, but still edible, a slice of very pungent but flavorful cheese, and a cup of water. Yet it was very satisfying.

Jelemi and Samas ate in silence, with the occasional grunt or gesture that one associates with people who have been living together for a very long time and feel little need for spoken communication. Kaspar used the time to gather his thoughts and reflect on what he had been told in the Hall of the Dead.

At the end of the meal, Samas cleared away the platters and cups, and Jelemi looked at Kaspar. The old man had piercing blue eyes and despite his feeble appearance and somewhat distracted speech, Kaspar was sure that his mind was neither feeble nor distracted, but a pose to put people off guard.

"I promised you some conversation before you depart tomorrow. So, what would you like to talk about?"

Kaspar said, "I think it would serve us both if I told you a story." Kaspar began with his exile, not embellishing his part or diminishing his faults, just telling the two men how he had come to fall to such low estate. He then recounted his encounter with Flynn, Kenner, and McGoin, and their travels.

While he spoke the candle burned down. When he had finished, Jelemi asked some questions, drawing out details Kaspar had missed or glossed over.

Kaspar knew it was past midnight by the end, yet he felt no need to sleep, so anxious he was to make some sense out of the insanity in which he was trapped. After a long silence, he asked, "Can you tell me what that armor is?"

"No," said Jelemi. "I can only tell you it is ancient, and evil, and cursed."

"Can you do something about the curse?"

"No. That would take the power of the gods."

"Well, then," said Kaspar, "can you intercede with the gods on my behalf?"

Samas said, "You need to go to a temple to ask for intercession."

Kaspar let his frustration show. "It was a temple that sent me here!"

Jelemi stood up. "The hour is late and you're tired. We can talk more over the morning meal."

"I will show you to your room." Samas said.

Kaspar followed the short monk through the main hall, which seemed devoid of furnishings, to a flight of stone steps at the rear. "Once," said Samas, "there were more than a thousand Keepers in the bastion. Now there are only three of us."

"Three? I've only seen two."

"Keeper Andani is down is down at Ispar-by-the-Sea, shopping for some things we need."

"That's . . . what? Three, four hundred miles from here?"

Samas nodded. "We go every five or so years, whether we need anything vital or not; we grow most of what we need here. We take turns. If we don't get away from the Bastion every once in a while, it can get tedious. I will go next."

"How long have you served here?"

Samas stopped to a door and said, "You may sleep here." He paused as if calculating. "I've been in the Bastion for four hundred and thirty-two years next Midsummer's Day."

Stunned, Kaspar said, "You don't look your age."

Samas laughed. "There are benefits to serving the gods." Then his tone grew somber. "But I think we need to recruit some new members. We asked the gods about this and are waiting for an answer."

"How long have you been waiting?"

"Not very long," said Samas. "Only twenty-seven years."

Kaspar said good night and entered the room, or rather, a monk's cell. There was a sleeping mat, an oil-lamp, flint and steel to light it, a coarse blanket, and a bowl and pitcher full of fresh water. A metal cup sat in the bowl.

Kaspar didn't know if he could sleep, so anxious he was to get his questions answered before he was asked to depart in the morning, but as soon as his head was on the mat, he fell asleep.

At dawn, Kaspar awoke. He found a tub at the end of the hall with enough water in which to bathe. He wished he had the means to wash his clothing, but decided that he'd rather be quickly dirty again than trudging down the mountain with the armor strapped to his back in wet garments.

In the kitchen, he found the two Keepers waiting for him. Jelemi beckoned him to sit down. He found a generous portion of hot oatmeal in a bowl, freshly baked bread, honey, cheese, and tea. He fell to with a nod of approval.

As Kaspar ate, Jelemi said, "We have considered your story and are at a loss as to why the good Father Elect of the Temple of Kalkin sent you to us. We have little knowledge that is not available to him."

"I have considered that there may be no reason more profound than that he wished his problem to become someone else's problem," observed Kaspar.

Jelemi and Samas exchanged startled looks, then started to laugh. "You know," said Samas, "we never considered that. It's a little too obvious, I think."

Kaspar nodded. "Often people overlook the obvious, I have found."

"Well, we hate to send you away with no help whatsoever," said Jelemi. "Why don't you stay an additional day and we'll think if there's anything we may have missed."

"That's welcome news. I thank you," said Kaspar. "I was just wishing earlier for the opportunity to wash my garments."

"We can accommodate you in that," said Samas. "When you've finished eating, find me in the garden and I'll show you were you can do your laundry."

The two Keepers rose from the table, leaving Kaspar alone. He helped himself to a second helping of oatmeal and cheese, and sat quietly, contented to have a day to rest after so many days of struggle.

Kaspar appeared at the table in the kitchen in time for supper. He felt rejuvenated. He had washed his clothing, though he felt awkward standing around naked waiting for the clothing to dry next to the fire. And then he had eaten a midday meal and taken a long nap. He knew tonight would be his last opportunity to get any information from the two Keepers, so he had spent the afternoon framing questions for them.

Striking up a conversational tone, Kaspar asked, "Would you tell me how your order came to be?"

Jelemi motioned to Samas and said, "He's a bit more of an historian than I am."

Samas said, "Little is known of the time before the Chaos Wars. It is said that man came from another world, through great rends in the sky. What is known is that an ancient race lived here before us."

"The Dragon Lords?" asked Kaspar.

"That is what men call them. They are known as the Ancient Ones by other races."

"We thought that perhaps the armor had something to do with them."

"It does, but not in the way you think," answered Samas.

Jelemi threw Samas a look that suggested to Kaspar that he had stumbled onto something they didn't want him to know about. "If it's not of the Dragon Lords, is it . . . booty or a trophy of some kind?"

Jelemi sat back with a sigh. "More of a reminder, I'll wager."

"You've discovered something about it since we last spoke?"

Samas nodded. "We have searched the archives and I must confess that I found the entire thing intriguing. It was not of this world, and the claim by the monk that it was somehow 'wrong' awoke a vague recollection. I read on and I think I know what he was talking about."

Jelemi again shot him a warning look, and Samas said, "Why don't we just tell him? He's probably going to be dead before he can say anything to anyone who may cause us trouble."

Jelemi stood up and in a scolding tone said, "Very well, but if someone has to explain to the gods why this man learned their secrets, it won't be me!" He nodded to Kaspar. "You two have a nice chat. I'm going to tend the chickens."

"What is it that Jelemi doesn't want you to say?" Kaspar asked.

"You said you were a noble, so how grounded are you in theology?"

Kaspar shrugged. "As much as the next layman, I suppose. I do my duty at the temples."

"But you don't believe?"

"I've seen and heard and read too much not to believe in the gods, Samas. But it is difficult at times to believe they are overly concerned with my choices in life."

"In the main, you are correct. The only issue of your life that matters is how you live it, and that is between you and Lims-Kragma. She will judge you and decide where upon the Wheel you return." He chuckled. "She's the only god that all men meet, eventually." He stood up. "Help me clear away these dishes."

Kaspar took the plates while Samas took the cutlery and cups. They moved to a wooden sink in which rested a bucket of soapy water. Samas said, "Scrape off the scraps into that bucket at your feet, please. We feed them to the chickens and pigs."

"You have pigs?"

"Oh, we have quite a nice little farm on the other side of the garden," said Samas as he started cleaning cups, first washing them in the soapy water, the dunking them in a bucket of clear water. "It's a little bit of a walk down the hillside, on a nice plateau. We could feed many more Keepers if we needed to. In any event, what you should know is that what is taught in the temples to the laity is but a small part of the truth about the gods. What the temples know, in turn, is also only a part of that truth, though a larger part than what they teach. And what we, the Keepers know, is more than the temples, though they would chafe to hear such.

"But what we know is only a small part again. Some theologians argue that even the gods' knowledge is limited, and there is only one being who knows all, a Great Mind, or godhead, a being so vast and all-knowing that our attempts even to understand its nature are pathetic attempts at abstraction.

"It is said that men created the gods, too. That the gods fulfil our expectations of them, which is why we need so many. It's difficult to conceive of a single being who can take responsibility for everything in this universe and the other universes we know of. So, man created gods for every conceivable function. I do not know if this is true, but I do know that each god does have a role.

"Above the lesser gods existed seven greater gods."

"I thought there were only five greater gods," said Kaspar.

"There are, now. But before the Chaos Wars there were seven. One died during the Chaos Wars—Arch-

Indar, the Goddess of Good. This caused a tremendous imbalance, for there was no agent to counteract the God of Evil. His name is never mentioned, for even to think it is to draw his attention to you and make you his minion."

"I can see that would pose a problem," said Kaspar, in a tone that suggested he didn't entirely believe what he was hearing. The Chaos Wars, to most scholars, was a creation legend, a mere story to explain how the world came to be the way it was.

Samas smiled. "I can see you don't believe me, but that doesn't matter. I'm not about to tell you his name." He winked. "Because I don't know it. Most theologians call him 'the Nameless One.' "

Kaspar grinned. "There was a time in my life when I would have openly scoffed at all this, but what I have gone through these last few years . . ." He shook his head. "I will try to be open-minded."

"To understand what a catastrophe this was, you have to understand something about the way the universe works. Nothing is destroyed. Can you understand that?"

Kaspar said, "But I've *seen* things destroyed."

"You've seen things transformed." Samas pointed to the wood bin. "If I take a piece of wood and put it in the hearth, what happens?"

"It burns."

"Would you say it was destroyed?"

"Yes," said Kaspar.

"But it's not, you see. It becomes heat, and light, and smoke, and ash. When a man dies, the body becomes corrupt, and like everything else in nature, it is part of a cycle. We bury bodies or we burn them, but it doesn't matter if the body feeds worms or turns to ash, it is transformed, not destroyed.

"But the mind and spirit, they live on. The spirit we

know goes to be weighed, and if worthy returns to a better place on the Wheel of Life. If less worthy, a lesser place. But what of the mind?"

Kaspar admitted to himself that he was now intrigued. "What of the mind?"

"That goes to the gods, you see. What you've experienced, what you've learned, is the entirety of universal understanding—every living being returns consciousness to the gods. And they in turn evolve."

"I think I understand."

"Good. Some time between the creation of the universe and the Chaos Wars something went terribly wrong. The Nameless One is the most likely culprit, but we do not know for certain. Even the living gods do not know. But at a critical time, when the universe was changing, a war erupted in heaven.

"The lesser gods rose against the greater gods, and with them rose the Dragon Lords to challenge both lesser and greater gods. The Dragon Lords were cast out of this universe, and left to wander in an alien dimension until the Riftwar."

"Really?"

"That was what that was all about. You didn't think it was something as petty as the Tsurani wanting to conquer a metal-rich world, did you?"

"I thought it had to do with Tsurani politics back on Kelewan."

Samas smiled as he dried off his hands. He motioned for Kaspar to return to the kitchen table. "You are an educated man, I see. No, whatever the invaders thought, it was the Nameless One behind the attack. You see, evil profits from extreme chaos or extreme order. Good profits from a balance between the two. With total order, there is no growth. With total chaos, everyone and everything is constantly at risk. In the end, you will discover that by its nature, evil is insanity."

"I'm not sure what you mean."

Samas looked at Kaspar as a tutor would a truculent child. "Surely, I don't need to explain this to you?"

Kaspar said, "I am truly not sure."

"Have you ever wronged a man . . . just to do him harm? Or have you always had a reason?"

Kaspar answered quickly. "There was always a reason."

"There you have it," said Samas as he sat down. He motioned for Kaspar to fetch over a cup of water for him. "You would never look at yourself as 'evil' no matter what the other fellow thought of what you did. It's in our nature. And that's the great secret of evil. It is never viewed as evil by those who perpetrate the evil."

Kaspar handed him the water cup and sat down. "Well, I have done things that I now question."

"So you've grown wiser with age. But at the time, the choices you made seemed reasonable." Samas held up his hand to cut off any debate. "Even if you thought they were questionable choices at the time, I'm sure you justified them as being necessary, 'the ends justifying the means.' Am I right?"

Kaspar nodded ruefully.

"If every choice was weighed independently on a moral basis—that is to say, without claiming justification like justice, revenge, or necessary ruthlessness—then far less evil would be done in the world. Every faith in every temple has one creed in common, in one form or another: 'Do as you would have be done to.'"

Kaspar sat back, crossing his arms over his chest. "I think I understand."

"Good, because if you do, then you can see that the only explanation for evil beyond the justifications men make is that it is insane. It is destructive and it lends itself to nothing useful. In short, it is madness."

"Keep going."

"You need a serious grasp of this concept before I can tell you the rest of what you need to know prior to your leaving." Samas cleared his throat and took another drink of water. "Evil is wasteful. It consumes, but it never creates."

"So, by its very nature the Nameless One must be insane?"

"Yes!" said Samas, slapping his palm on the table. "You do understand. The Nameless One has no more ability to be sane than a chicken can play a horn." Kaspar looked bemused by that example, and Samas pointed to his mouth. "No lips. You can teach a chicken all you want, but it'll never learn."

Kaspar found this amusing. "Very well, I'll embrace the notion that evil is insanity."

"Good, because then you'll understand what came next. When Arch-Indar died, the other Greater Gods—fearing that the Nameless One would be unopposed and there would be no balance—did something that has happened only this one time; they cooperated. The remaining Greater Gods, even the Abstainer, used their combined power to banish the Nameless One to another realm."

"So that left five Greater Gods?"

"Yes, though it may as well be four. Helbinor, the Abstainer . . . well, he doesn't do anything. He abstains." Samas shrugged. "It's one of those things that can drive a theologian to drink."

"If they were combining their power, why didn't they just destroy the Nameless One?"

Samas grinned. "Because nothing can be destroyed, do you see?"

Kaspar blinked. "Like the firewood. Yes, they could only . . . change him."

"And not very much, really. They couldn't change his nature, but they could change his location. So they found another realm, a dimension outside this one, and they found a world, one so vast that our world would be but a pebble on its beach. And there they bound him, and buried him deep within the heart of the greatest mountain on that planet. And there he resides today."

"So if he's in this other realm, why is he a problem?"

"I'll spare you the theology, but remember how I said if you knew his name, he could control you?"

Kaspar nodded.

"That's how powerful he is. Think of the Greater Gods as . . . controllers, forces of nature, if you will; not nature such as the wind and rain, but rather the essence of how the universe is put together—good, evil, the balance, the builder, the worker-from-within, the granter-of wishes, and the abstainer. The world of the physical and the mystical—all things are governed by these controllers."

"All right," said Kaspar. "Now, what does this have to do with the relic I carried up here?"

"We don't know. What we suspect is that it is from a different plane."

"Again, I don't understand," said Kaspar, looking confused.

"You've no doubt heard the expression, 'damn him to the seven lower hells!' "

Kaspar nodded.

"Well, there are not really seven levels of hell or seven levels of heaven. Or rather, they're the same thing. The gods reside in the first level, we in the second. Or some maintain they are the same, but two sub-levels."

"Wait a minute," said Kaspar. "I'm lost."

"Ever peel an onion?" Samas asked.

"No, but I've eaten many," said Kaspar.

"Then you know that that they are made up of many layers. Consider the universe as an onion, but made up of only seven layers. That's a bit arbitrary, but it's the agreed-upon number. In any event, assume we live on the highest level, save for the gods. At the lowest are beings so alien to us we can not even imagine them. In between are beings that range from totally alien creatures to those which are similar to us.

"Demons come from the fourth and fifth levels, and with great magic can exist in our world. They are able to feed on life energies here and survive, even thrive. The demon who engineered the Serpentwar, or the Emerald Queen's War as I think you know it, was from the fifth circle."

"Demon?" asked Kaspar, his eyes wide. "What demon?"

"I'll tell you that story some other time. In any event, if you've heard of beings called the Dread, they live in the sixth circle. They suck the very life energy out of anything they touch in this plane of reality. They can exist here, but if they did they would wither even the grass beneath their feet. The creatures from the seventh level cannot even survive here—they gather energy so quickly from the very air and light they would destroy themselves, along with a very large portion of the landscape around them.

"That armor, we think, is from the second circle, the plane of existence next down from ours. But we're only guessing, and we wouldn't advise you to make any decisions based upon that supposition."

Kaspar said, "No disrespect, Samas, but what is the point of the lecture?"

"So that you would realize how vast the arena is in which you play. The woman who gave you the disc?"

"Yes, the witch?"

"She is no witch. The image on that disc is that of Arch-Indar."

"But you said she was dead."

"She is. What you met was a memory of her."

Kaspar sat up, his mouth open in disbelief. "But I spoke with her! She waved her hand and Flynn fell asleep! She handed me that disc, and that's real enough."

"Oh, she's real. But she is only a memory of the Goddess. If she gains enough worshippers over the centuries, she may return. But for the time being you must realize how powerful the Greater Gods are. They are so powerful that the memory of one lives on as a self-aware, conscious being, an entity in her own right."

Kaspar sat back. "Ah, nothing is destroyed."

"Yes!" Samas said, clapping his hands in delight. "You do understand! It's as if you died, but a single hair from your head fell to the soil and had all your memories and a will of its own. That's a bad analogy, but it's the best I can do when I'm sober."

"I took you to be an abstemious order," said Kaspar with a laugh.

"We ran out of ale and wine three years ago. It's one of the reasons Keeper Andani went to Ispar by the Sea. Otherwise I'd be drinking more than water. This magician you told us of, Leso Varen—"

"Yes?"

"I think he is not mortal."

"You think he's a memory of the Nameless One?"

"No. I think he is a dream."

Kaspar was about to protest, then considered the admission he had made about Hildy.

Samas continued, "The Nameless One had relics from before the time he was banished, and over the centuries men have found them. All of them go mad, some sooner than others, if they keep those items. But those that do keep them for a long time gain powers from their master. They also become part of his mind, and long after the mortal body has perished, they live on as dreams in the mind of the god.

"I mention that to point out there are others loose who mean to return the Nameless One to our world."

"Why would they do that?"

"Because they are mad," said Samas.

Kaspar sat back. "You've convinced me that I play in a game so vast I doubt I can comprehend it. So let us just say the stakes are high. But I still do not know what it is I am to do."

Samas said, "I know. We have given you all the knowledge we have. There's only one more thing we may do for you."

"What is that?"

"Why, let you speak to the gods, of course."

FIFTEEN

KALKIN

Kaspar sat motionless.

Samas stood up. "Come along. We might as well go and see them now."

"The gods?" Kaspar said after a moment.

"Why, certainly."

"I thought your job was to protect the gods?"

Samas motioned for Kaspar to stand, and said, "You're hardly a threat. No, we protect the gods from being constantly annoyed and distracted by mortals. Prayer was created as a way for a man to let the gods know what he's concerned about. The temples have slightly more efficient means, but they're limited. A cleric of one order can hardly speak to the deity of another order. But there is a way to confront the gods directly. We guard protect their privacy in a manner of speaking. Come along."

Samas led Kaspar from the kitchen, through the

empty great hall, and entered a small room. There, he removed a torch from a large metal container holding a dozen or more. Opening a pouch at his belt, he removed flint and steel, handed the torch to Kaspar, then struck sparks into it, until a flame caught. He replaced the flint and steel into his pouch, took the torch from Kaspar and led him into a series of tunnels going directly into the heart of the mountain.

After walking for a few minutes, Kaspar said, "How do I speak to the gods?"

"As you would to anyone else, I suppose."

"You've never spoken to them?"

"No. I've had no reason to. We Keepers really don't, if you think about it. Our mandate is narrow; protecting the gods from . . . well, you'll see in a moment."

The tunnel was long and dark. Then Kaspar saw a light ahead. Samas said, "We're almost there."

"Why are you letting me talk to the gods if you're supposed to protect their privacy?"

"You'll see."

They reached a cavern, but one filled with light. In the middle of it sat the source of the light. It was a platform of a pure white substance that looked at first to be marble, but as Kaspar drew near, he saw that it was a single piece of translucent material. Two steps of the same material allowed one to mount the platform. A soft white glow from it was bright enough to illuminate the entire cavern, but was surprisingly free of harshness. Kaspar felt no discomfort looking at it.

"What do I do?" he asked softly.

Samas laughed. "Everyone who comes here whispers the first time."

Kaspar repeated the question in a conversational tone.

"Just walk onto the platform."

"That's all?"

"That's all."

Kaspar took a step and Samas said, "I suppose I should bid you farewell."

"Why? Won't I be coming back?"

Samas shrugged. "Maybe. Few people are given this opportunity. And a few manage to get into the Pavilion by other means." He looked as if he were trying to remember. "A pair of magicians managed it about thirty or forty years ago. I don't know what happened to them. And a hundred years ago—I was told this, but don't know how accurate the story is—two beings, men or something else walked into the Hall of the Dead, crossed the River of Death, and entered Lims-Kragma's Hall."

"Flynn just did that."

"But these two came back!" Samas took a step forward and extended his hand. "In any event, you've been good company, Kaspar of Olasko, and if you don't come back this way, I'll remember our time together."

"Well, all things considered, I hope I do see you again, Samas."

The Keeper smiled, and said, "Just walk to the middle."

Kaspar did as he was told and found a golden circle inscribed in the middle of the platform. He stepped into it.

Instantly he felt something. It wasn't a vibration, or a hum, but his body felt a tingle, as if energy was coursing through the very fiber of his body. Then a pair of golden spires rose up out of the platform, to his right and left, each spire a latticework of tiny golden threads. Kaspar's eyes couldn't quite make them out. They weren't metal, or light, or anything he readily recognized, but they were brilliant and he felt his pulse race at the sight of them.

They lengthened, seeming to grow out of the base, and crossed before Kaspar's face. Following the circle, they formed a helix as they rose. Kaspar saw other spires appear and soon he was confined in a golden cylinder of light.

Then everything vanished. Kaspar felt a cold beyond human endurance pass through him, a cold so stunning he could not even gasp.

Then there was total darkness.

Kaspar felt as if he was floating. Then he opened his eyes. The sun was on his face, and he felt a slight chill. As the floating sensation ceased, he realized he was on a hard surface.

He sat up.

He was on a marble floor. He reached out and touched the stone. Then he looked around. The floor stretched out in all directions, and his senses were confounded for a moment.

He stood up. The floor was punctuated at regular intervals by columns, crenellated depressions in the surface giving them texture. He moved to one and touched it. It felt smooth and looked like ivory.

Between the columns hung silken draperies of translucent white gauze which swayed with the breeze. He looked up and saw that there was a glass ceiling above, through which the sun shone down.

There were no other features and after a moment, he decided to move toward the source of the breeze.

After passing though half a dozen hangings, he saw one that wasn't occluded by the gauze, and what he saw made him pause. He was on top of a range of mountains, and below him he could see snow-capped peaks and clouds reflecting back the afternoon sunlight. He approached the edge cautiously and looked down.

How this place was suspended above the clouds was not apparent, but from the edge, Kaspar could see there was no physical connection with the mountains. The air should have been bitterly cold and thin, perhaps not even sufficient to breathe, but Kaspar found it plentiful and only slightly brisk.

"Quite a sight, isn't it?"

Kaspar turned around.

Where there had only been empty floor now rested a short pedestal, of the same white stone, topped by a flat slab upon which sat a man.

He was fair-skinned, with curly light brown hair and eyes and a strong jaw. His age was difficult to ascertain—for a moment he looked to be Kaspar's age, while an instant later he looked almost boyish. He wore a simple light blue tunic and white trousers, and he was barefoot.

"Yes," said Kaspar slowly. "It is a sight."

The man climbed off the column and when his feet touched the floor, the column vanished. "Few ever get a chance to see it. This is, in a manner of speaking, the Roof of the World." He came to stand next to Kaspar. "Like many things, I rarely bother to notice it, until I see someone else admiring it, and then I pause to remind myself of how striking it is.

"These are the two highest peaks on the world, did you know?"

"No," said Kaspar. "I did not."

"The southern peak is called The Elephant, and is only two feet shorter than the northern peak, which is called The Dragon. Can you imagine? Both over thirty thousand feet and only two feet difference between them?"

"Thirty thousand feet?" Kaspar said. "I should be freezing to death. I hunted giant rams in the mountains of my home, in the high passes which are over ten thousand feet, and some of my men were sick even at that altitude, and it was freezing even in summer. How can this be?"

The man smiled. "It's simple. You're not here."

"Where, then, am I?"

"You're somewhere else. Now, before you become overly concerned by this, you don't have a lot of time, so let's move on to why you're here."

"It's a long story."

"I know the story. You don't need to recount it, Kaspar."

"You know me?"

"I know everything there is to know about you, Kaspar, former Duke of Olasko, from the time you accidentally stepped on Talia's kitten's foot and she wouldn't speak to you for a week—"

"I was twelve!"

"—to what you had for breakfast with Samas."

"Who are you?"

"I am Kalkin."

Kaspar said nothing for a moment, then said, "The god?"

The man shrugged. "Labels, titles, categories, are all so . . . limiting. Just say I'm a 'being' and we'll get along."

"But . . ."

Kalkin held up his hand and his smile widened. "We don't have time for debate. Now, you have some questions, but let's save time and have me tell you some things, then you can ask a couple of your questions and then we can get you back to the bastion."

Kaspar could only nod.

Kalkin moved to sit down and suddenly there was a large pale blue divan where before there had been only hard floor. "Please, sit."

Kaspar looked around and saw another divan behind him. He sat down.

"I'd offer you something to eat or drink, except I know you're not hungry or thirsty. For some people, it puts them at ease."

"I'm not sure at this point that's possible," Kaspar said softly.

"So, then, where to begin?" Kalkin said, "How about with that thing you've been lugging around?"

"Yes," said Kaspar. "That would be a good place to start."

"It's not armor. It's a construction. What you would consider an animated machine. Imagine if you could have a toymaker build you a large wooden toy that could walk and, for the sake of argument, understand some basic commands and do your bidding. This is to that what a trebuchet is to a slingshot.

"That thing is called a *Talnoy*."

"Talnoy?"

"In the language of its creators it loosely translates to 'very hard to kill.' "

"Kill? I thought you said it was some sort of mechanical device."

"It is far more than that. It has . . . a spirit in it, or a soul. It's . . . not something that's easily explained. It's exactly what Brother Anshu said it was, something very wrong. The soul inside it was not put there willingly."

Kaspar shook his head. "That's evil."

Kalkin said, "Very. I trust you still remember most of Keeper Samas's instructions on the topic?"

"Yes."

"Good, because now I'm going to give you more to ponder. As you move from the higher to lower circles or planes, from what we call the First Level—" he made a circular motion in the air "—sort of where we are now, and you move to the Last Level, the laws that govern the universe change. It has been, argued—sometimes for centuries—that each realm has its own set of rules, its own 'right' and 'wrong,' its own 'good' and 'evil,' and that everything is relative. Others contend that good exists at one end of the spectrum and evil at the other.

"For the sake of simplicity, just accept that no matter what you think of such discussions, whatever exists in the fifth circle or plane should stay there!"

Kaspar said nothing.

"That thing, the Talnoy, should have stayed in the second circle of creation. It should never have come to Midkemia!"

"How did it get here?" asked Kaspar.

"Very long story, which you don't have time to hear."

"Why not, if you don't mind me asking?"

"Well, I do, but not as much as you will. You're dying."

Kaspar sat up. "What?"

"You're not really here. You're somewhere else, half-way between life and death, and the longer you linger, the closer you get to death, and once you cross that river . . ." Kalkin shrugged. "There's only so much I can do."

"But you're a god."

Kalkin waved this away. "I cannot stick my nose in Lims-Kragma's business. Once you're in her domain, she's the only one who can send you back. And she doesn't make a habit of it. So, knowing time is of the essence, let me make a few points.

"As I said," he held up a finger, "that thing you carry around should never have been brought to this world." Kaspar again looked about to speak, and Kalkin lost his smile. "Don't. All right, one of the Dragon Lords as you call them brought it here as booty. And it was hard-won and . . . well, they should not have tried to raid into that realm. In any event, it was before my time, and we—whom you call gods—only discovered it was here after the fact."

"Then why didn't you send it back?" asked Kaspar.

Kalkin laughed, a harsh barking sound, then shook his head. "Mortals!" He leaned forward. "Don't you think we would have if we could? *We are confined to this realm!* We are part of this world."

"But I was told the Nameless One was confined in another realm?"

Kalkin stood up, obviously impatient. "This always happens when you try to explain." He turned to face Kaspar. "You don't have time. So suffice it to say that when the gods you think of as Greater Gods, those Samas would call the Controllers, all put their minds to something, they could achieve it. Now, this has happened once!" He held up one finger and pointed to it. "Once. Got that?"

"You've made your point."

"Good, because now I'm about to make another."

Kalkin waved his hand and the pavilion vanished. They were in a gray void for a moment, then suddenly they were somewhere else.

They hovered in midair. It was night, and below them was a city, but one unlike anything Kaspar could have imagined. It was massive, without a hint of anything natural. Everywhere he looked, Kaspar could only see buildings, streets, bridges, and people. If one could call them people.

They looked roughly human, but their proportions were wrong, as if people had somehow been stretched, with legs and arms that were too long for their short torsos.

Their faces were also elongated but had enough variation that Kaspar recognized that they were as different from one another as people in any Midkemian city. A few might even have passed through the market square at Olasko with only an occasional odd glance. They were uniformly gray of skin, but so pale that it wasn't obvious. They wore different-colored clothing, but the colors were muted and dull—grays, greens, even the reds and orange hues lacked vibrancy. The females wore long dresses and some sported hats of an odd fashion, but the males seemed almost uniformly attired in tunics and trousers.

The city was all of dark stone and all in tones ranging from gray to absolute black. Nothing colorful was employed as decoration. Kaspar and Kalkin hovered over a main gate. The construction was unbelievable, for the wall was massive, wide enough that a boulevard topped it, with carts and pedestrians, and carriages pulled by something that looked like an elongated horse or mule, but with reptilian features. The gates below opened into a tunnel that led under this causeway and into a gigantic bailey, between the wall and the first . . . building? Kaspar realized that there were no individual shops or houses in sight. Everything was connected, as if this city was one massive building interrupted by streets and canals, with thousands or tens of thousands of openings. Even buildings that at first appeared to stand alone, upon closer inspection could be seen to be connected by bridges, enclosed tunnels, and halls. Kaspar's eye failed to catch much of the detail, for everything appeared to exist on three, four, or more levels, and the illumination was from thousands of torches, so the light was constantly flickering.

"Impressive, isn't it?" said Kalkin, and Kaspar turned to look down the road. The grass, if that was what it was, was colorless in the night, as were the distant trees.

"I thought you said you couldn't come here," said Kaspar.

"We're not here. We are merely looking. That's quite different. Look."

Kaspar looked and saw the city gates closing for the night. Everyone outside the gate hurried to get inside, and no effort was made to accommodate them. Those at the gates wore black armor not unlike the Talnoy, save they had open-faced helms and lacked the golden trim.

"Why is the gate open so late?"

"It isn't late," said Kalkin. "It's sundown."

"But the sky is black!"

"Yes," answered the god. "This world's sun puts out heat, but little light. Remember what I said before, the laws and rules here are different. If we were here in the flesh, your life would be measured in days. The air itself would slowly poison you. The heat of the sun would slowly blister your skin, and even at night you would find it uncomfortably hot. The water would taste like bitter sulfur and burn like acid."

The gate closed with a thunderous sound, as if two giant stones struck the earth. Then Kaspar realized that somehow the gates were now part of the wall: cleverly balanced stones, perhaps counterweighted somehow, turned so effortlessly that two men—or whatever these creatures were—could close them alone.

"Observe," said Kalkin, indicating the road.

A single wagon hurried toward the gate, pulled by one of the mule-like reptiles, and Kaspar saw it was driven frantically by a single creature. "What do you call these . . . people?"

"They call themselves the *Dasati*, which in their tongue means 'people.' They are as unlike people as dragons. Actually, dragons are more like people than these creatures. This is one of their worlds, Kosridi. It is a regional capital."

"One of their worlds?"

"Like the Tsurani and some other races, they have means to move from world to world. They are more aggressive than any nation in history."

"What is occurring?"

"A curfew of sorts. No one is permitted outside the city walls after the gates close."

"Why? Are there enemies close by?"

"The Dasati have no enemies . . . on this world, at least. But there are many perils."

The cart pulled up before the gate and the driver shouted frantically to those up on the wall. The Dasati on the causeway above the gate paused and looked down.

A chatter of conversation erupted and others hurried to watch the man in the cart. Then out of the darkness came a howl.

Kaspar's blood ran cold at the sound. "What is that?"

"Something analogous to our wolves."

Creatures raced out of the darkness, leaping across the dark landscape so rapidly that Kaspar only had a hint of their form. When they neared the wall, their hides reflected the torchlight, and Kaspar's mouth opened in astonishment.

If the things pulling wagons and carts were lizard-mules, this was a thing produced by a wolf mating with a horse. "What is it?"

"It is called a Zarkis," replied Kalkin.

The creatures were the size of a large pony, with ocher-colored fur around the muzzle, but otherwise they were dark gray in color, with black fur on their legs. Their heads were broad, flat, and the eyes wide set and yellow in the torchlight; and their fangs were as long as Kaspar's dagger.

They moved with astonishing speed and three had the beast of burden down in seconds.

Two others leapt from behind the wagon and one snatched the driver's head from his shoulders and a moment later, before the body could even collapse, the second creature bit the torso in half. Kalkin observed, "The pitch of life, if you will, the pace and rhythms, are far more extreme than your world's. Even the plants are tough and hard to kill. The predators of this world are beyond description. Even the prey animals would put up a fight you can hardly imagine should you hunt them. Think of a rabbit with teeth like a razor and the attitude of a wolverine. The people are as unforgiving."

"Why did no one help him?" asked Kaspar.

"Help is a matter of convenience to these people. A family member might have tried to drop him a rope, had there been time, a close friend might have promised to say goodbye to his mate, an acquaintance would not have laughed at the slaughter until after he was dead."

Then Kaspar realized everyone on the wall was laughing, as if they had witnessed a brilliant performance by a court fool. "They think this is funny?"

"Different rules, Kaspar." Kaspar looked at Kalkin and saw that the familiar smile was gone. "These creatures view horror as funny. It amuses them to see pain and suffering."

"I've seen games down in Kesh," said Kaspar. "I've seen men fight to the death, but they're cheering, not laughter. It's . . . a contest."

"Here, suffering is an entertainment. The weak are to be purged from the collective body of the race, suffering is exploited; weakness marks you as a victim, power marks you as an exploiter; everything is a negotiation between people of roughly the same power, for if you are stronger than another, you take what you wish, and if you are weaker, you find a powerful patron to protect you in exchange for service. Murder is a pastime, and charity is unknown and unimagined. The only thing close to kindness is reserved for family, for if you find another's child unattended, you kill it, for it may some day be a threat to your child. And you nurture your child, cultivating a sense of obligation and loyalty, against the day he may turn you out when you're too old to be useful. You gain power from your family, your physical strength, your ability to use magic, or the patronage of your gods—and they are every bit as unyielding as the people who worship them."

That was when Kaspar realized he had not seen a child anywhere. They must be hidden and protected by their mothers until they were old enough to defend themselves. "Harsh beyond sane words . . ." he whispered.

"Different rules," said Kalkin again.

With a blink they were somewhere else.

"At sundown the *Karana*, the ruler, reviews his army."

Kaspar looked and saw a palace, or something that reminded him of one, situated on the highest hill in the city. As they neared the central courtyard, Kaspar was astonished at the scale of everything. The palace itself was as big as the citadel in Opardum, and half again, and its central courtyard was easily a quarter of a mile on each side.

Kalkin indicated a balcony marked by a massive red banner that hung below it, a banner bearing a black glyph and surrounded by a circle made up of tiny swords. Atop it there stood a creature who looked much like the others, save that he carried himself with obvious authority. Several females hung behind him, and Kaspar expected by the standards of this race they were comely, for they wore raiment that was relatively skimpy compared to what he had seen on the streets, and of brighter colors. The ruler wore a red cloak with some sort of white fur at the collar. Under this, he wore black armor trimmed in gold, like the Talnoy's.

Across the courtyard thousands of armored figures marched, with drums pounding and horns blowing a dissonant flourish. "Those are Talnoys?" Kaspar asked.

"Yes," said Kalkin. "They are slaves to the Karana, and slaughter at his whim. They have conquered nations and worlds, and each is occupied by the soul of a murdered Dasati."

"What I've seen is chaos. How do these people keep order?"

"The same way a colony of ants or a hive of bees does, by instinct, by knowing who does what and not worrying about the fate of the individual. Should someone here be clever enough or powerful enough to slay the Karana, he would be the Karana the next day, and be hailed by those he ruled, for he had proven to be a stronger ruler, and therefore might protect his clients and vassals better."

Suddenly they were somewhere else, and Kaspar felt the air was much warmer.

"We are on another continent," said Kalkin. "It is afternoon here. Below, what you would consider 'games' are underway."

Kaspar looked down at a stadium at least three times larger than that in the city of Kesh. At least two hundred thousand of the creatures could be seated in it, he judged.

On the floor of the arena several areas had been fenced off. And in each of them horrors were underway.

A creature that looked like an elephant with a crocodile's hide and no trunk, but rather the face of a sloth, was being ridden around slowly, crushing people staked out to the floor.

In another area people were being set on fire and let

loose to run until they fell over and were consumed by flames.

Everywhere Kaspar looked he saw pain and suffering, and those in the seats above howled in laughter and pleasure. At many points along the terraces he saw couples aroused by the bloodshed to the point of mating, ignoring those around them.

A male Dasati was looking over the edge of the arena, where a pack of small doglike creatures were tearing people limb from limb. The spectator's neighbor stood up, put his foot to the first man's backside, and pushed him into the arena. As the startled man fell into the waiting maw of the slavering animals, those around the victim and the murderer gave in to paroxysms of laughter.

"Samas is right," said Kaspar. "Evil is insanity."

Suddenly they were back in the pavilion. The two light blue divans appeared and Kaspar sat down heavily. "Why did you show this to me?"

"Because now you begin to understand why that thing you've been hauling around for weeks needs to be got rid of."

"Well, if you can't send it back, can't you destroy it?"

Kalkin gave Kaspar a withering look.

"I know, if you could have, you would have." Kaspar sat back. "What am I to do?"

"We gods may not take that thing off this world, but you mortals can."

"How?"

"You must seek out those who've put you in your current predicament. You were hardly what one would term an innocent bystander, Kaspar, but you were never the main concern of these people. Your companion, Leso Varen, was. Samas has told you who the magician served, and perhaps even a little of that being's nature, but what you don't know is that your enemy, Talwin Hawkins, was also serving others: the Conclave of Shadows."

"I've never heard of them," said Kaspar.

"Of course not. They wouldn't be much of a secret organization if you had. Even Leso Varen was ignorant of them; he knew someone was opposing them, but not who."

"Where do I find them?"

Kalkin smiled. "That's a bit of a problem."

"You don't know? I thought you were the god of knowledge."

Kalkin laughed. "Me? Hardly. That worthy being was known as Wodan-Hospur before the Chaos Wars. He is one of the four missing gods. We don't know if he's dead or just . . . somewhere else. I merely take care of knowledge until he returns." With a grin he said, "In your nation you call me Banath!"

"The god of thieves!"

Kalkin bowed. "And Trickster and Prankster, and Walker in the Night, among other names. Who better to guard knowledge than a thief?" He stood. "Come now, we must return you. Your time here grows short."

"But where do I find the Conclave?"

"If you knew, and fell into the wrong hands before you found them, you could do much injury. By now others know the Talnoy exists and are no doubt looking for it. Which means they are looking for you as well."

"How do I hide something like that?"

"You don't," said Kalkin. "Remember when you killed the *wergon*, with the Talnoy's sword."

"The what?"

"That demonlike creature that killed McGoin?"

"Yes."

"And the Talnoy came to retrieve its sword?"

"Yes."

"Just take its sword and it will follow you."

"You mean I didn't have to carry it up the mountain?"

Kalkin tried not to laugh. He failed. "No," he said, spluttering. "You didn't."

Exasperated at being the butt of the joke, Kaspar said, "Well then, what do I do, dress it in a robe and call it brother?"

Kalkin laughed again, then gathered his wits. "No, but take that ring you carry in your purse and slip it on. Put your other hand upon the Talnoy and think of a monk, and it will look like a monk to any but the most powerful of clerics or magicians."

"It's a controlling ring?"

"Of sorts. The Karana can't be everywhere and someone's got to order these things around on the battlefield. It lets subordinates give tactical commands to the Talnoy. Just don't order it to attack the Karana or you'll burst into flames.

"Oh, and remember, the ring will drive you mad if you wear it for more than an hour or two at a time. But any time you need to instruct the creature, slip it on, tell it what you want, and it will do it. Just be sure to take it off as soon as you can. So, keep the instructions simple."

"How do I find the Conclave?"

"This is the tricky part. I can send you in the right direction. The problem with big magic is that the bigger it is, the easier it is for . . . certain people . . . to notice. So I can get you to the city of Sulth, or rather just outside it, with your treasure chest and the Talnoy, and from there you can buy a ship. Sail northwest for forty-five days, then cut straight west, and within another two weeks you'll start seeing familiar waters. Make for your home, and seek out Talwin Hawkins.

"If you can talk to him before he kills you, or before the

new Duke of Roldem has you executed on the spot, Hawkins can get you to the Conclave. Tell them what you have seen and what you know and bid them rid this world of the Talnoy. And press upon them it is urgent."

"Why?"

Kalkin grimaced, and there was no hint of humor left in him. "I failed to mention this, didn't I? Now that the Talnoy has been removed from the crypt in which it was hidden, and the protective wards around it removed, it's like a beacon light to the Dasati. Magical gates, or rifts, are starting to form. Little ones, not easily found, and they only stay open for minutes at a time, but the creature that killed McGoin was an inhabitant of Kosridi that blundered into a rift. And that thing represented no threat compared to a fully animated Talnoy. You know how hard it was to kill the wergon with conventional steel."

"Nearly impossible."

"Everything on Kosridi is hard to kill, and the Talnoy are among the hardest." Kalkin's expression became even more somber. "Soon, the rifts will be staying open longer, and they will be larger, and eventually a Dasati magician or cleric will discover it. It takes no imagination to know what will happen next.

"If their world is unpleasant and dangerous to you, this world is a lush paradise to them, for creatures may easily go from the lower to the higher realms. Remember what Samas told you about the true nature of the Emerald Queen: the demon who displaced her wanted to rule here and could operate outside the rules that bind us gods and you mortals. The Dasati's Karana would joyously add this world to his empire and delight for years in slaughtering humans for the entertainment of his people at home. Imagine facing an army of Talnoy in the field."

"We need magic."

"Yes, a lot. Get to Opardum. Find Talwin Hawkins, and have him take you to the leadership of the Conclave. Show them the Talnoy and get it off this world!" He paused, then added, "For if you do not, we shall have a struggle that will make the Riftwar seem trivial."

"So why the geas? Why not just . . . I don't know. Just have some of your temple priests bring this thing to you?"

Kalkin shook his head. "It's not my geas, or that of any other god. And it wasn't meant to bring it here. But I'll remove it so you can take that thing away."

"Then who did put the geas on it, and where was it supposed to go?" asked Kaspar.

"That doesn't matter," said Kalkin, and he waved his hand.

Suddenly Kaspar felt a shock run though his body and all was a gray void. He felt the air explode from his lungs, then hung for an instant in nothingness. Then he was on the ground in a stand of trees and next to him was his chest of treasure and the Talnoy.

Kaspar inhaled deeply and felt cold.

It was evening, and a few farmers' carts could be seen on the road from his vantage point. Kaspar, pulled the ring from his purse and slipped it on. He said to the Talnoy, "Look like an ugly manservant."

Suddenly the creature was replaced by a hideous-looking man. "Not that ugly," said Kaspar, and the face of the creature changed so that now the Talnoy looked like a commoner, wearing simple clothing, in service to a wandering mercenary. "Say something," Kaspar instructed.

"Something."

"Well, you can talk. Call me 'master.'"

"Master."

"If I give you an order, say 'yes, master,' and do it."

"Yes, master."

"Good enough to start. Now, pick up the chest and follow me."

"Yes, master."

Kaspar made his way out of the trees and onto the road. The ugly servant followed behind, carrying a small chest easily on his shoulder.

SIXTEEN

SULTH

Kaspar drank alone.

The Talnoy sat motionless in the room above, a small attic over an alehouse that wasn't usually rented out. He was avoiding taverns and inns until he found a ship, concerned about Kalkin's warning that others would be looking for the creature.

For that was how he thought of it now—a creature. He had spent some time over the previous four days experimenting with it, asking it questions, determining its capacity for independent action, and at the last he was convinced of two things: first, that the creature possessed enough faculty for independent thinking and making decisions that it could hardly be thought of as devoid of life; and second, that an army of such creatures would be almost impossible to defeat.

He also discovered he had found the limit to the time

he could wear the ring. He had identified the warning signs, for it was an alien feeling to him: blind fear. He had reached this alehouse with the Talnoy less than an hour after donning the ring and having the Talnoy disguise itself as a servant. By the time he had agreed to a price with the owner of the establishment and reached his room, Kaspar had felt very uneasy. He had wondered why, and left the ring on as an experiment. Sitting on his simple straw mattress, he had waited, leaving the Talnoy standing in the corner. Nearly half an hour after reaching the room, blind panic had started to sweep over him until he was certain something dire was outside the door. He had overcome the urge to draw his sword and attack whoever was outside, and had yanked the ring off his finger. Almost instantly the feelings of dread and fear had dropped away.

He had experimented and now knew he could wear the ring for no more than an hour and a half, and he could not use it for at least that length of time after removing it. If he put the ring back on after the minimal time had passed, the madness returned quickly. Kaspar had decided once or twice a day was safe, and that more than that was a risk.

He considered what else he knew about the Talnoy. It was ancient, yet appeared as . . . fit, for lack of a better word, as those he had seen on Kosridi. There were no signs of age or any lessening of its effectiveness. It was, for all intents and purposes, new.

Kaspar couldn't escape the feeling that he now was in over his head. Before, he had felt tasked—plagued even—by the geas that had driven him to take this thing to Kalkin. He also had a list of questions he wished he could have got answers to: Why had the geas been placed on it in the first place? If the geas wasn't intended as a compulsion to get the item to the gods for the very purpose he was now undertaking, then what had it been intended for? Kalkin had said it wasn't important to know, but Kaspar could hardly believe that was true. And why did Kalkin seem so troubled by the thought of those things entering Midkemia? Even if he was limited in his ability to leave Midkemia, couldn't the gods act if the Dasati invaded? Were the gods afraid of the Dasati?

He sipped his ale while waiting for Karbara, a man who passed for a shipbroker in this sorry excuse for a city. Karbara was supposed to appear shortly with news of a ship which would carry Kaspar home. Kaspar cursed fate for putting him in the middle of this enterprise, for it had felt doomed from the outset, but then he realized that it was his opportunity to return home without forfeiting his life. However, finding a ship was proving to be a problem.

Sulth was the biggest city on the western coast of Novindus, but that meant hardly anything. The only other city of any size was Port Punt down the coast. Most of the shipping was between the two cities, with a ship bound for one of the southern cities leaving every three or four months. The large ocean-going types of ships common to Olasko and the other Eastern Kingdoms were rare in these waters. And none of the larger ships in port were heading north. He would have to buy his own ship.

Kaspar turned as the door opened, and Karbara entered. He was a slightly built, anxious man, given to glancing around as if someone was following him. He came to Kaspar's table and said, "Found a ship."

"What is it?"

"A two-masted coaster with a square-rigged foresail and a jib, lanteen-rigged on the main, but it's got a deep draft for a coaster, and it's relatively new. The owner is giving up the sea to stay at home with his wife and children. It's the best I can do, but it's a bargain."

"How much?"

"Three hundred golden coins or the equivalent."

Kaspar considered. That was cheap by Olaskon standards, but everything down here was cheaper. It was more than a year's earnings for a master carpenter back home, twice that here, so the ship's captain could buy a handsome little inn or set up some other business with that. "When can I see it?"

"Tomorrow. They finish offloading cargo before noon, then she sits where she is. The captain is anxious to sell, so he might come down in price."

"I'll be there after dawn," said Kaspar, finishing up his ale.

"I'll meet you there," said Karbara, getting up. "And you'll have my price?"

"Ten percent of what I spend on the ship, yes."

"Good," said the thin man, and left.

Kaspar sat back. Something was wrong with Karbara. He was too nervous about the sale. Yes, for him, it was more than a full month's earnings, but Kaspar expected he had other sources of income. Kaspar understood betrayal, and he knew that early in the morning, when it was busy yet still gloomy, a lot of things could happen in an alley between here and the docks that might be overlooked by the local constabulary for a while.

Kaspar decided to get to bed early, and to ponder what he would do in the morning. He finished his ale, nodded goodnight to the owner of the alehouse, and went upstairs.

The Talnoy stood motionless in the corner of the room. So that no questions would be asked, Kaspar had secured a sleeping mat which he put on the floor. It was probably a needless caution, as the alehouse owner seemed indifferent to anything beyond collecting his rent.

The first night Kaspar slept in the room, he found it troubling to have the thing standing there. Several times during the night he awoke to find it hadn't moved. It was odd that while he had carried it from place to place it hadn't troubled him to sleep near the Talnoy. But now that he knew it was capable of independent action—even if only when Kaspar gave the commands—he found the presence of the device troubling. Still, he was tired, and finally he fell into a troubled sleep.

He tossed and turned most of the night, plagued by dreams of a vicious, loveless race living in a dark realm.

Kaspar moved slowly though the pre-dawn murk. An unseasonable fog had rolled in off the Bay of Sulth and noises seemed to come out of nowhere. The city was already awake and moving, with vendors pulling carts, shopkeepers getting ready for the morning's business, and wives hurrying to the vegetable market.

Kaspar had no idea where an attack might take place, but he had the sense to use a roundabout course to get to the docks. If anyone was waiting to ambush him along the way, they'd have to be mind readers. He had put on the ring before he left and told the Talnoy to kill anyone attempting to steal the chest. He marked the hour and vowed to return to the alehouse within safe time-limits.

He had stopped to tell the alehouse owner not to enter his room and made it clear that the "servant" had been instructed to use deadly force if anyone did. The owner of the establishment seemed slightly amused by that: he nodded and said he might send his brother-in-law to clean the room, though.

Kaspar found no one waiting for him along the path he had chosen, but then he knew that if Karbara was remotely clever, the ambush would be close to the docks, for there were less people likely to notice an altercation there, and fewer who might investigate if they did. He reached the docks at the western end, far from the designated meeting place. He moved in the gloom as the sky began to lighten. It would remain dark until the sun burned off the mist—not for another two hours or more.

Kaspar reached a point where he could see the outline of the ship at rest, a darker shape in the murk, delineated by fore and aft lanterns. From what little he could see, she might do.

He lingered for a few minutes, conscious of the ring on his finger, even though he felt none of the discomfort that marked his nearing the safe time-limit. As the sky lightened, he could make out the figure of Karbara pacing near the ship. Kaspar leaned into a doorway, content to wait until dawn to see what happened next.

For half an hour the sky lightened and Karbara paced. Dockworkers approached the ship and shouted to the sailors and they began to finish offloading the cargo they had started on the previous afternoon. Wagons and porters, hawkers, and thieves began to appear as the day broke.

Finally, Kaspar decided that if there was an ambush planned, it must by now have been aborted, for the docks were becoming too crowded for anything clandestine. Besides, he had left himself only a short while to speak to the captain and return to the inn.

Kaspar strolled up and said, "Good morning."

Karbara turned, and then smiled. "I thought you would be coming that way," he said, nodding in the opposite direction. Shaking his head, he said, "No matter. Good morning. Let's go aboard." He motioned to Kaspar to mount the gangplank.

Kaspar waved to Karbara to precede him. With a hesitation, then a shrug, the slight, nervous man mounted the gangplank. Kaspar wondered if the ambush might happen below decks. He kept his hand loosely on the hilt of his belt-knife.

They reached the main deck to find that a rotund man of middle years was directing the offloading of the cargo. He glanced over at Karbara, then Kaspar. "You the buyer?" he asked without preamble.

Kaspar said, "Perhaps. Tell me about your ship, Captain . . . ?"

"Berganda," he said, curtly. "She's less than ten years old. I traded in two older ships because she's faster and holds almost as much as the other two combined." He looked around. "She's fifty feet at the waterline—what we call a *bilander*. You can see we've got a big lanteen yard on the mainmast." He pointed to the large boom that nearly touched the stern. "You get a lot of canvas open to the wind in a reach, and while she's a bit of a pig in a following wind, if the breeze is spanking, you can reef the lanteen and run straight ahead. Otherwise it saves you the need for a mizzen sail. Anyway, my wife is eager for me to stay home and I've got a brother who has a wagon business, so while I know nothing about being a teamster, I do know cargo. She's fit, and if you know ships, you know at three hundred pieces of gold, she's a bargain." He pointed to Karbara, "But you pay him his fee."

"I'll pay his fee," said Kaspar. "And I'll give you five hundred, but you've got to sail her one more time."

"Where?"

"Across the Blue Sea, to the northern continent."

"Damn me, but that's a long voyage. I don't even know how to get there. All I've ever heard is you've got to sail out from the City of the Serpent River to the northeast. I guess we could sail along the north coast and head up from where the continent turns south . . . that's nearly a year."

"No," said Kaspar. "Once we clear Horsehead Cape, then it's forty-five days north by west, then due west for two weeks."

"Sail the other way?" said the Captain. "Very well. Always wanted to see that part of the world. I'll take three hundred now, and two hundred when we get back. How many passengers?"

"Two. Myself and my manservant."

"When do you want to leave?"

"As soon as possible."

"Very well, sir," said Captain Berganda. "You've bought yourself a ship. I call her the *Western Princess.* Care to rename her?"

Kaspar smiled. "No, *Princess* will do. How long to provision and crew?"

"Crew's no problem. My lads were grumbling about being out of work after today. They'll be happy to come aboard for another long cruise. Provisions? Give me two days. You say fifty-nine days or so? Let's say three months in case the winds are contrary. We should be ready to sail on the morning tide in three days' time."

Kaspar reached into his tunic and took out a small purse. "Here's one hundred pieces of gold to seal the bargain. I'll have the other two hundred for you this afternoon, and two hundred more when we reach Opardum."

"Opardum, you say?" The Captain grinned. "That the name of the land we're bound for?"

"The city. The nation is called Olasko."

"Sounds exotic and I look forward to seeing it." He took the gold then extended his hand and they shook to bind the deal.

Kaspar turned to Karbara and said, "I have your gold back at the alehouse. Come along."

Karbara hesitated. "Sir, I have another appointment shortly that I must not be late for. I will come by later today for my payment."

Kaspar clamped down on the thin man's shoulder and said, "Come now, this will only take a few minutes, and I am certain you're anxious to be paid."

The little man tried to twist out from under Kaspar's grasp and failed.

"What is the problem?" asked Kaspar. "You act as if you don't wish to return to the alehouse with me. Is something amiss?"

With a look bordering on panic, Karbara said, "No, sir, honestly, nothing. I just need to meet with another gentleman. It is *most* urgent."

"I insist," said Kaspar, digging in his thumb. The slight man looked as if he might faint, but he nodded and came along. "You're not worried are you, that I might return to the alehouse and discover someone's broken into my room and stolen my chest of treasure, are you?" Kaspar felt a sense of disquiet growing inside and knew that he needed to remove the ring soon.

At this Karbara turned to run, but Kaspar tripped him. "When we get back to the alehouse, if anything of mine is missing, I'll personally turn you over to the local constables, do you understand?"

Karbara began to weep, but Kaspar ignored his tears and half-led, half-dragged him along. They reached the alehouse and found the owner standing in the center of the room, his face drawn and his eyes wide. "You!" he said to Kaspar as they entered. "You'd better get up there!"

"Why?"

"Two men came in here as brazen as can be and walked

up the stairs without so much as a by-your-leave. I heard noises and got halfway up the stairs to investigate when I heard screams . . ." He shook his head frantically. "Well, I've sailed and fought and traveled . . . but, man, I've heard nothing like that in forty years. I don't know what happened to your manservant, but something dreadful has occurred and you'd best see to it. I've already sent a street boy for the constables."

Kaspar felt fear sweeping over him and knew he had only minutes to keep the ring on before the madness came. He pulled Karbara upstairs and entered his room. The Talnoy stood in the corner where he had left him, the chest still at his feet, but otherwise the room looked like an abattoir. Blood splattered the walls and floors, soaking completely through the blankets on the bed. Two men, or what was left of them, were piled on the floor. It was hard to recognize much that was human about them, as it appeared they had been methodically pulled apart, limb from limb. Two heads lay nearby, staring blankly up at the ceiling.

Karbara gave a whimper and fainted.

Kaspar shook his head. He slipped off the ring, and felt the approaching madness vanish. He took a deep breath. He would wait as long as possible before slipping it back on. He hoped the constables in this city were as slow to respond as they were in other places, for he needed an hour or more to pass before he could put the ring on again.

An hour passed, and Karbara stirred. Kaspar looked around and decided it was better to have the little would-be thief unconscious for a while longer, so he knelt and delivered a swift blow behind the man's ear. Karbara flopped once and fell silent.

Kaspar heard voices from below, and knew that even if the constables were slow in coming, the news of some problem in the room were spreading through the common room, and shortly would be the topic of street gossip in the neighborhood.

Taking a deep breath, Kaspar put the ring back on and instantly felt a small discomfort. He knew he must make straight to the ship and get the Talnoy out of sight. He went to the Talnoy and put his hand on its shoulder. "Manservant!" The creature's appearance changed instantly. "Pick up the chest and follow me. Say nothing to anyone unless I command it."

The creature bent over and shouldered the small chest effortlessly. He didn't have a spot of blood on him, and Kaspar realized the manservant disguise was an illusion, not a costume that could be splattered with gore. Unless he ordered it.

Kaspar turned and walked out of the room. At the bottom of the stairs, a few local men had gathered and were whispering as Kaspar and the Talnoy descended. Kaspar took out ten gold coins and handed them to the alehouse owner. "My friend passed out. Take a deep breath before you go in there. This is for the trouble of cleaning up and for telling the constables that I've left by the south gate if they ask, instead of the west gate. Sorry for the trouble, but they were thieves."

The owner took the coins without a word.

Kaspar led the Talnoy down to the docks and boarded the *Western Princess*. Captain Berganda said, "I thought I wouldn't see you for another couple of days."

"Change of plans. We're staying aboard, and if anyone asks, you've never seen us."

"Understood," said the large man. "You're the owner."

"Where's our cabin?"

"Well, I haven't moved out of the captain's cabin yet . . ."

"Stay there. Is there another?"

"Small one near mine. I'll have a boy show you." He

shouted for a cabin boy and when the youngster appeared, he instructed him to take Kaspar and the Talnoy to the cabin.

Kaspar told the boy that he'd eat in the cabin tonight, and as soon as the door closed, he pulled the ring off. Kaspar felt anxious and didn't know if it had been the ring or his concern about it, or worry he might be apprehended before he reached the docks. Unless the constables in this city were rigorous beyond his experience of such local officials, his roundabout route to the docks would have them seeking him through the south or western gates.

Kaspar sat on the lower bunk. There was another above him, but he made the Talnoy stand in the corner, next to the chest. Kaspar then settled in for two long, boring days of waiting until they departed Sulth.

No mention of the bloodshed at the alehouse reached Kaspar before they departed. If the captain or the crew had any concerns about his reasons for hiding in the cabin, they kept them to themselves. Finally, on the third morning, they got underway.

Kaspar waited until they were clear of the harbor and came up on deck. Captain Berganda said, "You're the owner, but once we've weighed anchor, I'm master."

"Understood," said Kaspar with a nod.

"If your course doesn't set us sailing off the edge of the world or into some monster's maw, we should be seeing your homeland in three months or less."

"If the gods want us to," said Kaspar with an ironic note.

"I always make an offering before leaving," said

Berganda. "I don't know if it does any good to have those priests praying for a safe voyage, but it can't hurt."

"No," said Kaspar, "Prayer can't hurt. Who knows, they might even listen now and again, right?"

"Oh, they listen all the time," said the seaman. "And they answer prayers. It's just that most often the answer is 'no.'"

Kaspar nodded, and couldn't find a reason to disagree.

He looked at the distant shore as they sailed south by southwest down the Bay of Sulth. It would be a long, and he hoped uneventful, voyage.

Kaspar watched the sea, the choppy waves sending spindrift dancing in the late afternoon sunlight. They had put forty-five days between the ship and Novindus. Kaspar had never felt any affection for the sea, but he had been aboard many ships voyaging from city to city as ruler of Olasko.

The *Western Princess* was a well-run little ship, and the crew knew their tasks. There was none of the iron discipline found on military ships, rather it had more of a family feel. These men had sailed with their captain for years, some of them for their entire adult lives.

Kaspar had fallen into a routine, mostly out of boredom, that began each day with his exercising on the deck. He would draw his sword and go through a vigorous workout, at first to the amusement of the crew, then to silent approval as his skills were shown. He would strip to his trousers and swing his blade for an hour, ignoring the weather unless it was blowing so fiercely he couldn't stand on deck. Then he would douse himself with a bucket of sea water, which was as close to a bath as he was going to get until they reached land.

Now they were on the westward leg. Kaspar stood quietly, thinking, letting his eyes rest on the constant surge of the sea. He had pondered his next move, for Kalkin was right about Talwin Hawkins. Though it was nearly a year since the battle of Opardum, Tal was likely to draw his sword and start carving Kaspar up before he could get out three words. Kaspar had an idea of what he was going to do, but he hadn't worked out the details yet.

"Captain!" came a shout from the lookout above.

"What is it?" shouted the captain.

"I don't know . . . something . . . off to starboard."

Kaspar had been on the port rail, so he crossed the ship. In the distance an enormous shimmering circle hung in the air.

"What in the name of the gods?" muttered a seaman, while others made protective signs.

The hair on the back of Kaspar's neck stood up. He didn't know if it was the few minutes spent on Kosridi, the time he had spent with the Talnoy, or just an intuitive moment, but he knew this was a rend in space, a rift as Kalkin had called it.

Suddenly water started pouring from the circle into the sea, brackish, dark, and stinking of sulfur as the wind carried its reek toward the ship. "Come to port!" shouted the Captain. "I don't know what that thing is, but we're showing it our stern!"

Sailors jumped to obey, while Kaspar watched in mute fascination as water from that lightless world poured into the Blue Sea. Where it struck the sea, the water roiled and sputtered, throwing up steam and smoke, as flickers of energy danced along the foamy edges. Then abruptly a head appeared in the circle, a monster of that ocean's deep unlike any mythical sea monster or real danger on Midkemia. It was black, and the head looked as if it was armored, sunlight gleaming off its hide. To Kaspar it appeared to be some sort of giant eel, with amber eyes that glowed in the lowering sun. The head had a crest of swept-back spikes as if to protect it from even larger predators—if that was remotely possible. Kaspar could hardly believe the size of the thing. It was already thirty feet out of the rift and more of it was coming, and it was getting bigger at the girth, so not even half of the creature was through. It could swallow this ship in three or four bites!

"Gods preserve us!" shouted the lookout.

The creature's fins came through, and Kaspar reckoned it must be over a hundred feet long! Men began calling out the names of gods and begging for mercy, as the creature was now looking at them and attempting to come through the rift faster.

Then abruptly the rift vanished, and a shock of wind was accompanied by the sound of distant thunder. Severed in two, the creature hung in mid-air, its eyes glazing over. It thrashed as it fell, spraying black-red blood everywhere. Then it plunged into the sea below, vanishing beneath the foam.

Suddenly it was as if the incident had only been imagined, for any sign of the event had gone, the creature vanishing below the waves, and the empty sky showing no signs of the rift.

Kaspar looked around. Ashen-faced sailors muttered prayers and clung to lines and rails, until the Captain's voice shouted for them to be about their duties.

Kaspar glanced at Captain Berganda, and their eyes locked across the gulf between them. For an instant the Captain's gaze seemed accusing, as if he sensed somehow that this terrible vision was linked to Kaspar being aboard the ship. Then he turned his attention to his ship and the moment was lost.

Kaspar looked around and knew that by the time they reached Olasko, the crew would be arguing over what it was they had seen, and the tale would become another bit of seaman's lore.

But Kaspar knew that what he had seen had been no vision. And he knew what it heralded. He heard a voice in his mind. He didn't know if it was his own recognition of what he had seen, or Kalkin whispering one last warning into his ear, but in his mind the words formed, "Time is short."

SEVENTEEN

Home

The lookout shouted.

"Land ho!" he cried, as Kaspar and Captain Berganda stood on the quarterdeck.

"Just where you said we'd be, and on the very day, too," said the Captain.

"I got my instructions from a very high source," said Kaspar, trying to find humor wherever he could. Since seeing the alien sea creature, he knew two of Kalkin's warnings to be true: the Talnoy was a magnet for the rifts and those on the other side would dominate this world swiftly. No matter what else occurred, he had to warn those in a position to do something about it. He had to find the Conclave of Shadows, even if it meant his death.

Not a selfless man by nature, Kaspar had come to realize that if those creatures invaded Midkemia, no one would survive, no matter how high born, where they hid, or what their skill with weapons. Eventually all would be slaughtered, either in the war, or as entertainment for those heartless beings. So his survival became secondary to those he cared about, even if there were only a handful. He found it odd there were so few of them: his sister, Natalia, and Jojanna and her son Jorgen, and in an odd way, the families of the men who had died on the ill-fated expedition that had begun all this. But even without them, it seemed impossible to consider standing idly by and watching the world of his birth be destroyed.

Kaspar shouted to the lookout. "What do you see?"

"Islands! Hundreds of 'em from the look of it."

"Turn north by northwest, Captain, and that'll put us on a tack for home," said Kaspar.

They sailed all day and by dawn the next day saw coastal shipping sailing close to land. Kaspar had already worked out his strategy for getting ashore and finding Talwin Hawkins. He had spent no time with any member of the criminal element of Opardum, but he had hanged enough of them, listened to confessions under torture, and read enough reports by the City Watch to have a few ideas of how to contact the man he assumed was the new master of Olasko.

By midday, they saw the city of Opardum rising against the escarpment behind the citadel. "Impressive," said Captain Berganda. "Tell me, Kaspar. How many ships leave from here bound to my city?"

With a grin, Kaspar said, "None."

Berganda fixed Kaspar with a narrow eye. "Before I tell the lads they're stranded and they chuck you overboard, owner or not, I assume you have a plan as to how we're getting home?"

"Yes," said Kaspar, his eyes now captivated by the rapidly-approaching city. "Keep the ship. Sell it again when you get back to Sulth. I just needed the passage home and it's worth the price."

"Well, then," said Berganda, with a laugh, "you're the finest man I've ever met and I'm proud to say I worked for you." He shook Kaspar's hand. "I think I'll take that gold you gave me and load up on rare items to sell at home. Who knows? If I make enough profit from this, maybe I'll get my brother-in-law to sell his caravan business and he'll come work for me!'"

Kaspar laughed. "A word of advice; find someone who speaks a language called Quegan, for it is closest to your speech anyone here knows, and learn a bit of the local tongue, else the merchants of my homeland will send you home with nothing to show."

"Advice noted," said Captain Berganda.

Kaspar settled in, impatiently watching as they drew near the harbor mouth. He couldn't believe the emotions that rose up within him, for until this moment he had no idea how much he had missed his homeland and how much he loved it.

Still, he realized he was returning as an outcast and an outlaw. If he couldn't avoid being recognized, he faced the possibility of summary execution.

Kaspar went over what he knew of docking procedures and cautioned the Captain that things might be different since he was home. He neglected to mention to Berganda the reason for his absence or the fact he really knew little of docking procedures because as Duke of Olasko, whenever he sailed into the harbor, everyone got out of his way.

It was almost sunset when they entered the harbor. An assistant pilot in a customs boat waved the *Western Princess* over to a mooring buoy and by hand signals got them to heave to and drop anchor. The young man in the boat shouted up, "Anyone speak Olaskon?"

This was Kaspar's first risk of being recognized, but he had to take it, for the Captain would want to know why he wasn't willing to translate. He shouted back, "I do."

"Stay here until morning. A customs officer will come aboard at first light. If anyone comes ashore, you'll all be hanged as smugglers!"

Kaspar shouted back, "We understand!" He translated for Berganda.

The Captain laughed. "Is he serious?"

"He's an earnest young officer in the duchy's service, so of course he's serious. But the threat, however, isn't. Smuggling mainly takes place in the islands we passed to the south. Anyone bold enough to try to smuggle right in the main harbor probably deserves to get away with it. No, they're just trying to ensure we don't come ashore, get drunk and start a brawl, and end up in jail before you can sell your cargo so they can fine you."

"If you say so, Kaspar," the Captain said, "However, I think once you're ashore, I'll have the boys stay here until morning."

"What will you do when the sailor who speaks Olaskon is missed?"

The Captain laughed again. "Nothing. We'll work out a way to communicate, and if anyone here speaks that Quegan language you say is related to ours, we'll get it across. That earnest young customs officer was obviously mistaken about which ship berthing this night had someone aboard who spoke your language. Must be a lot of foreign ships come into this harbor every day."

Kaspar laughed. "Play dumb and they'll buy it. Now, lower a boat as soon as it's dark and I'll tell your lads where to take me." He reached into his tunic. "Here's the other two hundred, and a hundred again. Just to make sure that if your brother-in-law decides to become a sailor, you'll have enough gold to make your wives a little less furious."

"Thanks for that," said the Captain. He passed the word that a boat was going over the side away from the docks after darkness fell.

Kaspar returned to his cabin and waited.

The inn was out of the way and quiet. It was the sort of place Kaspar had never once set foot in throughout his entire life in this city. It was a favorite of dockworkers, stevedores, teamsters, porters, and other rough men. It was the sort of place where men would look the other way.

Kaspar and the Talnoy had entered the inn two days earlier and had taken a room at the back, on the lower floor.

Kaspar was keeping a low profile, sniffing around, and trying to make contact with someone from Opardum's underworld. He had an idea about getting a message to the palace, to his sister, but he was still reeling from the news he had received earlier that day. He had just finished his midday meal when a pair of city constables entered the inn.

They had walked through the room, glancing here and there, and after a few minutes they had left. Kaspar was struck by one thing, and motioned the serving girl over.

"Yes, sir?"

"It's been a while since I was last in Opardum, but what was that crest those constables were wearing on their shoulders? I don't recognize it."

"It's a new coat-of-arms, sir. We have a new duke."

Feeling a chill, Kaspar played ignorant. "Oh, really? I've been at sea. What happened?"

She laughed. "You must have been on the other side of the world."

"Might as well have been," he said.

"Well, we had a war, and old Duke Kaspar was run out. I hear they banished him to some hellish place, but you know how gossip is. He's probably rotting at the bottom of his own dungeons. Duke Varian is in charge here now."

"Duke Varian?" said Kaspar with a sinking feeling in his stomach. Had Leso Varen managed somehow to turn things to his own advantage at the very end?

"Ya, nice enough bloke, come over from Roldem. Married the old Duke's sister, and now they're expecting a baby."

"Duke Varian Rodoski?"

"Ya, that's him. Seems a fair man for a noble."

After she left, Kaspar had almost laughed aloud. Half in relief, for despite his past attempts to kill Rodoski, Kaspar knew him to be a good man. He had been a loving husband before his wife had died, and he was a devoted father. It was a damned good state marriage as far as Kaspar could tell. It would bring stability to the region and make it nearly impossible for the vultures to try to pick at Olasko's bones.

However, hours later the loss of his duchy was still nettling him. He sat back. It wasn't *his* duchy. It was his home, true, but he no longer ruled here, nor would he reclaim his throne. What had begun as a mad plan for revenge had long since become a desperate race against an implacable menace that would destroy this city, his nation, his sister and her unborn child. No, Kaspar had to let old emotions go. Revenge was no longer viable . . . or even desirable. In fairness, had his and Tal Hawkins' positions been reversed, he would never have forgiven Tal. He would have killed him.

Kaspar stood up to return to the room and saw a man in

the corner looking at him. He had noticed the slender man when he had entered the inn earlier that afternoon, and had been struck by something vaguely familiar about him, but the man's features had remained hidden under a large hat and in the corner he was shrouded in darkness. A few times Kaspar had cast a glance his way, and every time the man seemed to be caught up in his own thoughts as he contemplated the contents of his ale mug. This time, however, the man's eyes locked with Kaspar's for the briefest of instances, before he glanced away and looked down, hunching over.

Kaspar made his way toward his room, then at the last moment he turned and in two strides crossed the gap between them. The other man was fast, as Kaspar had known he would be. Very fast for someone having to stand up and draw a weapon.

Kaspar barely parried the dagger's blow with his own dagger, then used his advantage in size and strength to push the man off balance. He went over the back of his chair and slammed his head against the wall.

Men were moving away, for brawls were common in this inn, and no one got involved until they knew who was fighting whom, especially when weapons were involved.

By the time the barman had come over, his cudgel striking the palm of his meaty hand, Kaspar had the man pinned to the wall, his dagger under Kaspar's boot, while Kaspar's blade was at the man's throat.

"Hello, Amafi," said Kaspar. "How would you like to arrange things so that neither Talwin Hawkins or I cut your throat?"

The former Quegan assassin, for more than a year body-servant to Talwin Hawkins before he had betrayed him and became a fugitive, said, "Magnificence! I barely recognized you."

With a grin, Kaspar whispered so the others in the room couldn't overhear. "But recognize me you did, and what were you about to do, barter my head for your freedom?"

"No, my lord, I never would have done such a thing," whispered Amafi in return. "I am, like yourself, a man fallen on hard times. For nearly a year I've lived hand to mouth, forced to menial labor to survive. I was afraid you'd recognize me. I was but waiting for you to retire so I could slip out unnoticed."

Kaspar stood up, and the barman sensed the fight was over, turned and went back to his station. Kaspar put out his hand and pulled the older man to his feet. "You're a liar and a traitor and I don't believe for an instant that as soon as I went to my room you wouldn't have been off to the citadel to barter my life for your freedom. However, it happens I have a use for you, one which will benefit us both in keeping our heads on our shoulders. Come, this is not the place for the two of us to swap stories."

"Agreed."

Kaspar went to the bar and purchased a bottle of wine and two cups. He motioned for the assassin to proceed down the hall ahead of him. "Forgive me, but it's going to be a while before I willingly turn my back on you."

"You are a wise man, Magnificence."

When they reached the room, Amafi opened the door when Kaspar indicated and took one step in, then froze. "It's all right," said Kaspar. "That's my . . . servant."

Amafi entered the room. "He . . . doesn't move."

"He's very good at standing very quietly," said Kaspar. "Sit on the bed." He moved to the window and sat on the sill. There was only a small table in the room and a very dirty washbasin and a pitcher of tepid water. Kaspar poured a cup of wine and handed it to Amafi, then poured one for himself. "I've got a long tale to tell, Amafi, but I'd like to hear yours first."

"There is little mystery. While I was in the service of Talwin Hawkins, I ensured I knew a quick way out wherever we were. It's an old habit, and while I knew no details, it was clear to me that my master was involved in something beyond my understanding, which always means trouble, eventually. While my master was exploring the citadel for a means to defeat you when you betrayed him . . ."

"I did, didn't I?"

"Sir. But then, I think he expected it. I judged him to be a man unable to break an oath, so he was counting on you betraying him first when he took service with you."

Kaspar laughed his barking laugh. "So, had I not sold him out to set up Rodoski's murder, he might still be in my service and I might still be Duke of Olasko?"

"Possibly, Magnificence. Who am I to know such things? In any event, when it was obvious to me that the citadel was going to fall, I merely waited and stripped a dead Keshian soldier of his uniform. I left the citadel with the victorious troops, and I speak fair Keshian, so no one noticed. I was just another dog soldier with blood on his tunic. There was enough looting and drunkenness on the way out to the harbor that it was simple to vanish into an empty building, lie low for a few days, then emerge. I've been attempting to leave Opardum ever since you vanished, but unfortunately, I lack means."

"A clever fellow like you? I would have thought it easy enough for you to get passage."

Amafi sighed. "Magnificence, I am past fifty years of age, and by trade I am an assassin. In my youth, you would never have made it to the table, let alone pushed me back before I could kill you.

"But now I am reduced to this low estate, and the only

other trade to which I may lay claim is body-servant to nobility, and how might I gain employment when the only reference I have is a man who would most happily kill me?"

Kaspar laughed. "Well, I have a proposition. As I said in the commons, I may have a way to keep Hawkins from cutting either of our throats, and more, get you safely away from here to somewhere you might retire."

"I have some small savings in Salvador. If I could get there . . . ?" He shrugged.

"Help me get to Tal Hawkins and I'll get you to Salvador. And there'll be more in it than whatever pitiful savings you might have. I'll set you up for life."

Amafi looked at Kaspar with a jaundiced eye. "That wouldn't take much if my life is measured in days."

Kaspar laughed. "You are a rogue, Amafi, and I should have your throat cut on general principle, but while I hardly trust you to be loyal, I do trust you to have a strong self-interest."

"So, you may not harbor any ill will because I deserted you in your hour of need—you are, after all, a wise and understanding man—"

Kaspar laughed. "Never, in my forty-odd years has anyone called me that."

Amafi shrugged. "In any event, you may forgive me my slight indiscretion, but my former master may not. After all, it was I who betrayed him to you."

"And I obliterated his nation, yet he forgave me. I think he'll be inclined to let you get out of the city rather than hang you once you've got us together. He'll have far more important things on his mind."

"Well, then, I am your man again, Magnificence. It has been a hard year, and from the look of you, for both of us. It took me nearly ten minutes to recognize you."

"Really?"

"You don't know how much you've changed? You must see yourself in a mirror, Magnificence. You will hardly recognize yourself."

"I could use a bath and new clothing," said Kaspar.

"Then instruct me as to what I must do, and then while I do it, go to the bathhouse tomorrow and then to a tailor. If I can find my former master, you should look your best when you meet."

"What do you mean 'find him'? I thought he would be here in the city, running things."

"Hardly. He left your former Captain Quentin Havrevulen, along with Counts Stolinko and Visniya to form a triumvirate to rule in your sister's name until they sorted things out. Which was accomplished when the King of Roldem named Duke Rodoski as the new Duke of Olasko and married him to your sister."

"The King of Roldem? And Kesh and Isles let that pass?"

"They had to: Hawkins made Olasko a province of Aranor, and both of them vassals to Roldem."

Kaspar sat back. "So we're part of Roldem now?"

"Yes, and so far it seems to be working. At least taxes haven't gone up, and no foreign armies march through the streets, so the populace is content."

"I underestimated Hawkins on more than one front. But where did he go?"

"Rumor is that he found a girl of his people and went back into the mountains. I will need a little gold to get information."

"You'll have it. And while I improve my appearance, I expect you to spend it wisely. Find out where my old enemy has gone. It is imperative I find him."

"Yes, Magnificence, though I find it odd you're so

anxious to find your former vassal and have no wish to kill him."

"Oh, I would love to kill him," said Kaspar. "I haven't changed that much, but there are far more important things than revenge afoot right now."

"Then I will do what I can."

Kaspar said, "That is all one can ask. Now, you sleep on the floor, and don't try anything crafty—my motionless servant over there is quite capable of pulling your arms out of their sockets if you attempt to kill me while I sleep."

Amafi glanced at the Talnoy and nodded. "It is a thing of baleful aspect, and while it may be nothing more than a suit of armor you have in the corner for reasons I can't begin to imagine, I would never think of doing such a thing, Magnificence. At least not when there is no profit in it."

Kaspar laughed, then lay down on the bed. "Blow out the candle and get some sleep. We have much to do tomorrow."

Amafi had been right. Few would recognize him. He regarded himself in the mirror, a fine piece of silver-backed polished glass. He had possessed one this fine up in the citadel, but he hadn't seen a good looking-glass since . . . He laughed.

The tailor said, "Sir?"

"Nothing, just thinking what old friends might say if they saw me now."

"They would say you're a man of unusually good judgment and rare taste, sir."

He had gone to a bathhouse and had got as clean as he

had been in a year. He then had a barber come and trim his hair to a respectable length, though shorter than he had worn it before his exile. His beard he had not trimmed as before, when he used to keep his upper lip shaved. It was thinned out and cut close, but he kept the moustache and wore the beard fuller along the jaw.

But his concerns over being recognized were considerably lessened. He hadn't been this thin since he was a youth. In the span of a well-lived lifetime, he had put on a certain bulk, though he prided himself on being fit. Now he was lean. He could see hollows in his cheeks and when he took off his old shirt and allowed the tailor to fit him with a new one, he could see his ribs.

Rather than wait for days, he had paid the tailor to make him a suitable ensemble in one day, though it meant standing for fittings repeatedly all afternoon. It didn't matter: he had nowhere to go and nothing else to do, so when it came time for him to confront those in power in Olasko these days, he might as well be presentable.

"That will do for the moment, sir," said the tailor, a man named Swan. "If you care to wait, I should have this finished within the hour."

He had sent for a boot-maker who had measured his foot and was now returning. "I have several that may do until I can finish the boots you ordered, sir."

Kaspar had simply introduced himself as a gentleman from Sulth, which was true. He didn't think either merchant cared that they had never heard of the city of Sulth as long as the gold marked the touchstone correctly. It would probably be wise to find a moneychanger and exchange some of his Novindus gold for the local coin.

While he was trying on boots and selecting a pair, Amafi returned. Kaspar paid the boot-maker and arranged to have the custom-made boots delivered to the inn where he was staying; then he took Amafi into a corner of the tailor's shop. "What have you found?"

"I have discovered a way to get a message to your sister, Magnificence. It will cost only a little gold, for the girl who works in the palace is a foolish child who is easily gulled. But it is dangerous, for should anyone discover she's bringing word to the Duchess from her brother she will babble like a brook."

"Such is the risk," said Kaspar. He took a small piece of folded vellum out of his tunic. "Send this to Talia tonight."

"The girl will be in a tavern near the citadel, for she has family working there. She helps out in the citadel's kitchen and laundry, but she does not live there. It may take a day or two for her to find a means to slip the note to your sister, but she claims she is able."

"Something troubles you, Amafi?"

The old assassin rubbed his hands as if they were cold. "Ayee," he said, a sound of pure exasperation, "you'll forgive me, Magnificence, but I have had a poor run lately; I tend to be picking the losing sides. I served Talwin and you betrayed him, then you, and you were in turn betrayed. I'm hoping my luck is due for a change."

"We both are," said Kaspar dryly. "Now go. Look for me tonight at the River House." He tossed a small purse to the man. "When you're done, come back and buy yourself some decent apparel. I can't have you coming to the River House looking like a rag-picker."

"Yes, Magnificence," said Amafi with a grin. "I shall serve."

Kaspar watched him leave and sighed. The chances were even that the wily old killer would sell him to the constables the first chance he got if he thought he could somehow avoid being confronted with his own malefactions, but Kaspar had to take risks at this point. His sister was the only one with authority who might keep him alive long enough to fulfil his mission.

Kaspar could feel it. He was close. Close to taking that infernal thing in his room to the palace, close to explaining the situation and, hopefully, finding Talwin Hawkins and through him, the Conclave of Shadows.

The River House was one of the finest dining establishments in Olasko, according to all reports. It had been opened in the last six months, so Kaspar had obviously never dined there, but he felt the need of a good meal. An epicurean, Kaspar hadn't had what he considered a decent meal since before his capture. If his time was short, he at least would live well for the last few days. Besides, he was convinced no one would recognize him given his relatively new appearance.

The owner were a couple from the Kingdom, a cook and his wife, and this had become to place to dine among the wealthy commons and minor nobility. In past years it had been the estate of a noble whom Kaspar's father had ruined. The home had changed hands several times, and most recently it had been something of an inn, with a brothel upstairs. Now it had been completely renovated and was providing meals at midday and at night in the fashion that had come from Bas-Tyra. With no bar or common room, it was neither inn nor tavern. Rather it was called a *restaurant*, in that language, a place to be restored. It was proving so popular in the Bas-Tyra province of the Kingdom of the Isles, that similar establishments were appearing in major cities throughout the region. It was a perfect place to dine for those with homes which were too small to entertain in, or for those whose means prevented them from having a cook on their staff.

The room was crowded. If the throng desiring to be seated tonight was an indication, the food would live up to its reputation. Kaspar had been forced to give the manager a healthy bribe to find him a small table in the corner, and only because it was early in the evening.

The corner suited Kaspar, as he could easily watch who came and went. Several familiar faces dotted the room, not people he knew well, but rich commoners and minor nobles of his court. He found it amusing that none of them noticed him there. He started slowly, with a cold white wine imported from the Kingdom, while he dined on shellfish and raw shrimp. The dishes were superb.

As he ate, Kaspar saw more familiar faces come into the room, yet no one gave him a second glance. He realized something about human nature; people do not recognize one another outside a familiar context unless they are very well acquainted. No one for a moment considered that the man in the corner might be a thinner, sunburned, fitter Kaspar of Olasko, because no one expected ever to see the former duke sitting in the corner of this establishment, dining at his leisure. At most someone might say, "I saw a fellow tonight who bore an uncanny resemblance to the old Duke. What do you think of that?"

The pretty woman who served him was named Magary, the cook's wife, and she was charming without being flirtatious—a welcome change from the coarse serving women he had encountered everywhere he had dined since his exile began. She recommended several dishes. By the second course, Kaspar was determined to at least taste everything she recommended, even if he couldn't finish every dish, for the flavors were stupendous.

The other woman serving customers was a regal-looking woman with reddish-blonde hair, who would have been called beautiful if it hadn't been for her aloof manner. She smiled, but there was little warmth in it.

Kaspar was trying a new dish—fresh field-greens with a vinegar and fruit compote on the side, covered in lemon juice and spices. The crunchy texture took some getting used to, but the flavors were wonderful. Magary poured Kaspar a different white wine and said, "The tartness of the dressing on the salad clashes with most wine, but I think you'll find this one goes well with it."

It did indeed, and Kaspar complimented her on the choice as he began another course, a whole stuffed squab with spices and a sauce that made him want to linger.

As he finished the bird, Kaspar saw Amafi entered the establishment, and point to Kaspar. The manager looked in Kaspar's direction and Kaspar waved the Quegan over to his table.

As Amafi sat down, Kaspar said, "You must try the squab. It is amazing."

"So I have heard, Magnificence."

"You look good," Kaspar said, indicating with a wave of his fork Amafi's new clothing.

"Thank you. It feels good to be clean again."

Magary came over and when she saw Amafi her face froze and she hesitated. She turned and vanished into the kitchen.

Amafi sat motionless for a moment, then stood, "Magnificence, we must leave, now!"

Kaspar sat back. "What?"

Amafi reached over and took him by the arm. "Now, sir, at once. I've been recognized."

Kaspar was halfway out of his chair when the girl returned from the kitchen with two men behind her, both dressed in white cooks' clothing. Before either Amafi or Kaspar could draw a weapon, one of the two men had a sword leveled at them.

"Well, if this isn't the most unexpected surprise of my life, I don't know what is," said Talwin Hawkins.

EIGHTEEN

CONFRONTATION

Kaspar stood motionless.

The gravity of the moment was not lost on him. He had found the man he sought, but if he said or did anything wrong he could be killed in an instant.

Pale blue eyes with cold murder in them regarded Kaspar. Tal Hawkins' mouth was set in a humorless grin. Diners saw his unsheathed sword and many began to rise from their tables nervously.

"Be seated and rest easy, my lords, ladies, and gentlemen. This is just a simple misunderstanding over the cost of the meal," said Tal. He motioned Amafi and Kaspar toward the kitchen door with his sword. "In there, if you please, gentlemen." And in a softer tone, "Remember that I can gut you before you can make a move in the wrong direction."

Kaspar edged toward the kitchen and said, "Amafi,

please don't try anything stupid. You're not as fast as you once were."

"Yes, my lord," said Amafi. "A fact of which I am painfully aware."

Once in the kitchen, Tal Hawkins motioned the two men to a table in the corner. "Take your swords and knives out, slowly, and that includes the two in your boots and the one behind your belt-buckle, Amafi, and place them all on the table."

The two men did so.

"I've witnessed many amazing things, Kaspar," Tal said, "but I confess, to have Magary come and tell me that she'd been serving Amafi for the last hour and then to come out and discover that he was dining with you, well, that is easily the most astonishing thing of all. How did you come back, and how could you be so brazen as to enter my establishment?"

"The truth is," Kaspar replied, "I had no idea you had become an innkeeper."

"This is not an inn, it is a restaurant. Lucien and his wife were my servants in Salador. When the war was over I sent for them and started this business, along with my wife." He indicated the quiet woman Kaspar had seen serving tables earlier. Now, she stood in the corner holding a long knife. "She knows who you are, Kaspar, and will happily gut you should I let her. Care to give me one reason why I shouldn't?"

"Because I have a very long, very strange story to tell you."

"And why should I listen to anything you have to say? Why shouldn't I just call the constables and have them frog-march you both to the citadel and let Duke Rodoski decide what to do with you . . . assuming, of course, that Teal lets you leave here alive?"

Kaspar said, "I need to whisper something to you." He put his hands behind his back. "On my word, I will not attempt to harm anyone in this kitchen, but when you hear what I have to say you will understand why no one else can know."

"Lucien," Tal said to the cook.

"Yes?"

"Take one of those swords and place the point against the neck of the former duke, here," said Tal. "Should he do anything, feel free to skewer him."

Lucien lifted a blade and grinned. "Yes, Tal."

Kaspar leaned over and spoke softly into his enemy's ear, "I need to take something to the Conclave of Shadows."

Talwin Hawkins, once known as Talon of the Silver Hawk, the last man of the Orosini, stood motionless for a long moment, and then laid down his sword. He turned to Amafi and said, "Sit here, and do not move."

"Yes, Magnificence," replied his former bodyservant.

To his wife, Tal said, "I will explain everything later."

She didn't look happy, but she nodded once and put the knife down.

Then, to the others Tal said, "Go back to work—if we have any customers left, they will want service."

Lucien, Magary, and Teal went back to work and the kitchen buzzed into action around them.

"I have a room at the back where we can speak privately," said Tal.

"One favor."

"*You're* asking *me* for a favor?" Tal stared at Kaspar in amazement.

"Please; you interrupted my meal. I was hoping, if you didn't mind, we could talk while I finished eating. This is simply the finest meal I've ever had."

Tal stood in mute astonishment for a moment, then with a shake of his head he laughed. "Improbability upon impossibility. Very well." He called over to Magary, "If you don't mind, would you serve this . . . gentleman the balance of his meal in the back room. And please bring two glasses for the wine."

Keeping his sword leveled at Kaspar, Tal motioned for him to move through a door at the back of the kitchen. Inside the room beyond stood a table with eight seats around it. "This is where the staff eat," Tal explained.

Kaspar nodded. He pulled out a chair and sat down. Tal remained standing as Magary appeared with the wine and two glasses. Tal indicated that Kaspar should pour, and he did.

"Tal, I'll bring in the beef in a few minutes," Magary said.

Tal nodded. "Close the door, please."

Kaspar took a long drink. "Before I begin, let me say that this establishment has stunned me, young Hawkins. Your talents never cease to amaze me. The selection of food and wine is unsurpassed."

"Been a while since you've had a good meal?"

Kaspar laughed. "Longer than you know; but even when compared to the citadel's cuisine, this is amazing fare. Had I but known, I would never have wasted you as an agent. I'd have made you the highest-paid cook in the Eastern Kingdoms."

"Most of the credit belongs to Lucien. We work well together, but he's the true visionary. Now, please begin." Tal sat down but kept his sword leveled at Kaspar.

"I have a long story to tell you, so perhaps we should wait until the next course is served so as not to be interrupted? It can be told only to a few people."

"Your request suggests as much."

A few minutes later, Magary appeared with a steaming plate of beef in gravy, garnished with spiced vegetables. After she left, Kaspar took a bite. "You outdo yourself with each dish, Talwin."

"If you live long enough, Kaspar, remind me to tell you how cooking helped me get off that rock."

"The Fortress of Despair?"

"Yes. I think you'll find the tale amusing."

"I wish that I could say the same of my story. I'll skip the early days of my exile, save to say that it was educational. Let me begin with that small city called Simarah, where I encountered three traders from Port Vykor named Flynn, Kenner, and McGoin."

Kaspar began to tell his story.

The night passed slowly. When the last guests had departed, Teal knocked and entered to see if her husband and the man who had destroyed their people were still engaged in conversation. Tal rose and approached her immediately, turning his back on Kaspar, and leaving his sword on the table within easy reach, so Teal knew that there would be no bloodshed.

Tal told her that he might be there all night, so she went to where Amafi sat waiting patiently and said, "My husband bids you to return to your inn. Your master will send word when it is time for you to rejoin him." As he stood, she added, "Both my husband and Kaspar instruct you not to try to leave the city."

Amafi shrugged. "I've been trying to leave for about a year now. I expect it is fate that I stay." He bowed to the young woman and departed.

She stared for a long time at the kitchen door. She

considered returning, but thought better of it, realizing that the man who had destroyed her world, and the man who had rescued her and her son from slavery were going to be in there for a long time. Eventually she turned and went upstairs to bed.

Kaspar and Tal were still at the table in the back room when Lucien, Magary, and Teal entered the kitchen in the morning. Tal had boiled some coffee and the two men had consumed several full pots.

As the others entered, Tal said, "I have something to tell you all." He motioned his wife over to his side and put his arm around her. "Teal, more than anyone, understands that this man is the author of unimaginable horrors."

Kaspar sat dispassionately, his face revealing nothing.

"I once forgave him for his crimes." Tal looked at his wife. "But I will not ask you to do the same, Teal. While I was educated and allowed to live the life of a young noble, you endured degradation. I only ask your forbearance and understanding: I must keep this man alive for a while longer."

At that, Kaspar smiled. "A long while, I hope."

"That is not in my hands. I am aiding a fugitive now, and while I do not like it, I have no choice. If the City Watch catches sight of you and word reaches Rodoski, I will have to use whatever sense of indebtedness the Duke may feel toward me to keep you off the gallows." He paused, then added, "Only a few can know about those things of which we spoke. I am forced to keep secrets from the woman I love," he looked at his wife, "who bears this insult with a dignity I could not possibly match."

Teal smiled slightly, and Kaspar was struck by her beauty. *Gods, what kind of man was I*, he wondered silently, *to ruin a life such as hers simply to satisfy mad political ambition?*

Kaspar stood up and bowed to Tal's young wife. "Madam," he began, "words will never heal the wounds I have given you. I do not expect your forgiveness. I just wish you to know that I deeply regret what I have done to you and your people, and that I feel unfathomable shame for my deeds."

Quietly, Eye of the Blue-Winged Teal spoke. "I am alive. I have a healthy son and a husband who cherishes me. My life has been good this last year."

Kaspar felt the moisture well in his eyes at the woman's quiet majesty. He said, "You put me in mind of another woman I know, to whom I owe a great deal. I will do what I can in the future to make sure that she and others like her do not suffer."

Teal inclined her head slightly.

Tal said, "Well, Kaspar and I have much to do in the next few days, but until then we have breakfast to make and a midday menu to prepare. Lucien, what are we serving today?"

Lucien grinned and started speaking about the ingredients they needed to purchase at the market and which dishes he thought would be likely to attract customers that day. Kaspar waited until the kitchen settled into its normal rhythm and then took Tal aside. "I assume you have means to reach those people?"

Tal didn't need to be told to whom he referred. "As I told you, I am no longer in their service. I have the means to let them know I need to speak to someone, but how long that will take . . .?" He shrugged.

Kaspar stood silent for a moment. "Could you get word to Talia that I'm still alive?"

Tal nodded. "Yes, though I do not haunt the halls of power any more." He waved his hand around the kitchen. "I find this life far more enjoyable. I think my grandfather would have difficulty understanding the appeal; the food of my people—" His eyes were distant for a moment.

Kaspar said nothing.

Tal broke from his momentary reverie. "I'm sure she'll wish to see you, but it may prove difficult. Until we can conceive of a way to convince her husband not to hang you, you would be well advised to stay out of sight. It should be easy, as you look different enough. You might have dined in peace the entire night and left, had Magary not recognized Amafi.

"In any event, we share a common cause until those you wish to speak with tell me otherwise." He grew reflective, then said flatly, "We may be allies for a while and I can live with that, but make no mistake, Kaspar: while I forgave you, I will never forget what you ordered, and to the end of my days, I will hold you in contempt." He paused. "As I hold myself in contempt for the things I did in your service."

Kaspar nodded. "Svetlana?"

Tal looked at him. "Not a night goes by when I do not think of her murder."

Kaspar sighed. Gently, he placed his hand on Tal's shoulder. "It is said by some that the gods show us their bitter humor by molding us into what we hate most in others."

Tal nodded again. "Go back to your inn and wait quietly. Try to avoid being seen. I will send word as soon as I have been contacted."

"I know this is difficult for you," Kaspar said, "but believe me when I say that we do have a common cause, for my description cannot do justice to what I saw."

"I understand. Try to keep Amafi out of sight, as well."

"I will. Good day."

Tal simply nodded.

Kaspar left the establishment and made his way quickly back to the inn. He strode through the common room to his own room, half-expecting Amafi to have disappeared, but instead he found the old assassin asleep on his bed. He awoke instantly when Kaspar closed the door behind him. "Magnificence, do we live another day?"

"We live another day." Looking at the motionless Talnoy standing in the corner, Kaspar wondered how many days they had. Then, looking back to Amafi, he said, "We need a bigger room."

Days went by and Kaspar waited patiently. Then, after a week of silence, a messenger arrived with a note from Tal. *Come to dinner*, was all it said. Kaspar said to Amafi, "I think something has come up. We are to dine at the River House tonight."

The rest of the day passed slowly for Kaspar, for he was anxious to get on with whatever task was necessary to see this thing to the end. The Talnoy stood in the corner, a daily reminder of the terror that was dimensions away, yet lurking in every shadow. The appearance of the rift at sea, and the terrible creature that had tried to come through it, reminded him of Kalkin's warning—that the Talnoy was a beacon to the other world and its continued existence increased the likelihood of a Dasati invasion tenfold with each passing day.

At last, early evening came, and Kaspar and Amafi dressed for dinner. They walked to the River House rather than renting a carriage. As Tal had observed, the less they did to call attention to themselves, the better.

They were almost at the restaurant when Amafi hesitated. "Magnificence, we are being followed."

"How many?"

"Two, at least."

"Agents of the Duke?"

"I don't think so. These men are hunters. Turn right at the next corner, and stay close."

As soon as they rounded the corner, Amafi grabbed Kaspar's arm and pulled him into a doorway. They waited in the shadows as the two men walked away. Both wore heavy, dark-gray cloaks and floppy hats which hid their features. They hurried along, unaware that Amafi and Kaspar had turned another corner a short distance away.

"Shall we follow, Magnificence?"

"No," said Kaspar. "We should not court trouble. Especially when it is looking for us." He stepped out of the doorway. "Come, back this way."

They returned to their original route, and soon arrived at the River House. Once inside, they were immediately shown upstairs to a room at the rear of the house. There they found Tal waiting with his wife and a man who Kaspar had seen once before, a tall white-haired magician.

Tal nodded a greeting. "Kaspar, I believe you remember Magnus."

"I could hardly forget."

Humorlessly, the magician said, "I see you survived the nomads."

"And many other things, too. What has Tal told you?"

"Things that should not be repeated here." Turning to Tal, Magnus said, "We shall return, soon." Then, to Amafi, he said, "Stay here with Tal."

Magnus stepped forward and put his hand on Kaspar's shoulder. Kaspar felt a buzz, saw a sudden blur of gray, and then found himself somewhere else, in the middle of the afternoon.

He could hear the birds in the trees as he looked around his new location. A large villa rested in a peaceful valley before him. Kaspar could see people milling around the villa, as well as other creatures which he could not identify. Yet, with all that he had seen so far, nothing shocked him for long.

"Where are we?"

"On my father's estate, on an island in the Bitter Sea."

"Your father was the short, earnest gentleman who convinced Tal to spare my life a year ago, correct?"

At that, the tall magician smiled. "Yes, that was my father. Come, he is expecting me to return and explain Tal's cryptic message. It is better that you tell him the tale yourself."

Magnus led Kaspar into the villa through a large rectangular building which framed a lovely garden. He led the former Duke of Olasko down a long corridor and into a very large room in which stood a desk and a massive collection of books, scrolls, and parchments organized on shelves, in wicker baskets, and some just piled in a corner on the floor. A short, bearded man in a black robe sat at the desk, his brow furrowed in concentration as he read something inscribed on a parchment.

When he looked up, he seemed mildly surprised. "Magnus, I didn't expect you to return with . . . Kaspar of Olasko, if I'm not mistaken?"

"You're not, Father," said Magnus. "Tal Hawkins sent word that he needed to speak with a member of the Conclave, and when I answered the summons he told me a strange and terrible story. It is a tale best recounted by this man."

"I am Pug, and this is my home," said the short man. "I do not recall if we were ever properly introduced," he added dryly.

Kaspar laughed. "I believe we were both somewhat distracted."

"What is this terrible tale that impels my son to break protocol and invite you here without my leave?" He threw his son a questioning look.

"If what he says is true, Father, it is most vital."

Pug said, "Very well. Hmm . . . I can't call you 'Your Grace' any more, can I?"

"Kaspar will do." He sat in the chair at the opposite side of the desk.

Pug waved the parchment he had been studying. "It's a bit of a coincidence that you should appear today; I was trying to understand something left behind at your citadel by your friend Leso Varen."

Kaspar laughed. "The last year has left me with the decided impression that *friend* is hardly the right term. *Manipulative parasite* describes him more accurately, I believe."

Pug sighed. "I almost wish he was still alive, because there are many questions that I would relish putting to him."

"Oh, he's alive."

Pug sat up straight. "Are you sure?"

Kaspar looked perplexed. "I did not see his body, but I have it on good authority that he's alive somewhere. The person who told me explained that he is like a cockroach—you can stamp on him all day, but he just won't die."

Pug laughed. "I've faced him directly and indirectly

upon a number of occasions, and that is as fair a description as I've heard. But I'm dubious. Who told you he was alive?"

"I believe she is called Arch-Indar."

Pug sat back, his face a mask of open astonishment. "She's a god."

"And a dead one, too," said Magnus.

"Well, I was told that she's actually just the memory of a god."

"By whom?"

"A Keeper who dwells in the mountains below the Pillars of Heaven, under the Pavilion of the Gods. He told me that before sending me to the Pavilion to speak with Kalkin."

Pug said, "You spoke to Kalkin?"

"Banath, yes," said Kaspar. "Arch-Indar directed me to the Keepers, who in turn led me to Kalkin. He was the one who told me to find you."

Pug sat back, then said to Magnus. "Inform your mother and send for Nakor. I think that they, too, will wish to hear this tale."

When his son had left, Pug said, "We'll try to keep this civilized and convivial, Kaspar, but I do wish to impress one thing upon you."

"Which is?"

"If your story doesn't live up to my son's estimation of importance, there will be consequences."

Kaspar said nothing.

Pug said, "I would like to believe that you are no longer Leso Varen's pawn, but that wish has little to do with the security of my people. If you do not convince me by the time you finish your tale you're done for, and you will not leave this island alive. Is that understood?"

"Understood." Kaspar was quiet for a minute, then he

said, "If it's not too much trouble, I was about to dine a moment ago, before our . . . journey here."

Pug smiled. "I think we can arrange for some food."

Kaspar sat back. He welcomed the prospect of a meal, but regretted that, if this was to be his last, it wasn't at the River House.

NINETEEN

CONSULTATION

Kaspar waited.

He had finished telling his story to Pug and the others, and as had been the case with the Keepers, he had been asked a lot of questions. Now they sat quietly as each member of the Conclave pondered what had been said.

The woman was named Miranda; but although she was Pug's wife and Magnus's mother, she looked no older than her son. She had dark hair and a penetrating gaze, and her manner indicated that she was considered an equal here; her simple blue robe hid none of the fact that she was trim and fit, and still youthful despite her years. The short man, Nakor, Kaspar remembered from his brief encounter with the magicians after the fall of his citadel. He wore a yellow robe, cut raggedly at the knees, and carried a wooden staff. From his shoulder hung a large travel bag. He had been grinning when he had entered the room, but as Kaspar's story unfolded, his grin had faded and now his expression was one of somber consideration. Magnus never lost his serious expression throughout.

"Very well," said Pug after a minute. "Your thoughts?"

Miranda crossed her arms. "I think we need to examine this Talnoy at once."

Magnus said, "I'm concerned about the news that Leso Varen is still alive. We have yet to uncover the location of that abominable rift he was working on in Opardum."

Nakor shook his head. "And I'm concerned over the fact that if he is still alive, Varen may also be looking for the Talnoy. The two men following Kaspar earlier today in Opardum may have been agents of the King of Roldem or the Duke of Olasko, but they also may have been Varen's agents."

Kaspar said, "Forgive me, but it's difficult to hear 'Duke of Olasko' in reference to someone else. In any event, does Varen have agents?"

"His organization is as impenetrable to us as ours is to him," Pug said. "We have many allies, and are a council, while Varen counts no other his equal, I believe, but reigns supreme over his minions."

"But you could be wrong," said Nakor.

"I'm still wrestling with what Kaspar saw on this other world," said Magnus. "How much of it is accurate?"

"It's what I saw," said Kaspar.

"It's what Kalkin showed you," said Nakor. With a grin, he added, "And Banath is not called the Trickster for nothing. Who knows what his agenda is?"

"Certainly not to see the world of Midkemia destroyed."

"No," said Miranda. "But there may be far more to it than merely a risk to humanity and the other intelligent races here. Nakor's right. Banath can have shown you only part of the truth. Just your description of these . . ."

"Dasati," supplied Kaspar.

". . . Dasati," continued Miranda, "leaves me wondering. Cruelty, I know. We've witnessed enough of it right here on Midkemia." She fixed Kaspar with a baleful look, but made no further comment. "We are . . . or rather, Kaspar is, only aware of what he was allowed to see. Logic dictates that there must be more to that society than simple cruelty and self-interest. To have reached such a plateau of power and organization requires a certain willingness to cooperate and make sacrifices."

"Different rules and laws, is what Kalkin said." Kaspar smiled. "I had such thoughts as well after seeing it. But I know enough about civic authority and ruling a population to know that you may hold sway through power and terror for a while, but you do not build a centuries-old culture that way."

"This is becoming abstract," Magnus said. "Perhaps they achieved their social pinnacle, and then changed. But whatever the cause, we need to worry about who they are now and what their intentions may be."

"If what I saw is accurate," said Kaspar, "they have no intentions yet, but if they become aware of us, then I suspect they will conquer first and ask questions later. Kalkin mentioned that the Dasati empire spanned worlds."

"Assumptions?" asked Pug.

"That we move quickly," said Magnus.

Miranda nodded. "I think we fetch this Talnoy here, now, and start examining it."

Nakor said, "I think I will venture to the temple of Banath in the City of Kesh, and see if any of my old friends there have any inkling of what Banath—or Kalkin," he nodded to Kaspar, "has to say on the subject. It would not surprise me to find out they know a great deal or nothing at all, but one should ask. I will return in two days." He left the room.

"Very well," said Pug. "We agree that time is of the essence, so Magnus, take Kaspar back to Opardum and fetch the Talnoy and bring it back here." To his wife he said, "You and I should discuss who is to work with us."

She nodded, and Kaspar stood up. He looked at Magnus and said, "Where to now?"

Magnus put his hand on Kaspar's shoulder and suddenly they were in the back room behind the kitchen of the River House. "Here," said Magnus.

Kaspar felt his knees go slightly weak for a moment then, gathering himself, he said, "I will never get used to that."

Magnus smiled. "Wait here while I speak to Tal."

In a few minutes Tal returned with Magnus. "The three of us should go to your room and collect that thing," Magnus said.

"Why the three of us?" asked Kaspar.

"Because we could use an extra sword and there aren't a lot of people I can take the time to explain things to," said Magnus impatiently. "Just come along and let's get on with it."

The three men left the River House and hurried to Kaspar's room at the inn. The hour was late and Tal had finished showing out the last customer before Kaspar and Magnus appeared. The streets echoed with their sound of their boots upon the cobbles, and they moved purposefully but alertly through the dark streets of Opardum.

As they neared the inn, Kaspar held up his hand. Whispering, he said, "Something's wrong."

"What?" asked Magnus.

"I see them," said Tal. "Two men in the shadows, one opposite the inn, lurking in a doorway, another just at the corner of the alley on this side of the building."

"I saw nothing," said Magnus.

Kaspar stepped back into the shadows, and motioned the others to follow suit. "If those are the same men who followed Amafi and me earlier tonight . . ." He glanced at the dark sky, "It is the same night, isn't it?"

Magnus nodded.

"If it is the same two, then Amafi was right and we're being followed." He glanced around. "If I hurry back and loop around and come down the alley quietly, I should be able to get a good look at the one at the corner without him being aware of it."

Tal said, "I'm more likely to do it without being noticed, Kaspar."

"Yes," said the former duke, "but you don't know what they looked like."

"Floppy hats, large cloaks?"

"Yes."

"Did you see their faces?"

"No."

"Then you don't know what they look like either. Wait here."

Kaspar and Magnus waited. "They must have followed Amafi here, and are now waiting to see when I'll show up."

"Perhaps others have already gone inside and taken your man?"

Kaspar chuckled. "Hardly. The Talnoy would have prevented that, given my instructions; anyone else who entered the room besides Amafi or myself was to be incapacitated."

About five minutes after Tal departed a commotion erupted in the alleyway, and Kaspar and Magnus saw the man opposite the door to the inn race toward the alley, drawing his sword.

Kaspar drew his own blade. "All right then, here we go!" He charged down the street and turned into the alley in time to see Tal standing over one fallen man and beating back the other with a furious assault. Kaspar stuck the point of his sword in the small of the man's back and shouted, "That's enough!"

The man froze and let his sword fall. Tal stepped forward and pulled the man's hat off, then Kaspar spun him around.

The man was a stranger. Kaspar looked at Tal and said, "You're more likely not to be noticed?"

Tal shrugged. "So I'm out of practice."

Magnus stepped up to the man and said, "Who sent you?"

The man looked at his fallen comrade and then at Magnus and Tal. Magnus said, "Do not try to deceive us, man. We have means to make you speak the truth!"

The dark-cloaked man lunged forward as if to attack Magnus, and Kaspar struck him hard across the face with the hilt of his sword. The man went face down onto the cobbles. Then he tried to get up. Too late, Magnus shouted, "Hold him!"

By the time Tal and Kaspar had hold of him, he was already convulsing. "He's taken poison," said Magnus.

Tal went to inspect the first man he had fought. "He's dead also."

Magnus knelt beside him, put his hand inside his shirt and pulled out a medallion. He swore. "Not again!"

"What is it?" asked Tal.

Magnus held out the medallion. It was a base metal of some sort, perhaps pewter, blacked. In bas-relief a single hawk had been inscribed. "What does this mean?" asked Kaspar.

"The Nighthawks," said Magnus.

"Who?" asked Kaspar.

Tal shrugged.

"The Guild of Death. It's been forty or more years since we encountered them. I'll let my father tell you more about them, but for the moment, we'd better make haste." He motioned for Kaspar to enter the inn first.

They went in and found the common room deserted, which was not unexpected this time of night. Kaspar went to his door and knocked twice. Amafi opened it, and said, "Magnificence! You are well!" Then he looked past Kaspar and said, "And not alone."

Kaspar motioned for the others to wait outside, entered the room and approached the Talnoy. Slipping on the ring he said, "Do not attack anyone." He took the ring off again and motioned for Magnus and Tal to enter. "Were you followed?" asked Kaspar of Amafi.

"Yes, by the same two men who followed us earlier. I sent word with a boy to the River House."

"He never got there," said Tal. "They must have stopped him."

Magnus said, "Then the boy is certainly dead." He looked over to the corner where the Talnoy stood motionless. He stood in front of it for a few moments, then said, "I know what the monk meant, Kaspar. There is a wrongness here that . . . I can't explain. But this thing does not belong in our world."

"Then," said Kaspar, "I suggest we take it to your father and see what he can do about getting it off this world."

Magnus shook his head. "No."

"What do you mean 'no'?" asked Kaspar. "I thought this was what we came for?"

"Tal? Do you sense it?"

Tal Hawkins stared at the silent black visage. He put his hand on the armor for a moment, then said, "Something . . ."

"Talwin has a knack few without magic ability have, the

ability to sense magic being used. Whatever foul arts trapped a soul within this armor is still strong and . . . dangerous." Magnus turned to look at Kaspar. "You may be safe, because the ring gives you control over this creature, but I am not. I will return to my father and consult with him."

Suddenly Magnus was gone.

Tal sat on the bed. "I hate it when he does that."

Kaspar sat at the other end. "I know."

They waited.

More than an hour passed, and suddenly Magnus reappeared. He said, "Father instructs me to bring you and the Talnoy to a specific place on the island where he and my mother have begun erecting wards to protect us from it, as well as to hide it from anyone seeking it."

"Hide it?" said Kaspar. "We're in Opardum, then in a moment, we'll be thousands of miles away. Why would anyone look for it on your island?"

"There are far more useful methods of detection than simply looking under rocks," said Magnus. "This thing contains alien magic, and the only reason Varen or his agents haven't found it is because they are not sure what they are looking for. Now that I have seen it, touched it, I could find this . . . artifact anywhere on this world."

Kaspar and Tal stood up, while Amafi stayed seated in the corner.

Magnus said, "Get the thing to stand in the middle of the room." To Tal he said, "I will send word if we need your help. Thank you for your part in this."

"Keep me informed, Magnus," Tal said. "I am willing to serve if need be."

Kaspar slipped on the ring and ordered the Talnoy to step forward and it did.

Magnus said, "Gather around."

"Magnificence?" questioned Amafi.

"You'd better come along, too," said Kaspar.

Amafi looked relieved. "Sir."

They gathered closely and Magnus put his hands on Kaspar and Amafi's shoulders; and suddenly the group was standing in a clearing behind the villa.

Amafi gaped at what he saw around him. It was late—nearly midnight at their present location—and still people were hurrying about on various errands. Many were foreign-looking in their apparel, and a few were clearly not human.

Kaspar said, "I think it'll take some getting used to."

"Magnificence, I agree."

Pug and Miranda stood nearby, and Kaspar saw they had appeared inside a circle defined by five points of amber crystal which glowed from within. "Step out of the circle, quickly," Pug instructed.

They did so, and Pug said, "Stand back." He waved his hands and Kaspar saw that Miranda and Magnus mimicked his movements. The crystals flared brightly for a moment, then the light was reduced to a faint glow.

Pug said, "Anyone looking for this will have to be a very powerful magician to locate it."

"Very powerful," echoed Miranda.

Pug said, "Let me have the ring, please."

Kaspar took the ring out of his pouch and handed it to Pug. The magician placed it on the palm of his hand and looked closely at it. "This is nothing made by the hand of mortal man, obviously."

Magnus said, "Both the ring and the artifact positively reek, Father."

"Once the wards hiding this thing in the cave were disturbed . . ." Pug started. "We may never know how that happened, but I have my suspicions."

Pug silently examined the Talnoy, while Kaspar, Amafi, Magnus, and Miranda waited outside the circle of wards. Others from the community gathered, and Amafi whispered, "Magnificence, what manner of place is this?" He stared at a creature with coal black skin and bright red eyes who was watching Pug intently.

"A school, if you can believe it," said Kaspar. Looking at Pug, he said, "And a great deal more."

The examination went on for more than an hour, but no one grew bored and departed. Everyone was content to stand quietly and observe, while Pug examined the Talnoy. Only an occasional whisper broke the night's quiet.

Finally, Pug said, "Let us go to my study."

Kaspar and Amafi followed Magnus, Miranda, and Pug, while the other inhabitants of the island dispersed, returning to whatever tasks awaited them, or to bed. Amafi looked from place to place as they walked through the large villa, the garden, and into the halls leading to Pug's private study.

Once inside, Pug said, "It is a very evil thing you have brought us, Kaspar."

Kaspar said, "I find that no surprise, Magician."

"I fear it is everything you said, and more," said Pug. He sat down at his desk and indicated for the others to be seated. Miranda came to stand behind her husband, putting her hands on his shoulders, while Magnus remained standing in the corner. Kaspar and Amafi took the two chairs opposite Pug. "I think we shall wait for Nakor to return before I make a final decision, but I am ready to concede that what you say you saw was indeed what menaces this world.

"Even one of these creatures would take some effort to

destroy, and an army of such . . ." Pug let the thought trail off. "We shall have an end to it, though." He was silent for a bit, then said, "Magnus, you had something else?"

Magnus stepped forward and put the Nighthawks medallion on the desk. "Two men tried to follow Kaspar in order, I believe, to find the Talnoy."

Pug sat back in his chair, an expression of disgust on his face. "The Guild of Death, after all these years."

"The Guild of Death?" prompted Kaspar.

Pug's dark eyes studied Kaspar's face. "There were, in reality, two guilds. The original was a brotherhood, a sort of extended family, who were among the most lethal assassins in the history of the Kingdom and Kesh. They operated out of Krondor, Kesh City, and Salador for nearly sixty years. Over that time they were infiltrated, or some members turned loyalties, but by the time people I knew began to encounter them they had been . . . subverted to serve dark forces. Before they had been a small group, no more than fifty, who killed by contract and mostly for political reasons. By the time my friends encountered them, they were already under the sway of those who sought to plunge the Kingdom into chaos.

"A dear friend, Duke James of Krondor, when he was old Prince Arutha's squire with my first son, William, and a student of mine discovered their stronghold, an old military fortress out in the Jal-Pur desert. He found hundreds of them trying to conjure a demon into our realm." Pug sighed. "Prince Arutha and his army killed hundreds of them down there.

"Later I met a man . . ." He looked at Kaspar. "You knew this man as Leso Varen. When I met him, he was called Sidi. He's had other names, as well. And other bodies, from what I can judge. You know who he works for?"

Kaspar said, "That was explained to me." He turned to Amafi and said, "And you don't need to know."

"Magnificence," said Amafi with a slight bow. "I rejoice in my ignorance."

"This man, Varen for now, is the . . . leader, for lack of a better term, of those who seek to open the doors to chaos and destruction and plunge this world into the sort of madness you've witnessed, Kaspar."

"I understand," said Kaspar, "so the point is, Varen was the leader of the Nighthawks."

"In a way, yes. He had other agents as well. In any event, if the Nighthawks are following you, it means only one thing. Varen is interested in you, and not because you were his host for several years. He may not know what it is you possess here." He pointed to the Talnoy. "But he knows something important has come your way. Most likely he had agents around the world looking for a sign of you, but most would be in Olasko against the possibility of your return."

Kaspar said, "Or they may have simply been looking for some magical sign of the Talnoy, and not realized who I was."

"Perhaps," said Miranda. "Trying to guess the enemy's next move is useful; trying to guess what they are thinking is pointless."

Pug nodded in agreement. "In any event I think you may safely leave this matter to us." He studied Kaspar. "You've still got accounts to settle. I believe you were under Varen's influence, but you have plenty of blood on your own hands. Still, if you'd like, I'll ask Talwin Hawkins to speak to the Duke on your behalf."

Kaspar laughed. "Thank you for that, Magician, but I doubt you've enough magic between the three of you here to convince Rodoski to let me remain in Olasko. I know I wouldn't if our places were reversed. Even if I behave myself, there are others who would use my presence as an excuse to undercut his authority. Moreover, now that Olasko is part of Roldem, King Carol would probably rather have an army of Talnoy in Opardum than me. No, I'll move on."

"You have plans?"

"Some, but they're not quite finalized. But one favor, if I might, Magician. Could you arrange it for me to see my sister once before I leave Olasko again?"

"Assuredly," said Pug. To Magnus he said, "Find our guests some rooms while I send a message to Talwin Hawkins." To Kaspar he said, "Stay here for a few days and when we can, we'll return you to Olasko. If Varen's Nighthawks are out looking for you, it wouldn't do to have you lingering in Opardum."

"Agreed."

Magnus motioned for Kaspar and Amafi to follow him and led them down a long hall into another wing of the villa. He escorted them to a comfortable room containing two beds. "Wait here," he instructed.

A few moments later he reappeared with a young sandy-haired and blue-eyed man, and said, "This is Malikai. I've asked him to see to any needs you may have while you're with us."

Kaspar smiled. "And to keep an eye on us as well?"

"Hardly necessary," said Magnus. "We're on an island, so there aren't a lot of places for you to go. But there are a few we'd rather not have you wander into, for your own safety. I don't know how long you're to be with us, so we'll see to some clothing as well as food while you're here."

Magnus departed and Malikai said, "Sirs? Is there anything you need right now?"

"Nothing more than a good night's sleep," said Kaspar, sitting and removing his boots. "We came from a bit farther east and I'm not sure what time it is here . . ."

"After midnight, sir."

"Well, then, we can still get in a solid night's sleep, Magnificence," said Amafi. He sat on the other bed.

Malikai said, "I'll be in the room next door until breakfast, gentlemen. I have classes in the morning, but should you need me, just ask any student you see to come fetch me. They'll know where I am. It's a small group here."

"Very well," said Kaspar. "I expect we'll have many questions, but as you have a busy morning ahead, we'll save them."

The boy left and Kaspar lay down, pulling a blanket over himself. Amafi did likewise and blew out the candle. Then he said, "Magnificence, what will you do now?"

"Sleep, Amafi."

"I mean, after we leave this place?"

Kaspar was quiet, then said, "I have some ideas, but nothing I'm ready to talk about. Good night, Amafi."

"Good night, Magnificence."

Kaspar lay there and realized it was a very good question. He had completely lost himself in getting the Talnoy and Kalkin's warning to the Conclave of Shadows, and beyond seeing his sister one more time, he really had no idea what he would do after that.

As tired as he was, sleep was slow in coming.

For three days Kaspar and Amafi were guests of Pug and his family at their villa. Kaspar discovered this was the almost legendary Sorcerer's Isle, where ships were kept away by a mix of rumor and magic. The rumors were of horrors visited on those who stopped at the island, and the magic consisted of several illusions that made the otherwise bucolic and tranquil isle appear less than hospitable to anyone sailing close enough to get a look.

The island was beautiful, and as it was now late spring in the north, in full bloom. Amafi and Kaspar both took the time to rest and refresh themselves after the rigors of their time in Opardum.

For the old assassin, it was his first trouble-free rest in a year, and for Kaspar it was a place to unburden himself from the terrible responsibility he had felt since meeting Flynn and the others. Both men enjoyed the relaxation.

On the morning of the fourth day, Malikai found Kaspar sitting on the verge of a large green behind the villa, listening to a lesson being conducted by an instructor who appeared to have slightly orange skin. Other than that, she was remarkably attractive. Kaspar could barely grasp the scope of her discussion, but as with the university in Novindus, the simple fact of all these eager young minds being educated fascinated him.

"Good day, Kaspar," said a woman's voice from behind him.

Kaspar turned and saw an unexpected face. "Rowena!" he said, rising. "Why . . . ?"

She smiled. "Here I am Alysandra, which is my real name."

Kaspar laughed. "So you were one of Pug's agents?"

"Yes, as was Tal."

Alysandra motioned for Kaspar to walk with her. "I almost died at the hands of that madman, you know."

Kaspar said, "At the end . . . things were out of control. I rarely understood what I was agreeing to."

"Oh, I don't hold you responsible," she said brightly, her smile as engaging as before. "After all, I was told to get close to Varen, to see if he had any weaknesses. He didn't find me interesting in that way. He did enjoy cutting me up bit by bit." She said the last matter-of-factly. "They did a lovely job of healing my wounds. Not a scar to be found."

Kaspar was at a loss. When he had known her as the Lady Rowena of Talsin, a third daughter of a minor noble of a backcountry barony in the land of Miskalon, she had been the most seductive woman he had encountered. Here, she was different. Her manner gave him the feeling that she viewed what happened to her in a distant fashion, as if it had happened to someone else.

"Well, even if you were following another's orders, it was while you were ostensibly under my protection. I allowed it to happen."

"That's all right, honestly. After all, I was there to kill you if I had the chance."

Kaspar stopped dead for a moment, then caught up with her. "You were?"

"Only after I found out what Leso was doing."

"Did you?"

"No, but they're still investigating what they found in the citadel. It's something . . . very strange according to those who know about such things."

"What about you?" he asked. "Now that you're well, will you return to your family?"

She laughed—the same musical laugh Kaspar remembered as they lay in one another's arms those many nights in Opardum. "Family? I have no family, or as close to a family as I will ever know. There's something wrong with me, Kaspar, or at least it seems that's what people think. It's not that I like to hurt people, it's just that I don't care if they're hurt. Do you see?"

And suddenly Kaspar did. "You're the perfect assassin."

"Well, I don't know about perfect, but I certainly feel no

remorse. I found you to be a great deal of fun, and as a lover you're considerate and very strong, but if you died now, I wouldn't care. So, Pug thinks it best for me to stay here and work for him."

Softly Kaspar said, "I agree."

She smiled and gripped his arm. "Well, I must go. But if you see your sister soon, tell her I said hello."

"I will," he said, and as he watched her walk away he felt a profound sadness.

Later that morning, Malikai found Kaspar and said, "Magnus would like to speak with you, sir."

Kaspar followed the young man, luxuriating in the scent of fresh blossoms and the feel of the sun on his back as he walked through the garden. Magnus was standing next to some very lush flowers of a type unknown to Kaspar. The pale magician said, "It has been arranged for you to visit your sister."

"When?"

"Now," said Magnus, putting his hand on Kaspar's shoulder.

Suddenly they were in the back room at the River House. "There's a private dining room at the back. She is waiting for you there."

Kaspar found his way to the rear of the dining room which was already crowded even though it was still early in the evening in Opardum. He entered the room and found Natalia sitting at the end of the table.

She rose and said, "Oh, Kaspar," and came to him. She was obviously pregnant. She kissed him and said, "I thought I'd never see you again."

"Nor I you."

She stepped back. "You look so different. You're so much thinner!"

He laughed. "And you're not."

She blushed. "Varian and I will have a son, so the midwives tell me, in another two months."

Kaspar calculated. "He didn't waste much time, did he?"

Natalia moved to her seat and took it, motioning for Kaspar to sit down. She rang a bell and Magary appeared. "You can begin serving now."

"Yes, Your Grace."

Kaspar laughed as Magary left. "Your Grace! That's right, you're now Duchess."

She leaned forward. "Kaspar, I know things have been . . . difficult."

He patted her hand. "That word doesn't do it justice. But I'm really fine."

"Varian is a good man. He and I will never . . . well, I respect him and he's gentle. He also is a wonderful father and he's a fine ruler. Your nation is in good hands."

Kaspar sighed. "Nation? No longer."

"Well, if it's any consolation, the next Duke of Olasko will have your blood in him."

Kaspar laughed out loud. Slapping the table, he said, "I can't begin to tell you how surprised I am that that particular bit of news actually does please me."

"I'm so glad."

Magary entered with soup, and from the smell of it, Kaspar knew he was going to enjoy it. When she left, Kaspar picked up a spoon and said, "I am doubly pleased to be meeting you here, my darling sister, for if this meal is like the first one I had here last week, you are in for a treat."

They talked throughout dinner and into the night. Kaspar sipped fortified wine and she had hot tea after supper. At the end, they found they had run out of things to talk about. And both knew why.

Tal entered and said, "Your Grace, your carriage awaits."

Natalia arose and came to kiss Tal on the cheek. "Thank you for my brother."

"You're more than welcome. I'll wait outside as you say goodbye."

When they were alone, Kaspar said, "Shall I walk you out?"

"No," she said. "Someone might recognize you, even at this late hour. It's best I go now." They stood holding hands for a silent minute.

Kaspar said at last, "I know. We may never see each other again."

"What will you do?"

"I don't know yet, but one thing I've discovered in the last year is that this world is a vast place, with great opportunities for someone who wishes to begin again. When I have begun again, I shall send word."

"May the gods protect you, dear brother." She kissed him and left quickly as if fleeing before tears overwhelmed her.

A minute later Tal re-entered the room. Kaspar said, "As she said, thank you."

Tal shrugged. "We both love her in our way."

Kaspar laughed. "Irony isn't your strong suit, but you see it, don't you?"

"That I could love your sister while wishing you dead?" He nodded. "I could never love Natalia the way a husband should love his wife."

"But you found the girl you were destined for?"

Tal shrugged, and his expression was one of mixed

regret and resignation. "Teal isn't the girl I knew in the village. She is . . . changed. She will never truly be happy, I think. She was raped so many times she doesn't even know who our son's father is. I treat him like my own, but . . . it'll never be the same for her. However, she has good days, weeks even." A faraway look came over his face. "She never cries, Kaspar. Never. I would welcome it if she did."

"You took on a burden."

"Who else was there to give her back a tiny bit of what you took away?"

Kaspar was silent: there was nothing he could say to defend himself. Finally he said, "Alysandra said to say hello. She is well."

Tal laughed, and there was a note of bitterness in it. "I was so young when I met her, I thought her the love of my life. It was a harsh lesson."

Kaspar said, "There's another one who never cries."

After a long pause, Tal said, "If you are fortunate and meet a woman you can love without reservation, do so. For then you'll know the gods have truly forgiven you."

Kaspar nodded. "I should be getting back. How is that arranged?"

Tal handed Kaspar an orb fashioned out of some golden metal which was much lighter than gold. "Press that button there and you will be back at the villa."

Kaspar said, "Then it is goodbye, young Talwin Hawkins, though not so young as when I met you. Shall we meet again?"

Tal smiled a rueful smile. "Where the Conclave is concerned, nothing is certain. As much as I can, Kaspar of Olasko, I hope you fare well."

"And you, Tal."

They didn't clasp hands, but they did lock gazes for a

moment, and something passed between them. Kaspar pressed the button on the orb and suddenly he was in Pug's study.

Pug looked up. "Was it an enjoyable visit?"

Kaspar said, "Very enjoyable. Thank you for your help. Tal did most of it. I just sent him a message." He paused. "You look tired."

"There are times I think I was born tired," said Pug. He smiled. "I remember being a lad back at the castle in Crydee, and while it was only a hundred or so years ago, it seems a lot longer."

Kaspar laughed. "You have wonderful beaches here, I have been told. You should go for a swim, lie in the sun for a day."

"I would if I could. But we have things to do."

"We?"

"Yes, rest, for tomorrow you and I will take a journey to see someone who may shed some additional light on the Talnoy."

"Who and where?" asked Kaspar.

"A friend of mine, who knows more about the Dragon Lords than anyone living."

"And where does he reside?"

"Elvandar. We are going to the court of the Elf Queen."

Kaspar said, "Talwin was right. You do never know what will happen next."

Twenty

Elvandar

Kaspar blinked.

One moment they had been on Sorcerer's Isle, and the next they were in a deep forest, standing on the banks of a river.

Pug said, "This is the Crydee River." Then he turned to ensure that the Talnoy was still with them.

"What now?" asked Kaspar.

"We wait," said Pug. "We won't have to wait long. The elves are vigilant at their boundaries."

"Why do we wait for them to come to us?"

"No one may enter Elvandar or the surrounding forest unbidden. To do so would invite dire consequences."

The temperature was brisk, but not uncomfortable. They had departed after breakfast, but as Elvandar was farther west than Sorcerer's Isle, it was still early morning at the time of their arrival.

For roughly an hour they waited, Kaspar sitting on the ground, Pug and the Talnoy standing motionlessly. Kaspar had spoken little to the magician in the time they were together. It was obvious that Pug was the leader of the Conclave, though no one had openly said as much. He didn't seem the sort of man to engage in idle chatter, and so far nothing Kaspar had seen had disabused him of that notion.

At last, Pug said, "They're here."

Kaspar looked across the river and saw nothing, but Pug called out, "Hello! It is Pug of Crydee!"

A laugh sounded from the other side of the river, and a voice called back, "Welcome to Elvandar, Pug of Crydee. You and those accompanying you may enter."

Pug beckoned to Kaspar and commanded the Talnoy to follow them across the ford. Kaspar, glancing behind him to make sure it was following, thought that it looked twice as menacing in the shadows of the forest. He had gratefully relinquished the ring to Pug, who seemed able to wear it for longer periods without apparent difficulty.

Across the river, among the trees, waited four elves. Kaspar noticed that one of them looked a little different to the others; he was broader of shoulder and had slightly less pronounced ears.

"Ho, Calis!" Pug said, smiling at the unusual-looking elf.

"Greetings, Pug." The young man looked no more than twenty-five years old. "You are always welcome. I've already sent a runner to inform my mother and father of your arrival."

"I'm afraid we must hie to the court by faster means."

"Sorry I won't be there to see you," said Calis.

"How is your family?"

"Ellia and the twins are fine." He looked at the Talnoy

and said, "Am I safe in assuming that this is what brought you to court?"

"Yes, I need to speak to your father about it."

Calis examined the Talnoy closely. "It has an evil aspect, but there is something in it—" he grimaced. "It reeks of death, Pug."

"I fear you're right," said Pug.

"Then we shall not keep you. It is good to see you again, Pug."

"And you."

Pug motioned for Kaspar to stand closer to him and suddenly they were in another part of the forest.

Kaspar's mouth opened.

Before him rose a truly awe-inspiring sight, a forest unique and otherworldly. They stood in a vast clearing. Before them, in its center, majestic oaks ascended to the very heavens. Each was easily three times the height of those in Olasko's hunting forests, and the colors!

Some were leafed in dark green, as befitted the season, but others were alive with red, gold, and orange. He saw one that he swore was tinged with blue, and several bore leaves as white as snow. Between the mighty boles, below the main canopy, arched vast walkways built upon massive branches. Stairs, seemingly carved out of the living trunks, spiralled up out of sight and platforms could be glimpsed between the foliage. Upon all of these constructions walked elves.

They were a stately people, but what Kaspar had read about them did not do them justice.

Some wore hunting leathers, like the sentry elves at the river, but others wore regal robes of rich hues, hand-stitched with threads of silver and white, gold and yellow. They moved with a fluid grace, an economy of motion that made them appear to glide rather than step.

"Breathtaking," Kaspar whispered.

"I've been here more times than I can count, and I still gape in awe," said Pug. "Follow me."

He led Kaspar toward a large sweeping stairway that curved out of sight around the trunk of one of the giant trees. Elven children played around its base, and several women sat observing them quietly as they worked at their sewing.

Pug exchanged greetings with many who passed them as they climbed. Kaspar felt that he couldn't take in the wonders fast enough. "This is a most marvellous place, Pug," he said.

"Indeed."

"It is more than its beauty . . . it's also the tranquillity of the place."

"Sadly, it has not always been so. A battle was fought at the place where we arrived between the elves and Tsurani invaders during the Riftwar. I was a captive on the Tsurani world, but I have heard the sad tale many times. This lush woodland has been watered with the blood of the long-lived too often."

Kaspar intuited what he meant by that, for the elves were rumored to live for centuries.

They reached a high pathway across several huge branches which led to a gigantic central court. Upon a large wooden dais rested two thrones, and upon these sat two people who looked as noble as their surroundings.

The woman's throne stood slightly higher than the man's. She wore a simple gown of winter-white, and he a brown tunic and trousers, but the simple clothing could not hide their majesty. Her ears were like the other elves', upswept, pointed, and without lobes, and her magnificent red-gold hair was gathered by a single golden circlet that allowed it to cascade loosely about her shoulders. Her almond-shaped eyes were blue with green flecks.

The man wore no adornment, but his body radiated

strength. Kaspar felt awed by his power. Pug had struck him as a man of subtle strength, but this man was strength personified. He must have stood at least six inches over six feet tall and was broad-shouldered, but something about him conveyed that his power came not just from his size, but from deep within, as well.

"Welcome, Pug!" the man said, rising to greet them. "You sent no word of your arrival."

Pug embraced him. "I fear we've arrived before the messenger that your son dispatched from the river. Time is of the essence." He turned to the woman and bowed. "Your Majesty."

She smiled and Kaspar was again dumbstruck. She was alien, but beautiful beyond measure. She nodded graciously. "You are welcome, Pug, as always. Who are these two with you?"

Pug said, "Queen Aglaranna, may I present Kaspar, lately Duke of Olasko, and now a . . . companion. And the creature behind him is our reason for being here."

The Queen inclined her head. "Welcome, Kaspar."

Kaspar said, "I am most astonished and gratified to be here, Majesty."

Pug said, to Kaspar, indicating the tall man, "And this is Tomas, Prince Consort of Elvandar and my boyhood friend."

Tomas gestured toward a circle of elves who sat on either side of the thrones. "These are the Queen's advisors." Nodding toward an elderly elf he said, "Tathar is first among the Spellweavers." The old elf was broad-shouldered and bearded; otherwise, despite his white hair, he looked much like his companions. He was dressed in rough-woven cloth and leather and sat at the Queen's right hand. On the other side of the dais, to Tomas's left, sat another elf. "And this is Acaila, first among the Eldar."

While Tathar possessed a certain rough-hewn look, Acaila appeared composed and spiritual, like a cleric. His features were thin from age, and his skin was almost translucent, like parchment.

Kaspar nodded a greeting to all of them.

Tomas asked, "So what is this thing that you have brought to us? It is not alive, is it?"

"In a manner of speaking, it is," said Pug. "I was hoping you could shed some light on it."

Tomas fixed the palest blue eyes that Kaspar had ever seen upon the thing and after a moment, they widened. "A Talnoy!" Tomas said softly. "Now I remember."

"Remember?" said Kaspar.

Pug said, "All will be explained." Turning back to Tomas, he asked, "What do you remember?"

Tomas's voice turned icy, as if another person spoke through him, and his gaze became distant. "We battled against a race called the Teld-Katha, on the world of Riska. They attempted to banish us from their skies using a hastily-constructed but mighty spell. They failed; instead, they created a rift.

"We destroyed the Teld-Katha, but never plundered their world, for we in turn were ambushed through that rift, and those that—" His eyes focused suddenly, and turning to Pug, he said, "You must destroy this somehow, and quickly!"

"Our initial examination leads me to believe that to do so may prove impossible."

Tomas looked to the two senior elves. "Tathar and Acaila, will you please use your wisdom to see what you can make of this creation?"

Both elves bowed and approached. Tathar said, "I need no spell to see that it is a foul thing; even in repose it exudes an evil strength."

Acaila said, "I will consult the archives."

"First, let us away to a quieter place," said Tomas. "Then, I will tell you all I know." To his wife, he said, "I beg the Queen's leave to depart for more cloistered quarters."

"Go, and I will join you this evening, husband."

Tomas bowed, then led Pug and the others away from the central court.

When they had reached a large room situated within the bole of a tree, Tomas said, "Pug, that thing may be the most dangerous creation in this world. How did you come by it?"

Pug deferred to Kaspar who told his story one more time.

When he was finished, Tomas said, "Here's what I remember about the war with the Dasati—"

Kaspar interrupted him, "Forgive me, but how can you remember something that happened before you were born?"

Tomas looked at Pug, who said, "I neglected to tell him."

"As impossible as this may sound," said Tomas, "I possess the memories of a Valheru, one of the Dragon Lords. It's as if I have lived two lives, but I'm afraid that time will not permit a long explanation." He looked around at the four men in the room with him and continued, "This was a time before the Chaos Wars, when the Valheru reigned the heavens. We had the power to fly between worlds and no one equaled us." His eyes grew misty in remembrance. "We had destroyed the Teld-Katha, whose last desperate act brought about the creation of the rift.

"Through that fissure came beings who attacked us without any hesitation. We eventually disposed of them and turned our attentions to the rift, sensing a great power through it—perhaps a power greater than anything we had ever encountered. So we turned away from Riska, and flew into the rift." Tomas looked away as if the memories were difficult. Softly he said, "It was the only time in his life when Ashen-Shugar knew fear."

He pointed to the Talnoy. "I can wield my golden sword, Pug, and if I strike the creature with all my might, I could damage it. With several blows, I could perhaps incapacitate it. But they use foul magic, and while it lies twitching on the ground, it heals. Within hours it will be whole and fighting again.

"The Dasati are a plague. There are millions of them, and their Talnoy number tens of thousands—perhaps hundreds of thousands. Even without the Talnoy, the Dasati were as difficult to kill as any mortal beings the Valheru had faced. Only during our struggle with the gods did we know greater danger. Even the demons of the Fifth Circle, or the Dread Lords, are more easily faced, for while they are individually more powerful, they lack numbers. Ashen-Shugar, Ruler of the Eagle's Reaches, and his great golden dragon Shuruga, slaughtered many, but for every one that fell another two took its place.

"After days of fighting, the first of the Valheru—Kindo-Raber, Master of Serpents—fell: he was pulled from the back of his dragon and torn apart by the Dasati. They ripped the flesh from his bones, Pug. They tore his great dragon apart as well. They are like soldier ants on the march: eventually, every living creature in their path falls.

"Many more Valheru died as we fled, and so fearful were we of the Dasati, that we closed the rift by destroying Riska."

"You destroyed an entire world?" asked Kaspar.

"We had the power. We used our strength to shred the mantle of the planet, causing great upheavals and earthquakes. We vented our rage upon that world in order to destroy the rift, and it literally shook itself apart."

"How did the thing get here?" asked Pug, pointing to the Talnoy.

Tomas said, "I do not know. Perhaps one of my brethren seized one as a trophy . . . though I can hardly believe it. We had to flee for our lives."

"No," said Pug. "It was someone else."

"But how; and more to the point, who?" asked Tomas. "Only Macros the Black knew enough of rift-magic to do this, and no matter how convoluted his plots were, I can't see him doing anything this dangerous."

Pug smiled. "Oh, I can. It's been a long time since I inherited Macros's island, and I must confess that because of the Serpentwar, the cataloguing and filing of his vast library has been sorely neglected." Pug sighed. "Perhaps I grew vain and believed there was nothing more to learn from his works. In any event, I will have some of my brightest students begin searching for some mention of this thing at once."

"Macros's chief fear was the return of the Dragon Host. He may have held that creature as security against the possibility." Tomas's expression changed to one of alarm. "One Talnoy would only annoy the Dragon Host, however an army of them—"

"You think there are more?" asked Pug. "How could there be, and why has no one discovered them?"

Kaspar said, "When my friends found the Talnoy, it had been buried inside solid rock. The vault had been exposed only because of an earthquake. Many wards had been placed around it, too."

Pug said, "That sounds like Macros." To Kaspar, he said, "Do you know where they found it?"

"I have an idea. Flynn did tell me where they discovered their treasures, and the name of the town close to that place. From what he said, it should only take a little gold to get the locals to show us the exact spot."

Pug said, "Good. We must find it as soon as possible."

"Forgive me," said Kaspar, "but I think you're overlooking the main threat here. The Talnoy isn't a danger at present. Rifts keep opening between our world and the realm of the Dasati. You should have seen the thing from the Dasati ocean that tried to get through one during my voyage home! These rifts will open more often, and stay open for longer unless you do something about it!"

"Creatures from the Second Circle have appeared here upon rare occasions in ages past," said Acaila. "The Eldar were first among the servants of the Valheru, and we still keep their lore.

"Even the smallest creature from that realm is potentially deadly and difficult to kill. A host of such beings would pose a threat too impossible to contemplate."

Tomas said, "Do I don my armor again?"

"It is not just Elvandar that is threatened," old Tathar said slowly, "but the entire world in which we live."

Kaspar said, "Forgive my asking, for I know little of magic and, to be honest, even that little is more than I would like."

Pug nodded, realizing he was speaking of Leso Varen's necromancy.

"But you've whisked us all over the world. Can't you just send this thing away like that?"

"It must have a specific destination."

"How about the sun?" offered Kaspar. "Can you send it that far?"

Pug laughed. "Perhaps, but I can only send it to a place I know, or one which is described to me in great detail. It works best by line of sight. I suppose I could look at the sun for a moment, then try to go there, but I'd rather not risk it." He sat back. "Though I think I have a solution for the short term: I will take the Talnoy out of Midkemia."

"Where?" asked Tomas.

"To the Assembly, upon Kelewan. The magicians there may have the means to understand this thing, and they are more numerous than my students at Sorcerer's Isle. Certainly, they can establish powerful enough wards to hide it again."

Kaspar said, "What of Stardock? My friends had thought to sell it to the magicians there."

Pug smiled. "I founded the Academy at Stardock. Trust me when I say that most of the real magical ability in Midkemia is on my island, and even when combined, Stardock and my students on Sorcerer's Isle lack the experience and ability of the Assembly.

"Taking it to Kelewan will remove the Talnoy from Midkemia, and reduce the likelihood of new rifts forming. Over time they may begin again, but as I said, the Great Ones may be able to duplicate the wards and give us all some time to study it."

Tathar said, "We shall examine the thing before you go. Perhaps we may discover something."

"You shall be our guests tonight," Tomas said, leading Kaspar and Pug to a room. "Rest here for the afternoon. Pug, when you have a moment, please?"

Pug nodded. "I will join you shortly." He turned to Kaspar who was sitting upon a down-filled mattress laid across a wooden bed. "My friend and I have much to discuss. Will you be all right here alone?"

"My head is swimming from all that I've seen and heard, Pug. Some time to rest and reflect will be very welcome."

Pug departed, and Kaspar lay down and let his mind

drift. Images of the past few months flashed before him; Jojanna and Jorgen, Flynn and the others, the chess matches with the General, and the sea voyage. Then something struck him.

He stood up and left the room. Heading back toward the Queen's court, he crossed over a bridge and saw Pug and Tomas speaking quietly on a platform below. "Pug!" he called.

Pug and Tomas looked up. "What?"

"I just thought of something." Kaspar looked around. "How do I get down there?"

Pug pointed. "The stairs are over there."

Kaspar hurried to join them.

"What is it?" asked Pug.

"Find out who put the geas on the Talnoy, and you'll know who buried it under the cliffs ages ago."

"Geas?" asked Tomas.

Kaspar explained. "When I met Flynn and the others they were the only survivors of a trade expedition to Novindus. They were under a geas. Everything else was secondary to getting the Talnoy to the Pavilion of the Gods—they even abandoned a fortune to do it. Someone wanted it called to the gods' attention very much."

Pug said, "I can't find fault with your reasoning."

"I didn't realize until just now, but since leaving the Pavilion I've had no strong desire to go anywhere. The geas seems to have gone."

"Fulfilled," said Tomas.

"Or it was removed by Kalkin! Is there any way to discern who might have been the author of that geas?"

Pug said, "Possibly. Magic is as much art as it is logic, and often a magician leaves . . . a signature, for lack of a better word." He looked at Kaspar. "If it had been your friend Leso Varen, I'd have sniffed it out in minutes. It wasn't."

"What about his belongings at the citadel?" asked Kaspar. "Did you find anything there that might tie him to this?"

"No," said Pug. "But Varen was trying to create a new type of rift—"

Tomas said, "New type? How do you mean?"

Pug sighed. "This is very complicated, so if I get too convoluted for you, ask me to stop and explain. Rifts are tears in the fabric of space. They require special knowledge and a great amount of energy to create. The energy that Varen was using is something that I'd never encountered before. But it reminded me of something I can't quite put my finger on."

"How is it different?" asked Kaspar.

"Varen used life energy, leeched from his victims during horrible torture and murder—much as Murmandamus gathered life energies when he tried to unlock the Lifestone."

Kaspar looked lost at these references, but Tomas said, "The Pantathians?"

Pug nodded. "Perhaps. Though we believed them finished, and have seen no sign of the Serpent Priests since the end of the Serpent War, but yes, it's possible. Let me go examine the Talnoy."

Pug vanished suddenly, and Kaspar stood looking at Tomas. "Forgive my ignorance, but you speak of things that are unknown to me."

Tomas grinned, and for a moment looked boyish. "My friend Pug can be abrupt when it comes to such things. Come with me and we'll fill in those gaps in your knowledge over a cup or two of good dwarven ale."

Kaspar nodded. "I'd enjoy that."

They moved away from the platform and Kaspar followed Tomas to what appeared to be family quarters.

For royalty, it was modest, Kaspar decided. Yet there was something regal in the manner and bearing of these people, so he assumed that they didn't need to be surrounded by the trappings of wealth to remind others of their importance.

Tomas poured two cups of cool ale and handed one to Kaspar. He motioned for the former Duke of Olasko to sit down and said, "My story is long and involved, and intertwined with many of the questions you're asking. If you wish to know of the Serpent Priests and the role they played in the Riftwar and the Great Uprising, then it truly begins when Pug and I were boys, working for my father in the kitchen at Castle Crydee . . ."

By the time Tomas had finished his tale, they had drunk several cups of ale and the candle beside Kaspar's chair had been lit. The Elf Queen entered the room, and Kaspar rose.

"Here you are," she said with a smile.

Kaspar bowed. "Majesty."

"Are you comfortable, Lord Kaspar?"

"Lord no longer, Majesty, but yes, I am more than comfortable. Your home is most restorative. I feel more content than I have in years."

Tomas smiled. "It is one of the benefits of living with elves."

"Your husband has just finished telling me an astonishing tale of his boyhood, the Riftwar and the Lifestone."

"The Lifestone was one of the most closely-guarded secrets of our time; only now that it no longer exists may we speak freely of it."

"When Tomas told me of your son, and how his alien

nature—combining human, Dragon Lord, and elf—proved to be the key to unlocking the Lifestone . . . well, I had an idea. I think I should speak with Pug about it."

Aglaranna stepped out of the doorway and said, "They are in the room which leads off the library, Kaspar."

"Come, I'll show you," said Tomas.

Kaspar bid goodbye to the Elf Queen and followed her consort along the tree-paths and branch-ways of Elvandar until he reached a tree of epic proportions. Of all the boles he had seen, this was easily the largest. It was seventy-five or eighty feet across, and in the middle of it stood an open doorway.

Tomas led Kaspar into the tree. Inside, Kaspar was astonished to see level after level of floors, with a central well that had a ladder running its entire depth. "This is our library," said Tomas. "It's unlike human libraries in that we keep a great deal more than books and tomes. It is also the place where we keep artifacts and other items of interest."

"Fascinating," said Kaspar. They circled around the central well and exited via a doorway opposite the one by which they had entered. Kaspar saw a large clearing on top of a nest of branches. Beyond it lay another room, and inside it Kaspar found Pug and the two elder elves examining the Talnoy.

Tomas said, "Kaspar has an idea, Pug."

Pug looked up. "We'd welcome one."

"If I understand what Tomas just told me, the Lifestone was created by the Dragon Lords to use against the gods, yes?"

"Yes," said Tomas. "That was its purpose, to take all the life energies on the world to use as a weapon against the gods."

"How?" asked Kaspar.

"What do you mean?"

"Well, after Tomas's son unlocked the Lifestone, freeing the captive life force within, your wife was able to conceive again, correct?"

"Yes," said Pug. "Though I don't see the relevance."

"Indulge me," asked Kaspar. "Now, allowing people to be born doesn't particularly strike me as the purpose of a weapon; nor does healing wounds, or all the other things which apparently happened to those who were exposed to it at the time."

Pun nodded.

"So, my point is, how was . . . Murmandamus?" He looked at Tomas.

"Yes, that was his name."

"How was Murmandamus going to utilize all the lives he took to command the Lifestone, and how were the Dragon Lords going to use it against the gods?"

Pug looked at Tomas, who said, "If the stone had been activated it would have swallowed up all the life force in the world. Everything from the largest dragon to the tiniest blade of grass would have withered. The gods would have lost their worshippers and their identity at the same time. The Valheru were convinced they could raid other planets and repopulate Midkemia."

"Madness," said Kaspar. "Keeper Samas instructed me a little in the nature of evil, and the conclusion he reached is that evil is pure madness."

"We agree," said Tomas. "We have seen the influence of evil, even here among the elves."

"So, then, the Pantathians sought to destroy all life on this world, including their own?"

Tomas said, "They were a twisted race, fashioned by one of the Valheru to worship her; Alma-Lodaka, whom they believed to be a goddess. In their mindless adherence to that faith they thought that upon her return she would exalt them to the rank of demigods, at her side. It was a sad and twisted perversion, an even more evil use of the Valheru's very essence," said Tomas.

"So here's my point. Why are you trying to find a logical answer for this thing being here when a mad one makes so much more sense?"

Pug looked at Tomas, and after a moment they both laughed. "Kaspar," said Pug, "do you have something specific in mind?"

"You say you've faced Leso Varen before, but he lived in my citadel for years. I dined with the man. I stood and watched him do things to people . . . madness is the only way to describe it. But while there may have been some sort of insane logic to what he did, how do we know it was logical from anyone else's point of view?"

"Go on," said Tomas.

"Where did the Pantathians live?"

"In the foothills of the Ratn'gary Mountains, south of the Necropolis," answered Tomas.

"Could it be, then, that the geas wasn't part of some clever plan for someone to find the Talnoy and take it to the gods, but rather, it was something that the Pantathians created to transport the creature to where they lived?"

"Why?" said Pug.

"Why?" repeated Kaspar, "Because they are mad! Somehow, one of these things got into this world. Perhaps it came through the rift with the Dragon Lords. Maybe one snatched it as booty and dropped it somewhere. But at some point it got buried and the Pantathians put wards around it to hide it. From whom, I have no idea. But perhaps they left the insurance that if anyone did accidentally discover it, it would try to get back to their home anyway."

"Why bury it there?" asked Tathar.

"I don't know. Maybe they didn't want someone else to find it, and hiding it was preferable to carrying it across the continent," said Kaspar. "Maybe their goddess told them to, but whatever the reason, perhaps there is no more design in this than Flynn and his friends stumbling across something that was no more than an ancient booby-trap."

"If so, then the Pantathians' madness has served us," said Acaila. "For had the geas not been invoked, this thing would have stayed in that vault undisturbed, and when rifts began appearing no one would have the slightest inkling as to why they were happening."

"Until an army of Talnoy descended upon us," said Kaspar.

"I will have Magnus take it to Kelewan," said Pug. "I think I will try to seek where the Talnoy came from in Novindus." He turned to Kaspar, "Will you help me locate the cave from which it was taken?"

Kaspar shrugged. "I will do what I can."

Pug said, "Now, there is one other concern."

"The Nighthawks," said Tomas. "Yes, that worries me."

Kaspar said, "Can Leso Varen be back in power, so quickly? Talwin Hawkins broke his neck."

Pug said, "I have faced him several times and over the years I have gathered other testimonies to his handiwork. For example, years past, a baron of Land's End died trying to conjure a horror in a failed attempt to save his dying wife, and the son of a noble in Aranor tried to murder his entire family on the night of his betrothal. Also a lord of Kesh freely betrayed state secrets to the Kingdom of Roldem for no reason whatsoever before taking his own life.

"Yes, if he possesses the power I think he does, he could be back within a year of his 'death,' and sending those in his employ on their dark missions once more." Pug looked at

Kaspar. "There's a particularly dangerous and repellent spell whereby a magician can trap his own soul in a vessel, bottle, or any sealed container. As long as the vessel is kept intact, it doesn't matter what happens to the body. If another body is close to the vessel at the time the previous body dies, the soul of the magician takes that body over.

"Varen could look like anyone now. He could be a young boy, or a beautiful woman. He could mask his identity from any but myself—I have faced him too many times not to recognize him within minutes."

Kaspar said, "You've got to find that jar."

"Some day I will," said Pug.

Tomas sighed, "Then let us dine, my friends, and tomorrow you may set about whatever unhappy tasks you must face; but until then ease your minds and hearts."

Kaspar and Pug exchanged glances. Both knew that while the night would be enjoyable, neither would be able to relax.

TWENTY-ONE

CONFLAGRATION

Kaspar waited patiently.

He and Pug were about to depart from Elvandar and were awaiting the appearance of the Queen and Tomas at the morning court. The Talnoy stood motionless behind Kaspar.

When the royal couple arrived, everyone stood and bowed. The Queen assumed her place upon the throne. "We thank you for your warning of this dangerous turn of events, Pug. Thanks to you, as well, Kaspar of Olasko."

Kaspar bowed to the Queen. "Majesty, your graciousness matches your beauty. You humble a proud man with your generosity and kindness."

Aglaranna smiled. "I know that your past is dark, Lord Kaspar, but I sense that you are struggling to find a better path. You have our good wishes for your success in this endeavor."

"Again, your graciousness humbles me, Majesty," said Kaspar.

"It is time?" the Queen said, looking at Pug.

Pug said, "We have to depart now for Sorcerer's Isle, with Her Majesty's leave."

Queen Aglaranna smiled and inclined her head. "Go with our affection and best wishes for a safe journey, friend Pug. You are always welcome at our court."

Tomas shook Kaspar's hand. "I hope we meet again under less dire circumstances. As my wife said, I wish you well on a better path than the one you have trodden so far."

"I hope that I may some day return to visit, Tomas."

To Pug, Tomas said, "You know my vow, never to leave Elvandar save to protect it, but Tathar has convinced me this threat is far graver than the Tsurani invasion. Should you need me, you have only to call."

Pug said, "I pray I never have such need, but if you get the call, know I will not make it lightly."

"I know."

Pug slipped on the ring that commanded the Talnoy and said, "Approach." The creature obeyed.

Pug slipped the ring off and handed it back to Kaspar, who slipped it into his belt-pouch. Pug put his hand on Kaspar's shoulder and said, "Elvandar is protected by wards unlike any in the world. I will need the cooperation of the Spellweavers to depart directly to my home. Otherwise I would need to take us to the riverbank, and we would have to cross the ford again." He nodded to Tathar.

The old spellweaver inclined his head, and began a chant, one that was quickly picked up by the other spellweavers. "In a moment, we will be able to—"

Suddenly, there was something wrong, frighteningly wrong. A thrumming sound filled the air, tearing at

Kaspar's ears. The pain stabbed at him, making him falter as he raised his hands to his head.

Kaspar's eyes watered from the pain. Blinking away tears, he fell to his knees, and saw that many in the Queen's court had also been driven down. The Queen sat back on her throne, her eyes shut tightly, her face a mask of torment. Tomas stood up, obviously in discomfort, but able to bear the distress more easily than the others.

Kaspar felt his stomach knot as waves of nausea swept through him. He turned to where Pug stood and saw the magician struggling to focus.

Pug's face was set in a grimace, but his eyes were focused and clear. He raised his hand above his head, and shouted a harsh-sounding incantation. The horrible noise ceased. For a moment, everyone was still, stunned by the unexpected event, then the skies above them exploded into flames.

For an instant, Kaspar felt the heat of an open oven wash over him, threatening to sear his lungs and blister his skin. But Pug had another response, and with a wave of his hand the crown of flames descending from the sky was repelled. It washed over an invisible dome of energy, but Kaspar still felt nearly-unbearable heat.

The spellweavers were still reeling. The attack from above seemed to have taken its toll on those responsible for protecting Elvandar as much as it had on the trees surrounding the court.

Everywhere he looked, Kaspar saw flames in the heads of the trees. The ancient oaks were faring better than those in the forests surrounding the center of Elvandar. Through the branches and boles, Kaspar could see fire in every direction. And he could hear shouts and screams.

Pug shouted, "Tathar! It has been years since I cast weather-magic. Can you bring rain?"

The old elf shook his head. "The breach of the protective barriers has stunned us, but we will try."

The elves knelt together and began to discuss what they would do. "Quickly," urged Pug as he kept the central court protected.

Kaspar looked around and wondered what was happening to those people in Elvandar who dwelled in places unprotected by the black-clad magician's spell. Those on the ground or on the lower platforms should be safe, for the fires were only burning the topmost branches, but those with homes in the higher platforms were surely doomed.

Kaspar had seen a canopy-fire in the forests of Olasko when he was a child. His father had taken him hunting one summer during a dry year and a lightning storm had started a fire above them in the mountains. The boy had stood and watched as flames leapt from treetop to treetop, racing as fast as the animals below fleeing the conflagration. It had been a terrible thing to witness.

Suddenly another terrible feeling struck Kaspar, a chill that seemed to run down his spine and into the pit of his stomach. He drew his sword without conscious thought, and every elf turned, looking around. Something was there that hadn't been present a moment before.

Then Kaspar saw the shadow—the fleeting image of the faint figure of a man, caught by the corner of his eye. "There!" he shouted, pointing at the flickering shape.

A flurry of action erupted. Kaspar looked around in astonishment as elven spellweavers collapsed on all sides. Only ancient Tathar stood like a deep-rooted oak, his hands moving through the air as he sought to protect the Queen. Tomas was at his wife's side in a single step, and swept her up in his arms. He carried her as easily as if she were a child to the relative safety of their private quarters, a short distance away.

Kaspar turned, looking for another glimpse of the figure he had seen. He saw nothing.

With one hand held high, Pug willed away the threatening flames, and with the other he invoked a new spell. Blinding blue light erupted from his hands, and its brilliance outlined the entire court in stark relief, throwing harsh highlights and black shadows. In the middle of the court, looking around as if seeking something, stood the silhouette of a man holding a sword. Then there were two. Then a third.

Pug cried out, "Death-dancers!"

Kaspar tried to make sense of them: they were human-shaped, but without features or dimension, silhouettes given form, like large cutouts from a material so black that it reflected no light. Kaspar knew that without the magic Pug had cast, these things would have been invisible to the eye.

The elves raced into action. Throughout Elvandar Kaspar could hear shouts and screams, and the sound of steel ringing out.

Then a death-dancer stood before him, and the former Duke was fighting for his life. Kaspar had never faced anything so fast and focused before. He parried, for all he could do was defend. He didn't have time to think about a riposte or an attack. He was simply trying to stay alive.

When Tomas returned, he held a golden sword. With a crushing blow he sliced hard across the shoulder of the creature battling Kaspar and it howled, a thin, wailing cry. The death-dancer turned to engage Tomas, and Kaspar thrust hard, his blade striking the creature in the back. It wailed again, but seemed only slightly slowed by the blow.

Then something pushed past Kaspar, and in his peripheral vision he saw two more death-dancers pick up the Talnoy and begin to carry it away.

Kaspar pulled the ring from his belt-pouch and slipped it on. Instantly he felt the odd sensation that accompanied wearing the ring. He leapt after the fleeing death-dancers, and in the instant that he touched the Talnoy's shoulder, said, "Kill the death-dancers."

Kaspar stopped as the Talnoy came alive. It raised its legs, knees bent, then kicked upward until its legs were almost straight in the air. In a move that would have dislocated a human's shoulders, it pushed off and broke the underarm hold of the two death-dancers, shooting itself high into the air. It tucked and flipped and twisted, and when it came down it landed on its feet facing the enemy, the black sword in its hands.

The Talnoy took a step forward. Moving with inhuman quickness it scythed through both death-dancers at the waist. Both turned to smoke and vanished with a cry. Then it turned to intercept a death-dancer that had just dispatched two elf warriors. The black, featureless dancer turned, as if sensing the Talnoy's attack, and raised its blade. The Talnoy slashed downward with incredible force, and the death-dancer recoiled from the impact. Then the Talnoy delivered another thundering blow and the death-dancer fell back as if shrinking in on itself. The third blow of the black blade sliced through its shadowy sword and cut into the apparition's neck. It lost coherence, and before Kaspar's eyes turned to smoke and blew away on the breeze.

Before Kaspar could understand what he was seeing, the Talnoy was upon a fourth death-dancer, while Tomas struck down another with both hands on his sword, a blow that could have cut through an anvil. The death-dancer crumbled and evaporated.

Tomas looked around, but while the elves and humans were gathering their wits, the Talnoy set off at a full run, moving as easily and quickly as the elves through the trees.

Tathar slapped his palms together and thunder erupted above them. Rain started to fall.

Kaspar hesitated for a moment, then when Tomas and Pug hurried after the otherworld creation, he followed. As he ran, Kaspar grew angry. *These monsters, these death-dancers*, he thought, *how dare they invade the most tranquil and wonderful place I have ever seen!* A small part of his mind realized that this emotion heralded the first hint of madness that came from wearing the ring, and that within the hour he must remove it; but for now the risk to Elvandar was still too great.

Kaspar was puffing as he ran up a flight of stairs. He reached the top—his eyes and lungs burning from the acrid smoke that filled the air—just in time to see Pug vanish out of sight. The rain was banking the fires above, but the heat was filling the air with steam.

Kaspar caught his breath. He saw Tomas, upon another platform, vault over a wooden railing and vanish below. Kaspar ran to the railing and looked down, just as Tomas landed lightly on his feet forty feet below on another immense platform, where several elves lay sprawled in pools of blood. Kaspar couldn't see through the foliage and smoke as Tomas moved out of sight, but he could hear conflict a short distance away. He cast about, saw stairs leading down and hurried to get to where the fighting was.

By the time he reached the lower platform, the conflict had moved again. He continued to hurry toward the sound of fighting, but always it stayed ahead of him. The pace of combat was furious, far more manic than anything Kaspar had experienced during battle.

At the next platform, he had to stop to catch his breath. He could barely stand, let alone fight. His lungs felt seared by the steam and smoke. He leaned forward, hands on his thighs, coughing and spitting. In the distance he could hear the sounds of fighting abate, and then suddenly it was quiet.

Kaspar stood slightly bent over, breathing hard and hearing only the sound of the driving rain as the fury of the storm increased. He took one last deep breath and hurried toward the last place he had heard fighting.

When he reached the location of the final struggle, he found Tomas, Pug, and the Talnoy standing amidst a scene of carnage. Four elves lay in grotesque postures of death, while another dozen nursed wounds that ranged from minor to life-threatening.

Elves from all parts of the community were rushing to aid the injured. "What just happened?" asked Kaspar.

Pug turned, and with an upraised hand indicated that Kaspar should remain silent. When Tomas turned to face him, Kaspar understood.

Never in his life had Kaspar seen such a look of outrage. In the hushed voice of fury, Tomas said, "Who dares?" He looked at the fallen bodies and the volume of his voice rose, "Who *dares* to visit this upon my people?"

"Someone who wants that," said Pug, pointing to the Talnoy. "They may not know exactly what it is, but they know it's important. They have sensed powerful dark magic afoot in the land, and they want to control it."

Kaspar said, "How do you know that?" He took the ring off at last.

Pug said, "There are no other possible reasons. Moreover, I'm certain because I know who sent the death-dancers."

"Who?"

Pug looked at Kaspar and Kaspar saw a mask of controlled rage, no less fearsome to behold than Tomas's, and possibly even more so because of his iron control.

Softly, Pug said, "Your old friend, Leso Varen." He

looked around and made an encompassing gesture. "This proves that he is back, for he is the only magician powerful enough to create this many death-dancers."

"Why here?" gasped Kaspar.

Pug pointed to the Talnoy. "He must have sensed its presence when Tathar and the spellweavers breached the defenses of Elvandar to allow me to leave." Pug looked at Tomas. "I feel responsible, for had I only transported us to the river, he never would have violated your sanctuary."

Tomas shook his head. "No, old friend. It is not your fault. And I believe he might have broken through our wards anyway. Remember, when you were prisoner on the Tsurani world, it took the skills of Macros the Black to repulse the Tsurani Great Ones when they attacked. If they could pass through our defenses, why not Varen?"

Pug nodded. "Perhaps you're right. I will send Miranda to you after I return home, to consult with Tathar and the others about strengthening your defenses." He looked at the smoke-filled air, listening to the cries of anguish and pain, and said, "This cannot happen again."

Kaspar could only nod mutely in agreement.

It was a somber meeting in the Queen's Court as the council learned the extent of the damage. Sixteen elves had sacrificed their lives to protect their homeland. Another dozen had been killed in the fires, three of them children.

Pug took Kaspar aside while Aglaranna and Tomas listened to more tales of the defense. "What you have to understand is that these people only have a child once in a century or longer. This is the greatest loss they have endured since the Riftwar. They will be mourning for many years to come."

Kaspar quietly said, "I sensed such was the case. It is a tragedy."

Acaila spoke to the Queen. "Our wards were swept away, Majesty. It was as if someone had studied them for a very long time, silently, unobtrusively, and passively. At the moment they fell away, two other spells hit. The flames were little more than a simple fire-spell, but on a massive scale." He turned toward Pug. "It was not because of your departure, my friend. Had the wards been at full strength, I think the outcome would have been the same."

Tathar stepped forward, his old eyes deeply shaded by his bushy white brows, yet they seemed alight with anger. "It is as Acaila says, Pug. This was no chance attack." He looked at the motionless Talnoy. "Sensing that thing's presence here may have caused your old enemy to seize the moment, but the efficiency of the assault and the thoroughness of the preparation necessary to breach our wards, fire the trees, and transport that many death-dancers into the heart of our forest speaks of detailed, patient planning. No, the assault on Elvandar must already have been decided upon a long time ago. It was only the timing that may have been left to the last minute."

Pug nodded at the old elf. "Varen must have been preparing to attack Elvandar as a contingency, for he could not have known we would bring it here. It was an effective plan, and simple in design, but one requiring great arts. The disorientation spell was cast as the wards fell, and the sudden transportation of the death-dancers was no mean feat. It is clear that the attack was a diversion—a massive, bloody, and cruel distraction—so they could spirit away the Talnoy."

Pug sighed. "But even so, I cannot help but feel that had I not brought this artifact here, you might have been spared all this."

Tomas said, "Then rest your mind, Pug." He looked at the Talnoy. "The irony is that, had that thing not been under Kaspar's control, we would have suffered far more injury. I would have eventually destroyed the death-dancers, but many more of our people would have perished. Now that I have seen what that thing can do, I know this much: you must resolve this matter swiftly, for an army of such creatures turned upon us would be a certain end to us all." He stepped close to his friend. "My memories as Ashen-Shugar are one thing, but my experiences here as Tomas are another. Pug, the entire might of the Kingdom and Kesh combined, all the magicians of Stardock and Sorcerer's Isle, all of them together could not withstand ten thousand of these things. Act with haste."

"We must be away, and quickly," Pug agreed. "It is clear that Varen is again in charge of forces that rival the Conclave, and he is acting boldly, even recklessly. To breach the wards that protect Elvandar is no trivial feat, and to send in two dozen death-dancers—" he looked at his boyhood friend and the Queen "—is as monstrous a feat as the creation of that Talnoy, for each death-dancer is created by the willing relinquishment of the soul to the magician, the sort of deed only a fanatic would consent to."

Kaspar saw Tomas return to Aglaranna's side and lean over for a moment of quiet conversation with his wife. For her part, the Queen held his hand and seemed to be reacting with concern in her eyes. Finally she looked down as if in resignation, and Tomas kissed her, then moved away. He walked passed Pug and Kaspar and said, "Wait here, please," and went into the royal quarters.

He soon emerged, and Kaspar was again struck by the man's uncanny appearance. Now he wore a white tabard over a suit of golden armor and carried a white shield. Displayed on both tabard and shield was a golden dragon.

On Tomas's head glinted a golden helm; a dragon's head rested upon his pate and golden wings swept down on either side.

Quietly Pug said, "This is as close as any living man can come to seeing one of the Dragon Lords in the flesh."

Tomas returned to his wife, conferred briefly once more, and then turned to the assembled elves. "My friends, I will send word for both Prince Calin and Prince Calis to return at once and serve here in my stead. I vowed never to depart Elvandar save at the time of her greatest need. We have been attacked with no just cause, and our beloved brothers and sisters have been slain. A war has come to us, and it is a war, make no mistake. I surrender my place as Warleader of Elvandar to Prince Calin, until my return."

Kaspar said, "Where's—"

Pug cut him off. "With us."

Tomas came to stand beside Pug. "I will accompany you, my old friend. I will not return to Elvandar until this business is settled."

"It may take a while."

With a bitter smile, Tomas said, "As long as it takes, Pug. As long as it takes."

Pug nodded once. Then he put his hand upon Tomas's arm. "As long as it takes."

Pug, Tomas, Kaspar, and the Talnoy vanished.

TWENTY-TWO

ASSAULT

Kaspar blinked.

One minute they were standing in Elvandar, then suddenly they were back on Sorcerer's Isle, and in an instant, Kaspar knew something was terribly wrong here, too. He could smell the smoke in the air—not the faint scent of the wood fires in the hearths or kitchens, but thick clouds of roiling smoke, as bitter and as blinding as it had been moments earlier in Elvandar. He turned and blinked back tears.

An inferno raged in the villa.

The bodies of students and warriors in black armor lay strewn about the landscape. Pug cursed, took one look at a fallen warrior and almost spat. "Black Slayers!"

Tomas suddenly took to his heels, and Kaspar heard the sound of conflict. He slipped on the ring, touched the Talnoy lightly and shouted, "Follow me!'

Pug shouted, "Miranda!" once, then vanished.

Kaspar caught up with Tomas as the white-and-gold-clad warrior crashed into the rear of a group of Black Slayers who were being kept at bay by the desperate incantations of half-a-dozen students, who were frantically casting wards and offensive spells which quickly lost their effectiveness. Kaspar struck one Slayer as hard as he could from behind, cleaving it between neck and shoulder. The black-armored figure crumpled, and Kaspar was relieved to see that the things could die.

He backed away toward the Talnoy and commanded, "Kill these Black Slayers!"

The Talnoy leapt to work beside Tomas and between them, the Black Slayers were dispatched in less than a minute. Tomas looked around and shouted, "Are there more?"

One of the students, her face streaked with tears, dirt, and blood said, "They're everywhere."

Kaspar and Tomas turned and Kaspar shouted to the Talnoy, "Follow me!"

The three of them ran until they found more Slayers rampaging through a library, throwing everything that would burn into a fire.

Tomas let loose a primeval roar of anger and surged forward. Kaspar was about to order the Talnoy into the battle, but before he could give the order Tomas had decapitated one Slayer, cleaved another from armpit to groin, and was cutting down a third. The fourth and fifth died before Kaspar could decide what to do.

Tomas looked around and started running toward the sound of more fighting. Kaspar instructed the Talnoy to follow Tomas and kill Black Slayers on sight. The Talnoy turned and sprinted after Tomas. Kaspar labored to keep up, but in seconds the other two were out of sight.

Then rain started to fall.

Kaspar realized that someone was summoning rain as the Spellweavers in Elvandar had. He stopped, trying to get his bearings amidst the smoke and confusion. He couldn't see a thing in the library, so he went back into the courtyard.

His lungs still hurt from all the smoke he had inhaled in Elvandar, so Kaspar stopped again to gather his wits. He wasn't doing well with the smoke, and the coughing he endured brought up a bitter, acid taste in his throat. *If I live through this*, he thought, *I hope they have a healer who can keep me from getting pneumonia*.

He coughed and spat, and hurried on.

A long pasture rolled away from the villa and on its far side stood a wooded area. Kaspar saw students fleeing for the trees, hoping to hide in their shelter.

A Black Slayer emerged from a doorway barely ten feet from Kaspar, and saw the fleeing students. He failed to look in Kaspar's direction, so the former Duke of Olasko drew his sword and threw it with as much force as he could, for he knew he would never be able to overtake the black-armored warrior.

The slayer was taken squarely in the back and Kaspar's sword knocked him to his knees. Kaspar was behind the fallen warrior, picking up his sword, before the slayer had time to recover. With the precision of a master chef carving a roast, Kaspar inserted the point of his sword in a gap below the Slayer's armpit, thrust, and turned his blade. The man inside cried out in very human pain, and Kaspar suddenly realized that these were not supernatural creatures, just fanatical men in gaudy black armor.

The realization lifted his spirits. At least he was facing something he could kill.

Another coughing-fit wracked Kaspar's body and he was forced to take a moment to catch his breath. He listened for the sounds of struggle and caught the sound of a conflict that seemed close at hand.

He hurried into a room in one of the buildings near the kitchen and found two dead Slayers, nearly cut in two. He had no idea if the Talnoy or Tomas had killed them, but considered the question academic.

Kaspar heard a woman scream and followed the sound down a long hallway which connected the outbuilding to the main house. He saw a blue-robed figure vanish around a corner, and a few feet closer found the body of a woman.

Kaspar ran to where she lay and knelt beside her. He had recognized her the moment he had seen her; it was Alysandra, lying still in a pool of her own blood. His stomach sank. For an instant he wondered why he was so upset; they had been lovers, but it had been a relationship of attraction, not love. She had been Pug's agent and would have killed him without remorse if ordered to. Despite that, he still felt a pang of sorrow at seeing her corpse, her face a mask of surprise and confusion. He reached out, gently closed her eyes, and then stood up.

Then he ran around the corner, after the man in blue.

Kaspar stood drenched in his own perspiration, the result of having encountered a pair of Black Slayers who were obviously fleeing either Tomas or the Talnoy.

Both had been severely wounded which had allowed Kaspar to despatch them swiftly, though it had still been a close thing. The smoke had seared his lungs and he could hardly breathe. He knew that men died from too much smoke in battle, and he now wondered if that might prove to be his mode of death.

Coughing up blood, Kaspar looked at the two dead figures in black. The Slayers looked formidable and were good warriors, but Kaspar had seen better over the years. It was their eagerness to die serving their master that made them so dangerous. Of course, the fact that they had fled from an opponent proved they weren't entirely without reason.

The Talnoy came into view and Kaspar shouted, "Come here!" The creature responded to his voice, despite having no contact with him. Kaspar realized belatedly that he only needed to touch it once—when donning the ring—to place it under his command. That made sense; it would be impossible for a commander to race around a battlefield touching each and every Talnoy under his command.

"Follow me," Kaspar said, and they went in search of any more invaders.

Kaspar tried to find his way though the villa's long hall. Smoke had reduced visibility to a few feet, and he was almost blind. Gathering his wits, he said to the Talnoy, "If I fall, pick me up and carry me to safety."

In the haze ahead of him Kaspar saw an exit, and he hurried to it. Once outside he discovered that he was totally disoriented. He thought he'd find himself outside the villa, on the slope leading down to the meadow, but instead he looked out upon the central garden.

The courtyard stood as an incongruous contrast to the charred buildings surrounding it. Somehow the flames hadn't touched the greenery or the pools, but the smoke was still thick here.

Kaspar stood still for a moment, deciding which way looked the most promising as a safe exit from the burning building. For a moment, he was free of the waves of heat which had blanketed him inside. He considered remaining in the center of the garden, dousing himself in one of the pools, and waiting for the fire to burn out, but then he felt a stab of panic rising up inside him, and realized that the ring was starting to affect him. He was about to take it off when the wind changed and a billow of smoke swept toward him. As he considered which way to move, a figure emerged calmly from the cloud.

For a moment, Kaspar thought it was Tomas, for the man was very tall, but as he drew closer, Kaspar could see he was not as broad-shouldered as Pug's friend. The man's hair was blond and fell loosely to his shoulders. His eyes blazed a vivid green, gleaming from tears caused by the smoke. He had a square, lean jaw, and looked to be no more than twenty-five years old. He wore a pale blue robe. Kaspar realized that he was the man who had vanished around the corner moments before he had found Alysandra's body.

When he saw Kaspar, he smiled in recognition. "Kaspar! What an unexpected surprise."

Kaspar paused, for other than in flight, he had never seen this man before.

Then the man's eyes fell on the Talnoy and he said, "Delightful! I have been looking everywhere for this thing." He took a step toward it. "I'll relieve you of him now."

Then Kaspar realized. "Varen!"

The magician grinned. "Do you like the new me? That trollop who tried to kill me—Lady Rowena—reminded me of pleasures I had not indulged in for years." His grin widened. "So, I thought a younger body would be the perfect thing to get me into a better mood.

Dying can be so traumatic!" He motioned over his shoulder. "Funny thing, though, I ran into her a few minutes ago and I must say she looked quite a bit better than the last time I saw her hanging from my wall—well, it was your wall, strictly speaking; as it was your citadel. She looked very confused as to why I was killing her. I couldn't decide if it was funnier to let her die without knowing or to tell her. Sad to say, by the time I'd decided, she was dead anyway."

"Why?"

"Because it pleased me to see her die," said the magician. "But that's the problem with death, once they die, the fun stops! Torturing a corpse is hardly sport. There are spells that can bring people back, I know, but . . . well, the reanimated aren't quite as receptive to pain as the living. You can make them do any number of amusing things, but suffering just seems beyond them." Regarding Kaspar's sword, he added, "It seems you've changed your alliances."

"It's a long story," said Kaspar.

"Well, I'd love to pull up a chair and chat with you, for I'm sure it's a very interesting tale, but time is pressing and there are some people nearby who wish me a great deal of harm, so I must be on my way. I must confess, though, I only had a slight inkling of what it was I was seeking—its aura is very alien—but as soon as I caught wind of it, I knew it would be something special; something fun, guaranteed to create chaos and generally annoy my foes. However, I'm a little disappointed; it just doesn't look . . . big enough."

Kaspar dropped the point of his sword. "You may have some problems gaining control over it. You could use my help," said Kaspar.

Varen said, "You propose a bargain?" He grinned. "Well, it's nice to see that you appreciate the difficulty of this situation. Don't worry, I'll manage to find a way to control the creature. After all, if you could discover the knack, it shouldn't take me long. Now, my old host, it is time to say goodbye."

Suddenly, Kaspar realized Varen meant to kill him.

The magician pulled back his hand and a strange light started to form around it. "Sorry, Kaspar, but if you've switched to the other side, I can't leave you around to help them." His eyes grew wide, and Kaspar saw that no matter what his appearance, Varen was still as mad as he had always been. "This is going to hurt, a great deal," he said, smiling.

Varen's hand shot forward, and Kaspar fell away to the side; the magician's fingers missed him by inches.

"Kill him!" Kaspar shouted.

Varen's eyes widened. He looked down and saw a black blade protruding from the pit of his stomach. Blood began to gush out of his nose and mouth. Looking up at Kaspar, he managed to gasp, "I should have thought of that." Then he collapsed.

Kaspar backed away from Leso Varen's corpse and stood up. He remembered what Hildy had told him about cockroaches. Varen looked dead, but for all Kaspar knew he might be waking up somewhere else in a new body at this very moment.

Kaspar's head swam, but he knew the ring's impending madness was not the only problem he faced. He was likely to die from smoke inhalation if he didn't find a way out soon.

"Find the safest way out of here," he ordered the Talnoy, and the creature turned at once and headed for a door billowing smoke. It might well be the safest way, Kaspar thought, but that didn't mean that it was completely without peril.

He followed the Talnoy into the smoke-filled hall,

through another door, and saw with relief that he was on the other side of the house. He started to follow the creature, but a spasm of coughing doubled him over.

Suddenly Kaspar couldn't breathe. Within moments, he was on his knees and the Talnoy had disappeared from sight. He crawled forward and fell face-first onto what felt like damp soil, not stonework. He tried to get up but collapsed, and then spun away into darkness.

Kaspar awoke and coughed. His lungs hurt a little, but surprisingly less than he would have thought, given how dreadful he had felt during the fires. Amafi was sitting in the corner. "Magnificence! You are awake."

"Thank you for telling me."

"I am surprised, that is all. The funny little man gave you something to drink last night and said you would be fine, but you were close to death when they brought you here."

Kaspar sat up and looked around. "Where are we?"

"In one of the buildings untouched by the fire," said Amafi. "Many of the students were killed, Magnificence, and many more wounded. Most of the buildings were severely damaged, but these people are amazing. As you might suspect, several of the magicians are using their arts to repair the place. It should be as good as new in a month, so I have been told."

Kaspar said, "Where are my clothes?"

Amafi reached into a chest at the foot of Kaspar's bed and handed a soft bundle to him, "Cleaned and ready, Magnificence."

Kaspar stood and found himself only a little light-headed. "For how long was I asleep?"

"Three days, Magnificence. The Talnoy picked you up and carried you to safety, otherwise the building would have fallen on you where you lay. The little man, Nakor, prepared a draft which had you breathing easily again in minutes, once we'd administered it."

"How did you manage to survive all the slaughter?" asked Kaspar as he sat up and pulled his boots on.

"I hid when I could, fought when required, and had good fortune, Magnificence."

Kaspar stood. "Ah, brevity. Very good, Amafi." He said, "How are Pug and his family?"

"Well enough," said Amafi, shaking his head with a sad expression. "But bereft. Many of those lost were very young. The black-armored invaders were indiscriminate; their mission was carnage."

"Did you see the blond magician who led them?" asked Kaspar, moving toward the door.

"Yes."

"That was our old friend Leso Varen."

Amafi nodded. "So Pug said, Magnificence. He said he could sense who he was despite the change in appearance. Actually, Varen was looking very well until the Talnoy gutted him."

They left the room and Kaspar asked, "Where can I find Pug?"

"I'll show you, Magnificence."

Amafi led him outside and at once Kaspar saw the extent of the damage. Only a portion of one hall was left intact, but the garden had been miraculously spared. Already workers were repairing the damage, and Kaspar paused for a moment to marvel at them.

A girl no more than fourteen years old stood next to a pile of cut lumber. Her hand was outstretched as she used her mind to move a timber to the top of two charred, but still sturdy, supports. When the beam was in place, two young men hammered iron nails into the wood and called down for her to send another up to them.

At other locations more mundane approaches were being used, and the sound of hammers and saws filled the air.

"The dead?" asked Kaspar.

"They held the rites last night, Magnificence. The boy, Malikai, was one of those slain."

Kaspar said nothing, but he felt regret.

They entered a building previously used to house farming equipment, from the look of the plow, harnesses, and other items stacked outside the door.

Pug sat on a simple stool in the middle of the room; a blackened kitchen table serving as his desk, a stack of papers before him. He looked up. "Kaspar, you seem to have survived."

"Pug," said the former duke. "I have you to thank for that."

"Nakor, actually," said Pug as he stood up. "He had a potion in that bottomless bag of his which healed your lungs from the smoke damage. He used it many times on the first night."

Pug came and leaned against the table. "We found you at the feet of the Talnoy and found the blue-clad magician gutted in the garden."

"The Talnoy killed him and carried me to safety."

Pug said, "Varen?"

Kaspar said, "It *was* Varen, and he's dead again . . . if that means anything." He looked at Pug and said, "You were right. He was after the Talnoy. It killed him."

Miranda entered the room and it was obvious that she had overhead the last exchange. Without preamble she said, "That thing has to be taken away from here. They didn't know exactly where it was at the time of the attack, but they knew it had to be here or in Elvandar."

"Otherwise he wouldn't have divided his forces," said a voice from outside.

Kaspar turned to see Tomas standing in the doorway.

"And he'd have thrown the death-dancers and the Black Slayers at us together, completely overwhelming us."

Pug nodded. "Varen will be back. Until we find the vessel housing his soul, he will keep coming back."

Kaspar said, "Then that's what we must do."

Pug smiled. "We?"

Kaspar shrugged. "I was left with the impression, when last we spoke, that my options around here are limited."

Pug nodded. "They are. Come, let's take a walk."

As Miranda and Tomas moved aside to let them exit the hut, Pug said, "I'll be back shortly." He paused and said to Miranda, "Have Magnus prepare to take the Talnoy to Kelewan. We'll have the Assembly turn their best minds to the problem."

She nodded. "After what's happened here, we'll need the help."

Pug smiled and touched her arm. "And send for Caleb. I want him to work with Kaspar on tracking Varen down."

She said, "I'll take care of it."

To Tomas, Pug said, "Why don't you return to your family for a while? I think Varen depleted his resources in these two attacks."

"I agree, but when the time comes to deal with that monster, I will be there."

"Yes," said Pug. "Nakor will see you back to Elvandar, unless you want to summon a dragon?"

Tomas grinned. "I could, but they tend to get irritated when the trip doesn't involve something dangerous. I'll find Nakor." To Kaspar he said, "Fare well, Kaspar. I'm certain we shall meet again."

They shook hands. "It has been an honor, Tomas," Kaspar said.

Pug indicated that Kaspar should walk with him, and when they were alone he said, "It is good that you've decided to join us."

Kaspar laughed. "I assumed there wasn't much choice!"

"There's always a choice, but in this case, your alternative was not particularly attractive. You're a man of guile, wit, and perception, and you possess a certain ruthlessness that we shall most certainly need before all this is done; and know that it is far from done. This new struggle has only just begun. We have learned a bitter lesson; we have grown complacent in the defense of our home. We will never make that mistake again."

Kaspar said, "When do we begin?"

Pug said, "Now. Come, let us make plans."

The former duke, now an agent of the Conclave of Shadows, and the former kitchen boy, now the most powerful magician in Midkemia, walked down the hill toward the meadow and began to make plans.

Epilogue

Missions

Magnus bowed.

A group of five magicians wearing black robes returned the greeting. One of them stepped forward and said, "Greetings, son of Milamber. You are a welcome sight to these old eyes."

Magnus smiled. "You're generous, Joshanu." He looked to the other four Great Ones of the Assembly of Magicians. "It is good to see you all."

He stepped off the dais upon which the rift machine rested, the twin of the one kept in Stardock on Midkemia. The room was large, but relatively empty save for the rift machine and the five men who waited around it. They had been warned of Magnus's arrival by a signal system initiated years before. The room was all of stone, and cold for this hot planet, but it was well lit by oil lamps set in sconces on the wall.

"What is this thing that follows you?" asked one of the other magicians.

Speaking perfect Tsurani, Magnus answered, "It is the reason for my visit. It's a man-made construction, yet it contains a living spirit. It belongs to the Second Circle," he said, using the Tsurani terminology for the second level of reality.

This piqued their interest. "Really?" said a tall, reed-thin magician.

"Yes, Shumaka," said Magnus. "I knew you would be especially interested." To the entire group, he said, "My father begs the Assembly for their wisdom. If I may prevail upon you to gather as many of your brethren as you can, I would like to address them all."

A short, stout magician smiled. "I shall spread the word. I am certain that when the news of this thing has spread, every member will be in attendance. Come, let us find you some quarters and let you rest. How soon would you wish to speak?"

Magnus slipped the ring on his finger and instantly felt the tingle of alien magic. "Follow," he instructed the Talnoy, touching it lightly.

One thing the magician had discovered since being charged with transporting the Talnoy to Kelewan was that it responded to any language. Therefore, it was Magnus's opinion that it could read the thoughts of the ring-wearer, and the vocalization was only really necessary for clarity of the command.

They led Magnus and the Talnoy through the heart of the city of magicians. The vast building covered an entire island, much as Stardock dominated the island upon which it stood. This one, however, dwarfed its imitator and was truly ancient, while Stardock was less than a century old.

No one knew more about rift-magic than Pug, and

Magnus carried a set of messages from his father to various members of the assembly detailing what he knew, what he surmised, what he suspected and what he feared. Magnus had read the communiqués; they were not designed to reassure.

Still, the Talnoy was away from his home and Varen was, if not stopped, then at least slowed considerably.

But the last thing his father had said to him before he departed troubled him deeply.

Pug had embraced his son and whispered in his ear, "I fear the time of subtle conflict is behind us, and that now we once again face open war."

Magnus hoped his father was wrong, but suspected that he was right.

Nakor swore as he bumped his head against the ceiling of the cave. It had taken him nearly a week to find it, using the information Kaspar had provided him. He ducked under the low overhang, torch in one hand, walking staff in the other.

He had used one of Pug's Tsurani spheres to magically transport himself near to where Kaspar thought the Talnoy had been discovered: Shingazi's Landing. He had left Sorcerer's Isle in the middle of the afternoon, and had landed in Novindus during the dead of night.

Nakor left his rooms in Shingazi's Landing, and walked until he was out of sight of the town. Then he used one of Pug's tricks, and used the sphere to transport himself by line-of-sight. It was slow compared to the instantaneous jumps made from point to known point, but it was dangerous to attempt traveling in this way to unknown destinations, as the sphere could easily land the user inside solid rock.

He had found the village the Kingdom traders had used as their base of operations in the northern regions of the Eastlands, and after spending some gold and asking the right questions, he had located the cave.

Nakor looked at the devastation the grave-robbers had left behind them and balanced the torch between a pair of large rocks to light the cavern. Porcelain jars with unreadable writing upon them were now tiny shards, and clay tablets had also been smashed. Nakor sighed. "Such a mess."

He felt Pug's arrival before he heard him call out his name. "In here!" he shouted, and a light appeared in the tunnel a few moments later.

Pug came to stand beside his friend. "What have you found?"

"This," said Nakor. He knelt and picked up a clay shard. "Perhaps if we took these back with us, the students could piece them together, and we might learn something?"

"This has all the hallmarks of a Pantathian burial vault," said Pug. "Look." He pointed to some armor. "That's Pantathian."

"What's back here?" said Nakor.

Pug held up his hand and light sprang forth, bathing the rear of the cavern. "Looks like rock."

"You, of all people, should look beyond the obvious, Pug." Nakor walked to the rear of the cave and examined the wall. Then he began to bang on the stones with his walking stick.

Pug knelt and examined something in the corner. "Did you look at these ward-markers?"

"Yes," said Nakor. "Macros put them there."

Pug stood up. "So, Macros the Black stumbled across a Pantathian burial chamber in which the Talnoy rested, and instead of ridding the world of it, he put some wards around it and left it here for us to find."

"Well," said Nakor, "if you couldn't destroy it, what makes you think Macros could?" He glanced back and saw that Pug wore a wry smile. "You still think of him as more powerful than you, but that's not so, at least it hasn't been true for some time." Nakor went back to examining the wall. "Besides, he was very busy for a few years."

Pug said, "You could say that. But he never made any mention of it in his papers, to me, or to his daughter."

"He didn't spend a lot of time with your wife, Pug."

"But this is important. It's as dangerous as anything I've seen so far."

With a rumble, the rear wall began to move and Nakor let out a satisfied grunt. "Found it!"

Pug hurried to stand next to the Isalani. "What do you think?"

"I think that if the Talnoy was out there, whatever is hiding in here must be very important indeed."

"And perhaps dangerous," said Pug.

Nakor retrieved his torch and they headed down into the tunnel. They had walked about a mile when the floor began to level off. Nakor said, "There's a cavern ahead. Can't see much with this light, though."

Pug raised his hand and a light as bright as day streamed from his palm.

"Gods," Nakor whispered. "We have a problem, Pug."

The walls of the chamber rose a hundred feet or more, but the floor was less than ten feet below them. The cavern floor stretched out in a huge circle, and on it, lined up neatly as if in waiting, stood line after line, row after row of Talnoy.

"There must be hundreds," Pug whispered.

"Thousands. We have a problem," Nakor repeated.